Everything Is Combustible

Everything Is Combustible

Television, CBGB's and
Five Decades of Rock and Roll

The Memoirs of an Alchemical Guitarist

RICHARD LLOYD

Beech Hill Publishing Company
Mount Desert, Maine

Richard Lloyd Management:
Bill Carlton/NMM email: nolaminates@gmail.com

Plowboy Records
C/O Ben Ewing
154 Franklin Road
Brentwood, TN 37207
Email: bewing@plowboyrecords.com

BEECH HILL PUBLISHING COMPANY
Mount Desert, Maine / www.beechhillpublishingcompany.com

ISBN: 978-0-9976937-8-2
Printed in the United States of America

1 2 3 4 5 TS - P 22 21 20 19 18

The names and identifying characteristics of some incidental
characters (persons) in this book have been changed.

To the memory of my grandparents
John and Catherine Ewing (Pa Pa and Me Ma)

To my loving wife, Sheila Lloyd,
my mother, Virginia Lloyd,
and my son, Dylan Lloyd

The generations roll along . . .

Contents

Foreword

I have known the guitarist and songwriter Richard Lloyd for more than thirty years, but no matter how well you think you know Richard, there is always another surprise. Once I was crossing Times Square when I ran into the photographer Bob Gruen doing a shoot with a group of dreadlocked musicians. Bob introduced me to the Wailers, Bob Marley's band. We talked for a few minutes before I said I had to run, I was meeting Richard Lloyd. Al Anderson, the Wailers' guitarist said,

"Richard Lloyd! The guitar player?"

"That's right."

"From Television?"

"Yes."

"From Montclair High School?"

"Huh?"

It turned out that the future guitarists of Television, the center of CBGB's, and the Wailers, center of reggae, started out as teenagers playing together in a New Jersey basement. I was witness to their coffee shop reunion. Richard's influence appears where you least expect it.

Richard Lloyd is one of the most original thinkers I have ever known and he has faced down some of the worst demons. Since childhood he has lived on the line between inspiration and madness. He was institutionalized as a teenager, became a rock sensation in his mid-twenties, beat drug addiction through guts and discipline, and stayed sober for twenty years—only to backslide when it seemed like the coast was clear, a downward spiral that cost him his marriage, many of his friendships, his band and almost his life. That he pulled himself up from the bottom and began again was more than inspiring—it seemed impossible. Then again, a lot of Richard's life seems impossible.

I have seen Richard at his best and worst, but this book surprised me again and again. It is a harrowing journey in which the supporting characters include not only criminals, quack psychiatrists, junkies and holy men, but Keith Moon, Jimi Hendrix, Keith Richards, and the cast and crew of CBGB's—a group with Richard at its bull's eye.

Richard has been a profound but often unrecognized influence on rock 'n' roll. As co-founder of the great band Television he was a direct influence on dozens of acts, including U2 and R.E.M. Richard literally built the stage at CBGB's, where Television established a scene that soon included Patti Smith, the Ramones, Blondie, and Talking Heads and set off a musical revolution that spread around the world.

Richard Lloyd's place in rock history was established before he was thirty years old, but his adventures continued. He made a series of fine solo albums and worked as a sideman and session musician. He married and raised a son. He explored spiritual and philosophical disciplines with a scholar's attention. He worked in an office. He was a guitar teacher. He made background music for TV shows. He is the rare rock legend who has also lived for years as a civilian. He has always had a writer's sensibility—the gift for standing slightly outside himself and observing.

Combine that with a photographic memory and an almost penitential honesty and you have the makings of a great memoir.

Richard Lloyd is a man who, when told by Keith Richards' mother that his band would never be as great as her son's group, agreed with her and told her why: "At the end of the day, Keith and I are organ grinders, and Keith has the best monkey."

That is the observation of a thinker, a wit and—it turns out—a vivid and compelling writer. That's Richard Lloyd.

—Bill Flanagan
New York, New York
April 2017

Prologue: Waiting for the Rollercoaster

I have read my fair share of biographies and autobiographies and memoirs, many of them connected with rock 'n' roll. Some biographies and autobiographies try my patience with fantastic genealogies; how so-and-so's great-grandfather crossed the Atlantic in a rowboat with 39 cents and how he begat the grandfather who begat the father of the person whose biography I am reading. They also usually include how their ancestors met their respective spouses, what they did for a living and all manner of uninteresting (at least to me) set ups, to help me understand the roots of the person. I drag myself through these books waiting for the magical moment I'm interested in—when the person becomes aware of his destiny, how it approaches him, how it takes him for a ride and how he reacts to it. I usually know something about the person to begin with—why else buy their biography? And I know the measure of their success or tragedy, or both.

I slog through the first third of the book like someone waiting in line to ride a rollercoaster. I'm waiting for that moment when they've been strapped in and there is no turning back. That's the magic moment when the chain underneath grabs the car and starts to pull it up. The car reaches the top and slowly arches its way over into the freefall. Then come the ups and downs, changes in gravity, torque—sometimes dangerous, sometimes exhilarating. The rollercoaster ride began for me when I was born on this lunatic asylum planet.

This book is a memoir—not an autobiography. I'm not sure I know the difference but I can imagine that an autobiography traces a person's own history somewhat chronologically, factually, perhaps even objectively, whereas a memoir is based on first-person memory. Memory has its own rules, first of all that it is subjective—no one else sees the objective events from the same perspective. Events on their own have no meaning. Human beings append meaning to events, and these meanings do not exist except invisibly, within each person. Autobiographies are meant to delineate a person's life; memoirs allow you to understand them a bit and to share their lives from the inside.

So this book is a memoir. I often ask people to recount to me their first memories, whether it is sight or sound or an entire panorama. I am often surprised by how difficult this exercise can be, and how uncertain the phenomenon of memory can be. In my case it is not like that. My first memory is as firm as the earth upon which I stand.

There is a game that young people play. They sit across from one another and they make a declaration: "I am dreaming and you are part of my dream." They both say this back and forth until neither is certain. How can we know what is real, and if our memories are truthful? I suppose that one is left to one's own inner devices. I have always had very strong memories. I spent much effort and self-destructive behavior seeing if I could efface that photographic memory, but nothing I have ever done has attenuated it in the slightest.

This book began as stories spoken aloud in the tradition of oral storytelling. The method is ancient in origin, going back to a time when the storyteller and the audience had an intimate connection. Stories were told in a conversational manner and tended to be detail laden and lyrical. While this may not align with the current bon ton literary trend toward writing that is rigidly concise and pithy, it suits my approach because I have an eidetic memory, and I am a musician and songwriter by profession.

1 Hello Pittsburgh

I was born at 8:15 PM, October 25, 1951, in Pittsburgh, Pennsylvania. I only know that it was Pittsburgh because I was told that it was Pittsburgh. Pittsburgh is just a word, and my memories are full of hearsay.

All of our memories are full of hearsay which sometimes gets mixed up with our factual and sensory impressions, so that things get all jumbled up and we hardly know what we remember. But we have no choice except to follow this twisted memory, because it is all we have to stand on.

1951 was only six years after the end of World War II, and it was the beginning of the Cold War between the United States and the Soviet Union. People at that time were in a strange halfway state—between the exhilaration of recovery from war and the threat of nuclear anni-hilation. Pittsburgh was one of the central eastern industrial cities that forged steel and sent it to Detroit and other places for the manufacture of cars and skyscrapers. I was thrown into this cast of time in a steel town, on the wrong side of the river, on the wrong side of the tracks.

I was born downtown at Northside General Hospital, and my young parents lived nearby in my paternal grand-parents' house. My father's name was Joseph Alt, and he was a tall, lanky youngster of German heritage—alt means old in German. I was christened Richard John Alt, which is what my birth certificate read until I had my name changed legally at the age of nine to Richard Lloyd. Lloyd is the name of my stepfather, David Lloyd.

My mother's name was Virginia Ewing until she married at the age of 18. I am one-half German and one-quarter each of Scottish and Irish—the Northern European mix. My parents broke up when I was three months old and I went to live with my mother and my maternal grandparents, John and Catherine Ewing. They lived in Homestead, Pennsylvania, a suburb of Pittsburgh and the home of US Steel and Bethlehem Steel.

Homestead had a lively history and what I clearly remember is that it was built on a huge hill at the bottom of which were the railroad tracks, the shipping yards, the steel mills and the river. I think it was the Ohio River but it could have been the Monongahela or the Susquehanna. That's why the football stadium was called Three Rivers Stadium—the three rivers meet in Pittsburgh. Homestead was rather rundown, what I call upper-lower class rather than lower-middle class. The roofs on all the houses were orange from the dust and smudge spewed by the steel mills and the whole town was completely saturated with two things: churches and taverns.

Most people worked in the steel mills and the others got jobs out at the coal mines nearby. These were the two main jobs that came up like a Chinese menu: pick either A or B: steel mill or coal mine. Across the river was a much better and more affluent neighborhood, just out of reach by bridge. I can truly say I was born on the wrong side of the tracks and on the wrong side of the river.

I can only imagine my mother being destroyed by her divorce from my father when I was an infant. I hardly saw him after that. He joined the Navy when I was three and I have never seen him since nor do I care to. There is no doubt that my mother wanted to get the hell out of her parents' house, somehow, anyhow—she wanted to become an actress, which brought her eventually to New York. She sent for me when I was six.

My mother had her first job as a soda jerk downtown. A tall, blonde, handsome boy would come in at lunchtime to order soda. My mother was 17 and my father was probably 18, and he began to come in more often and linger, and they fell in love. Soon after that they got married and my mother became pregnant with me. What my father did for a living at 18 was a riot. Down the block was a burlesque house. The cigarette girls would circulate through the audience in between the acts of strippers and comedians while young men would walk around with wristwatches up and down their arms, offering them for sale. That's what my father did—sold wristwatches in a strip club. That might be one step above being a hawker in a carnival because you get to see the girls. But my parents fell in love and from what I was told they got married and, boing, my mother got pregnant with me. That's the easy part.

The hard part for young people on this people-farm called Earth is to find stability in relationships, especially when they have not yet found themselves on the exit from their families and neighborhoods, and these relationships are usually volatile and doomed. My own biological parents were no different. They were not off to a terrific beginning.

After I was born we moved into my father's parents' house and immediately there was fighting. My mother's mother-in-law didn't like her and thought her son had married too early. There was a breaking point at which my mother said she knew she was leaving—she called the diaper service and told them to change the address where they delivered the diapers to her parents' house. Then she called her parents and asked if she could come home and bring the baby.

It must have been a devastating time for my mother. She was left with a broken marriage and a young baby. I'm sure she felt that she was a failure, and that feeling probably lasted a long time. I vaguely remember my paternal grandparents, but those memories are so vague that they don't allow any clear pictures to emerge. I was three years old when my father joined the Navy and became a welder. Right before he shipped out, he came over and brought me a sailor suit just like the one he was wearing. I put it on and he bounced me around on his knee laughing and told some joke that made me pee my pants. With a big splotch of piss somewhat over my crotch he then picked me up and handed me to my mother and said, "Here—you take it." And then he said goodbye. Goodbye Joe, hello Pittsburgh.

2 Something of my Birth

My mother reports that on the day I was born she felt she was going to give birth and went to the hospital. They told her to go home because they expected the birth would occur the next day. She started to leave but changed her mind and went back. After they admitted her, she claims she went into labor and finally gave birth to me.

My mother reports that, when I was first brought to her, I seemed to look at her in a very serious way and that I seemed to be an old man. She says that I was "checking her out" and that it scared her, but after a minute or so my eyes softened and I turned into a baby, closed my eyes and went to sleep. She thinks that I was making sure that she really was my mother. I believe this story because I was not born a "child." I was always very old. Later I became a child, but only a little bit. I was looking at her to assess what I had gotten myself into.

My first crystal clear memory is of being in the crib in the living room of my grandparents' house in Pittsburgh. I was trying to stand up. Since my mother says I was walking around at nine months, this was quite a bit before then. I was practicing standing by holding onto the bars of the crib. My legs were shaking and my head was too big to hold up and kept wobbling. At a certain point my hands began to give way and I knew that I was going to fall, so I let go and attempted to sit down. I fell upon my cushy diaper and then upon my back. I remember hoping that my head would not get banged, causing me to lose consciousness. I wondered how much muscle control I would be able to exercise during the fall. I didn't bang my head on the padded bottom of the crib and I didn't lose consciousness, so I rolled my head back and forth looking at my splayed-out arms.

When I looked to the left side I saw my left hand and it was sort of chubby. I flexed it into a fist using my will and a series of thoughts came to me in a kind of musical chord. How did I get here in the human body? Had I done something wrong? I will have to learn to coordinate this body and I will have to learn to walk and talk, and I will have to interact with all the others who are in similar bodies. None of them seem to be aware of any problem with this, and they seem to be satisfied being here. But I am stuck here in their midst where I will probably fall asleep the same as they have. I'm going to have to be here for quite a number of years and I have a great deal of work ahead of me.

I had a distinct knowledge that I had been elsewhere before this body and that this "elsewhere" was not constrained by the laws that inform this physical place. This memory of a place of greater freedom haunted me. I continued to have this memory of a place from which I had been somehow forced to leave to come here to be born. This place seemed to be, and still seems, just out of reach.

Between the ages of one and two I began consciously trying to find my way back to this memory because I did not want to lose it. It was faint and ethereal as I tried to follow it back. I would sit on my heels and be still for as long as possible and try to remember. I gathered my attention and spent long periods of time trying to follow its delicate pathway back. As I became more and more quiet I noticed certain things that were in the way.

First, I noticed that my body's breathing stood in the way of my attention. I began to practice ceasing breathing so that I could pay better attention to this faint and ethereal thread. I did not "hold" my breath. I would just find a relaxed place, and not breathe. Then I also noticed the drum in my chest that would not stop beating. I saw that my way was blocked. I tried to stop my heartbeat by my own volition in order to pay better attention, but I found that I could not stop it. This noise was preventing me from being able to fully gather my attention. I felt that if I could find absolute stillness I would be able to connect with what I was seeking. This went on daily whenever I was alone. Then something new started happening when I was about two years old. It became possible for me to simply not breathe for long periods of time.

I remember thinking that the length of time that I was not breathing was supposed to be impossible. I thought to myself that this consensus of belief about man and his possible authority over himself and his body and the phenomenal world was wrong and seriously limited and that the weight of this consensus was what kept things the way they were. I also felt that I could not allow my new understanding to be seen. I imagine that other children find out similar things about the consensus restraints that humans are subject to, and then abandon their own inner authority at an early age. Maybe it is just fantasy and magical thinking as the nervous system grows and forms.

One day, while in a kneeling position in the living

room, something dramatic happened. While not breathing it became more and more effortless to just sit, and I came "loose." "I" floated out of the body and moved upward sort of like a kite in a gentle wind. I looked back and there was my little body sitting quietly, not breathing. I seemed to be attached by some sort of stretchy thread or line. I was now freer but still tethered and I thought about exploring.

I wondered how long I could stretch the line before it would detach from the body. I wondered if I could go through the walls and leave the room—but then I realized several things. One was that I was inexperienced. What if the line detached and I was out of sight of the body and could not find my way back? It seemed that I was alone, but what if there were other powers further out that I might run into? What would I do then? I also began to wonder how long the body could continue not breathing with me away from it. Everyone else was on the other side of the house. I began to get frightened. What if they came into the room before I could get back into the body? What would they think? And what if I did let go and let the body die? I remember thinking that this would be completely unfair and cruel to my guardians. They would not understand anything about what happened. Even if I was able to go to a better place, I couldn't leave them with the misery of that.

I began to return to the body but I found that I could not reconnect. I kept passing through the body as if I were a ghost. I began to panic. After quite a bit of this panic I managed to align myself with the body but found that I didn't know how to fully reconnect. I managed to find some "snaps" in various places of the body which allowed me to reattach—sort of like the snaps which hold your blue jeans together or which hold a diving helmet on.

I decided to start breathing before someone caught me, but I found that I had forgotten how to engage the muscles. Breathing was not such an established habit at my tender age. This really threw me into a panic and I thought that I might have to watch the body die. It seemed the body could have remained that way for quite some time without any danger, but after I reattached, some sort of timer came into play and I needed to act before a deadline. Just like a guy trying to start a motorcycle or lawnmower, I kept trying, and finally, somehow, I got the body to gas and it began to breathe.

Sometime later I went to my mother and grandmother and asked them if they knew anything about breathing and meditation. In a delicate way I described a little of what I had been doing and that I'd been having some "experiences." Both of them told me that they had no experience in any such matters. Realizing that I had no mentor, I decided to stop these experiments.

I distinctly remember several other things from that year. It surprised me that I could understand most of what people were saying. I knew that I did not know how to talk very well, but I remember being curious as to how I knew the meaning of words that people spoke. I remember that I hadn't worked on this—so it seemed strange that I could understand the language that people used around me.

There was something else: there were other kinds of knowledge available to me. I knew that I could understand most of what people were saying although there were some words I didn't understand and had to guess from context, but when I was thinking to myself it was not in language. I wondered what form my own thinking was in. It was a kind of direct perception coupled with the concept. It is very hard to explain in language, but this form is more like pictures, or metaphoric pictures. It occurred to me that I would learn language and how to speak and slowly I would come to use this language as the main form of thinking like everyone else.

There was something else very curious. I could see other people, including the adults around me, in such a way that I could see their emotional condition in a kind of picture thinking. The amazing thing was that they did not need to speak words out loud. When they did speak, I noticed that their words and this "picture thinking" that went on inside of them did not conform. This led me to conclude that people were disjointed—that they had lost an elemental connection to their own inner selves, and most importantly, they were unconsciously lying because their words and their motives did not conform to each other. This was very strange to my "I" within myself, which experienced the kind of unity where my thinking and my feeling moved in the same direction. My thinking and feeling were overlain and overlapped, whereas in the adult it seemed there were two or three people in one package: one was the words and their concern about what the other organisms were thinking about them, and their other was their true, or inner, movement. I noticed that being with adults at that time was like experiencing a double exposure as if my eyes were slightly crossed. It was not altogether comfortable, but when I was a little older it started to recede. The focus and depth of my vision was changing. Eventually I lost much of this force of vision and could only hear the words.

I no longer practiced stopping my breathing, but I did begin "playing" with my breathing and performing various exercises. This was when I was three or four years old. I did all sorts of breathing exercises: huffing and puffing, segmented breathing, breathing through one nostril or the other or alternating the nostril in various patterns, counting the breaths, and changing the ratios of the inhalations and exhalations. I imagined the breath to be a substance I could direct to different parts of the body: pretending that the breath was a pneumatic drill or saw, imagining that the breath could move out on objects and buckle the walls, that it could reach different distances, that it would change my shape, either enlarging or shrinking me.

I also had another interesting experience, which later on, when I read the yogic literature, I was surprised to find listed. At times I sweated, tingled, vibrated, swooned and began to shake. I occasionally began to jerk and hop around the room like an insect. I began to fade out for various short lengths of time, beginning to pass out and waking up in other parts of the room. The final straw occurred one afternoon while performing my breathing exercises. I buzzed out, and when I woke up and opened my eyes, I was lying on my back looking at a piece of wood. I thought I might have died and was looking at the inside of the coffin. After my senses came back fully, I realized that I was under a large table. How I had gotten there is anybody's guess, but I began to worry that I would crack my head or damage my body in some irreparable way if I kept it up, so I retired from the breathing exercises.

3 First Birthday Party

The first birthday party I remember was when I turned three. I was given a red car with pedals. When the cake was brought out and my mother asked me to blow out the candles and make a wish—I said no. My mother asked me again—and I still said no. She asked again and said that the candles were burning down and the children wanted their cake and I should make a wish and blow out the candles. I looked up at her said, "Mother, I am housed, fed, clothed, cleaned, and loved. I don't have anything to wish for."

My mother became frantic at that point and said that I didn't have to tell anybody what my wish was but to please blow out the candles. While I could handle this, I still didn't want anything, so I wished that everyone else present would get their wishes, and if I gained, it would be collaterally.

I really didn't have a desire for anything special, but when I saw that red car I went nuts. Everybody wanted to drive it and I wanted to drive it by myself. We all got in a big line and everybody got a turn driving my little red car. I was very proud of it. I guess I did want something but we were so poor that I had denied myself the idea of wanting something.

We had a tiny piano with 28 keys that were in tune and I used to play it often. I would play one note and just listen to it fade away. I wondered how it could fade into nothing and

I concluded that it couldn't—that the note would go on and on, out into the universe. I would play two notes at a time and I wrote a number of pieces which sounded very Baroque, but when it came to playing three notes at a time I was stymied—sometimes it sounded good and sometimes it didn't. I asked my grandmother if she could teach me how to play the piano and she said "I'm sorry honey, I don't know how to play the piano—perhaps you could ask your mother." I asked my mother and she said, in a kind of exasperated tone, that she didn't know how to play the piano either. Her tone made me realize that she was thinking of herself and her lack because we were so poor. And when I asked for piano lessons I was told we were too poor to afford it.

I went back to my 28-key piano and I played whenever I could. I invented some musical pieces and improvised, always from an emotional motivation, and I was consciously conjoining the music to emotions. Sometimes I got frustrated and would play with my fists and perform glissandos with my thumbnail. Some of the keys eventually broke because of my fist performances. That was the end of my piano playing. Now that I understand music better, I can't stand keyboard instruments because they are never really in tune and you can't bend notes on them. That's one of the reasons I love the guitar, the sitar and the harmonica—because you can bend notes on each of them. You can bend notes on the saxophone, too, but I didn't have the breath control.

This all happened in Homestead where my grandparents were renting the upper floors of their house to different tenants. We set up a little rubber swimming pool in the backyard to splash in during the summer. By that time I was spending the school year in New York and only went to Homestead for summer vacation with my grandparents.

One summer when I was eight I went out into the woods with some boys and one said, "Oh look, black-berries." It was suggested that I eat some of these berries because they were delicious. When I asked the other kids if they wanted any they said no—they had had their fill. What I didn't know was that the blackberries were growing in a poison ivy patch and I was getting internal poison ivy poisoning. I don't know if you know what it's like when your insides itch all the way from your mouth to your ass, but it was just another experience. My face swelled up and I looked like Linda Blair in *The Exorcist* with my skin cracking open and oozing pus.

I was taken to the hospital where I was told there was nothing they could do. During grand rounds the doctors came just to see me because most of them would never get to see internal poison ivy poisoning. Then I was sent home to New York, somewhat delirious. We went by bus and my grandmother came with me. The bus had to make extra stops so she could get cold water to put on my forehead. I was passing in and out of consciousness, but by the time we got to New York I was able to get off the bus on my own two feet. My mother didn't immediately recognize me and said, "Where's Richard?" My grandmother explained about the poison ivy poisoning and pointed at me and my mother blanched. I saw a photo booth that offered four photos for a quarter. I wanted some evidence of myself in that condition but my mother said, "I am not having my son look like that in any photograph—you look like a monster." I'm still angry at her for that because I like evidence of my own conditions.

4 Richard Discovers Electricity and Other Experiments

When I was about four we got one of the first televisions on the block. I think it was a Zenith. It took several minutes to warm up while there was only a little dot of light in the middle of the screen. There were only three channels and each channel only broadcast for a couple of hours each day. I remember my grandfather getting anxious about it needing to be turned on at least five minutes before watching a show. We would sit in a kind of panic hoping that the TV set would warm up in time. I was warned about the electricity and told never to touch the plug.

This piqued my curiosity and I began wondering what this stuff was that they called "electricity." I also wondered why there was a warning attached to it. I decided to find out for myself when everyone else was in another part of the house. I turned the television on and pulled the plug halfway out of its socket. I licked the thumb and forefinger of my right hand and grabbed it between the plug and the socket. Electricity roared through my hand and up my arm to my shoulder. Immediately I learned several things about it; it was as powerful as anything else I had ever experienced. Second, it had no concern for me—I'm not sure evil is the right word, but the electricity really didn't care. It was clearly looking for something. I remember thinking that if it got into my chest it would take me over. It would oust me. I knew that I needed to fight it and let go. Luckily, although my fingers seemed to be stuck to the plug, I managed to get them open and was released. My right arm buzzed for several hours. I felt it for several days, and I still have a memory of the sensation. I was a little concerned that my arm would buzz permanently, so I was relieved when it faded.

Between the ages of four and five I began experimenting with my senses. I would walk around the house with a blindfold on or with my eyes closed, trying to sense the walls and furniture by touch alone. My mother didn't like this and made me stop. I also used earplugs or my fingers to shut off my hearing so I could try to listen to inner sounds. I would plug up one ear for a day to see what it was like and on the next day switch to the other ear. I put plugs in my nostrils so that I could pay attention to the right or left nostril independently. I realized that far more information comes in through the visual sense than is necessary for the organism to act upon.

People usually blink about 15 times a minute with brief visual interruptions. I wondered what it would be like if the blinks were backwards. I began walking around with my eyes closed and I blinked them open only every once in a while. I wanted to find out how little visual information I could carry on with. I used to cross the street and walk on the sidewalk in this way, with my eyes closed except for the fastest possible blinking to find out what had changed. It made the world appear like a flipbook.

I had ongoing experiences connected with time—one of which continued until I became a teenager. I would suddenly experience the world slowing down. Everything would begin moving in slow motion so that I had an indefinite time to think about my own movement and participation in events. Mostly this was extremely pleasant, but sometimes it was frightening. It might have been some sort of epileptic event.

When I entered school at the age of six a lot of these activities got put aside because no one else shared these interests. When I would bring up any of my own questions or interests, I got stares or worse.

5 "What Do You Want to Be When You Grow Up?"

Children are always asked what they want to be when they grow up. Aside from the fact that I didn't want to be on this planet in the first place, in this condition of stricture, with these people who were obviously insane, I had no idea how to answer this question. You know, children give all sorts of answers when they are younger that are meaningless later on, except for those rare cases where the child sees something that shapes their entire life. There may have been such a moment in my life. If so, it would've been that first memory and all that took place before I reached the age of five.

"What do you want to be when you grow up?" Doctor, lawyer, astronaut, scientist, writer, artist, fireman, policeman, construction worker, etc. Hardly any child answers with the job that they will end up doing. In other words, when you ask a child what he wants to be when he grows up he will almost never reveal what he is going to end up doing. I have never heard a child say that he wanted to be a waiter in a restaurant, or a financial analyst for some bank, or sell pretzels as a street vendor. He dreams something of grandeur, whatever that might be in his little mind, or if he is more of an old soul, he will refuse to answer the question or say, "I don't know."

That ought to conclude the matter, but it hardly ever does because adults enjoy prodding their poor little neighbors for an answer to this insulting question. It comes from the same part of adults that makes them want to tickle children, I suppose.

I was asked that question a lot. I didn't have an answer. I didn't want to have an answer. I had a lot of questions. Most of my questions were directed back into the substance of myself. What was I? Why was I? How did I come to be in this thing, in this place, in these circumstances? Did I have a purpose? Was there a task I was meant to achieve? Was I stranded on a farm planet as a punishment? Was it some kind of penance to be human, or was it something grand? Having adults ask me what I wanted to be when I grew up never ceased to be annoying in the same way that a mosquito is annoying to a person who is trying to concentrate. "What do you want to be when you grow up?" is a kind of rash—like poison ivy. For the adult, not getting the child's answer is the scratching which keeps making them ask it over and over again, until by virtue of fatigue, the child blurts out some stupid response that the child knows is bullshit. It is one of the ways in which we learn how to survive socially. It is more training in how to lie.

I don't remember what I said, but I know it was something out of exasperation. Being asked that question often, by enough people, began to inculcate into me the notion that answering the question to myself, internally, was something important. So, I tried to ask the question of myself. I didn't get a straight answer.

6 Cough Syrup, Death, Hypnosis and an Early Psychedelic Experience

When I was five I developed a terrible cough that sounded like a dying moose. The doctor advised that I should be in bed under a steam tent. I spent lots of time in bed with Vicks VapoRub all over my chest and a machine sending steam into the tent. The cough was probably caused by rheumatic fever and whooping cough. The doctor prescribed a cough syrup that tasted like Coke and probably had a narcotic or a small amount of cocaine in it. Remember, this was about 1955. I was given a teaspoon of it every once in a while. I remember looking at it and that was the first time I had the desire to take some extra, but I didn't because I was a good boy.

I loved this Coke syrup while I was in the steam tent for weeks. One night I thought that I was going to die. I stayed awake all night long coughing my guts out until the light came in the morning. Then I heard the church bells, because it was Sunday, and a poem suddenly came to me. It was something like, "Death, get thee now from thy soft bed. Up thy cherished marble steps shall I ascend, when the bell doth toll for me." This was really strange because I had never heard or used archaic English before.

I used thee, thou, thy, doth, and some of the piano

pieces I wrote then were Baroque and extremely classical. I remember writing the poem and a deep male voice came to me from the corner of the room saying "There is no death." It wasn't said in an emphatic way, but in a matter-of-fact way, and it came right after I had written the poem—a true auditory hallucination in four words. It was so compelling that I have believed it ever since. I've had these events from time to time, and they have always been correct. I've never heard frightening, paranoid voices, but only good voices, and only rarely.

I went to doctors and dentists when I was young, like most kids. One dentist had a poster of the moon on a window shade. He always pulled it down and told me to watch it and imagine that I was in a spaceship going to the moon. Then he would give me an injection and start working on my teeth. I now recognize this was a hypnotic procedure. Doctors and dentists were being taught medical hypnosis in those years, promulgated mostly by a guy named Dave Elman. He had been a stage hypnotist and when his father was dying of cancer and in great pain, he wondered if hypnosis could help him, and it did. Elman quit the stage and began teaching dentists and doctors his quick trance techniques.

When I was seven or eight I had some sort of dental problem and the dentist put some liquid on a cloth— probably ether (it smelled like roses) and he told me to breathe it in and relax. I fought like the devil and they had to hold me down and press the cloth against my face until I passed out. I went on to have an intense psyche-delic trip with colored squares turning into circles and geometric shapes flying around. It seemed as though I could see through my eyelids and I could hear the doctor talking to his nurse. I was in this state for a couple of hours. My parents carried me out, put me in the car and took me home. That was a profound early experience for me, brought on by a chemical.

7 Turning Upside Down Inside and the Power of Silence

When my two cousins and I were about seven or eight years old, we began learning something about yoga because there was an early morning television show about it. I remember thinking that if I could have run off and become a yogi or a fakir I would. I could never get my legs into the full lotus position and I despaired at my lack of postures which showed me how little "will" we all have. I wanted to get in that position more than anything—but couldn't get it. I always tried experiments to see how much of myself was amenable to my volitional will. I was consistently amazed at how resistant the body and thinking and senses were to any kind of control whatsoever. I felt daunted by the stubborn refusal of the body to accede to my wishes.

My cousins and I were doing imitation yoga postures. My cousin Billy declared that he had learned something from his uncle that was real yoga because his uncle had been to India. His younger brother Ronnie was especially upset that Billy had been taught something that he hadn't. We asked Billy to show us. He said he could move his "I." He got into a headstand and said he was going to move his "I" from his head to his abdomen. He counted 1 to 3 and then proceeded to do it. It was very weird. You could tell that his center was now in his abdomen, and when he spoke, it seemed as though his mouth moved but his voice was coming from his belly in a kind of telepathy. He then flipped it back and came down from the headstand.

He said that he could show us how to do it, so we all got into headstands. He said that first you get into a physical headstand which turns everything upside down. Then you do "an inner headstand," turning yourself within yourself. Since I had had the experience of becoming detached from my body earlier, I was a little bit wary. Ronnie kept trying but couldn't get it so Billy said he would help him. We were all upside down. I could sense Billy "walking" over to Ronnie's right side (not in the physical sense) and he put his hands on Ronnie and turned him upside down inside himself. I was still upside down physically and psychically, so I decided to try it. It was a little like folding over at the waist and diving off a diving board. There was a little leap of faith. It took two or three times before I turned over like an egg timer. Then I was upside down inside my upside down physical body. It was very strange. I began to feel nauseous and disoriented. I "flipped" myself back and felt better. Billy and Ronnie stayed as they were for a little while longer and then came down. Then they began fighting because Ronnie was jealous. I was bedazzled. I knew then that there was a real yoga that was very different from the regular concept that normal people play at. The experience also showed me that the identification with the head (or even the body) was extremely temporary, fragile and malleable. I kept practicing yogic postures, but never tried Billy's "trick" again.

I also tried every spiritual discipline that I heard about. One of the most humorous of these was somewhat along the line of Mauna, which is the practice of intentional silence. It's done in both Western and Eastern mysticism. I heard about it and thought that it sounded delicious. I decided to practice silence. I said to myself that I would not talk either outwardly or inwardly. I felt like I was doing very well at it until I ran into other people.

People don't like it when you don't talk. They get very uncomfortable. I remember my grandmother looking at me strangely and asking me, "Are you all right?" Of course, I wasn't supposed to answer. This only concerned her more. It was practically the same thing with the children who were playing. Nobody played silently—the children played with a good deal of chatter. When they noticed that I wasn't participating in talk, they made me the center of attention. The children were especially good at breaking my ability to remain silent, either by persistently nagging me for periods of time, or by getting nasty, sarcastic and angry or by tickling, wrestling and even punching. After a bit of this treatment I would finally reach the end of my rope and blurt something out. Doing that released the pressure but ruined my practice.

I thought about writing on a card: "I am practicing silence today." But then I thought that would be cheating and would sully my practice by having a bridge to fall back on. I saw I was really getting nowhere if I tried to practice this around other people, especially children, so I finally did make a card and carried it in my pocket. That turned out to be an absolute disaster. A little girl grabbed it out of my hand and made it the object of the entire neighborhood's goofs and glee, while I became the central object of derision. I learned a lot from this and anything else I might have tried with other people. The first thing I learned was that I couldn't find others who had any interest whatsoever in what I was interested in. Second, I learned that other people have an instinctual negative response to interests like mine. I really don't know if it was instinctual in all the others or if it was socially-supported enhanced negativity which ran up against my hopes and interests, but I do know that others would repeatedly throw these interests against the rocks.

This is the beginning of my story—a story of one with the lodestone, a mad, crazy, careening out of control, fighting with my guardian angels rock 'n' roll story. The story of an old soul acting like a juvenile delinquent on a reform school planet. Remember the story of Jacob and the angels with whom he wrestled all night? He wrestled with those angels and he got something out of it, something profound and devoutly to be wished for, but he also got a broken hip. There is a price to be paid. I have never been afraid to pay it.

8 Catholic School, God and the Devil

I remember kindergarten as something absolutely wonderful. There were toys and play time and nap time (which I couldn't stand because I was awake) and just a general sort of bliss at learning anything and being able to play with new things.

Then I entered first grade. What a horror. I was handed a pencil and a notebook, and told to sit down at a desk. In my innocence, I pleaded, "Where are the toys?" I was told, "Well, you're a big boy now and you get to sit at a desk—isn't that nice?" NO! It wasn't nice, and although I made do, it is not something I would do to our children. Children need to amble out their youth in the middle of the forest before being told to sit in a chair six hours a day for 12 years or more.

I had been placed in a Catholic school. My family was traditionally Catholic, although nobody seemed to go to church except on special occasions. But my grandmother had statues in her bedroom of the little Lord Jesus with the world in his hand and of mother Mary, and she cherished them.

I asked my grandmother about it and she said that because her husband (my grandfather John Ewing) was an avowed atheist, she stopped going to church and practiced Christianity inwardly—going about cooking and cleaning without complaint or any outward sign of bitterness or negativity. She was a loving, caring person.

There I was in Catholic school. I took Latin and was an altar boy, which I thoroughly enjoyed for half a year—I don't know why I stopped but it was not from being molested, because I was not. And I was never hit by any of the nuns although I was screamed at a lot, so I never developed the kind of hatred that many lapsed Catholics have against the church. I now realize that the church is the aggregate of the people in it, and they are a completely mixed bunch.

From the time I was born I could not understand how the world could be such a mess with people so unpleasant to one another. Then I was told there had come a savior to save us from our sins—that is, our flaws and faults, lies and insults. Well if that was the case I couldn't understand how this savior could've ever been a success. People were still nasty or alternately kindhearted in a haphazard way.

Nonetheless, many people seemed to worship this Jesus as the savior, and in my own private thoughts I began to ponder this. I began to wish that I could be of help to Jesus. At the same time I couldn't fathom how he had failed. I wanted to be a saint to help Jesus, or be his assistant or someone like his brother. Sometimes I was jealous of Jesus, and I suppose I wanted to be God.

This is a difficult subject because I knew that I was not him, and I recognized that I was weak and had flaws. Yet I also knew that I could be a force aligned with the same purpose for which he had come into the world—to awaken the interned from their unconsciousness, except for the fact that I had no real will to work with. Neither my body or my emotions would obey me, and my thoughts yielded very little power. I was shaken by my urge to replace Jesus, and felt competitive with him, as siblings would. I was an only child, but Jesus was my brother—a real man.

This made me wonder if perhaps I was the devil who will break something in a big tantrum because he can't have it. So, I wanted to be a saint. Later on I learned that most saints are not paid well or well-known so I gave up on that wish. I couldn't fathom spending my life force only to end up anonymous, like a gear inside a clock. My ego was way bigger than that. I remember being disappointed that these saints were so poorly treated and so poorly paid, like unappreciated servants.

We were often taken to church in Catholic school. The church made me feel claustrophobic and nauseous. It was just about one of the worst feelings imaginable, like being dragged to one's death, or like a walk to the gallows. I wondered if there was something wrong with me. Again, I thought perhaps the devil had gotten into me. In any case, something was seriously wrong if I was having such a negative reaction to being in a place I had been told was holy and good. In hindsight, I may have been aware unconsciously that the devil in fact was in the church and this was my reaction to being in such a place—a place corrupted and thoroughly infiltrated by the enemy. I realized that I was not a saint and my status, position, responsibilities and duties in this incarnation fell under a different title.

It was later that I heard the idea of the bodhisattva. These are beings who have perfected themselves and earn the right to Nirvana or heaven, but when they get there they discover that everyone else has been left behind. As a result their peace is not complete. It is disturbed by compassion for others. So, they decide to return to the earth to be born again and to forgo their own salvation and remain on earth until all are saved. This sounded right up my alley—I started praying for the chance to perform the act of the bodhisattva.

I vowed that I would take on all the suffering of others—that I would go to hell in their place and they could have my merit, if I had any. This one was a difficult pill to swallow, but like a man who cuts a deal with God when he is in big trouble, I cut the deal and prayed for this. It was my prayer for several years. And whenever I was asked to make a wish on my birthday candles, or if I got a wishbone, my wish was always that the other person would get their wish, or that everyone in the universe would get their wishes. At the beginning this was really my only wish, and I couldn't find any other "wish" in me asking for my own fulfillment.

It seemed to me that the world was so bad off that this was the only wish worth bothering about. After a while, the cautionary thought crept up on me that most people have very shallow wishes and that, if they came true, it would be really bad for them and everybody else, so I began tempering my wish with the idea that they should get their wish only if it was good for them. This was the beginning of my lifelong interest in the idea of wish. I wondered how much actual power there might be in wishing. Something in me knew that there was a very powerful aspect in a wish—more powerful even than prayer. But I could not understand the choices that other people made when they were given the opportunity to make a wish. None of the things that other people talked about wishing for seemed important.

It seemed to me that the most common wishes were either for objects, like a new red bike, or for unattainable goals like instant world peace. I felt it was a shame to be frittering away what might be our most powerful device— and one which might be directly connected to a real will in us.

Again, I wondered about myself and I pondered what my role was to be in this life. Although I wished with all my heart to be a bodhisattva, I also recognized that this was not the right title for me. The question of why I had been forced to be born in this time and place constantly nagged at me. It never ceased from plaguing my thoughts. Much later when I was a young adult I realized that I had once been the Yogi who had achieved a great deal. There had come a time when I had reached a crossroads in my practice. One way led to work on myself in private leading to the goal of emancipation. The other way was to turn back to the community—the city and the people—and to work on myself through service to others. I saw clearly that I had chosen the first way, and in doing so I had achieved a great deal. But there had come a time when I also realized that I had reached a cul-de-sac— that this route to salvation was flawed, and that I had to turn back and return to work with others.

In order to facilitate this I had to be born again. I saw this extremely clearly and deeply. The matter of its truth has never wavered, and it has been a hard truth. I could see, from the very beginning, that facing this and being with other people was the very last thing I ever really wanted to do. Plainly speaking, I hated people and as a general rule thought that humans as a species didn't know what they were doing.

So I kicked against the goad, and wrestled with the forces which it had born me. In this wrestling, I gained a great deal of a particular "something" and developed an enormous, strange kind of sensitivity, like the safecracker who uses sandpaper on his fingers so that the nerve endings are revealed and he can feel the tumblers fall. But this is another story, for later.

9 The Intoxicated Cartoon

When I was little I watched cartoons, both on television and at the movies. The movies cost thirty-five cents back then. I lived on the wrong side of the river and on the wrong side of the tracks, which meant that we were very poor and thirty-five cents was a big deal. The theater used to show two, sometimes three movies on Saturdays. There were 20 minutes of cartoons in between each movie. The cartoons were filled with ridiculous violence, and usually the happiest character in any given cartoon was the intoxicated character. He was usually portrayed holding a bottle with a skull and crossbones on the label and a big smile on his face. There were usually X's across his eyes, meaning that he was completely zonked. Whenever there was cartoon violence, the intoxicated cartoon character seemed immune—nothing ever happened to him. He was completely protected by his intoxication. It was a very strong image for me.

Back home at my grandparents' house, there wasn't a lot of fighting—just the usual bickering over money, since we had so little, but there was a lot of love and very little meanness. The only time my grandmother and grandfather got into it was after my grandfather went on a binge. He was a binge drinker and usually the binges occurred when he was going out with one of his brothers, most often my uncle Earl, or when he went to one of his Lodge meetings.

At that time my grandfather resembled Ralph Kramden from *The Honeymooners,* and his fate, especially his financial fate, closely resembled that hapless soul we used to laugh at on our black-and-white television. He was always trying to come up with schemes to lift us from the day-to-day penny-pinching and the worrying about paying the bills. None of these schemes ever worked. He bought a laminating machine, and thought that everyone would want to have their precious family pictures laminated to ensure their longevity. But everybody laughed at him and nobody wanted his services. Years later, the laminating business took off. He was just ahead of the loop.

Another thing he did was buy a mimeographing machine, thinking that he could get good business out of the local school system or churches because they would need all sorts of things printed out. Unfortunately, he bought the machine before he found out that the school system already had their own machines, and the largest town councils weren't interested either. So the laminating and mimeographing machines ended up in the basement, where they became my personal toys when I was ten or so, and I had tremendous hours of fun mimeographing and laminating all sorts of nonsense. He taught me to use each of them so that I could be his assistant.

My grandmother only yelled at my grandfather when he came home drunk. After that he would challenge me to a peeing contest where we would both head into the bathroom and empty our bladders. Of course I could never compete with the gallon of beer which he had stored away under his growing waistline, so I would always empty out and stand amazed for the next couple of minutes while he drained the firehose. He never got mean when he drank—

just woozy, so I could never understand why my grand-mother got so angry and called my uncle Earl a bad influence.

Everybody smoked. I couldn't understand why the adults smoked. When the cigarettes ran out, my grand-mother would give me a note and I would go to the store to buy them. My grandparents had a real reluctance to run out of cigarettes, which I also couldn't understand, but I could tell they absolutely needed them. I pondered the question: why do the adults take poisons?

When they drank, they wobbled around and seemed stupider and more likely to have accidents and get into fights. When they smoked they would have giant coughing fits. I figured there must be something really good going on to pay such a heavy price in the loss of their health and capacities. I thought about this for a long time and was determined to get to the bottom of it. So finally, when I was nine years old, I slipped a cigarette out of my grand-mother's pack of 20 after she had smoked a couple. They never used to count the cigarettes, but they would know if I took the first one or if I took the last one.

I was practicing being sneaky. I got some matches and hid my cigarette while I thought about how and where and when I was going to smoke it. I had a friend who was willing to experiment and share in the adventure and we began talking about finding a place. I think it took about two weeks before we settled on a garage that was usually unlocked and located down the alleyway. The owners were never home during the day. After gathering the cigarette and the matches, the two of us clandestinely climbed into the garage. It was empty and we felt pretty safe. The moment had come. I lit the cigarette, took a drag and passed it to my friend. I had inhaled the smoke but it forced its way back out of me in a little coughing spasm. I was going to have to get used to this. My friend was trying just as hard as I was, and he was having just as much luck. But we managed to smoke a cigarette between us, getting pretty dizzy and a little sick. We waited half an hour before we dared to leave the garage. I walked home, went into the bathroom, brushed my teeth and washed my face and hands.

This was the kind of adventure and experiment that I was going to have to repeat, because I still could not understand why the adults smoked or took poisons. I would find out, in a big way, pretty soon.

10 Junior High Heroin and
   Big Angel/ Big Devil

I went to Junior High at PS3 in Greenwich Village. The year after I left, it became a reform school. PS3 had several classes for highly intelligent children. The majority of the kids were poor and it was a very diverse school—white, black, Chinese, Jewish—the school was in the deepest part of the west side of Greenwich Village.

One day my friends and I went to a tenement and there were a bunch of kids listening to The Velvet Underground and shooting up heroin. I took one look and said, "Oh no! They are just sleeping through that music." I left, and I never listened to the Velvet Underground again until people started comparing Television to them.

I didn't want to hear songs about heroin while my junior high school friends were shooting up. Of course, I had already tried heroin—really strong white heroin that was sold in one and two dollar bags, those little envelopes the post office workers put stamps in. We would take a little bit and snort it, getting completely bonkers-stoned, with intermittent bouts of vomiting, nodding out and dreaming. I only did that for a couple of months, but certainly not steadily. I wasn't into nodding out at that time. By my late teens I had gone through just about every drug known to man. But I never dove into just anything and I was not a garbage head. I always investigated first.

After Junior High, I took an entrance examination to allow me to attend a specialized high school focusing on science. There were three in the city: Stuyvesant, Bronx Science and Brooklyn Tech, all which required entrance tests. About 20,000 kids would take the test for less than 300 seats in each of the three schools. I passed the entrance exam and decided upon Stuyvesant because it had a heavy emphasis on science and it was based in Manhattan where I lived. I didn't want to travel to the Bronx and I certainly wasn't interested in technology at the time.

At Stuyvesant there was a mix of brilliant teachers and average teachers. I had figured out that the average IQ of the students was higher than the average IQ of the teachers, so I decided not to do homework, thinking it was only a forced autodidactism after which they would give me tests. I loved tests so I would read the textbooks in a month—the entire textbook—and then wait for the tests which I always did well on. I declared to the teachers that I was not going to hand in homework. This got me sent down to the principal's office where I explained my position. I was told that as long as I passed the tests I could not get a failing grade. That suited me fine. I also went to my psychiatrist and asked him to write a letter freeing me from any team sports, although I did very well in gymnastics. Climbing ropes, parallel bars, sprinting, long jump—I excelled in all of these and I had very strong legs from bicycling. That took care of my body, and I loved to learn and hardly ever missed a day of school. My music touched upon my emotional center, so all three parts of me were being educated—body, mind and emotions (spirit).

I was also deep into using amphetamines and barbiturates. One time I took barbiturates before going to school and started nodding out in class. The teacher sent me to the nurse who decided that I had the flu and let me lay on a cart until I felt better. I slept until 4:30 PM when the nurse wanted to go home and told me to go see a doctor. I wobbled out of school with nobody any wiser. I used to be able to get away with all sorts of nonsense with my angelic face disguising the little devils inside. I subscribe to the slogan Big Angel/Big Devil—you can't have one without the other or you are unbalanced. I wasn't afraid of my devils and in fact got to be very good friends with them. They know more about mankind than the angels do. They have all the secrets whereas the angels only worship.

11 Teenage Activity

In my early teens I went to a summer camp run by a local community center. That was two weeks of utter joy. We did all the usual camp pranks to people like short-sheeting them, or filling their pillows with shaving cream. One thing happened that was kind of sad. We were out on a hike and there was one kid we couldn't find. He had somehow fallen into the latrine and couldn't climb back up because of the slime on the sides of the bottom. He had sliced his leg up pretty badly on a nail on the way down and spent six hours trying to get back up. After that his parents came and took him back home. We all thought it was a great joke but it was really quite sad.

The boys' and girls' camps were across the lake from one another. One night toward the end of camp we snuck across and had a great time until the camp director caught us and shooed us back over to the boys' side while jeering at us about camp rules. But what was he going to do? He couldn't kick us out and it was almost the end of the term. We had nothing but fun.

I had been in the Boy Scouts, but quit after three years, preferring to spend time with my fellows—the druggies. I had smoked a cigarette when I was nine, broken into the liquor cabinet when I was 10, and then the medical cabinet, stealing my grandmother's amphetamines and sleeping pills because she said she didn't like the way they made her feel.

I was reading books about James Bond and Sherlock Holmes and they both used drugs extensively so I thought I should try them out. I enjoyed it immensely, especially the uppers. Later on I got into downers deeply—about as deep as you can get with barbiturates. By then I was a little James Bond and Sherlock Holmes all rolled up into one. Of course I didn't have any cocaine at the time, so I made up for that later.

We used to drink beer while bowling and the kid that I bowled with approached me one time in school when we were in seventh grade. He asked me if I would smoke pot with him because he was afraid of what it might do to him, and he wanted help because he had gotten it from an older student and really wanted to try it. I asked him to give me two weeks to think it over so I could undertake research, at which time I would give him a definitive answer.

I spent much of the next two weeks in the New York Public Library researching marijuana—both medical studies and testimonials from people like jazz legend Mezz Mezzrow and other jazz musicians. I also studied drugs more generally, reading *Confessions of an English Opium Eater*, by De Quincey, and Baudelaire's *Artificial Paradises*, as well as the rest of the French drug users at the turn of the 20th century. My school had shown us anti-drug movies which only made us want to try them more. And my studies at the library showed me there was nothing wrong with marijuana—it poses no great health hazards. At the end of those two weeks I told my friend I would smoke with him.

One day after school we went up to his house. He was one of those misfits with a mother who was destroyed—she just lay on the couch in the darkness of her living room, and so we tiptoed around her and went to his room where we rolled up a joint and mixed it with tobacco so it wouldn't be too strong. As it turns out it wasn't strong at all, in fact it wasn't anything.

We smoked it and kept looking at each other, asking each other if we were high—

"I don't know, what about you do you feel anything?"

"I don't know—let's get a mirror and see if our pupils are enlarged."

That was the thing I was afraid of—that my parents would see my pupils super wide open and figure out what I had been doing.

It wasn't until a couple of weeks later that we went over to another kid's house. He had gotten some pot from his older brother. When we smoked that pot, OH BOY DID WE GET STONED. The giggles began, and they wouldn't stop—outright laughing for maybe an hour or two, followed by the munchies. I don't remember what we ate, but we found something in the kitchen. Who can remember when they're busy laughing at everything and anything?

Around the same time my parents enrolled me in a martial arts school named after Jerome Mackey, the man who operated it. Mackey ran an entire karate school franchise with much success. He taught three types of martial arts and had Japanese guys with black belts as teachers.

I started with Judo, and I liked it a great deal but I could never get past the white belt because I would not pin anybody during the competitions. I suppose I could have, but I preferred to lose. In some ways, this was the same as when I was learning to walk. In order to learn to walk you have to learn to fall, which is the first thing they teach you in Judo. So in order to succeed, you have to learn to fail, and you have to fail a lot. After a fist fight in the fifth grade, I didn't want to fight anybody for any reason what-soever, especially not just to earn a colored piece of cloth. So I left Judo and entered Shotokan karate, which is the hardest style in terms of its mechanics—it is very hard-edged karate.

I took the subway there and I used to bound up the stairs to the second floor where the dojo was. After an hour of the class I could barely walk down the stairs—that's how tough it was. My legs would wobble and unless I held on to the banister, I would've fallen down the stairs. I had always loved hiking and climbing when I was in the scouts. At school I used to get an A in gymnasium because I was very lithe and loved climbing ropes and doing parallel bars. What I couldn't stand was the highly competitive mindset of team sports—a group of people who had to win and a group of people who had to lose.

My hate and disgust for that aspect of team sports began when I was about six years old. I was given a foot-ball for Christmas, and took it out into the alley, where the boys wanted to play touch football. All went well until the third scrimmage when I was handed the ball and one of the other bigger boys tackled me. He punched the ball out of my arms and ran off with it yelling "Touchdown!" I told him we were playing touch football and he said, "That's for sissies, this is real football like my dad taught me." I looked at him deeply and I could see that he was empty, so I handed him my football and told him, "Here take this, it's yours." He looked a little bit confused, but I turned and walked back to my house and shut the door behind me. I never played another sport like that in my life, except a little bit of baseball. I don't even like ping-pong, because somebody wins and somebody loses and I would prefer to lose and get it over with.

So there I was in karate class with a white belt, and after every competition, the Japanese sensei would put some Japanese character on my belt meaning "courageous" or "good spirit," or some other nonsense, but he couldn't give me a yellow belt because I hadn't won anything. I stayed a white belt for about a year until my hair grew too long. The sensei told me to get a haircut or leave the dojo and I chose to leave.

I wasn't going to let anyone tell me to cut my hair. My parents bugged me about it, and I wasn't going to let them talk me into it either. The revolution had begun. The Beatles and the Stones and the rest of the English invasion started, and everybody began growing their hair in long styles. When the teachers complained about it, I showed them pictures of men in the Middle Ages who had hair as long, and even longer than we did. Some of them wore wigs—but who cares. Long hair came and went and came again. So I quit karate and judo in the dojo even though I wanted to learn Aikido very badly. But I wasn't going to let it get in the way of my hair.

I also took drum lessons for about three and a half years. I started wanting to play the drums when I was ten but my family was so poor all they could afford for me was one drum at a time—one for my birthday and one for Christmas.

As a drummer, I wanted to be able to play like Mitch Mitchell or Micky Waller or John Bonham and especially like Ringo, which is why the brand I chose for my full kit was Ludwig Pink Champagne Sparkle. I took lessons from a guy who was the ghostwriter for Cozy Cole and other big band drummers. They would play and my teacher would annotate what they were doing for their books. He taught strictly cross stick drumming—no matched grip for him, and he taught big band style, whereas I wanted to learn rock 'n' roll but I was stuck with him. But I really loved the guy—he was somebody special and mentored me really well. He taught me how to build a drum solo and play the Lindy and the special time stuff like 5/4 and 9/8 by breaking them up into smaller parts.

Those years were great for me. Everything was happening. The American rock explosion had started with the LA bands like the Doors and the Byrds, and the San Francisco bands like the Grateful Dead. When I went to my friend Danny's house he always had the best new records. Danny turned me on to the first Jimi Hendrix record and the first Pink Floyd record.

I had already developed a secret desire to play guitar as my primary instrument. I'm still interested in the drums and like to play them a great deal to this day, but something definitive happened that altered my course. I had a hallucinatory experience while playing my set. My drums lost all their color—like in the Wizard of Oz in Kansas—and everything became grayscale. The drums didn't sound as good anymore, and I heard a voice—an auditory hallucination that told me, "You need to play a melody instrument."

I mustered the guts to tell my drum instructor. He nearly wept, and told me that I could have been a really great drummer and that he was sorry to see me go. But go I went, and I've never looked back because the past is always present to me. Inside are encyclopedias .of experience. Going into my memory is like going into a house that is full of rooms, like a huge mansion where the maid hasn't been for years and the whole place is in disarray.

Many people I've met live in the basement of their house. Not only are they unaware of their own inner encyclopedias but also of their own potentials and possibilities—they are taken by society's hypnotic force and become ordinary. Although the ordinary is already extraordinary, I was not ordinary and I am not ordinary in that sense of being hypnotized like many others into the small world of the basement which is lit by candle and contains games like "I have money" or "I am handsome" or "I am beautiful, powerful, luxurious and sexy." I've never played those games because I am able to be honest with myself. I've been in almost all the rooms of my house at least long enough to see that they exist and that they have special powers. Each one has a different power, potential or possibility.

12 The Whole World Is Sex

Everybody has epiphanies, those moments where you see something deeply—an aspect of super reality that lifts you out of your horizontal daydream. I'm not kidding when I say that perhaps I had a kind of epilepsy—grand mal, petite mal, weird mal. The terms come from the French and mean big bad, little bad and in my case, weird bad. I don't think that it was bad and I don't think that I ever lost consciousness. I never fell down and had convulsions, but I might've floated off somewhere, gotten glassy eyes and drifted to the edge of the universe. I could look back on the earth from a vast distance.

I was sitting in class one day in the fifth grade when one struck me. It was before puberty. I can't remember what the teacher said. It was nothing provocative—just some ordinary something about something connected with something that we were supposed to learn about something—when it happened. They say epilepsy is a kind of electrical storm in the brain. If so, this was a pretty good sized thunderstorm.

I looked at the child in front of me, a red-haired girl, when I realized suddenly that she was the result of sex between her parents. I don't know how I can convey to you the surety of that understanding—that she was the result of sex, that she was made out of sex—100% sex. I turned my head and looked at another child and had the same realization. I looked all around the room and all I could see were packages of sex. Then I imagined even further, throughout the school building, the neighborhood, the city, the state, the country, the continent, the whole world.

Everybody in it and everything in it was completely and thoroughly made of sex. Then I had another realization—there's a lot of sex that does not result in children. If children are the result of sex, what is the result of sex that doesn't result in children? I started running statistics. There were seven billion people on planet Earth, all having sex, or trying to, and all made out of sex. What percentage of sex results in the birth of children? Each child might represent a package of concentrated sex, compounded by all the sex that their parents had had between conceptions. The whole world was packed like an overloaded and overinflated canister of oxygen. The canister was filled with sex.

The question became, does everybody get packed with the same amount of sex like tuna cans? Sometimes when I looked at women on the street I could see the weight of the sex that they were carrying around and I would ask myself, "How does she do it? How does she carry around all that sex? Isn't it heavy?" Other people seemed lighter, so I had to ask myself, "Is the sex hidden, or did they get less at the factory?" If your parents screwed a lot, but they only had one child as a result, does that child have more sex as a result? Does the screwing pack it in, or does it spill it out so the child gets less. My brain became a world full of questions and ponderings.

The entire earth was a canister of sexual pressure, the enormity of which squeezed so hard that babies popped out all over the earth, like bubbles on the surface of a large pot of boiling water. I could barely think. I was overloaded with this vision. For several weeks I could not look at anyone without seeing this deep impression that the whole world was sex. In fact, although I managed to tone it down, this impression has never left me. And when I look at you I have to prevent that vision from overtaking me. It doesn't make me feel sexually aroused—it's just pure science, pondering and realization. That is something I cannot get rid of.

13 Valence

In the seventh grade, I experienced an epiphany over chemistry. I loved chemistry, but even more so when my epiphany extended to atoms and molecules. I realized that every atom has electrons spinning around in groups of up to eight on a level, and for a level to have more means that the electrons start a new level. Atoms that get close to one another can share electrons if their valences match—that is, if one atom has five electrons in its outer shell and the other atom has three, then they fall in love and have sex. Is sexual activity more than in and out, and out and in? If one atom's electron leaves and circles the other atom and then returns, the two atoms hook up. It's that simple—chemistry is sex. That made it very exciting to study chemistry and playing in the chemistry lab was just like being a voyeur or matchmaker. I guess you might call that alchemy.

Geng Moon Eng was one of my good friends in the seventh grade. His parents owned the Chinese laundry on West 4th Street near Sixth Avenue, right next to a pastry shop where we got sweets after school. My friendship with Geng was based on our mutual love of chemistry. We used to look at chemical equipment catalogs the way the other kids looked at toy catalogs. We often went over to the big chemical supply store on Hudson Street, where we would ogle at Pyrex test tubes and retorts. We would buy chemicals in bulk and perform experiments because we both had pretty good chemistry sets. Of course, being 12 years old, our main goal was combustion, that is, blowing things up! I loved mixing lithium, the soft white metal, with water. It would cause the lithium to explode in a white-hot flame. Dazzling.

We also got fireworks in Chinatown and would open the little firecrackers in order to collect a big pile of gunpowder. There was nothing finer for young men of that age than to blow up a mailbox or drop a quarter stick of dynamite (called an ashcan) down a toilet to blow out the pipes.

One day after school we got some powdered phosphorus and gunpowder. We were going to mix them together to make a delightful little boom-boom. We were in the back of Geng's parents' laundry, surrounded by those packages of folded shirts and laundry wrapped in that brownish wrapping paper tied up with string.

We cleared a space and filled a large test tube halfway up with gunpowder. Our friend Abe was out front on the lookout in case the parents came back. They had gone out leaving Geng in charge of the store. I folded a card in half and put a pile of phosphorus on it. Then I began tapping it lightly into the test tube. The phosphorus was kind of clumpy, and so I took a pencil and very carefully tapped the end of the card to get the phosphorus to slide into the test tube. A little cloud of phosphorus accumulated in the air.

All of a sudden everything blew up in our hands. The entire room was filled with smoke and I couldn't see anything. I couldn't see Geng who had been standing two feet away from me. I was in shock, and because I couldn't see anything, I bumped into a lot of things as I walked out of the store towards the street. Smoke was billowing out of the back room and heading towards the front door. Abe was running towards me shouting something. That was when I realized I was deaf. The explosion had completely cut off my hearing. Abe's lips were moving and he was yelling at me, but I couldn't hear a word. Finally I figured out he was asking me where Geng was. I didn't know what to tell him. From my perspective he had simply gone up in a puff of smoke. I pointed towards the back and then walked outside into an unreal world. The city moved on with the traffic, pedestrians, streetlights and conversations. It was a silent movie. I couldn't even hear the normal sounds you hear from inside your own body. Pure silence. No ringing, no nothing.

I looked down and saw blood dripping off my fingertips onto my shoes. My white shirt was mostly red, although I didn't feel anything particularly painful. A few minutes later, Abe showed up through the smoke holding onto Geng. We convened on the street outside the laundry. Geng was terrified of how his parents might react so he had put out the fire with his bare hands. They were burned and full of pieces like a weird set of test gloves—black and red with shards of glass sticking out of them. Parts of his shirt had been burned as well as his face and hair. My hearing was still 90% gone but started to come back ever so slightly, such that if someone yelled it sounded like whispering in the distance. We were trying to figure out what to do and how to resolve this without his parents finding out what had happened.

We actually considered getting a box of Band-Aids and trying to cover up our wounds, changing our shirts, and trying to clean up the laundry, which at this point was completely filled with smoke from top to bottom and front to back. We could not see into the store at all. We opened the front door and waved our arms around trying to clear the smoke, but it wasn't doing very much good. My fingertips were still dripping blood and I couldn't wave my arms around without blood splattering all over the place. After about 10 minutes of panic we gave up and realized that we needed to walk over to St. Vincent's Hospital about three blocks away. We locked up the laundry while it was still full of smoke and walked over to the emergency room.

At the hospital we were separated and treated. I had several pieces of shrapnel in my forearms and torso. That's what was causing the bleeding. The staff told me that they felt it was too dangerous to try to remove the phosphorus and that if any of it got in my bloodstream it would kill me rather quickly. So they left the lumps of phosphorus/gunpowder where they were and assured me that my body would encapsulate them and that I could probably live with them permanently—which I have to this day.

My friend Geng was not so lucky. He had serious burns on both hands and his face and another wound like mine. I never saw him after that—his parents were hard Chinese, and they grounded him for a year and forbade him from ever seeing me again. Sometimes people ask me about those lumps on my arms and I tell them that when I was 11 years old I was in an explosion in a Chinese laundry. After the incident, when people came in to pick up their shirts, the old saying should have been reversed so that it read, "Sorry, ticket no laundry—due to explosion."

14 The Hypnosis and Slang Study Groups

In junior high school I formed two study groups. One was a hypnosis study group. I had always been interested in hypnosis, believing the adults to be under a kind of hypnotic trance that was socially driven, and which dampened the potential of human beings. I already believed that human beings had secret powers and potentialities that they never used, and I began to study hypnosis and human suggestibility. I put together a group of about 10 of us who would go to somebody's house after school where I would hypnotize them. They all wanted to be hypnotized and nobody wanted to learn how to hypnotize me, which was kind of a drag. I've almost always been in a leadership position by default. We did all kinds of hypnotic tricks like arm levitation or putting a person between two chairs and standing on them. It was a lot of fun and opened a lot of eyes.

The other group was a slang study and invention group. I recognized that English was a very fluid language and that slang always existed—mostly we had words like *boss* and *cool, groovy* and *out of sight*. I know people today who go to Japan to teach English slang because the Japanese learn English but haven't got a clue about slang. Imagine a guy coming to New York and hearing his friends say, "Let's go hang out and I'll set you up with a blind date and we can get down with some chicks." They wouldn't know what the hell you were talking about. I thought that slang invention would be a nifty way of studying human suggestibility.

The group would get together once a week and invent a word or phrase and append our own meaning to it. Then we would try to get it "pushed" into the school population like a virus or meme.

We discovered that, if you used the slang word that you had invented and the person you were talking to asked you where you had heard it, and you said you invented it yourself, then the virus would die on the vine—the slang word simply wouldn't get used. But if you said, "I heard it from some older kids" or "I heard it during summer vacation where the camp counselors taught it to us," then the slang word had a chance to take off.

Once I was talking to a kid about the slang invention group and he asked me for an example. So I made up one on the spot: "Bluff or All Bluff." Let's say a group of guys go out on the town and one of them spots a beautiful girl across the way. But he's too shy to go up to her because she's beautiful and he thinks he's not good enough for her. The rest of the group then say, "Go find out if she is Bluff or All Bluff." So the guy would be driven by group peer pressure to go over and talk to the girl. If she was a good person and blessed with great beauty on the outside, so that no normal guy approached her and she got hit on by fools and stupid jocks, he might sit down and talk with her and maybe they would become boyfriend and girlfriend—that would mean she was Bluff. But if she was conceited and full of herself she would be considered All Bluff, and the guy could return to the table and tell his friends, "Don't bother with her—she's All Bluff." Then nobody would bother trying to pick her up because she was an arrogant and conceited girl. The same slang would work with guys. If a group of them went out and one of the girls saw a handsome guy, she could be induced to go over and find out if he was Bluff, meaning his outside beauty had not ruined his inside, or All Bluff, meaning he was full of himself and conceited. That way all the girls could stay away from him and he would be left to wonder why he couldn't get a date. It would get around school and you would say don't bother with him or her because they are All Bluff—a very useful slang tool for separating the wheat from the chaff.

Slang words change from year to year and at that time what was said in New York wasn't said in the Midwest until three or four years later—it was the same thing with fashion. We kids who grew up in Greenwich Village knew that we were on the top of the rocket in the '60s. New York had Be-Ins and Love-Ins in 1966, and was ahead of San Francisco or LA, or any other place in terms of being the place to be. San Francisco really started to happen in 1967. The fashion that was in vogue in New York wasn't seen for three years in other parts of the country—it was the same with slang. It would start in New York and garner speed, passing through the region and perhaps through the country. But it took a long time. So a word like "Boss" meaning good or groovy only had a national shelf life of about ten years before it was turned over by another word—like "Rad" in the '80s.

I ran the two study groups for a couple of years, but in my spare time I was slowly drifting towards Danny's house. He was the host to a clique of druggies that I joined. We would sit around on acid and listen to all the new records. We were stoned cold on pot, hash and psychedelic heads. From the time I discovered pot until I was in my 20s, I stopped drinking, only to pick it up again when everything else had run its course. Danny's room was like his own little apartment where nobody bothered us while we smoked, dropped and later took STP, which is like a three day super-acid trip. When STP started coming around it was said that if you took it, you never came down. It took me six months of investigation before I tried it. By then I had observed that people did come down after a couple of days.

15 Samantha

My friend Danny's older brother Matt, who sold me pot, also sold me my first Stratocaster. He came into Danny's room and said, "I can't stand this guitar. It won't stay in tune no matter what I do. I wish I could sell it and I'd sell it cheap." Man, as soon as he said that I jumped up from my chair and asked how much he'd take. He said $200, so I went home and asked my parents about this deal. They said no because I was a good drummer and a drummer can always find work, but there are a million guitarists and you have to be special. However, I really don't think I had a choice in the matter. I was meant to play guitar. So I went back to Matt and Danny and asked to be fronted some acid or hash. That means that they would give it to you and you could give them the money later. I sold it for an exact profit of $200. I came back to Danny's house and I asked if Matt was around. When I found him I said, "I'm ready to buy that Stratocaster off of you, here's $200." By this time he was wary and starting to change his mind. I had to talk him into it by reminding him that we had shook on it and he couldn't renege now. So, I got my first Stratocaster and I was in love. I called her Samantha. I've never given a name to another guitar since. Samantha was stolen from me in a daytime mugging at knife point in Washington Square Park.

I don't think New York is as dangerous as people

think it is, but when you're young and vulnerable and in a neighborhood that's even a touch sordid, you have to be careful. I was being careful, but I was watched and Samantha was taken away from me. Bummer. It was only an object. I've never really cared much about objects because after all, when you die you have to give up the whole world and everything in it, including everyone you've ever loved and anything you've ever had. I believe that anything that you have *has you*, because otherwise you wouldn't look for things you lose. When you lose something and look for it you are its slave. I hardly ever lose anything—things cling to me, which is one reason why I'm so cluttered. Memories too—they have clung to me and are my constant companions.

16 Raising the Ritalin Roof

I had friends who lived all over the city. I often visited Steve who also lived in the West Village. One day Steve mentioned that his little brother had some kind of psychiatric problem—he was hyperactive and had attention deficit.

This was in the mid-60s before Attention Deficit Disorder became a well-known catch phrase. Steve mentioned that his brother was being prescribed Ritalin pills, which were calming him down. He also said that he had read that Ritalin calms down young children who were hyperactive, but for older kids and adults who took it, it acted like speed; that is, it was a kind of amphetamine. We loved amphetamines and took them whenever we could find them, so Steve suggested that we steal some of his brother's medication.

I thought about it for a while—about a minute—and then I said, "Sure go ahead and get us a couple of them." Steve snuck off and came back in a few minutes with the booty— some white pills.

"How many should we take?" I asked.

"I don't know, my brother takes one a couple of times a day, but he's little; I guess we should take several each."

We went into the kitchen, got some juice and swallowed the pills down. Then we went back to Steve's room and waited. We didn't have to wait very long before we both noticed something—shimmering waves of feeling groovy, very bodily. The amphetamines I had taken previously were Benzedrine, dextroamphetamine sulfate, or biphetamines, which are a combination of amphetamine and methadrine. Those acted strongly on consciousness— the mind and the body—followed by a crazy feeling of being like Superman with everything sped up.

This Ritalin was very different. It was decidedly delicious and very deeply felt first in the bottom of the body. With the waves of sensual pleasure traveling up through the body, the mind began doing a strange dance, slowing down and speeding up at the same time.

I had some strange experiences like this earlier in my childhood, where the outer world would seem to move in slow motion—I mean REALLY slow, like a *Twilight Zone* show where someone walks around and everybody else is moving like the hour hand of a clock. At the same time, my mind would speed up until I could no longer talk because my thoughts wouldn't fit into any verbal package. It was like a figure skater who spins with his arms out, and then, as he brings his arms towards his body, the spinning gets faster and faster.

With Ritalin, it was more like a gyroscope; that is, even though it is spinning, it maintains a directional center. In other words, it doesn't involve getting dizzy and losing coherence, but rather thinking at a speed which is usually impossible. What I had in my youth was a kind of petit mal epilepsy of the temporal lobe. I'm sure of it because I would trance out from time to time and everything would speed up or slow down.

Steve and I were feeling this amazing rush and began

telling each other about it. It was super exciting and neither of us felt like moving any parts of our body, except for our tongues and mouths, because we were feeling the acceleration. The body was as still as a candle flame in a windowless room, while the mind rushed like Ray Millan's vision at the end of the movie *The Man with the X-Ray Eyes*.

We started telling each other stories. I can't remember all of them because they were a madhouse—a flood of marvelous myths and fables and archetypes. Everything Steve and I had in our brains—entire storehouses of personal as well as archetypal memories were gushing up like a Texas oil well that had just struck pay dirt. Neither of us could stop it. We were both talking out of our heads and each one listening was flooded with associations, every new story stimulated by the other one, both of us dying to get a story out. Our bodies felt heavy like they were loaded down with sand—but we managed to move our chairs so we faced each other. Neither of us wanted to move, only to talk, and give way to the seemingly endless waves of insights.

It was getting harder and harder not to interrupt each other when Steve said he thought he had a good idea. There was an egg timer in the kitchen. We could each talk for three minutes and then turn the egg timer over. It seemed like a fabulous idea except for one fact—neither of us felt as if we could get up. Our bodies felt like boat anchors and our tongues were like sails flapping in the wind. We agreed that we would both get up together and try. What an effort! It took something like two minutes to stand up and it was a hilarious walk into the kitchen. Every new step, every new twitch of a muscle, brought us gales of laughter.

I thought we might die of laughter on the way, but eventually we reached the kitchen and like a slow motion movie, I saw Steve's arm reach out and grab the egg timer. I was laughing so hard at the thought of going back to his room that I couldn't breathe or tell him why it was so funny. To return—to turn around and head back after moving in one direction—seemed to be the silliest thing a man could ever do. Why would anyone ever go anywhere whatsoever if they were only going to turn around and undo the going that they just went? It seemed unbelievably ludicrous.

We got back to the chairs and put a small table between us where we placed the egg timer. We began turning the egg timer over and over and taking turns to talk. It was still difficult to wait three minutes because of all the important things to say that were being generated by listening to Steve. The explosion of tickled synapses that every new word and phrase generated was hard to keep to myself. This activity went on for several hours until Steve's parents came home. After knocking, they opened the door to see us facing each other with an egg timer between us. His mother asked, "What on earth are you boys doing?"

What kind of answer could we give?

17 Psychiatry Is Nuts

In my late teens I had become thoroughly sick of living at home where my parents practiced a double standard. They didn't want me to do drugs, smoke or drink, and yet they did all three, with pills in the pill cabinet, an alcohol stash and smoking. I decided to teach them a lesson. I went to the pill cabinet in the bathroom at night and I poured every single pill down the drain. Then I woke them up and told them I had taken every single pill in the house. They thought I was trying to commit suicide so they took me to Lincoln Hospital on 59th St. and Ninth Avenue.

The doctor who examined me in the emergency room could tell that I hadn't taken anything, but told me he was going to have my stomach pumped to teach me a lesson. I thought that was great—a new experience. He put a tube up my nose and down into my stomach, and of course no pills came out. He had a conference with my parents and they decided to send me to the psychiatric unit which was upstairs in what was called Tower 10. This was one of three floors dedicated to psychiatry, and it had the poshest units you could imagine. I had one roommate who was completely depressed but the surroundings were actually very nice. I liked being in the hospital. It gave me a sense of cleanliness and security that I didn't have at home where there were arguments and fights all the time.

I was supposed to be there for two weeks and during

the second week they began to give me limited passes for four or six hours. I was supposed to use the passes to go home so that I might get accustomed to being there. I did not want to be at home and when I returned to the hospital I was manic and giddy, happy to be back. The psychiatrist took me into his office and sat me down:

"You're back on drugs, aren't you?"

"I haven't taken any drugs. I'm just happy to be in the hospital," I said, and it was true.

"No. You're back on drugs," he replied.

I declared that I was not and it turned into one of those stupid games where he said yes and I said no until he finally put his foot down. He told me he was not going to release me but was going to send me to the state hospital at Creedmoor, which was an infamous facility on Long Island.

I was placed in Building 40, which they called the flight deck, and I was remanded for 90 days of observation. When I realized I had lost the battle of whether or not I was on drugs, I decided to act out. I was pretty manic. In order to transport me, I had to be shackled and tied down to a gurney. I was mad as hell about being sent to a state mental institution where the possibility of getting out was almost non-existent.

This place was where they housed the insane, the weird people, and it made *One Flew over the Cuckoo's Nest* look like kindergarten. The flight deck was where people were brought initially, and many of them were completely mad.

My roommate had a religious fixation and created an altar on one of the windowsills. He would put food from the meals in his pocket like corn and mashed potatoes, and then offer it to God on his altar. Often the staff would catch him and just wag their fingers and say, "You can't take food back to the ward." Another man was brought in after I had been there about a week. He was a criminally insane homosexual rapist. He had to be completely restrained because he would grab anybody's testicles or penis and yank on them, trying to pull them off. I think he might've been a cannibal as well. He would plead with me to loosen his bonds, but if I got close he would simply grab at my genitals, so I learned never to get near him. He was there about three weeks before they moved him deeper into the cavernous belly of the institution.

In Building 40 there were wards through which I travelled to go for meals. I went through wards full of misshapen human beings with watermelon shaped heads, monkey people, and childlike adults who were kept in cages with large balls and toys. It was insane to be insane and I was sane—which of course meant that I was insane, so I made some friends among the insane. On the way to meals we all passed through a ward that was full of people with elephantiasis. Many were in wheelchairs that had holes in them for defecating and urinating right onto the floor. These people had to be hosed down in order to be cleansed. The floor in that ward was slanted towards three drains in the middle of the floor where the water and human waste could flow down into the drains. I used to hold my nose because the stench was so bad, and there were always employees continuously mopping up after these people who were also deranged. Every once in a while, one of these people would get out of the wheelchair-toilets and lie on the floor, rolling around and getting themselves and anything they came in contact with filthy.

Another ward housed a man in a cage who would try to grab people from between the bars. The entire line walking to the cafeteria would walk on one side to stay away from him. He was all hairy and even had hair all over his face. I was told that he was a werewolf. Even though his area had no windows, whenever a full moon came up he appeared to grow more hair on his forehead and cheeks and became violently insane. Then the staff would put him in a special cage. I saw things that you would not believe with your own eyes, including the ward with people who had weirdly shaped heads. They were retarded beyond belief—these were the throwaway children, probably born into families that just didn't want to take care of them or couldn't handle them, so they were relegated to a life inside a cage.

As the days went by, having seen all this, I began to get bored. Every once in a while I freaked out and asked to be released, which meant that I would be injected with some tremendous tranquilizers like Thorazine and Mellaril. When I experienced side effects from these drugs, the staff, instead of taking me off the drugs, would add a new drug intended to combat the side effects. The side effects caused terrible spasms and symptoms similar to Parkinson's disease—shaking of my limbs and getting my spine locked up in weird positions that I couldn't get out of. All of this was drug-induced.

Over time I became increasingly calm and resigned to being there. As happened whenever I was in a mental hospital, my parents were told that it wasn't certain that I would ever get out. But after a time I would come down from the mania and go into a depression, which at least looked better to the doctors.

They did electroshock therapy there. I remember people coming out of the treatment room and walking into walls because they were so dazed. Then they would be told to sit down, and they were quiet. They were then considered to be "improved."

I also learned the Catch-22 of mental hospitals. The doctors walked down the ward once a day in a small group. They would stop and ask the patients how they were doing. Most patients would say stuff like, "Doc I'm much better now and I'm ready to go home," or "Send me home, Doc, I'm better and cured." Those people were never sent home. Occasionally they would stop and talk to a patient who would say, "I'm fine—whatever you decide, Doctor. Being here has done me a lot of good and I wouldn't mind staying," or "I'll go if you decide on that." Then the doctor would talk to his secretary and say something to the effect of, "I want to see that man at 1 pm in my office." Lo and behold, sometime in the next few days, that person would be packing up and going home. If you wanted to go home, they kept you. but if you didn't mind being there, they let you out—a completely insane approach which might have a point in its favor.

After 90 days in Creedmoor I was released but kept taking Thorazine and Mellaril. I found that my sex drive was completely gone. I told my doctor about it and he said there was nothing he could do—it was a side effect that I would have to live with. When I told him about some of the other weird side effects he just added a medication. His way of trying to cover over side effects with even more drugs made me angry as hell.

Eventually I stopped taking the psychiatric medications. I went back to the drugs I knew about for self-medicating— marijuana and hashish, amphetamines and barbiturates and inhalants. Once I got so nuts from not sleeping that I began to hear the guitar riff from "Over, Under, Sideways, Down" by the Yardbirds coming through my air conditioner all night long, Other times, I put silver foil over my windows because I could not stand the sunlight—thinking it would melt me.

About that time my parents were planning to move to New Jersey. I thought about "going crazy" again because I was terrified of going to New Jersey and would have rather been in a mental hospital in New York—but I didn't want to be in a state mental institution again, where I might not get out. I had been lucky to get out of Creedmoor, but, to tell you the truth, it was a nightmare which I also enjoyed in a sense, because I enjoy all experiences. I remember telling myself that very few people got the opportunity that I did—to visit the inside of a real mental institution prior to the reforms that occurred in the late 70s.

I thought perhaps I could stay in New York but I simply was not that strong yet, and although my father got me a job as a foot messenger, I didn't make enough money to survive there, so I had to go with them to New Jersey. Ironically, going to Montclair turned out to be a godsend. I was given an expansive separate floor at the top of the house where nobody would bother me, and I got to go crazy as much as I wanted. Eventually I got into such a mania that I didn't sleep for days on end, and bought a bunch of clocks, set them all at different times, and spread them throughout the room. I would have the radio and the television and the record player all playing at the same time—sensory overload.

That summer I went crazy again. I was manic-depressive and the manias were completely exacerbated by the use of ups and downs and sideways drugs. A friend of mine found out that you could get high from Sominex, a drug containing scopolamine hydrobromide. This drug was supposed to put a person to sleep if they took one or two tablets. Scopolamine was one of the ingredients in witches' brew during the Middle Ages, and it is derived from deadly nightshade, as was Belladonna.

This friend of mine decided we would take 20 each to go on a scopolamine trip. It was one of the worst bummers I've ever been on, and it lasted days. We spent most of the time on the roof or in the stairwell of my building and I was afraid to go home because I would exhibit symptoms. One of the symptoms involved strange spiritual creatures whom I could not look at, but that would appear in the periphery of my vision. It finally got so bad that I began talking to the hallucination, saying things like: "I won't look at you" or "So, you won't go away" or "I need to talk to you." This didn't help matters, and it took about three days for all of the effects to fade off.

One day I decided to go to the corner of Christopher and Columbus Streets (we lived near there) and tried to climb down a manhole hoping to find China. The cops came along and saw me pulling on the manhole. They stopped me and asked me what I was doing. When I tried to explain myself they arrested me and took me to jail. I called my parents and they told me the cops thought that I was nuts and should be in a hospital.

I might have been a danger to myself, climbing down manholes and walking down the middle of the street in a karate gee, stopping cars and going, "Beep beep, where's the aliens?" People must have called the police. This time my parents couldn't smooth anything over or get me out of it, and so they signed me in, and I was sent to another institution which is quite famous—Greystone State Mental

Hospital in New Jersey. This is where Bob Dylan used to visit Woody Guthrie when Woody was on his way out.

There I was on the flight deck of Greystone State, tied to a wheelchair because I was completely manic and out of control. I was there for three months, and the doctors wanted to give me electroshock therapy but my parents would not sign for it—they completely refused it. However, the doctors convinced my parents that there was a chemical shock therapy that would help me. It turned out to be something called insulin shock therapy, and my parents signed for that.

The way it worked was as follows. An overload of insulin would put me to sleep. The moment I began to wake up they would inject me once again. They kept me asleep for about a week injecting me every time I began to wake up. When the insulin didn't work anymore, and I began waking up within 15 minutes of the injection, they switched me to a strong stimulant like methamphetamine and amphetamine.

Then they put me in a rubber room—I swear by the love of God—they put me in a rubber room with a tiny window where they had to look in on me every 15 minutes to make sure I was still alive. This juxtaposition of sleeping and stimulants would freak anybody out. I thrashed and bashed against the walls, which weren't actually rubber but merely padded. Of course, I thought this was another experience that was very rare and I was privileged to be treated like a test dog in outer space.

After a couple days, I had worn myself out. They let me out and made me sit on a bench on the side of the ward. I was in a kind of daze. My friend Albert Anderson had been trying to visit me there, but the staff kept telling him that I was in seclusion. Eventually they let Albert come to see me. When he saw me he began crying. When I asked him why, he said, "Richard, they've killed you. I look at you and I can't find you—you're gone." I told Albert that I'd be back to normal after a while, which was true.

Electroshock was administered at Greystone as well. Every so often the shock carts would go by and a line of people scheduled to receive it would form. Electroshock was their big gun, but every once in a while things would go awry and I would hear the alarm go off—code blue—which meant that somebody's heart had stopped and all the attendants and nurses would freak out, running around with the paddles and the carts to bring the person back.

I'm very glad my parents didn't sign for that. I heard later that Lou Reed received a number of electroshock treatments and had recovered. Eventually I recovered from the chemical shock therapy and the doctors decided that they would let me out, but only on one condition—that I go into a drug rehab program in Newark, New Jersey. I agreed to that—anything to get out of Greystone. I was driven to one of those drug rehab halfway houses where you live for a year or so with people screaming at you and making you do all sorts of ridiculous things like wearing signs that say "I'm stupid."

We were all brought into a strange room full of elders who would scream all sorts of nonsense and abuse at us. It was meant to break us down. They were in the middle of what they called a "work marathon" and it had been going on for 24 hours. After welcoming me, they gave me a toothbrush and told me that my job was to follow a man with a broom made of old straw (that was falling apart) as he swept the rug. I was to follow him with the toothbrush and clean up after him on my hands and knees. This lasted about two days before I started to think I would be better off just walking out. I didn't know if they had the legal right to hold me there, even though Greystone had made it a condition of my release, but I finally decided I was going to leave. I remember the staff begging me to stay, and saying that I would go back to drugs. I retorted that of course I was going back to drugs—they were much better than this place. They begged and pleaded with me. As I walked out with my small bag of things, they continued to yell at me, saying that I would be back, and that I was making a mistake, and that I belonged there and all sorts of other nonsense.

I walked all the way from Newark to my house in Montclair. My parents asked me what happened. I told them truthfully, and they debated whether or not they should call the hospital, which they did. They were told that any patient who walks away from the hospital is free— the hospital has no authority to bring them back if they're capable of walking away, and that's that.

Among other drugs that I was on, Elavil exacerbated the symptoms of what admittedly looked like psychosis. Psychiatric medication was in the dark ages in those days, and it would take many more hospital visits until I finally found my way. During my stay at Greystone I realized that if I didn't take alcohol with drugs I probably wouldn't go insane, so I stopped drinking, and it's true—I didn't go "insane" again. That is if I was ever insane to begin with. I do not think that people who think they are insane are really insane—have a look at the state of the human race. But, practically speaking, I didn't have another manic episode for quite some time.

A flashback to Creedmoor at this point portends a worthwhile story. After I got out of Creedmoor in my teens, I went back to drugs and alcohol and started going into manic episodes again. When my parents decided to sign me into a mental hospital again and were driving me through Manhattan to take me there, we got stuck in a traffic jam and I saw an opportunity. I opened the car door and jumped out, and although my father got out and chased me, I was much quicker and escaped. I went to Central Park and hung my leather jacket on a branch and took off my shoes. I always knew I was going insane when I went barefoot.

This time I went completely bonkers and wanted to get out of this world. I walked from Central Park down to the World Trade Center and into that vast metro-complex where I found elevators that eventually took me up to the hundred and sixth floor. I entered an office and asked where the World Trade Center was—that is, where was the trading center where I could change worlds? They called security—the World Trade Center had its own police—and as I found out, they also had jail cells on the hundred and third floor, one of which they put me in. They had three cells then, and I was the only person there. They called an ambulance, which took me to Bellevue where I stayed for another two weeks. Sanity is insanity. I didn't cut off my ear or ever harm myself or anyone else—except for the emotional pain that I felt for putting my parents through hell when they were trying their best.

After I left my parents' house and moved out on my own, I was my own man, and I stayed out of mental hospitals for a very long time, although I was going into manic episodes between my depressions. My friends thought my manic episodes were exciting, which they were—from being super-deeply shy I became absolutely gregarious. Suddenly I could talk to strangers left and right. When I was manic it seemed like girls were more interested in me, in contrast to those times when I was super depressed and would just sit on my windowsill drinking wine.

I have been in several mental hospitals since then for various lengths of time due to mania and acting out of control, but it has been nothing like the experiences I had as a teenager in state mental institutions. I will never forget those. Frankly, I am proud to have been through those experiences. While I haven't been to the moon, or climbed Mount Everest, I have been to two old state mental institutions and several rehabs during the dark ages of treatment.

There was a second time I ended up in Bellevue years later, and that was for a depression combined with manic-depression. A strange thing happened that time which soured me on psychiatrists almost permanently. The psychiatrist there asked me what I did. I told him I was a guitarist who made records. He began to take notes, so I asked him what he was writing down. He told me he had noted that my statement that I was a guitarist who made records was part of my delusions. I insisted that I truly was a recording artist, a musician who had recorded records that were doing quite well, such as Television's debut. He dismissed me as delusional. I phoned my girlfriend and asked her to bring in the three records I had already done— Television's *Marquee Moon*, *Adventure* and my first solo record, *Alchemy*. She asked me, "Why Richard?" I said, "Just bring them please"—and so she did during her next visit.

The next time I was scheduled to see the psychiatrist I

took the three records in with me and slapped them down on his desk and asked him, "Whose name is that? Whose picture is that? And you told me I was delusional. What have you got to say now?" He turned to his writing pad and I could see that he wrote down only one word—"Angry," and then he proceeded not to talk about his mistake at all, but just prodded me for more garbage information. That time I was in Bellevue for two weeks.

I have not been in mental hospitals since then, but at least I know that when I'm put into them, I will get out—by my wits or just from coming down.

18 Richard Meets Velvert and Wakes up Jimi

Jimi Hendrix lived a block away from Blimpie's, on Sixth Avenue and 11th Street. The kids that hung around Blimpie's would see Jimi walking down the street every once in a while, sometimes holding hands with his girlfriend. In New York celebrities weren't bothered but sometimes we would just say "Hey Jimi, how's it going?" He was always very friendly and would say hello back to us. Sometimes my friend Velvert Turner would hang out at Blimpie's, and if Jimi walked by, then Velvert would split with him—if Jimi wasn't hanging out with a girl.

I should tell you something about Velvert and his relationship with Jimi Hendrix. His mother, Helen Turner, told me that Velvert once saw Jimi on TV and started jumping up and down and screaming "I know that guy— I've got to find him!" And somehow, he actually found Jimi, and Jimi took him on like a little brother. Velvert became Jimi's protégé.

Here's how we met: One member of our group was named Zeke, and once when we were at his house, we pooled our money to buy some hash. Then someone left to get the hash. We were salivating over the prospect of some great hash when the phone rang. It was Zeke's parents, who weren't home, and they were making sure that everything was all right.

Zeke shushed us and told them that everything was fine and he was doing his homework. We all let out a sigh. Waiting for drugs can sometimes be a real drag, especially if they never arrive and your money is gone. So when the phone rang again, we were all excited. Zeke answered it and talked for a minute and then put the phone down and said, "Oh no, it's this guy I know, Velvert."

The other kids start talking about Velvert without even having met him. Zeke had met him, and described him as a scrawny black kid from Brooklyn who was clearly out of his mind because he was claiming to know Jimi Hendrix. Everybody was laughing and wondering about this Velvert character's very strange first name. His mother told me later that "Velvert" was his given name on his birth certificate.

Ten minutes later Zeke's doorbell rang, and he ran to the window to see if it was the hash, but it was Velvert. He turned around and said "No, not yet. It's just that kid, Velvert!" and he buzzed him in. The doorbell rang and Zeke opened it. There was Velvert and instantaneously I knew, I KNEW, that he knew Jimi Hendrix.

All the other kids were giggling and laughing and began pointing at Velvert saying, "You know Jimi Hendrix? You really know Jimi Hendrix—then prove it!"

I said, "Listen guys, how do you know he doesn't know Jimi? I think he does because Jimi doesn't live on Mars and he's a human being and he has to know other people—why not this kid?"

Nobody believed Velvert and they were taunting him, when suddenly he spoke up. "Jimi happens to be in town because he is doing a concert tonight—and I can call him up at his hotel and prove that I know him."

So we all headed into the kitchen and sat around the table. Zeke brought Velvert the telephone. Velvert dialed some number that was clearly a hotel, and then he asked for someone—but it wasn't Jimi Hendrix. Everybody started laughing and saying, "You didn't even ask for Jimi Hendrix!"

And Velvert said, "You don't think he stays in hotels under his own name do you? Does he want you or just anybody to call him? Of course not. Now I will ask you a question. Does anybody remember the name I asked for? Because if you did, and knew the hotel, you could call Jimi."

Velvert said all this while the front desk at the hotel was ringing the room he had asked for. He had the phone to his head and let it ring a number of times. Finally Velvert said, "He must not be there. But I did call Jimi Hendrix, here, listen." He handed the phone to Zeke who put it to his ear and then handed it to the next guy who then handed it to the next guy who then he handed it to me.

I listened to it ring once and then during the second ring I heard a pickup—and that unmistakable voice. It was Jimi, who said, "Hey man, what's up? Who is this?"

Obviously I wasn't going to say, "It's Richard, Jimi," because he didn't know me from Adam, so I stood up and said, "It's Velvert, man," and I handed the phone to Velvert who began talking and took the phone over into a corner where he spoke in a low voice. They were having a conversation, but I was getting grilled by all the other kids asking, "Was it really him? Was it really Jimi Hendrix?"

I said, "Yes, it was—nobody else sounds like that—we obviously woke him up from a nap because he sounded sleepy."

"What did he say?"

"None of your business. Ask Velvert when he gets off the phone."

Velvert got off the phone, triumphant, and told us Jimi was doing a concert that night and he was invited.

As we walked back into the living room everyone was abuzz and forgot all about the hash. Here was a guy who actually knew Jimi Hendrix—this weird, scrawny black kid from Brooklyn named Velvert, who then said, "Yeah, Jimi is playing a concert tonight and he told me I could bring somebody, and I'm going to bring…"

Everyone began raising their hands, urgently petitioning Velvert to go with him to the show. Velvert put his right hand and right finger up in the air and started doing pirouettes saying "I'm going to bring… I'm going to bring… I'm going to bring – YOU!" And lo and behold he was pointing at me.

I was the only person in that room who hadn't asked to be taken along.

19 The Guitar Lesson without a Guitar and Black Roman Orgy

After Velvert Turner and I became friends, he would come over to my house where I kept my guitar and we would trade licks back and forth. When Jimi got his apartment on 12th Street, around the corner from Blimpie's, Velvert would go up there and Jimi would teach him guitar, using a large mirror that was in Jimi's apartment to transpose his left-handed playing into right-handed viewing. Jimi used to carry a small hand mirror around. When someone would play a lick he liked, he would ask them to repeat it, and then use the mirror to transpose it into a left-handed version.

By then, Jimi had already spent years traversing the Chitlin Circuit with various bands, once getting himself kicked out of Little Richard's band because his antics stole some of the spotlight from Richard, who felt he should be the prettiest and the most appreciated person on stage. Jimi also played with the Isley Brothers, where he learned all sorts of funk and soul guitar playing.

When Jimi was teaching Velvert how to play guitar, he used his own songs as the templates to show Velvert various things. Because I was one of Velvert's best friends, had a guitar, and only lived five blocks from Jimi, Velvert would leave Jimi's and come straight to me. He would show me the latest stuff that Jimi was teaching him. I think the first thing we learned were the bends that started "Highway Child." We also learned the beginning of "Purple Haze" and all sorts of other things that Jimi was teaching him, including methodologies of practice which were various things that he liked to do to warm up.

I cherished these visits not only because they cemented our friendship, but also because they were the link to my own guitar mentorship—getting lessons secondhand, literally minutes after Jimi taught them.

Velvert was a very strange bird and sometimes he would turn his back on me and play something Jimi had taught him. Then he would give me the guitar and see if I could play it back by aural memory. At that time I couldn't learn from records so I would get frustrated with Velvert's tomfoolery, but most of the time he was pretty straightforward with me. One incident, however, remains in my memory indelibly.

Whenever Velvert came over after visiting Jimi he had a special glow about him—I suppose anyone would that had a close relationship with him. Jimi recognized that I was one of Velvert's best friends, so eventually I got to hang out in the studio and at his concerts without Velvert's presence. But, in the beginning, I had to depend on Velvert.

One day Velvert called me especially excited, and said that he simply HAD to come over and show me what Jimi had taught him. I got out the guitar, but when he arrived Velvert mentioned that what he had been taught had nothing to do with the guitar but something else entirely, and that we should go take a walk. I was curious and practically scratching my head. We walked around the West Village until we got to Sixth Avenue and 8th Street and Velvert suddenly said, "We should go to Central Park."

I indicated that the subway was on that block and it would take us right there. Velvert said no—that we should hitchhike. I ridiculed the idea saying that no one hitchhiked in New York City, and Velvert said, "Oh yeah, watch this!"

As the light turned green, Velvert popped out from between two cars and stuck out his thumb. The first vehicle that came along, a green station wagon, pulled over and the guy rolled down the window and asked,

"Where are you boys going to?"

"Central Park."

"Well I'm going up just that way. Come on and get in and I'll drop you off."

We both huddled in the back seat as the guy drove up Sixth Avenue to 59th Street. He dropped us off right in front of the park. All the while I had been wondering how Velvert had done that! He just stuck out his thumb and pulled over the first car as though his thumb was magnetic.

We walked through the park in a leisurely manner while Velvert told me some of the other things that Jimi had taught him—casting spells and other voodoo and magic and things that his Cherokee grandmother had taught him. Some of these things sounded outrageous. One involved a curse that utilized a book of matches and some gestures. I've never used it and I would not advise anyone else to use it because it could backfire. It could be that Jimi did do things like this, and that they did backfire.

After we finished walking through the park, Velvert stated that we should go downtown by subway. The subway station was right there. I suggested we use it, but Velvert refused. He said that we should walk around until we found a different subway station, one that I should pick, with the promise that when we went down into the subway station he would show me something else that Jimi had taught him. So we walked around a while until we were almost lost. I finally saw another station.

I walked down the steps, put my token in the turnstile and went through. Velvert had told me to turn around and make sure I looked at him carefully when I got there. Velvert walked down the stairs, turned and walked right through a turnstile without putting a token in.

I couldn't believe my eyes. This was like a Houdini trick. I tested the other turnstiles, none of which moved. These were days when the turnstiles were huge and yellow with four arms. A person could jump over them or climb under them, but it was impossible to walk through like Velvert had. I asked him how he did it, and he wouldn't tell me, except to say that Jimi had taught him. It didn't seem to be a feat of stage magic. I still don't know how he did it, except that I believe he did do it because of the other things he had been shown by Jimi which were extraordinary.

In November 1969 Jimi had disbanded the Experience, and was trying to put a new band together—in which to play New Year's Eve and New Year's Day shows at the Fillmore East. The New Year's Day show later resulted in a live record and Jimi signed the rights over to Capitol Records to settle an old contract dispute.

There was a Mob-run club called Salvation in the West Village. Velvert invited me to the club and told me to wait for him there so we could get in for free. He was very late getting there, and I began to get worried so I bought a ticket to get in. I still have it—it is ticket #41 and cost $10. The ticket read "Black Roman Orgy—Music by Hendrix, Gypsy Sun, and Rainbows."

I headed downstairs into the club to find that the music had been halted because the PA kept feeding back and Jimi had become frustrated and stopped the show. I missed that 15 minutes and I'm sorry that he didn't get to play and satisfy himself and his friends. After that, the party started.

Jimi was sitting at a large round table with his back to the main room of the club, and he was leaning up against a large mirror. There was an empty seat there, so I sat down. I wasn't sitting next to Jimi but the guy between me and Jimi got up to go to the bathroom or something and I was pushed over by other newcomers who wanted to sit down. I ended up sitting directly on Jimi's left while he was talking to Buddy Cox, who was sitting on his right. There was a girl going around under the table giving blow jobs to people, but when she came to him, he waved her off and then she came to me and I did the same. I didn't want to have sloppy fifths and thought to myself, who knows what's been in that mouth? And anyway, I followed Jimi's example because I didn't want to get a blow job while sitting right next to him—after all I was 17 years old at this point.

After some time, Jimi turned and began talking with me. I usually spent my time around rock stars silently, not wishing to reduce my chances of being allowed to stay around them longer, but here was Jimi talking to me and there wasn't much I could do except say things like "uh huh" and "yeah." Jimi was talking about the rings of Saturn and other nonsense about the solar system. It was space dribble.

We were all very drunk. There were bottles of Portuguese wines, Lancers and also Mateus which was Jimi's chosen drink that night. He began telling me that he was "not long for this world," that people wouldn't let him out of the box and wanted him to be a circus clown and he wanted to play music, but they wouldn't let him. He went on and on with the self-pitying routine until I couldn't stand it anymore, and I began to talk back to him—in a nice way of course.

"Don't worry what other people say or think. Man, you can do whatever you want because people love you, and your guitar playing and your music, and I respect you and I love your music and guitar playing."

Jimi started to talk about "Mickey Mouse" and the rings of Saturn again and the lights began flickering, to indicate that the party was over because it was 4 AM, when bars in New York had to close. Frankly, while Jimi was talking, I couldn't understand half of what he said because he would change speeds, first speaking in a slower drawl, followed by what seemed like 50 words in two seconds, all about space and space creatures and "Mickey Mouse."

When the lights came on everybody groaned because nobody really wanted the party to end, but people soon began to flee like cockroaches in the light. Eventually we pushed the table away from us and stood up. I was still standing next to Jimi and couldn't get away because of the crowd—everyone was putting on their jackets. Jimi turned his back to me and started putting on his satin jacket, first one arm, then the other, when suddenly he turned around and punched me three times, pretty hard with a left-handed flurry—a left to the face, a right to the stomach, and another left to the face.

All I could do was absorb the blows and sit down. I heard a bunch of muttering and the words, "Somebody tried to beat Jimi up—we'll kill him," and I realized they were talking about me. I hadn't laid a hand on Jimi—it was the other way around. I sat there thinking that he packed a pretty good punch for a scrawny guy, but I wasn't hurt and in my magical thinking I had absorbed the force of the blows and kept that force within myself, not allowing it to dissipate. I realized I had received something no one else had—a measure of Jimi's true force, but I did not dare to get up.

Jimi and everybody else eventually left while I sat there. I waited 45 minutes before the guy who was putting tables up and sweeping the floor told me I had to leave because he had to lock up. I was still frightened of the people who had muttered the comment about killing me, so I walked up the stairs very hesitantly, looking from side to side.

Across the street from the club was a parking lot, and Jimi's Corvette was sitting there. He rolled down the window and crooked his finger to call me over, so I walked over to the window where he reached out and took my hands. He started crying and sobbing. His tears were all over my hands and he was rubbing them in while apologizing.

"I'm sorry—I'm so sorry," he said over and over again.

"It's no problem, Jimi—just get home and go to sleep. You didn't hurt me," I said.

Jimi would not let go of my hands, and this went on for about 15 minutes before I finally talked him into going home. He turned, still with tears in his eyes, rolled up the window, started the Corvette, and drove away.

What was I going to do? I was absolutely filled with energy from this extraordinary experience.

The thought did not occur to me to never wash my hands again—that would have been stupid anyway. I did realize, however, that not only had I received a measure of Jimi's force, but also a measure of his compassion, and I have kept these dear to my heart.

I decided not to walk straight home that night, but started off in the opposite direction to get some air and just to think. Suddenly, Velvert jumped out from a doorway and nearly scared the shit out of me. He asked me if he could walk with me and asked which way I was going. I told him I was just going to walk around aimlessly while thinking. Velvert knew Jimi had hit me. He asked me if I knew why. I said it didn't matter—that it had been a good thing, and that it didn't bother me at all. Velvert pressed the issue again, and I told him why, but then Velvert told me that I needed to figure it out for myself.

Years later I learned that "Mickey Mouse" was a derogatory term meaning that someone or something was cheesy, full of shit. I had tried to cheer Jimi up and he couldn't stand being patronized, which I can certainly understand—but I was not patronizing him. I was just sick of hearing him talk about his woes and did not fully understand that everything he was saying was true. He was not "long for the world" and the mobsters had him by the balls. I walked a while longer with Velvert, who, as it turned out, had arrived at the club late and had only talked to Jimi after he came out of the club.

"Oh Man, I think I beat up your friend," Jimi had said.

Velvert knew it was me, and had waited in hiding to see what would happen next.

After walking together for a while longer, Velvert told me that he had to go home and we parted ways for the night. I turned to walk home slowly, savoring the air in the autumn coolness, and pondered what this event had to do with me, and my fate or destiny.

20 Buddy's Got a Gun

Velvert and I spent a lot of time trying to get into the various nightclubs where we thought the rock stars and Jimi would be hanging out. One of the most famous was Steve Paul's The Scene, which was on West 46th Street right off of Eighth Avenue. It was a dingy little alcove in the basement. We would walk down the flight of stairs and run into the door man, Teddy, who would either charge admission and let us in—or tell us to fuck off.

We were 16 years old and broke, so we were usually told to turn around and walk back up the stairs. We developed a strategy whereby we would grab onto the coattails of whomever we knew was going to get in because of their fame, and we would try to join their entourage. If we were walking in with Jimi there was no problem. The Chambers Brothers were a group who always took us under their wings. They usually arrived en masse and were happy to allow us to join the band at least until we passed the doorman. Because Velvert and I were black and white teenagers, as friends we could finagle our way into most situations like a frisky molecule with a high valence. If it was a band like Traffic, I would ask Jim Capaldi or Chris Wood. If it was a funky group, well, Velvert was already Jimi's friend and protégé, so people were quite willing to lend him a hand.

We were both in school, so I don't know how we always ended up carousing until 4 AM or later, but we did. The legal drinking age in New York was 18, so we got away with murder. I don't think either of us looked anything like 18, but we were young, enthusiastic and crafty, and we would always cadge drinks when the bartender would end service.

One night we rode in on the coattails of the Chambers Brothers. Buddy Guy was the headliner with John Hammond, Jr. second on the bill. Buddy is one of the greatest electric guitarists of all time, and I've always included his name when people asked me for my influences. It was nice to get to meet him, but that's for later. Steve Paul's The Scene was like many of the other famous rock 'n' roll clubs. Like CBGB's later on, it was a dump. The main room was small and L-shaped, with the stage in front on the right. There were about 20 circular tables with four chairs each. The dressing room was on the left side in the back.

We had heard that Jimi was going to come down and jam with Buddy so we were just hanging out. Buddy's band back then was pretty road hardened—a real Chicago blues band. A few members of the band and Buddy's manager were sitting on a couch. Buddy wasn't there and his manager said that he had gone out for a bite to eat. His guitar was sitting there in a hardshell case, beckoning us with its magic. Velvert opened the case and Buddy's manager said, "Hey man, you better not do that. You know how to play that thing?" Velvert answered, "Yeah a little— you think Buddy would mind if we looked at it?" It was that incredible Stratocaster which you can see on the cover of Buddy's early records. Velvert picked it up, sat down and fiddled around with it a little bit. "Man, this thing is beautiful. You try it," and he handed it to me. I played a few riffs but was pretty nervous, and not that good yet. I didn't want to get caught with it in my hands if Buddy walked in. I handed it back to Velvert.

Velvert started playing some of the stuff that Jimi was

teaching him, including some pretty flamboyant bends, when the worst possible thing happened. The high E string broke! Just like that, pop. Velvert looked around at Buddy's band members and his manager and said, "Oh I'm so sorry, does Buddy have an extra set of strings? We will replace it and he'll never even know." Buddy's manager said, "How the fuck do I know? Look in his case." Velvert and I looked in the case but we couldn't find any strings.

"Doesn't Buddy keep an extra set of strings?" Velvert was starting to shake. Buddy's manager started talking again with Buddy's band members who were sitting in the room drinking, tittered amongst themselves.

"Man, you best fix that guitar. That's the only guitar Buddy's got, and he's got to play next. Let me tell you, he's going to be MAD, and one more thing—BUDDY'S GOT A GUN and is not afraid to use it!"

I thought Velvert might crap his pants. We didn't know how angry Buddy could get. After searching the whole room, Velvert finally found some extra strings in a big guitar case which belonged to John Hammond who was out onstage.

"Let's see, what kind of string was that high E? Probably a 10 gauge… Here's one. I guess I'll borrow it from John Hammond. He won't mind, I hope. I promise, I'll get one too, and later on replace this one."

Velvert restrung the guitar and all seemed well. We both breathed a special sigh of relief, and there was an audible "whew" heard through the whole room.

Five minutes later Buddy came in. Velvert held four fingers to his lips as if to say shush and nobody said anything. Buddy picked up his guitar, strummed a chord and said, "All right, time to go onstage." Velvert had done a good job of tuning it. The guitar sounded okay.

We got a table to watch the show. Buddy was fantastic

even back then, and he could play the hell out of the guitar. Because he did so many showman moves and overbends— when you bend a string more than a musical whole step— the guitar tended to go out of tune during the show. Buddy had a great technique where he would continue to play with his left hand and reach over with his right hand and turn the tuning knobs. About halfway through the show the brand-new string started to slack off and go out of tune. It hadn't mellowed like the other strings and it started slipping flat. Buddy reached over and turned the knob, but the weirdest thing happened.

The tuning of the string got worse as Buddy turned the knob. The tuning pegs should be turned counterclockwise to raise the pitch and clockwise to lower the pitch. Velvert had put the string on backwards so that to raise the pitch one had to turn the tuning peg the wrong way. This was because Velvert was learning guitar from Jimi, who is left-handed but played a right-handed guitar, which means that the tuning pegs are upside down, requiring him turn the knobs the other way.

You should've seen the look on Buddy's face. It was a combination of horror, surprise, confusion and a growing anger. Velvert looked at me, and I looked back at him.

"What the hell did you do?"

"I don't know, I just put the string on. I must've put it on backwards! What if Buddy really does have a gun? We gotta get out of here."

"Nah, I think we should stay. I don't think Buddy is going to shoot anybody, and he is playing great and I thought you said Jimi is coming—don't you want to wait for that?"

"No, I want to get out of here before Buddy finds out what happened. I can explain it later but I don't want to have to explain it tonight."

Well, we were best friends. I didn't want to stay without him, and it wouldn't have been fair to try to keep him there when he looked like he had seen a ghost, so we hightailed it back through the curtain and up the stairs along the street—the city street that knows nothing and keeps its mouth shut.

Buddy, I don't think anybody ever told you about what happened that night, but now you know. Velvert never meant any harm, and he is gone now, but I extend an apology to you on his behalf.

21 Hash Magic and Zeppelin Tales

In July, 1969, I went to Central Park to hear Led Zeppelin play at the Wollman skating rink. I went early so I could figure out a way to get in. Even though there were ticket beggars getting tickets, I was not allowed to beg. My friends and I had formed a type of "union" or club where we were supposed to get into the show, and backstage, without ever paying. Unfortunately, I couldn't get in and didn't want to sit on the rocks outside listening without seeing the band so I bought a ticket, which was a big no-no in our club.

I went in and sat on the aisle at the end of a row. I began to think magically:

"How am I going to get backstage? I belong backstage. I do not belong in the audience. I am not an audience member. I belong backstage. What is going to happen to bring me backstage?"

Then I saw a girl coming up the aisle asking various people something I could not hear, so I called her over to me.

"What are you looking for?" I asked.

"Drugs for Percy," she said.

I didn't know who Percy was so she explained to me that that was the Led Zeppelin singers' nickname. So I told her:

"You're in luck—I have a piece of the world's finest hashish in my pocket which I'd be happy to share with the band."

"Fine, give it to me and I'll make sure it gets to the band."

"No," I said, "Where my hash goes, I go. I will personally give it to the band."

"I can't do that and I can't get you backstage," she replied.

"Yes you can, and you can try going up the aisle and asking other people until you get lucky—but you're not going to get anything better than my offer."

So she left me and went up the aisle until she got to the end and started down another aisle. She eventually came back over to me and said, "Come on, I will try," and we walked down the aisle to the security entrance and she said, "Wait here and I will try to get you in."

Richard Cole was the tour manager and he was back there where I could see him. At the time I didn't know what he looked like or that he was Zeppelin's longtime tour manager, but she went up to him and I watched him give her a backstage pass. She brought it back, I put it on, and entered the backstage area. My magical thinking had worked. She took me into an empty room and told me to wait there while she got Percy (Robert Plant). After a few minutes the door opened and Robert walked in without speaking. I knocked off a piece of hash from my large chunk and gave it to him. He thanked me, and then split. So did the girl. So, I opened the door and started walking around with my backstage pass on.

People were going in and out of the band room. A short distance away was a guitar technician fiddling with several guitars which I assumed belonged to Jimmy Page. I thought to myself. "I deserve a guitar lesson from Jimmy Page, but I'm probably not going to get one here since he has to go onstage soon," so I approached Jimmy's guitar tech and started chatting with him.

I asked him how long he had been Jimmy's guitar roadie, and he said a couple of years. I said that he was probably a very good guitarist on his own to be Jimmy's guitar tech.

"I'm all right mate," he replied.

"No, I'll bet you're awfully good and I want to ask you a favor. I would like you to show me what Jimmy does to warm up. I'm not interested in learning any Zeppelin songs. I'm just interested to know what Jimmy does to practice or to warm up. Would you be willing to show me that?"

"Just a minute," he said.

He put the guitars down on the guitar table and took two out of the rack and handed me one.

"I'd be happy to show you some things. Let's find an empty room," he said.

And so we did. He began to show me what he had learned from Jimmy Page and was saying things like, "He does a lot of this... And he does a lot of this... And he always uses this note—see?" He showed me a lot of what Jimmy did and I could tell that it was spot on. So I got my guitar lesson from Jimmy page secondhand, just like I was getting guitar lessons from Jimi Hendrix secondhand—through Velvert.

I thanked him for the lesson and walked into the band room. I found a chair sitting opposite a couch near the food table. I sat there and remained silent. This was my strategy—remaining silent so I would last longer than if I opened my mouth and began talking. Sometimes people would talk to me and I did answer them, but otherwise I would keep my mouth shut because I wasn't interested in becoming friends with any of the rock stars. I just wanted to grab some of their aura and digest it. This had to do with my magical thinking. So I sat there and watched the band carefully, trying to absorb their energy as they began to get ready to go onstage.

At one point, Richard Cole came in and shooed everybody out while cursing and yelling,

"Alright, the band have to get ready for the show. Everybody out—get the fuck out! You, everybody, get the fuck out of here, God dammit."

I didn't think that was very polite, and he hadn't addressed me personally, so I sat there while everybody else filed out. There had been quite a large group of people, and they all followed Cole's directive and left the room until only I was left, sitting in the chair, stock still and silent. Then Richard left the room and closed the door behind him.

Now the band itself—the four of them—were the only people in the room. They began to discuss the setlist and what each one of them would be wearing.

I just sat, and watched, and absorbed what I could of their energy. They were revving up to go onstage and that palpable energy was what I wanted to feel, and I did. After sitting there for ten minutes or so, Robert Plant turned and took notice of me. He looked shocked that there was this kid sitting there in the dressing room by himself along with the band. Robert opened the door and yelled out, "Richard, Richard, come over here!" When Richard Cole got there Robert said to him, while pointing at me, "What is he doing in here?"

Cole said he didn't know and walked over to me.

"Excuse me, but would you please mind leaving?"

"Of course not, now that you've asked me politely."

I immediately got up and walked out of the dressing room.

It was almost time for the show. I left the backstage area and tried to return to my seat, but it was taken, so I went backstage again after the band went on and watched from the wings. I had a very good look at their drummer John Bonham who was absolutely incredible. He did a drum solo where he used his forearms instead of sticks, and I wondered how he could possibly do that without breaking his forearms. He was hitting the drums really hard and even doing rim-shots. I watched the band for a while and then went out into the house again because I really couldn't see Jimmy—he was turned away from me mostly, or in profile.

I watched the band from the front for a while and realized just how good they were—they were incredible. I decided I had better leave and go home and practice the stuff their roadie had shown to me. When it came time for the encore I stayed for a moment and then split—rushing to the subway and down to my house in the West Village. I had also been invited to go see Zeppelin in Queens where they were going to be playing in the next couple of days, so I planned for that, and I practiced, and practiced.

Buddy Guy was going to be the opening act at the Queens show, so that night I left early because I wanted to meet him. I got there so early that nobody was there except Buddy's bass player. I went into the dressing room and offered to share some hash with him and he said he had never tried any. I took out my pipe, filled it, began smoking it and passed it to him. He took a drag and said, "Whew, I feel really stoned." It was very good hash. He offered me a drink. He was drinking Mr. Boston's Lemon Flavored Gin. It was not a terrifically tempting drink, but of course I had to share some with him, because we were becoming buddies. He said he was so stoned that he might not be able to play that night. I said, "Sure you will." Soon the rest of the band came in, and the bass player introduced me to everyone, including Buddy.

Buddy was talking with his bandmates but then asked me about myself. I told him I was a guitarist basically just starting out, and that I admired his guitar playing. Buddy offered me a drink, and he was drinking J&B scotch. By this time, I was so stoned on the hash that I guess the J&B, and the Mr. Boston's Lemon Flavored Gin did not mix well in my stomach, and I began getting dizzy.

Buddy had turned away from me, and when he turned back he said, "Man, you are turning green. You better go lie down." I went to the corner where there was a couch and got terribly sick. After a moment or two, I started projectile vomiting. This was awful and I couldn't stop it, and the band gathered up their things and abandoned the room because they couldn't take it. I couldn't blame them. I remember the door opening at one point. Robert Plant looked in and saw the mess so he didn't get any hash that night.

I had completely embarrassed myself. The next thing I remember was the janitor waking me up. I asked him when the band was going on. The janitor said the show was already over, everybody had left and he was just cleaning up. So I got myself together and I split. I took the subway home, sick as a dog for a day and a half. Since then, anytime I've run into Buddy, I've asked him if he remembers me, and he says, "Oh yeah!" He invited me to visit him in

Chicago if I was ever there, and talked about how good the fried chicken was. But after that night I was too embarrassed to show up.

I tell this story because it is true—certainly not because it is anything glamorous. In fact, it shows you the underbelly of disgusting behavior that alcoholism and drug use encourage. I still feel bad years later for that night. I had missed my opportunity to make new friends and to get invited back anytime soon.

22 Woodstock

When I was 17 my stepfather, whom I refer to as my father, drove me to Woodstock. I actually bought tickets. We drove there but had to stop about ten miles from the site because the entire road was clogged with cars. We got out and walked the last ten miles. As we came up over the hill and saw massive numbers of people, I started walking away from him saying, "Bye Dad, I'll see you later," and he said, "Get home safe, son."

One of the reasons my father had decided to drive me up to Woodstock was that he wanted to see Ravi Shankar play, but we had missed him, so my father simply walked the ten miles back to the car and somehow extricated himself from the traffic. He told me later it took him about ten hours to get home when normally it would have taken two and a half.

There I was at the biggest rock festival there had ever been, a landmark event in the history of the 60s. There were masses and masses of people. When I walked past the broken-down fences I threw my tickets away, which I don't really regret because I don't mind not having pictures, mementos or souvenirs—I have my brain which is the most important storage unit in the world. Scientists never have (and they never will) find a limit to the storage capacity of the human brain. The brain is not like a computer where you fill it up and then have to get rid of something in order to put something new in it. Anything you learn you can retain if you like, and then learn something new.

The images in my mind of Woodstock are burned in like everything else in my life. I spent the entire three days awake except for one brief moment when I sat down during Sly and the Family Stone playing "I Want to Take You Higher." I just nodded off, but not for too long because the Who came next. Their music woke me back up and I didn't sleep again until I got home. This was all without drugs. I heard all the rumors about bad acid. I had had plenty of acid trips before then and was no longer really using psychedelics. I hardly even smoked pot at Woodstock—I might've had a puffer from somebody else's joint, but I didn't carry any drugs, and I didn't use any other drugs. I could stay awake naturally for three days back then, which often led to a mania—but I was certainly sane at Woodstock.

I don't remember the first act I saw, but I remember much of the music—it went on and on. The last act was Hendrix, and for some reason he didn't go on until the morning of the next day although he was supposed to close the show that previous evening. I knew he was exhausted, and I thought the band was ragged, and halfway through I left in order to beat the crowd. I felt a little discouraged because I had seen Jimi playing better than that so many times. His playing of the Star-Spangled Banner didn't mean a thing to me—just another jam. I didn't realize how important it would become in musical history.

I made my way back to the road and caught a ride to New York where I arrived at my house and fell out of the car. I probably slept for 24 hours. It was one of those times when I woke up either at dawn or dusk, wasn't sure which, and had to wait until it either got darker or lighter to find out. That happened to me a lot when I was taking downers and barbiturates.

More than enough has been written about Woodstock. I don't need to add to it, except to say that I was there and I'm proud to have been there. I spent a lot of time near the stage and sometimes behind it, using my magical thinking to get backstage. I never jumped in the mud but there was plenty on my shoes, so I hardly sat down the whole time. I meandered through the crowd studying people like the anthropologist from another planet that I am.

23 Adventures at the Fillmore East

I began going to the Fillmore when it was called the Village Theater. The first show I went to was the Grateful Dead, and it seemed like they played forever, which they did. I went home before they were finished but thoroughly enjoyed it because I loved their first record, and that was the kind of San Francisco blues they were doing at the time. I don't know how many acts I saw at the Fillmore. One was Jeff Beck with Rod Stewart, Micky Waller on drums and Ronnie Wood on bass. This was before Led Zeppelin had shown up on the scene and Jeff Beck was one of my favorite influences. Early on, I would always mention Hendrix, Beck and Buddy Guy if someone asked me who was influencing me. Of course I was also influenced by Magic Sam, Mike Bloomfield, Roy Buchanan, and so many other guitarists like the three Kings—Albert, B.B. and Freddie. There are just too many guitarists that I admire to try to make a list, so trust me, I liked all the great guitarists.

In 1962 I was invited over to my friend Eric's house who put on an early Dylan record. I thought it was very good but I didn't like it because the record had no electric guitar. I told Eric to call me when Dylan had electric guitars. It only took three years.

Velvert and I used to go to the Fillmore often, although I'd go often by myself as well. I remember the first Allman Brothers show there. While I was backstage they were having a huge party. In the midst of it was a guy tuning guitars with this strange instrument called a Stroboconn. It had whirling wheels that would stand still when the string was in tune. I couldn't believe he was able to tune while a huge, noisy party was going on.

Duane Allman's slide playing was incredibly sharp. I think he was playing through Fender Bandmaster amps. He is the only guitarist I ever held my ears closed for—I could still hear him but that treble was driving me crazy. At most Allman Brothers shows I would walk up the aisle and put my head inside the PA system to hear the guitars even louder. But at the Fillmore show I didn't do that. I actually moved back to soften the blow. Like the Grateful Dead, they had two drummers going at once, which was wonderful but strange.

I remember the Doors first visit to the Fillmore East and how incredibly and wonderfully sloppy they were. I should say loose, because of what happened when I discussed forming a band with Ray Manzarek some years later. I had lunch with him and accidentally told him that I had seen the Doors when they first played the Fillmore and I loved how sloppy they were. I think he took that as an offense. That band never happened because the singer we chose was on methadone and was a shut-in who never left his house. We couldn't get him to rehearsal. I saw the Doors twice in the early days. Jim Morrison had an incredible sex appeal that even the boys could feel.

I saw the Who several times, but the show I remember best was at the Fillmore in the early summer of 1969. That night there was a fire next door and everybody was evacuated except Velvert and me. This was the introduction of their rock opera *Tommy* and Bill Graham had filled the backstage area with pinball machines and lots of wonderful food.

While backstage I happened to see a jam going on between Pete Townshend and John Sebastian from the Lovin' Spoonful. Keith Moon wanted to get in on it and demanded some cardboard boxes and they were brought to him. Keith went nuts on the boxes while a few other people joined the jam. During the show a fire broke out at a supermarket next door. Although there was no smoke in the theater, a guy went onstage and announced that there was a fire next door and everyone had to evacuate. Roger Daltrey grabbed the guy and Pete Townshend kicked him in the nuts—Townshend was arrested later for this. It turned out that it was an off-duty fireman or policeman who got kicked. The Who wouldn't stand for anybody coming on the stage and didn't mind fighting stage invaders to get them off. About a minute later the music stopped again. Another guy went onstage and announced that there was a fire next door and the fire department was insisting that the entire theater be evacuated.

Velvert and I were backstage and we moved very slowly toward the exit until everybody was gone but the two of us. Velvert looked at me and said, "Do you want to leave?" I said, "Do you want to leave? I don't smell smoke and I want to stay." So we went back in the dressing room and played pinball and ate the band's food until people started filing back in. These were the kind of adventures Velvert and I had almost weekly.

Velvert could mimic Jimi's voice perfectly. He would often call up the Fillmore and get us on the guest list until one day the guy there told Velvert he had just spoken with Jimi and Jimi was in Hawaii. We were banned from the

Fillmore—"You'll never get in here again." Well, that lasted about two weeks and then we began getting in again.

The first time I saw the Grateful Dead I was smart enough to go before the security showed up. I walked right in and listened to their sound check. Between songs I asked Jerry Garcia if he could put me on the guest list. Jerry said no but he asked Phil Lesh for me. Phil said he had no guests in New York and he would get me on the guest list. Richard Lloyd+1. That was before I met Velvert.

You could say we went to the Fillmore so often that we lived there, but we also went to other clubs and theaters to see shows. Unfortunately, I missed the Yardbirds show at the Anderson Theater and that was really Led Zeppelin's beginning. Years later Hilly Krystal took the place over and Television got to play there. The '60s was an amazing time, and we kids in Greenwich Village took full advantage of it, sometimes going to chess clubs were Bob Dylan would be playing at another table, or the coffee shops where you could order a cup of coffee and sit for a couple of hours watching people come and go.

24 Montclair and the Reefer Gun

In the summer of 1969 my parents moved to Montclair, New Jersey and enrolled me in the Montclair High School to repeat the 12th grade. On the first day, everyone lined up to get their schedules, and it got quite crowded. I wondered how I could announce my presence. I decided beforehand that I would borrow a saxophone, which I could not play to save my life, and sit on the bench across the street and blow the sax until I knocked myself unconscious. About a half hour before school began, I started blowing the saxophone like Sun Ra. Some girls walked by and asked what I was doing and giggled at me, but I didn't care. I was blowing my ass off. Then a black kid came over and asked if I was a musician. I said yes. He asked me if I played saxophone. I said no. He asked me what instrument I played and I told him guitar. He asked me why the hell I was playing the saxophone and making such a stir and I said "I was calling you." This was halfway true—I didn't know why I was blowing the saxophone except that I wanted to make a racket, but I did know that if anyone engaged me in conversation about being a musician I would be in with at least one person. That person turned out to be Albert Anderson.

I don't remember much about the school itself except that Albert Anderson and I started fiddling with a guitar in a hallway that was set aside as a senior lounge. Pretty soon we were joined by another fellow who was in a band with Albert, and we would pass the guitar between us. We began to draw a crowd, and a little over three months later the student lounge was completely packed with kids of all grades.

There was a phone booth where we would smoke cigarettes and pot and the staff were none the wiser. We talked to many kids who were cutting class and going to the senior lounge with us. I'd say that at one point there ended up being about 300 kids in that long hallway. It had a couple of steps in the middle where we would sit and play the guitar. The whole thing turned into a gigantic party and the administration decided to shut us down. They got rid of our senior lounge altogether. After that we would just cut school completely, but while our hall parties were going on they were really something else.

I barely remember anything about the classes. I had already learned all the things that were taught in 12th grade so I didn't pay attention and just took the tests. When they started the graduation ceremonies and parties and crap like that, I quit again. Everybody warned me to have a Plan B and get a diploma in case being a guitarist didn't work out, but I had already decided that it WAS going to work out because I had made a wish. Wish is the most powerful thing a human being has if it's coupled with will and turns on an internal compass called the lodestone.

Lodestone is a natural magnet in stone by which you will always know which direction you're going in, and by-and-by I learned to tack. Tacking, a sailing term, is what you do when the current and the wind is against you, by turning the sail to catch the wind, so that you're going sideways but forward just a little bit. When you get to the edge you turn around and go the other way and tack left and right, back and forth, until the last tack brings you to your goal. An outside observer on the shore would always think you're headed in the wrong direction except for one brief instant, where in calculus, the bow and stern are actually pointed towards your chosen port or goal.

My parents had a large three-story house where I had the entire top floor. I met two girls who were best friends and they wanted to make a bet with me as to whether I could wear them out sexually. One was a curly haired blonde that I had a crush on, the other was a little plumper—I didn't know her too well. They looked at each other and told me that I couldn't do that, but I said I could wear them out, so they said okay. We went to my house and told my mother that we were part of a study group, so she let us go upstairs, thinking that three would not engage in any hanky-panky. Boy, was she wrong. I had a hard on like concrete. When it was all over, we sauntered past my mother who happily said "Goodbye!" to the three of us.

There was another girl who ran me all over town and was desired by everybody. I had been warned off of her because she had left broken hearts all over the place. She had a collection of ten records about evil women, including Santana's "Evil Ways." I steered clear of her, and even forgot she existed, until one day she showed up in the back of a car I was riding in. She had dyed her hair so I didn't recognize her at first and I said "I didn't know they grew things like this in New Jersey." I became one of her boyfriends—she probably had three that she was juggling. She was a strange girl, a model doing runway shows, and she kept me dangling for a couple of months until finally I got her hands into my pants and she went, "Ooohhh." I said, "What's going on, is it the biggest you've touched?" She said, "No I've touched bigger, but never harder." From that point on I decided I was going to make a record named "Harder Than You Are"—but I never got around to it.

When we first moved to New Jersey I thought I'd get beat up because of my long hair, but I found the kids were the same—close enough to New York to get the picture. I was invited to a party about a month after we got there, but I was bashful to go because I thought it would be full of jocks. The night of the party, I went anyway, and I was immediately invited into the kitchen where there were a group of guys sitting around a bale of pot—about 20 pounds. I knew immediately that I was in hog heaven and made good friends with all of them. The guy who gave the party was named Larry. He had some honest to God real opium, and he gave me some.

When you eat it, you are supposed to eat a piece the size of the little joint of your little finger, but he gave me a piece the size of my thumb. When it began to come on I went into a delirium and was invited to go into the hippie bus parked out front so I could be by myself.

I had all sorts of weird dreams and visions that were as real as reality itself. One of them involved being on a flying carpet over Morocco where I could look down and see the architecture. I swear to this day that if you flew me over Morocco I could tell you the exact place. The carpet kept flying until it came to Egypt and landed in front of a woman who was knitting a three-dimensional man out of gold thread. The man was about half done and I couldn't help but wonder if he was going to come alive when she finished. I remember this in vivid detail, and I can put myself back in that state without the drug. That's what a lot of these drugs were for me—doorways to altered states of consciousness that allowed me to become a mystic, criminal, doctor, chemist, adventurer and psychedelic explorer all in one. Any door that gets opened that way can be opened without the help of the drug. It's a matter of seeing the potential that is built into you but which you've never discovered before.

I lay in the bus all night long having myriad dreams like in Coolidge's *Kubla Khan*. The opium made me itchy all over so I spent the night scratching myself and taking off my clothes so that I could scratch every inch of my body. It was scratch and dream, and I had won the lottery.

After that night, I began to hang out at Larry's house and met Brian, who was Larry's contact. He began to front me pounds of pot which I would sell, then smoke up all my profit. When I got a pound of pot or several ounces of hashish, I would sit in my room and pick parts of it out and throw it all over the place. That way, when I ran out, I could find some of it by getting on my hands and knees with a pair of tweezers and rummaging through the carpet.

I had so much pot that I could get all my friends stoned to the point of being unable to walk. I had also devised a reefer gun. How did it work? I used large metal pipes with chambers in them. I bought several and put the chambers together which I then stuffed with pot. Next, I bought a fish tank air pump which I attached to the bowl and unscrewed it in half. I would light the inside, then screw it back together and turn on the air pump. It would burn about a quarter pound of pot in five minutes. Then I turned my walk-in closet into a drug den.

I moved my stereo into the closet which had enough space for three or four people, and I put pillows in there to sit on. In this way the reefer pipe, or reefer gun as I called it, would thicken the air with marijuana smoke because the closet wasn't that large. In early sessions, the smoke would sting our eyes. We could hardly stand it until I bought some goggles. Three or four of us would sit in there with our goggles while firing the reefer gun at each other until the entire closet was one big cloud and we couldn't see each other. Eventually someone would drop out, saying they couldn't take it anymore—they were too stoned to do anything except open the closet door and flop out. Then we would push the rest of their body out and close the door again. I felt it was my duty at the time to get people very stoned—to a point they had never been to before in their lives.

Albert Anderson became one of my best friends. He was a great guitarist and was also on the football team—one of the stars who was probably headed for the NFL. Albert was deathly afraid of his mother, so it took me about three months to get him to smoke pot at all. When I did finally get him his wings, he became a pot fiend and one of the only guys who could keep up with me. Later on, after we lost touch, he went to England and was asked to become the lead guitar player in the Wailers—Bob Marley and the Wailers. That's Albert playing lead guitar on "No Woman, No Cry," and he still tours with the Wailers even though Bob has passed on. If I had not turned Albert onto pot he could never have joined the Wailers, because Bob smoked a spliff as big as your mother's ass, and to be in the Wailers you had to love marijuana because it is a sacrament in the Rastafarian world. Albert fit right in, and as a result, Bob did me a psychic favor once and saved my life when I was nearly dead in the hospital and the doctors were going to put a pig valve in my heart because I was sick with endocarditis for the second time. That's a story for later.

25 True Wish

After I left high school I tried college but couldn't stand it. It seemed like high school plus to me—with all sorts of instant romances brewing and teasing and all that other crap. I wasn't given the choice of what to study in the first year so I lasted about three days and quit. I knew I was going to be a guitarist. I didn't need to ruin that by staying in school. I believe in something called macro quantum collapse, which is difficult to explain but I will try. Perhaps some of you know something about quantum mechanics and the Heisenberg principle wherein you can't measure the location and the velocity of an object at the same time because one will be skewed. You can learn the location of a particle, but not the velocity or vice versa, never both at same time.

Everybody in this world has choices. And everybody in the world has potentialities and possibilities. Let's imagine I go out my front door. How many possibilities do I have in terms of movement? I count about six—I can turn right or left which accounts for two of them. I can go across the street forward or I can return to the house which is another two. I can cross the street and then go right or left which accounts for another two. So let's imagine I turn right. Now I can no longer turn left, and I speak in the past tense about it because once I turn right I've made a decision that collapses all my other potentials and possibilities. So I turn right and I walk to the corner.

Now I have eight possibilities—I can turn right and continue on the same sidewalk or I could turn around and go back the way I came, or I can cross the street and continue on the same side of the street or I could cross the street and change sides of the street. I think you get the idea.

As soon as you make a decision, all the other potentials and possibilities vanish. Even though this is not the quantum world, but the macro world, the same principles apply. Until a decision is made, everything is open—everything that is available from your present position, the position from which all the choices you've made since birth have brought you.

Of course, there are choices you don't seem to get to make. You were born from one woman, in one place, at one time, and no one else was—even twins are born at different times, so you are unique. As you grow you gain greater and greater degrees of freedom from those decisions made by other people until, as an adult, you are supposed to be making your own decisions based on your level of maturity.

With that maturity, or lack thereof, as a basis, you will make correct or incorrect decisions which bring you on a course towards your goal, or away from your goal. These decisions will bring you closer to your line of destiny, or closer to your line of fate (fate and destiny are not necessarily the same thing) or simply leave you stranded in the realm of accident, where things go willy-nilly, where they will. Even the Zen idea of effortless effort and going with the flow does not mean that you are like a leaf on a river being swept down the river as the river wants. Most people live their lives like that leaf, but there is another way. That way is to recapture your decision-making power and start making decisions that are based upon your goal, whatever it is.

In my case, it was a decision to become a renowned guitarist, and to make an irrevocable impact on rock 'n' roll history. I may not have done it myself, but it did happen. Certain things could not have taken place without me, and would not have taken place without me and all the others who, through confluence, were brought together. Make no bones about it—these are powerful concepts which can change your life if you wish them to, because a true wish is the most powerful thing in the world.

What do I mean by a true wish? Is it in opposition to something called a false wish? Absolutely. The true wish is the wish of the heart and—if you've accreted one—the soul. I do not believe that everyone is born with a soul, although this will surely be debated, and I suppose it depends upon one's definition of soul. My definition of soul is that which accretes around the essence of a person. Experience coats a person's inner self just like the pearl is accreted around the irritants in the oyster. The value is in the irritant which stays in place and becomes a permanent reminding factor of the call to one's destiny. Not every person has a destiny or recognizes it, but it is essential to acquiring a soul. Other people have other definitions and so be it, but these are mine.

26 Boston and John Lee Hooker

After Montclair, I moved back to New York City. I could see there was really nothing going on there, so when a bunch of my friends from Montclair were moving to Boston, I decided to join them. I moved into a place at 309 Beacon Street on the first floor. It turned out that everybody was dirt poor and my place was a flophouse.

My friends and I got so drunk and stoned one night that I threatened to kill myself with a big butcher knife. The knife was taken off of me by a guy named Ston, one of the rougher kids I lived with. We knocked down the stairwell banister in the fight, and as I was climbing the stairs behind him, he kicked me, knocking out a piece of my molar. That has served as a reminder of the incident ever since—a permanent reminder because I can put my tongue there and feel the hole any time. What did we do to survive? We sold drugs and beat drugs—fake amphetamine—white powder in tinfoil.

We had quite a few customers out in the sticks where they couldn't tell amphetamine from flowers. We all really hated being beat artists. One day out there in the sticks I saw a business that was hiring bicycle pushcarts to sell Italian ices—that is, they were hiring people to sell it, and they paid by a count of the paper cups. I remember pedaling into downtown Boston over a bunch of hills with a huge crate in front of me full of Italian ices. I actually made good money—sometimes $100 a day. Whereas other people bought cups to be able to cheat the owner, I never did so, always figuring I made enough money, and I had enough bad karma on me already.

I've always been a believer in fast karma. I found out that if I did something wrong, five minutes later I might break a toe or something worse. It's inevitable, so it keeps me in balance and in check with my conscience. I think that the first time anybody litters or lies they begin to soil their conscience. Religion would say you're soiling your soul but I don't believe in that. I believe your conscience is your soul because it is a piece of the divine love and wisdom that exists in the universe. The devil is just a scapegoat, like Judas Iscariot. Anyway, I sold Italian ices for about six months and I spent two years in Boston before moving to Los Angeles.

After we got evicted from our first apartment, my friends and I moved into an apartment with a loft. We certainly deserved to be ceremoniously kicked out of our first apartment. We didn't destroy the apartment though; the only damage was to the banister where I had the fight with Ston.

Not everybody had a room in our new place and some people shared. We would pool our money to buy a submarine sandwich which we would cut in fifths—that was our food for the day. Other times we would get a loaf of white bread and a bottle of mayonnaise and eat mayonnaise sandwiches and play guitar. If I had a little extra money I would buy a bottle of wine and sit on the windowsill looking down at the pedestrians and cars and Boston itself.

I used to get into the Jazz Workshop for free, and I don't know how, but a little bit of magic goes a long way.

One time John Lee Hooker was playing and I decided to go. I walked around the club and into the backstage area—it was unguarded. John Lee Hooker was there, along with most of his bandmates, drinking and talking and then drinking and talking some more. I was an 18-year-old kid, and when John stopped talking to his bandmates, he turned to me. I was sitting about 15 feet away on a chair near the door when our conversation began.

"And you, Sonny, what you do?"

"Well, I play guitar," I said.

"What's your name?"

"Richard," I replied.

"Are you good?" he asked.

I kind of shook my head and shrugged my shoulders and said, "Sort of okay." He interrupted me and lifted his voice.

"No, no, no, you one of the greats—I can see's it. Now come on over here and I'll tell you the secret of playing the electric guitar."

He had a thick country accent. I stood up and brought my chair over next to him, and sat down. He actually cupped his hands and turned to me and whispered ear to ear.

"Richie, I'm going to tell you the secret of playing electric guitar—all them cats playing six string are shit. Here's the secret of what you do. You go home and you take off all the strings but one, and you learn that one string up and down and down and up and you bend it and shake it until the women go, 'Woo hoo.' Then you take a second string and you put it on, Richie, and you play them two strings up and down and down and up and you bend them and you shake them until the women go, 'Woo hoo' and the men go, 'Ahhh.' And Richie, by the time you finished with your six string, you will be a master of the electric guitar!"

That is verbatim. Jimi Hendrix had already taught us how to play vertically—that is up and down the neck on a single string rather than across the strings. Two of his solos on his first record are done in one string—"I Don't Live Today" is done entirely on the G string except for the last note, and the solo on "One Rainy Wish" is entirely on the B string, so I knew what John Lee Hooker meant. I didn't have the money to be taking my strings off and on, so I never did exactly what he told me to do, but I have always played vertically as well as across the strings. It was one of the first things that Jimi taught Velvert, and Velvert showed me.

After giving me his secret to the electric guitar, John got excited and said, "I'm going to have you up on stage to take a solo with us," and I said, "No, no, no," but he interrupted me saying, "Yes, yes, yes."

"I'm going to call upon you and if you don't show up I'm going to have them turn the lights on and find you, and if you go home, I am going to have somebody chase you down—you gonna come up and play with the band and that's the end of the story!"

Well, to say I was nervous in 1970 to be playing lead guitar with John Lee Hooker was an understatement. This would be the first time I would be playing in front of people who had paid to see an artist—of course they hadn't paid to see me, but if John brought me up on stage there's nothing I could do about it except try my best, which I did. I stood near the back of the crowd thinking maybe he had forgotten about me because he didn't call me up right away, but then I heard him say, "Now I'm going to bring up a promising young guitar player who is going to be one of the greats. Come on up here, Richie Lloyd." He had them turn the house lights on and pointed at me, crooking his finger as if to say, "Come on over here." I ambled up on to the stage. His entire band were rolling their eyes, and I couldn't blame them, but one of their guitarists handed me a spare guitar and plugged me into an amplifier.

John started a boogie which went on and on until he started soloing. Then he passed the solo on to the next guy, who passed it to the next guy and so on until it got to me. Then he turned his head and said, "And now, let's hear it for Richie Lloyd." I never let anybody use a nickname on me, but who was I to tell John Lee Hooker what to call me? He could have called me Juju and I would've responded. John Lee Hooker was one of the greats.

I started my solo and my legs were shaking. There should've been cymbals between my knees because they were knocking so hard. It was 12 bar blues, and I thought I'd have to go around once but John was just working me, and he took me around three times before he began to sing again. Thank God, I had made it without making too much of a fool of myself. I fought the solo as hard as I could and gave it everything I had and then he demanded more—a prime lesson in working with a band. You have to be prepared for them to demand more of you than you've got. They say 110%, but it's real—like a marathon sometimes. You get your first wind, and your second wind, and your third wind and so forth, until your hands feel like they're going to fall off and your fingers buzz like they've been electrified. That's what it felt like, and I climbed off the stage to some mild applause. Then I ran to the bar and had a few stiff ones. After the show, I thanked John for the opportunity and went my way.

Somehow the seasons went by, and I ended up in one of those vagrant rooming houses where you pay by the week. I had a nice room and a large ledge on which to sit and look out the window while I drank my wine. Later on, I moved to a different place where I had a roommate. Several funny things happened there. We had been smoking pot in a bong when we heard a knock at the door. In these rooming houses you don't just open the door for anybody, and this knock was rather insistent. I could hear the guy on the other side say, "Open up, its Joe, you know, Joe, come on, open up and let me in, it's Joe!" Well I made the mistake of opening the door, but slowly, and then the door was shoved open and several guys in suits barged in followed by about eight policemen. One of the guys pulled out a picture and put it up next to my face. He glanced back and forth and back and forth between the picture and me. Then he did the same thing to my roommate who was on the bed. After ascertaining that we were not whoever he was looking for, he apologized for busting in. They all backed out, not turning their backs on us for an instant, and they had their guns drawn. One of the patrolmen took a look at the bong and wrinkled his nose, but there was nothing he could do about that. It seems they were looking for a killer, because they had been downstairs evacuating some of the other tenants, and had told them to turn their music up loud in case of gunfire.

Another time I was drinking hard and taking some downers. I had a Heineken bottle in my hand and I resembled the guy who hits his forehead with the ice cream—I couldn't get the Heineken bottle to my mouth because I was so stoned. Even with one eye closed everything was triple and I kept spilling the Heineken over my shoulder onto the velvet cape I was wearing. I tipped so far back that I fell over backwards and hit my rear end on the edge of the bed and lost consciousness. I dreamed I was in World War I in the trenches, and I could hear people screaming for help as they lay wounded. Slowly, as I regained consciousness, I realized that it was me who was screaming at the top of my lungs. I had probably broken my tailbone and I couldn't move for three days. Eventually I wobbled over to the emergency room where they gave me a rubber doughnut to sit on and a prescription for 40 Percodans. I took a couple and they dulled the pain, but I began to think I was wasting them on physical pain and wasn't getting high. I stopped taking them and bore the pain until it started to fade.

I have a huge tolerance for pain. I thought to myself, if these things work on physical pain, I bet they work on emotional and mental pain as well, a considerable amount of which I was in as an undiagnosed manic-depressive—or as they call it now, bipolar. Boy, was I bipolar all right. When I was depressed I couldn't get out of bed for 30 hours at a time until my head started zapping me with electric shocks and I had to get vertical for a little while. Then I would lie down again, completely depressed and drunk, or I would go on a manic binge, staying awake for days on end and doing all sorts of incredibly risky, stupid things that I've never regretted.

27 California

I went to California in 1972. I spent quite a bit of my time in San Francisco, hitchhiking up there and back. I loved San Francisco because it was a pedestrian town—one of the few in the United States where you can simply walk around or take the trolley, and I knew the town from when I had been a child visiting my grandparents.

I went to see David Bowie the first time he played San Francisco at Winterland, and it was less than one-third full. Bowie wasn't known yet, but he was doing the Ziggy bit with the "Spiders from Mars." I don't know what got me in or why I was interested. In Los Angeles, I had met members of MainMan, the management company, including Leee Childers and Cherry Vanilla with whom I became lifelong friends. They might have told me David was going to be big.

I was intrigued by this very skinny guy who kept changing costumes—Bowie as Ziggy. David's guitar player was really good, but at one point he played a solo and David went down on him as if he was blowing him—and half the audience turned and walked out, saying things like, "I'm not going to listen to this fag anymore!" and "This is disgusting, let's get out of here!" By the end of the concert there were only about 100 people left. What was interesting to me sociologically was that three months later David played Los Angeles and you couldn't get a ticket no matter how you tried—he was that hot.

I met a girl in San Francisco who lived out in the woods and I ended up spending three months with her, waking up to the cold fog that was always present in the mornings. She was totally beautiful and we were in love, but eventually I got bored and went back to San Francisco proper even though I had no place to stay. There I met a black girl who was cute and we shacked up at some place across the bay. We screwed like rabbits for two weeks. I had never been with a black girl before, but it seemed so absolutely normal because most of my best friends during my teenage years were black. She was an outrageous lay. She had shorter hair than me, but she was fine—really fine. We had two weeks of great love before I moved out and traveled back down to Los Angeles. I had my electric guitar with me in a hardshell case and a suitcase full of clothes. I hitchhiked out of the city.

It wasn't hard to hitchhike back then, and I was a pretty savvy boy, so I never got into too much trouble with freaks picking me up. I was thoroughly freaky myself, so there wasn't much that I didn't expect, and I was always able to get myself out of situations I didn't like. I ended up in a group of four or five people who were all hitchhikers at the junction of the highway and Route 1, a beautiful scenic road along the Pacific Coast. It had just reopened after mudslides and my group was deciding which way to go. We split up, and some of us went to the main highway while a couple of us decided to go via Route 1.

We got a ride as far as Monterey and then we found ourselves stranded because two things happened. One was that not many cars were taking the road, as the mudslides had resumed behind us and the road wasn't clear yet. There just weren't that many cars on the road. So we started walking. There were four of us to begin with—myself, another kid and a couple. We walked and walked with the Pacific Ocean sounding on our right.

Eventually the couple became tired and decided to sleep by the side of the road. It didn't look like there was going to be any chance to get a ride on Highway 1. I was determined to keep on walking with the remaining guy—I don't remember his name if I ever knew it—so we did. I had a suitcase in one hand and my guitar case in the other. I was wearing three-inch high heels like Slade—different colors on three different levels of the heels and soles. My traveling companion had a backpack. Looking at it objectively, I must've looked quite ridiculous—like something out of a circus. But I was determined to walk back to Los Angeles if I had to.

We walked up and down the hills passing street lights every quarter mile. There was hardly any moonlight. When we would dip down, the light would disappear and we had to keep our eyes down on the ground to stay on the road. Then we would walk up the hill and the light would reappear to give us a sense of distance and direction. Having passed quarter-mile by quarter-mile we began to get tired and my companion begged me to stop, lay down by the side of the road and wait until morning. I kept telling him no. He said he was afraid to sleep alone in the darkness. He clung to me and we kept walking until he just couldn't take it anymore. I kept walking while he cried after me to wait for him. Finally, he dropped off, and I was walking alone down Highway 1 with my guitar case in one hand and my suitcase in the other.

I was still determined to keep walking even if it meant I had to walk all the way to Los Angeles. Eventually my shoulders began to ache terribly from carrying both objects and I knew that I could only keep one. I decided to keep my guitar with its hardshell case. I knelt down on the road and stuffed the guitar case with as much of my precious clothing as would fit. Then I got my gumption up. I took the suitcase and began twirling like a discus thrower with two hands on the handle until finally I let it fly. Off it went into the Pacific Ocean and I said "Hello Japan," realizing it would never make it across the Pacific and would instead float for a little while and then sink. It was still a gracious gesture to donate my clothes to the Japanese. Then I continued walking with my guitar case, switching it hand-to-hand so that I could continue through the night. I eventually reached San Simeon and the Hearst Castle, a quite famous tourist spot. From there I easily hitched a ride to Los Angeles.

Another time, when I was very drunk, I decided I was going to head from Los Angeles to San Francisco that night. It was about three or four in the morning when I got to the entrance of the highway. I had some cardboard and was going to write "San Francisco" on it, but I was too drunk to write. I glanced up at a light pole and noticed a sign saying "San Francisco." I figured that I could climb the pole, get the sign and use it to hitchhike on the highway. The sign was bolted down, and I was up there trying to loosen it. Then I heard honking. I looked down and it was the police—the dreaded LAPD. They were looking up at me and laughing. Then they told me to get down.

After I climbed down they asked me, "What the hell are you doing?" I told them the truth—that I was trying to get the sign because I was too drunk to write out my own name let alone the words "San Francisco." They didn't arrest me for public drunkenness but they told me that I had better beat it and go home. I wobbled off and walked all the way to Silver Lake where I was living with Richard Cromelin.

Then there was the time I was picked up for public intoxication. When the police got me back to the station, they kept insisting that I was some guy who had pissed on a lady's lawn in a neighborhood that was miles away. I think they were just trying to clear a case, but I refused to make a false confession. After a couple of hours they just let me go. By then I'd sobered up and they realized I wasn't going to admit to something I didn't do, so they had no choice but to let me go.

On another occasion, while walking to Silver Lake, I decided to stop for a beer and play the pinball machine that was in a bar on Sunset Boulevard. I went in and ordered a Heineken. I was drinking my beer and playing the pinball machine when two cops came in and asked me to go outside with them. I asked them if I could finish my beer and they said no. I asked them if I could finish my pinball game and they said no. I left the bottle on the pinball machine and walked outside with them. They asked me for my ID and said, "We saw you duck in here. Why were you walking in here—to escape us?" I said I wasn't and they said I was. This went back and forth a couple times, until one of the cops said that he had a warrant out on me. I had failed to pay a five dollar jaywalking ticket. This was Friday night and they took me to jail where I spent the weekend because there was no judge for service until Monday morning. Very strange—spending a weekend in jail for five dollars.

I got that ticket because I was used to jaywalking all over the place in New York. I had been warned never to jaywalk in Los Angeles. One day I was on Hollywood Boulevard and there was nobody around—no people and no cars in sight. As soon as I put my foot in the street I heard a siren. That's the way the LAPD operated. The ticket was only for five dollars and I had eight days to pay, but I forgot about it. My adventures in Los Angeles continued.

28 Keith Moon and the Sartorial Splendor

Out in Los Angeles, I was mostly falling into swimming pools at rock 'n' roll parties given by large record companies. I was staying at the house of the rock 'n' roll music writer Richard Cromelin. We were constantly on the lookout for free food and backstage passes and whatever else we could finagle out of Richard's status.

One night Richard and I were backstage at a Mott the Hoople concert. There was a party going on even before the band took the stage. Quite a few celebrities were there, most of whom I didn't give a rat's ass about. Suddenly I bumped into someone, turned around, and lo and behold, my face was two inches away from Keith Moon's forehead. He was dressed in a full tuxedo and had a martini in his hand. I can't remember whether it had an olive or an onion, but I thought to myself, "Where the hell did he get a martini?"

I also don't remember exactly how the conversation began, but it .was probably something along the lines of, "Oh excuse me, quarters seem to be pretty close around here," which I would've said because I almost knocked his hat off with my nose. In any case, he was in a fine and charming mood, with the martini, or perhaps the results of the previous martinis, working their inevitable magic as they do on us alcoholics, taking us on a roller coaster ride through the full gamut of emotions. Keith was in the bloom of cheerfulness, probably just a brief stop on the way to maudlin or lascivious.

We made small talk and chitchat—talking about nothing and laughing at each other's jokes when somehow the conversation landed on clothes the way a fly will land on shit after floating around the room haphazardly. Keith seemed to feel as if he were making quite an impression, which to tell the truth, he was. Backstage, at a rock 'n' roll concert, in a full tuxedo, drinking martinis in the top hat when everyone else was dressed on a rock star groovy or California hippie tie-dye bent.

Well, I was really not about to let him get away without giving him props for looking like he was at a wedding, so I told him, "You are truly one beautiful cat, Keith, but I, I am dressed to the teeth."

He looked me up and down, lingering over his assessment of my rags. Remember that this was in 1972. I was dressed in triple-colored platform shoes, skintight pants with absolutely no underwear and some gorgeous shirt that was probably really a girl's blouse and which shimmered like the wings of a butterfly. I had long dirty blonde hair with Brian Jones bangs so good that when Mick Jagger first laid eyes on me he did a double take that I can still remember.

I had a beer in one hand and a hard drink in the other. And if I didn't have a cigarette hanging out of my mouth like Humphrey Bogart, it was only because I was between ashtrays. I looked at Keith while he sized me up. Anyway, he was going to have to admit that I was no slouch and he retorted, "Well, you are dressed up pretty good, but I am dressed to the nines. There is no comparison."

I knew I needed a good retort. While we were certainly

the two best dressed dudes there, it was clear that I was chic, while he looked out of place at a rock 'n' roll gig. I think my actual words were "Keith, I am heavenly, and you look like you're at a wedding."

Well he bristled and laughed it off, and came back with another zinger. We were both having fun, and it was turning into a classic food fight of words.

"Richard, I'll have you know that I am Top of the Pops, and you are bottom of the pickle barrel, mate!" I said, "Keith, I'll have you know, that I've already been propositioned by both men and women 13 times tonight, and you look like a penguin!" Back and forth it went...

Then, all of a sudden, it turned ... ugly. And in a hurry. Keith's face fell and I could tell that it wasn't fun for him anymore. I had been playing with one big cat and the cat's temper turned. I saw another Keith Moon. I recognized this one too, and frankly I saw the homicidal glaze come over his eyes.

Now it wasn't so much fun for me either. I made a tactical decision. After all, I was a nobody, and I'd been going toe to toe with Keith fucking Moon, for Christ's sake. I know my place sometimes and I summed up the angles quickly. Polite is right. That's the way to get along, as the old blues tune goes. So I took off my imaginary hat to him and I bowed, deep, in a kind of Elizabethan solo, and I said, honest to God—

"Oh, highly esteemed and most visibly High Lord Keith Moon, it is as clear as a spring stream on a sunny afternoon that you are the one in sartorial splendor, and peasant I, dressed in paltry rags, I beg your indulgence and kindness oh kind sir, for departing from what is most evident, only for your amusement! I meant no harm, because, oh my God, just LOOK AT YOU, radiant like the sun in the sky!"

He was taken aback by my effluence, and I could see the gears turning inside his mental assessment Rolodex. Half a minute later a sly smile came over him and he returned to the loveable Keith I had originally had before me.

"You are putting me on, pulling my leg?" he said with a quizzical Gemini look on his childlike face.

"Yes sir, Mr. Moon, as surely as the sun sets in the west, I've been putting a good one over on you."

"Well then," he said, "let me buy you a drink!"

Well the drinks were free that night, but with that he put his arm around me and we stumbled over to the open bar where he proceeded to "buy" me a drink with a big flourish, and we partied on into the night.

29 Richard Cromelin's House

One evening at Richard Cromelin's house there was a knock at the door. When Richard opened it, it was Jim Kweskin of the Jug Band fame, along with a Mafioso guy carrying a gun. Richard had printed a mixed review of one of Jim's shows, and Jim was there to pay a visit. Kweskin scared the living shit out of the two of us.

Jim kept telling Richard that he should not have written reviews that were negative. He asked Richard if he was afraid, and we BOTH nodded our heads yes. Jim said that was good and that he wanted us to be fearful for our lives. I guess that was his way of making a point.

Jim was involved in something called "The Process," which was a cult much like Charles Manson's. He told the Mafioso guy with the gun to put me in the bedroom and close the door. Once I was in there I could hear them screaming at Richard even more. I thought about climbing out the window, but I was paralyzed. I imagined the headlines that would appear the next day about the killing of a rock music columnist and an unknown person. I sat there in the room trembling until they yelled that I could come out. They told me to sit on the couch with Richard. Then they left. Talk about journalistic freedom and the lack thereof! How would you like to be visited by an artist who threatens to kill you because you didn't give them a good review?

I slept through the San Fernando Earthquake at Richard's house. I woke up with all kinds of books and records scattered around me on the floor. I didn't wake up earlier because I had been very drunk the night before. I checked the door but it was still locked from the inside and none of the windows had been broken or opened. I couldn't figure out what had happened. I thought we might have been burglarized while I slept. Later I found out it was an earthquake that had been powerful enough to knock the water out of swimming pools all over Los Angeles. I had always wanted to be in an earthquake for the sake of the experience—and now I had slept through one.

I didn't fully experience an earthquake until 1992 when Television was touring in Japan. The rest of the band slept through it. When I told them there had been an earthquake early in the morning, they didn't believe me. All the news was written in Japanese so there was no way to prove it to the band. Being in an earthquake is strange because everything looks and feels like it's swimming. The room sways but in a different way than the wind causes something to sway. The building that I was in swayed like it was floating in a swimming pool. Luckily, we were in a hotel designed to withstand earthquakes—the Prince Hotel. It was next to a Buddhist temple where I would often go to sit and write and light incense. None of the band were interested in that, but we all enjoyed eating sushi together.

30 Lotus to New Orleans and New York

Led Zeppelin were staying at the Hyatt House in Los Angeles. They had renamed it the Riot House and the place was usually packed with people trying to see the band. I went to an event there held by Rodney Bingenheimer. There were a lot of Led Zeppelin groupies around, particularly in the room where photographs were being taken. I stayed away from there because I didn't think too much of the groupies. They were much too young and skinny for me to be interested in, plus they were all over the Led Zeppelin people, and I was a nobody at the time.

In early 1973 I heard about the Mercer Arts Center and the New York Dolls. Finally, there was a scene in New York that I could make use of so I decided to leave Los Angeles and I began looking for a ride. I settled on travelling with a guy who was driving to New York the long way. He had a Lotus Europa.

When I leaned on the car he said "Don't do that, your hand will go right through it—it's fiberglass." I asked him, "What happens if you're in an accident?" He said, "Well, if you're in an accident you die—but it's got the world's best braking and second best steering so you shouldn't get in an accident." That was enough for me. It was a two-seater. This thing could MOVE.

In the early spring of 1973 we set out, usually doing about 90 miles an hour, except when somebody tried to keep up with us. Then we would floor it until we couldn't see the chaser anymore. I got to see a tornado up close in Arkansas, which was very cool. I was looking at the black clouds when I saw a pimple grow downwards and it began to evolve into a tornado. Before it reached the ground I saw material on the ground start to go upward toward it—the vortex was about 200 yards above the ground. We slowed down to let the tornado catch up to us. When it was close enough that we felt some fear, my friend stepped on the gas and we went up to about 120 mph, leaving the tornado in the dust. When I say dust, I mean dust. The tornado dragged everything under it, tearing it to shreds and then pulling it up into the sky. I was not Dorothy so I did not want to go to Oz, at least not yet.

We drove up into cowboy country from Arkansas and then through the Dakotas where we stopped in some bars that weren't too friendly. Me with my long hair—I didn't invite friendly stares. I would ask my friend to leave before we got killed. Then we rode down the Mississippi on various highways until we reached New Orleans. We decided to stay there for two weeks. Those were two incredibly wonderful weeks. Led Zeppelin was in town, and although it seemed like I was following them around, I wasn't.

I did find a couple of things I was looking for. One was a woman who put out food every day for a dollar or two. It was all the rice and beans you could eat and a little bit of protein such as chicken. It was amazing how gracious everybody was in New Orleans. One day I was sitting at a bar drinking when all of a sudden I noticed that it was light outside. I asked the bartender, "Don't you ever close?" And he said, "Nah, by law we have to close one hour per year in order to clean up, but we never close in New Orleans." I thought that was incredible.

The other thing I found was a girl—a girl to sleep with and to be with and to show me around the town. She was a beautiful woman named Margaret. I wrote a song about her but I couldn't find a rhyme for Margaret so I changed her name to Anna, and wrote "Losin' Anna," which was originally played entirely on slide guitar in the key of D tuning.

Margaret was incredible and I felt bad when the two weeks came to an end and we had to go. But we HAD to go—we were heading to New York where there was now a scene I could investigate. My guitar playing was getting better all the time, so I felt that the time was close for my fate to take over and create the conditions for me to become a well-known and influential guitarist.

But something untoward happened while we were in New Orleans that I only found out about later when I arrived in New York. The Mercer Arts Center collapsed. I mean the building fell in and that was the end of the scene! When I got back to New York the scene had disappeared. I hung around a while until the New York Dolls were playing at the Hotel Diplomat, and hearing nothing but good things, I decided to go see them. It was an eye-opener.

The Hotel Diplomat is a pretty large place, with a high stage and room for about a thousand people. The place was packed. Everybody was dressed to the nines in their best and craziest clothing. As would happen, I felt like an anthropologist from another planet. Very few people were paying attention to the band. They were mostly paying attention to each other and gabbing and leaning into each other's ear to tell secrets. I found the audience to be just as interesting, if not more so, than the band, and this was the

New York Dolls at their height. They seemed sloppy but were very interesting and I thought that perhaps something amazing was going to come out of New York pretty soon.

I found out about Andy Warhol and the Factory, and where they all hung out—Max's Kansas City. I finagled my way into the back room there where I became a regular fixture. Leee Childers and Cherry Vanilla and some other people from MainMan were there as well as other freaks I knew from Los Angeles. Max's attracted people of every sexual persuasion and look, and there was always an amazing party every single night of the week in the back room.

There was a great jukebox that I took a girl behind one night to make love. I pulled the jukebox away from the wall and we had sex right there on the floor. That was a "one jukebox stand" because I never got the girl's name. There was just some instant chemistry and kissing and then sex and we couldn't be bothered going to anybody's house because we didn't want to leave the party. I swear that nobody noticed us—although of course that isn't quite true. I didn't notice anything but me and her. The whole place could've been staring at us with binoculars and I wouldn't have noticed. That's the kind of place Max's was. I kept going there during Television's run at CBGB's— right up until we made a record and had to go on tour.

31 Moving in with Terry Ork

In 1973, I started living with Terry Ork at his house in Chinatown. Before that I had no place to live and I was spending every night drinking and carousing at Max's Kansas City. My friends and I would go in the afternoon for the free chicken wings and other bits of food that Max's would put out. Sometimes it was our only meal, and later we would all return at the witching hour.

I had a job as a dishwasher but when they moved me to the night shift, I only lasted a few days because it inter-fered with my partying. I spent all my time at the bar looking for a girlfriend or boyfriend as the case may be. I was always decidedly heterosexual, but I didn't have qualms. I used to fall in love immediately, and with almost everybody. If the conversation was interesting I would declare my love, "I love you, take me home with you to-night and marry me, maybe next week." Surprisingly, this often worked, but when it didn't, I was dependent upon those who were interested in me.

A lot of people knew that I had no place to stay and that I was a floater. Terry Ork offered me a place to stay. I had just spent two weeks sleeping on the floor at Danny Fields' house. Danny was already a legendary publicist who had managed Iggy and the Stooges and later went on to manage the Ramones. Danny was very kind to me. He knew I was a vagabond, but a pretty one. He also knew that my type tended to find a place to crash and make every effort to never leave, so he laid down some ground rules. I could stay for exactly two weeks, and then I would have to find another place. He also agreed that no sex would be involved.

After a couple of days at Danny's house he began to renege on that last part of the agreement and chased me around the house a couple of times. Danny is a wonderful person, and I felt bad not being able to feel comfortable giving him what he desired. It was a strange thing because the world I was living in was strongly sexual—every kind of sexual. I even called myself a try-sexual, that is, I would try anything. I had tried homosexuality, and I tried it a lot, but I was coming to a place where I realized that I would never really be comfortable continuing that exploration. Finally, Danny had a solution that he felt might be negotiable. He suggested that I should simply stand there in front of him while he pleasured himself. We tried that a couple of times, but even then I was not comfortable. I'm sorry Danny.

After the two weeks I was homeless again with my hobo sack and guitar. Terry Ork told me that he had a large loft in Chinatown with an extra room and that his roommate had just moved out. He said that I was welcome— that I could move in right away. The terms were as follows: Terry would pay the rent and all the bills; I would provide companionship and whatever drugs I could scrounge up. That sounded fine to me. In fact it was the best deal I was ever offered because it led to so much more.

Terry's loft was enormous—right in the middle of Chinatown on East Broadway. He had the third floor. My room was in the front and got lots of light. His room, or

151

rather the rest of the loft, consisted of a kitchen and bathroom and the usual living room and bedroom with giant metal window guards against the back windows. It was a terrific space with a working fireplace in the living room. It was over a Chinese restaurant and bar which was frequented by Chinese gangs. Going in there after dark was somewhat like going into the Hell's Angels' clubhouse. I mean it was DANGEROUS. We did it anyway to get take-away beer. We rarely drank in the bar itself. We were only allowed to do that after couple years of steadily buying the take-away.

Our street was full of Chinese restaurants. They would put out enormous amounts of garbage every night, so the neighborhood was overrun with rats. Occasionally the rats got into the apartment. One afternoon I came home and saw my first big rat. I went into shock because the rat was the size of a large fat cat and was lying on its side in the hallway. It had been poisoned but wasn't dead yet. It was so big that I needed a shovel to pick it up. Terry held open a giant garbage bag and I dumped the rat in, first letting it lay there for a couple of hours to make sure that it was more dead than alive.

Another time I was practicing guitar in the living room when I saw this giant shadow move across the floor—another humongous rat. It crept along the side of the wall and stopped near the brick fireplace. I slowly crept to the other side of the room where there was a pile of bricks from the construction that was going on. I picked up a large red brick and brought it back to the middle of the room being careful not to disturb the rat who was thankfully sitting in one place—right in front of the fireplace. I had one chance. If I missed there would've been mayhem.

I lifted the brick and took aim. With all my might, and with a prayer, I hurled the brick at the rat and caught it in its mid rib cage. It didn't move. I waited a minute and then slowly inched my way towards this thing. I could see blood and guts from the hole where the brick had landed. I had been damn lucky killing a 12 pound rat from six feet away with a building brick. I went to get the shovel, but Terry wasn't at home to hold the garbage bag. I opened the window and heaved it out into the vestibule in the back. It probably made a tasty snack for the other rats in that part of town which certainly outnumbered humans. Those were the only two gigantic ones we saw, but we used to put out poison and snap traps to catch the smaller ones. The small ones were too stupid to avoid getting caught, and the big ones couldn't care less—they would stare you down. If you didn't back up, you were the stupid one.

That's the way it went at Terry's house that summer. Terry worked at Andy Warhol's Factory at night. He was one of the people who did piecework on the silkscreen, making copies of various Warhol's—electric chairs, Marilyn Monroe, the car crash, and the soup cans. They were then taken to Andy to sign, after which they were shipped to the various galleries that sold his work.

32 Summer of the Superglued Dishes

During the summer of 1973, while I was living in Terry Ork's loft, I was doing what I had been doing for many years. I was playing electric guitar during the day, and going out to bars, nightspots and taverns at night, seeing bands, drinking and trying to have sex with every woman on the planet.

When I practiced playing my electric guitar I never used an amplifier, thinking that would only mask any faulty playing and make me more self-conscious in the negative sense—more people would get to hear how crappy I was at the time. I have never thought that I was blessed with instantaneous talent. This has been a very good thing because it keeps me hungry and desperate. I have rubbed noses with many of the greatest guitar players on the planet. Part of my guitar practice involved imagining that inspectors were listening to me practice and pointing out how weak my playing really was.

Anytime I'm in the studio recording electric guitar, I imagine that several amazing players are there and they are commenting. I don't care about what anybody else thinks, but I am looking to impress my invisible friends—those guitar players with whom I wish to be a peer. I don't go in for hero worship and I am guru proof, but this meant that some of my recorded solos such as those on *Marquee Moon* like "Elevation" and "See No Evil" are melodically perfect, and cannot be faulted by Jimmy Page, Jimi Hendrix, Jeff Beck or anyone else for that matter. Those solos were constructed under the direct imaginary criticism of those personages and for all my self-deprecation, low self-esteem and perfectionism, those solos meet the criteria. That's why I often played them live exactly as they were recorded because they had been honed to the point that they could not be improved upon. I will often start a solo the same way and go in a different direction or try something new altogether, but they are classic in the sense that all the solos that I've loved over the years are classic—they are melodic, they contain dynamics, they use the entire fretboard intelligently, they do not fritter away notes, and they avoid that very tiresome and well-known riff of endless triplets that has the nickname "look at me, look at me, look at me."

While I was living at Terry's house, I needed money badly. I usually woke up between 2 and 4 PM, got something to eat from the refrigerator, and started practicing my guitar. I kept this up until Terry came home from his day job. Then we would figure out dinner and plans for the night which usually included going to Max's back room, where all the fabulous people were.

At some point I decided to "get a job." I needed my own money and was sick of living off handouts. Since I didn't have any diplomas and didn't want to do anything that would shackle me to a career, I decided to become a restaurant worker. I didn't want to be a waiter because I didn't want anyone to see me working, and I couldn't cook at the time, so I decided to become a dish washer. A friend of mine got me a job at an expensive French restaurant in the West Village. It was a place with only about 12 tables and a fancy menu including a lot of broiled fish and cheese dishes and au gratin. A lot of the dishes were baked on metal plates and they did not have a dishwasher because they did not want the noise to be heard by the romantic and fantastic clientele who ate overpriced meals and drank overpriced vintage wines in long stemmed glasses with rims as thin as the end of a razor blade. It's a wonder the patrons didn't cut themselves on the edge of the glasses.

I was stationed in front of the deep double sink in the kitchen. The dishes and plates and metal baking dishes were brought to me and placed in a file for me to wash, alongside racks filled with dirty wine glasses. The customers ate by candlelight, which meant wine glasses that looked clean after being washed by hand in the kitchen under fluorescent lighting would show fingerprints and smudges when placed on the candlelit table. If even one glass out of twelve showed a fingerprint the waiter would bring them all back to me to be re-washed. This drove me crazy. And fish and cheese baked on a metal plate acts like crazy glue. No amount of elbow grease could get them clean in a short amount of time. They needed to be cleaned and soaked in boiling water and cleaned again and soaked and cleaned again. All the while the owner would come in the kitchen screaming at me to hurry up and hurling epithets like, "What the fuck is the matter with you? I need those dishes. I need those dishes now! And how come you can't clean no sparkling wine glasses. I'm going to make you clean them all night long until I don't see a single smudge you motherfucking asshole." For this I was being paid five dollars a night!

I lasted two weeks, and one night when it got particularly rough, I quit on the spot.

"You can't quit on me!" the owner said.

"Oh yes I can—you pay me by the day so I don't have to give you any notice."

"I am not paying for you tonight."

"NO! You will never be able to get another sucker to do this job for the amount of money you pay me and with the way you abuse people. You should wash the fucking dishes yourself—after all you are the owner!"

"But I'll give you a raise. I will give you $10 a night. How about that?"

"It is worth a lot more than $10 for me to leave you stranded, after the way you mistreated me, it serves you right. Do the damn dishes yourself!"

I threw down my apron, pushed him aside and walked out into the cool air. Man I felt great! There was all that abuse while I had humbled myself for weeks, and I hadn't said boo to him the entire time. I had suffered and thought that it was a good experience to be an employee and slave, but I had finally had enough and I picked my moment perfectly. I could hear all of his customers calling for his attention as I walked out, "Where's my food? Where is that wine I ordered?" "The service here sucks." Man, those were some sweet words.

I still needed money so I got another job washing dishes at a coffee shop. It was open 24 hours a day and I was put on the day shift. They had an automatic dishwasher and the pay was better. They had me do some bussing, but I never saw anyone I knew, so it didn't bother me too much. Mostly I hid in the back. After a month they decided to put me on the night shift. Right away I knew my days there were numbered. I decided right then that I was not going to let work interfere with my partying—that would've been nonsense, because my partying was a component of my long-term goal which was to direct my fate toward my ultimate destiny—to make records and join the pantheon of the world's great guitar players.

Hanging out at Max's was certainly more in line with my interests than washing dishes in a coffee shop. Was I going to climb the corporate ladder at the coffee shop? Was my fate to be a waiter or restaurant owner or manager? No way. So, after a couple of days I quit. They couldn't understand it when I told them that I was quitting because I would rather waste my life away in an alcoholic stupor than wash dishes. They didn't understand it when I explained that the night shift was keeping me from hanging out with artists, musicians and transsexuals. I don't think they would have ever understood. I just have a different way of thinking than most people. I'm not ashamed of it. Life is just a testing ground anyway. I went back to my life of almost indigent poverty. At least I had a place to lie down and live that was pretty stable, where my one suitcase and one guitar were safe while I roamed the streets looking for trouble.

33 The Wailers and
the Art of Walking Out

One night I was in the back room of Max's and a couple of people told me I should go upstairs to see this great artist who was sort of like Mitch Ryder & the Detroit Wheels— real American rock 'n' roll—and that the guy was going to get really big. The second floor of Max's could hold about 60 or 75 people if they were crushed together. Not too much was going on in the back room so I went upstairs. There were about 12 people there. A band of black guys came on the stage and started doing this hypnotic music with a really great bass player. The guitarist was playing ska offbeats. The singer had really long dreads and was shaking them around and jumping up and down while he sang. I began to get bored because every tune sounded like it was played at the same tempo and speed. I tried to hold out, but after about five seemingly identical songs at the same tempo, I left and went back downstairs where I picked up a girl in the front bar. We went to the back room for a while and then off to her house for some shenanigans.

Did anybody guess? I had just walked out on Bob Marley and the Wailers who were touring the *Catch a Fire* album. It was certainly not Mitch Ryder & the Detroit Wheels but the Wailers were opening for Bruce Springsteen, and I had just walked out on several of the greatest artists who were about to blow up and become unusually successful. No matter how good or bad the guitarist was, I always walked out about halfway through. If they were totally great like Jimmy Page it led me to think to myself that I had better get home and practice. If they weren't that good, I would leave in the middle, saying to myself I might as well go home and practice. I've walked out on the greatest bands on earth for either of those reasons. I almost stayed for entire shows at the Fillmore often enough, but then for some reason Arthur Brown always came on. He would sing his one hit, "Fire," wearing something like a Carmen Miranda hat that was lit on fire. I made a vow that I would stay through the double shows of the Grateful Dead at the Fillmore but I left before they were finished—and it was dawn when I walked out.

34 Reno Sweeney's: Part One

Terry Ork managed a store named Cinemabilia during the day, which was on 13th Street off of Fifth Avenue. They sold movie posters, film scripts and memorabilia. There was nothing Terry would rather do on his day off than go to the movies all day long, so it was a perfect job for him, as day jobs go.

Richard Meyers (Hell) worked there, and Robert (Bob) Quine also worked there later on. As for me, I usually slept all day, and was up all night. I began practicing in the late afternoon. I had an old Fender Telecaster that I'd bought at the original Guitar Center on Sunset Boulevard in LA in 1971. I practiced on that guitar with a religious fervor, but quietly, because I did not own an amplifier. I practiced without an amplifier for many years, not only because I didn't own one, but because I didn't feel that I was good enough yet, and in my practice, I didn't want anyone else to hear what I was doing. I was self-conscious to the extreme. I practiced hour after hour in anticipation of when I would get the call.

One day in the autumn of '73 Terry came back from work while I was practicing my guitar. He told me that one of the people who worked at the store had a friend who "did what I did." I felt a slight insult in that Terry would insinuate that he knew what "I did," so I asked him what it was he thought I did.

"Well, you play guitar all day long alone, without a band or an amplifier. That's what this other guy does and he's going to be doing a short set on open mic night at a club in the Village, and I thought you might want to go see him play."

Frankly, I couldn't imagine why I would want to go see someone doing what I did. After all, I was already doing it, and I didn't see why watching someone else play the guitar was going to help me whatsoever. Seeing somebody else play only took time away from my own practice, and I didn't have an interest in going to watch other guitarists play if it was to absorb any of their ideas—or steal any of their licks—because that could have compromised my own originality. I gave Terry a "maybe," and asked him to remind me when the time drew closer.

A couple of weeks later Terry came home early again while I was busy playing guitar.

"Oh, do you remember the other guitarist I told you about? Well he's playing tonight at Reno Sweeney's. He's only getting 10 minutes and is supposed to be going on at 8 o'clock. Do you want to go with me?"

I replied that I was busy playing my own guitar and I wasn't sure I wanted to stop to see someone else. Terry started to get ready while I continued playing until about 7:45, when I broke a string. This irritated the hell out of me because I didn't have a replacement string and it was too late to go to the music store. I was short on money so I told Terry to wait a minute while I got ready to go. We got dressed, left the loft in Chinatown, and grabbed a cab.

Reno Sweeney's was a pretentious off-Broadway supper club that catered to Broadway wannabes and show business types that swarm around like flies on shit, hoping to get discovered and network their way up that era's American Idol ladder. Reno Sweeney's biggest draws were people like Liza Minelli or Peter Lemongello, or that guy who wrote Copacabana in Rio, or some other schlock. It was definitely not Rock 'n' Roll. We walked down a couple of steps on the south side of 13th Street and entered a kind of piano bar with fake palm trees and a small stage toward the back on the left. There were about 12 tables.

I looked around and felt like gagging. This was definitely the kind of place that I would avoid on principle. The atmosphere contained a kind of glamorous poison—a miasma of ambition towards glitz and gayness. As we entered this house of weirdos I felt a certain kind of defiant pride in my own anti-glamorous dignity and stance of rebellious rock 'n' roll.

We saw Richard Hell and his girlfriend talking to the hostess about getting a table. They had basically walked in with us, and we joined them. Richard was explaining that he was friends with one of the performers and he requested a nice table. Since it was just the two of them, the hostess was trying to avoid giving them a whole table, so it made sense for us to join them, and we were shown to one of the tables near the stage. Our waitress soon appeared, and explained that there was a two drink minimum. We blurted out that we were only going to be there for 10 minutes to see one performance but she insisted. We ordered both drinks, which meant that there were eight drinks in front of four people before the performer even came onstage. Tom Miller (Verlaine) was the name of the guitarist we were there to see.

35 Reno Sweeney's: Part Two

At a couple of minutes after eight we saw the door open halfway. In came a guy who was carrying a small Fender tweed amplifier and an electric guitar in a bag on his shoulder. He looked very unhappy dragging his burden along with him. Richard Hell saw him struggling through the double doors at the front and got up and ran over to help. We could hear and see them. Richard asked Tom if he wanted any help and Tom muttered something.

Richard took some of Tom's items and helped carry them to the stage. Then Richard and Tom went back towards the front door and had a talk. Hush-hush. I vividly recall Tom wearing a ratty off-white T-shirt which had age holes in it. Richard told Tom that he didn't look quite right. Richard grabbed his T-shirt, stuck his fingers in the holes and ripped it, emphasizing the poverty of it and revealing more skin. He ripped it to the extent that it fell off Tom's right shoulder. We could see underarm hair and one nipple. Richard leaned back and looked at him the way you look at a painting that you're trying to hang the right way and he said, "That's better." They said a few other things back and forth to each other in quiet voices, and then Richard returned to our table while somebody from the club asked who the next performer was. Richard responded and said the guy with the ripped T-shirt was next and that he would be on in a minute. The manager of the club told him to hurry it up.

Tom walked over to the stage lackadaisically and began slowly taking out his stuff. He wanted to put his amplifier on the chair and Richard helped him set up, which bothered the management. Sometimes those old amplifiers make a loud thump when you turn them on, and that's what happened. Upon hearing the thump, the club manager ran over. He had been eyeing us at the table with all the drinks, where we were yukking it up and laughing at the palm trees and all of the idiots who would frequent such a place. The manager had set his sights on the character on stage with the ripped-up clothing and electric guitar. He told Tom and Richard that the music was too loud. Tom and Richard started to argue with the manager saying that Tom hadn't even played anything yet, so how could it be too loud? The manager made them agree to turn it down and insisted that this was an acoustic club for singers playing along with the piano, not a venue for loud guitars. After Tom and Richard promised that they wouldn't go crazy, the manager turned and walked away. This was all perfect to me—just the kind of confrontation that made life exciting, and meant that there was to be a stance taken in rebelliousness.

Tom adjusted his guitar and amplifier, tested a few sounds and then proceeded to play three songs. Of course I didn't know the title of the songs at the time but one of them was "Venus De Milo" and one of the others was probably "Double Exposure." There was no doubt in my mind that this person had something both strange and recognizable. I had been close enough to successful artists and rock stars to recognize the chemistry of that elusive "It" and Tom had "It."

But the best part was the fact that Tom was clearly a misfit in the most positive sense of its meaning. He was filled with that constrained energy which I also had within me, like a watch that is wound so tight that the springs are ready to go kerflooey. His singing was impassioned although far from pitch perfect. His lyrics were oblique but full of double entendre, even triple entendre, and he had a strange angular look and hands too large for the guitar, which meant that he played chords in that strange way that I remember from Hendrix, with the thumb way over on the fretboard.

Terry Ork had his own vision. His was a strange mix of Marxism and leftist socialist views coupled with a vision of himself as being a patron of the arts like the Renaissance De Medici's. He often worked in the middle of the night making copies of Andy Warhol's silk screens, and he was envious of Andy's ability to act as a catalyst for so many happenings and artists. Terry wanted to sponsor a band like Andy had with the Velvet Underground. I had been biding my time practicing and waiting for that magic moment when the universe would open up to me and allow me to join the pantheon of those who furthered rock 'n' roll history. Terry had already been talking about forming a band around me, and I'd been putting him off until I felt ready. I had some underlying concerns about my own talents and ability to lead a band in the way that I felt would be necessary to achieve my own aim. I was very close to being able to do this, but I knew that I was missing some element.

Jesus told the parable of the talents, and it goes something like this: The kingdom of heaven is like a man who had three servants. As the man was going on a trip he gave each of his servants some talents (money) and told them to invest the talents wisely so that they would receive a return on them when they came home. Of the three servants, one was given 10 talents, another was given five and the third servant was given two talents. The servant with 10 talents invested wisely so that when the master came home, the servant presented him with 20 talents, and the master said, "Well done." The servant who had been given five talents also invested wisely and proffered a return of 10, where-upon the master also said, "Well done." But the servant who had been given two talents had not earned anything. He only returned the two talents to the master, and they were dirty. The master asked him why he had not earned anything, and the servant replied that he was afraid of the master and that if he invested his talents he might lose them rather than earn anything. Instead he dug a hole and hid them so he could give them back to the master when he returned. The master was infuriated that the third serv-ant expected his money to earn something in this way, and if the servant was afraid, at least he could have put the money in the bank and earned interest by combining his money with the money belonging to the moneylenders.

In my mind this parable played out in my looking for a band. I realized that most people, myself included, were in the position of the third servant. There are very few people to whom are given enough talents for them to turn a profit all by themselves. Most people have to join forces with others. This is true in rock 'n' roll—perhaps especially in rock 'n' roll—because of the concept of the band. Even the Beatles and the Rolling Stones involved a joining of forces and no single member could have had the kind of success that they had together. So when Terry offered to form a band around me, I had trepidations, and was looking for others of equal and matching strengths to my own—something like looking for pieces of a jigsaw puzzle.

There is another idea that relates to my thinking at the time which has to do with the original meaning of the word "symbol." The word now means something that stands for something else, usually unseen and elusive. The word originally meant a small clay tablet that would be broken in half, with one half given to a traveling messenger. When the messenger arrived, he would be asked for the symbol, and the two halves of the broken symbol acted like a lock and key identifying the correct match, which then told the receiver that the messenger could be trusted. When I went looking for other musicians, I was looking for the person with the "symbol" which matched my half.

While Tom was playing the second song, "Venus De Milo," I leaned toward Terry and tried to talk to him about the excitement I was feeling.

"Terry, forget about forming a band around me. This guy has something special but he is missing something. What he is missing I have. And Terry, I am missing something and I know it, and what I am missing, he has. You want to form a band and have it be successful. I want to tell you this and make you a promise. If you put me and this guy together, you will have the band you are looking for."

I was positively giddy with the certainty that I could embellish or augment perfectly what Tom was doing—that together, we could be a symbol in its original alchemical and magical meaning.

Tom played his three songs and packed up. Richard Hell went to talk to him and to help him out a little. We finished our two drinks and said hello to Tom, thanked him and said goodbye, then said goodbye to Richard and his girlfriend.

In the cab going back down to Chinatown I reiterated

what I had been trying to say in the club—that Terry ought to form a band by putting Tom and me together. When we got back home I said it a third time. Before I went to my room to go to sleep, I said it to Terry a fourth time, and the next day I said it again. Terry said he would ask Richard Hell to speak to Tom when he got back to work, because Tom would often come by and they would both go out to lunch. Tom worked at the Strand bookstore, which was only a few blocks from Cinemabilia. In the meantime, I continued to play my unamplified Telecaster by myself.

36 Television Rehearsing

Terry got us together, and Television began rehearsing five or six hours a day. It was a wonderful experience. Tom was definitely the leader, although in the beginning, if we did 10 songs, Tom would sing four and Richard Hell would sing four, and I would sing two, neither of which were my own songs. Hell wrote his own lyrics and Tom wrote the music. Hell never practiced the bass on his own, so it was important for us to practice together every day, as well as try to get Billy Ficca to play a regular beat because the rhythm section was all out of whack. It didn't matter in the beginning because we put on a show.

Tom was on fire, playing leads that were so wacky that they could have come directly from outer space. I was still growing but could play anything Tom asked me to play and make it seem as if it was my own, as well as adding my own parts. I had always wanted to be a lead guitar player so there was an ongoing struggle between Tom and me as to who would play the solos. We finally settled on an arrangement where we would split them roughly 50-50 which later became 60-40, and that worked out pretty well.

We had certain keys that would go to Tom and certain keys that would go to me. For instance, Tom didn't like playing lead in the key of G, so I got those songs—"See No Evil" for instance, or "Psychotic Reaction," both in the key of G, as well as some songs in the key of C. Tom liked to solo in D and we split the key of E pretty much evenly. We would trade back and forth on some songs to see who could come up with a better solo. It was all about the songs and the music.

Tom took great pains to try to teach Richard Hell how to play bass and was deeply frustrated by the fact that he would not practice at home. Richard was more interested in the act, the look, but to tell you the truth, I enjoyed his bass playing. It was wacky and loopy and the tone he got reminded me of Paul McCartney if he had been completely stoned on some kind of psychedelic booze. Richard used to bring in a rotgut whiskey called Wilson's which I would share with him.

Billy Ficca was southern Italian and had a stubborn streak. He insisted that he play the drums his way, which caused Tom to nearly pull his hair out. Only one or two of Billy's riffs drove me crazy. I had studied drums big-band style, cross stick like Billy, and Billy had this one fill that I called "Billy falls down the stairs," because it sounded like a guy falling down the stairs and hitting everything in sight. I would swear he didn't land on the one, and he would swear he did, and we would get into big arguments it.

Drummers have a strange count—an inner count that would go 1-e and uh 2-e and uh 3-e and uh 4-e and uh. So I would say he landed on the 1-e and Billy would say he landed on the one. But at least we didn't do any songs in 5/4 or 9/8 like Dave Brubeck. We did have a couple of songs in 6/4. I sang one of them called "What I Heard" which was about a guy with his head on the railroad tracks committing suicide. It was about what he heard while he waited for the train with his ear on the track.

The other song I sang was called "Hot Dog" which was

a take on jailhouse rock. Tom had "Double Exposure," "Venus De Milo," "I'm Going to Find You" and "Kingdom Come"—which was very different than the version of "Kingdom Come" that ended up on his solo album. That song was one of our fortes—the big ending song of the set that would go on for 10 minutes with a drum solo so we could go out and smoke cigarettes or go to the bathroom while Billy went crazy.

Billy could play a great drum solo. I was taught how to build a drum solo by William Kessler and I knew exactly what Billy was doing and it was quite good. Billy would also hit the shells, the cymbal stands and anything else within reach. He was always drumming. I used to say that he drummed continuously, occasionally interrupted by songs, because we could take a break and he would keep drumming. We would go out to eat hamburgers, drink coffee and come back and Billy would still be soloing. Damn, when Billy was on, he was the best, and his high-hat work was unbelievable. It still is.

We rehearsed and we rehearsed and we rehearsed. Terry Ork had some guys film us rehearsing in his loft—some of that footage is still floating around. Our first show was also filmed, although I haven't seen it in many years. That was a fun time. Richard Hell had songs like "That's All I know (Right Now)" and "High-Heeled Wheels." His song, "The Blank Generation" didn't come along until quite a bit later as a take on the Beat Generation. I enjoyed Richard's crazy singing. He would go into a kind of weird falsetto with exaggerated gestures, leaping and knocking the microphone stand over without a care in the world.

All four of us were having the time of our lives except for Tom who also had to serve as musical director. The music was as important to him as anything because he wrote most of it. Some of his songs got reworked and thrown out so we had a whole bunch of songs that never made it on a record. Tom was very sensitive about that, and he would seemingly throw a song away over nothing. I guess he was tired of singing it, or couldn't stand Billy's part, or the bass playing, or maybe my part for that matter. But we all sat around writing the songs together under Tom's direction, and it was really a band, where we made decisions by votes. If we had a tie, Terry Ork would cast the deciding vote.

At the time, we couldn't get a gig anywhere to save our lives. The most we could ask for was occasionally opening for other bands that had a record out or were on tour. We knew that would not get us as far as having our own place to play, so we rented a small theater that had 88 seats—the Townhouse Theater. We rented it for March 2, 1974, and we decided to put an advertisement in the *Village Voice*. It cost $200 for the smallest ad, and we made our own posters and put them up all over town.

We wanted quotes to go in the advertisement so Terry invited people to see us play, including Nicholas Ray who had directed *Rebel Without a Cause*. Nicholas didn't want to come see us but Terry promised him a gallon of Gallo wine, which he proceeded to drink up. Finally, in a drunken stupor, he said, "You guys are four cats with a passion." Lenny Kaye also gave us a quote. Danny Fields gave us a quote without even seeing us because he said that anybody who approached him for a quote with the bravado it required had to be very good and he didn't even need to see them.

We had these three little blurbs in the advertisement

along with a picture of ourselves. We plastered the West and East Villages with posters. I had bleached my hair which meant I could change it to any color I wanted. I wanted blue hair. I didn't want to get stuck with permanently blue hair, thinking that I might get my ass kicked for being gay, so I used food coloring. That way I could make it all kinds of colors—but I found out soon enough why that didn't work.

We hired the hall, we got some lights in, and we bought cases of beer in Chinatown where it's cheap because we thought we could sell beers during the show to make a little money. It turns out we sold very little beer and ended up drinking most of it ourselves, but Tom didn't drink, so it was mostly consumed by Terry, Richard Hell and me. Right after we got together, Tom changed his last name to Verlaine and Richard Meyers changed his last name to Hell so that they were now Tom Verlaine and Richard Hell, the two best buddies who had come up from the sticks to take New York by storm as poets—at least that's what Richard thought.

But Tom was already into music and that wasn't going to change. Tom and Richard had done a number of poetry readings and put out a little booklet called *Wanna Go Out?* with a composite picture of the two of them on the cover. Nice little book of poems. I have done a great deal of reading, including poems, and used to go to poetry readings with little books like those made for helping people with speech defects. I would open it up and begin extemporaneously inventing a poem. People would come up to me afterward and say that my poems were good. Sometimes they asked if they could see my book, but when I handed it to them they would look confused because it wasn't a book of poems at all—I had made them up on the spot.

william ork presents

TELEVISION

Tom Verlaine   Richard Hell   Richard Lloyd   Billy Ficca

Love'll come pump in your soul two feet deep.
Two minutes later alligators'll chew you in your sleep.

Killers. Sharp as tacks . . . They made me cry.
— Scott Cohen, INTERVIEW

They're finally here — in full pathological innocence . . . Color, skin, guitars: *Love in Spurts, Eat The Light, Enfant Terrible.*

— Danny Fields, SIXTEEN

Four cats with a passion.

— Nicholas Ray, director
REBEL WITHOUT A CAUSE

Saturday March 2

9:00 P.M.   Townhouse   Theater   120   W. 44th $2.00

Television

Surprise, surprise, when the time came for our show, there were actually quite a few people who came to hear us—88 seats and most of them were filled. We did two sets with an intermission. During the intermission, I ran into the bathroom. The food coloring I had put in my hair was running down my face and onto my clothes because of the heat onstage from the lights and my sweating. I washed it all out and ended up with a hair color that looked like straw, a kind of yellowish white.

Tom had been bugging me to cut my hair and I refused, but when I accidently turned it straw colored, he went crazy over it and said that I had finally found my look. He didn't want me to change it again, but my hair was pretty dry—you could bend a strand and it would snap apart.

Tom and Richard had this thing between them that in hindsight I call, "universal contempt"—that is, the two of them felt that they were the "special two," and other people were nothing but insects bothering them. I received some of that treatment. Before we went onstage Tom would blow his nose and then tilt his head back and demand that I look up into his nose to check if it was clean. He was neurotic about it, but I now realize that it was so that he could look down his nose at me. I always told him it was clean and after a while I refused to do it. He got Richard Hell to do it once or twice and then Richard refused and that was the end of that, but it was a long time before he stopped asking.

The Townhouse show was a rousing success, although we were probably a complete train wreck musically with Richard leaping around the stage, and me crouching, and Tom going nuts the way he did in the very beginning. We were an act as much as we were a musical performance, but Tom didn't like that bugging, and asked us both to stand still and stop jumping around—he said it was "false." I explained to him that my movements were generated by enthusiasm and excitement and that I was not going to stand stock still, but that I would tone it down so that it would only be "real."

This was the beginning of Tom taking over the band. He asserted himself musically but also in many other ways. He would scream and yell at Richard Hell because he didn't play the bass and had to be taught every single note time and time again. I was valuable on my own so I didn't get quite the treatment that Richard did from Tom. He always had a hidden respect for me which only came out once in a while. As far as Richard Hell was concerned, I could have been an insect for all he cared. Although we drank whiskey together and the three of us hung out with Billy a lot, when rehearsal was over we never hung out with each other. I've been to Tom's house maybe four times in my life, and he's never been to mine.

After that first show we realized that we couldn't continue to hire halls on our own, or book our own shows and get the PA and all the other things that were necessary for a rock 'n' roll show. We began to think about looking for a dive where we could be the house band and build an audience. We were contemplating that for a couple of weeks before Tom said he might've found a place—and that turned out to be CBGB's.

37 Hilly on a Stepladder

Tom asked if anybody was willing to go with him to ask the owner of the dive bar if he was going to have live music. I volunteered as always while Richard Hell hung back drinking whiskey and Billy practiced his drums.

As we approached the location, I realized I had seen a few bands play there previously. Hilly Krystal, the owner, was up on a stepladder repairing the new awning and affixing the weird Gothic lettering that his ex-wife had drawn up—that is still the iconic CBGB's logo. Tom and I looked up at him and asked him if he was going to have live music and he said "Wait till I get off this ladder and I will give you a tour." When Tom asked Hilly about playing there, he said no about four times—that he was not going to have rock music in his club. We protested that ours was like no other rock music he had ever heard.

The very next day I went with Terry Ork and witnessed him talk Hilly into letting us play on Sunday, March 29, 1974. Hilly was usually closed on Sunday and Terry promised him that he would make more money at the bar on that Sunday than his best day because he was going to invite a lot of alcoholics, and if not, Terry said he would make up the difference out of his own pocket. Hilly agreed.

On the day of our first show we took our amps and drums and put them in a taxicab along with Billy and we took the bus up to the Bowery to CBGB's where we met

Hilly and helped him schlep equipment in. That first night there weren't that many people there but it was enough to keep us going. Our first professional gig earned each of us one dollar, but we were elated. Wow. After that, Hilly gave us three Sundays in a row for a month of Sundays.

Originally Hilly was going to put the CBGB's stage in the front of the building facing backwards like a drive-in movie, but we talked him out of that by saying, "You'll get noise complaints." He said, "I'm not going to have loud music," so we said, "You're going to charge people at the door, right? They're going to be talking right next to the band and that'll disturb everyone." Hilly said "Hmmm." The clincher was my telling Hilly that, if a patron wanted to leave early, they had to walk in front of the band which would be demoralizing for everyone—especially for the band.

There was already a stage on the left-hand side, but Hilly asked us where we thought we should put the stage. Tom suggested that it be put on the right-hand side, slightly toward the middle, so that the people on the end of the bar, which was very long, could see it. That way we could have dressing rooms in the bathroom with the kitchen behind. Hilly got Merv, the wonderful first bartender at CBGB's, and a couple others including myself, to move the stage and rebuild it in three tiers. That was my idea because I thought it would put the drummer far enough back that he wouldn't drive us crazy. It was also a kind of drum riser that would make the drummer look like Ringo because the Beatles always had a very tall drum riser. We divided the stage into two other levels, with the second level for the amplifiers and personal stuff we would take on stage. The bottom level was for the front people and singers with microphones set up.

This stage design also lifted the amplifiers, making it easier for the singers to hear them. The bottom level was only about a foot off the floor. Playing that way sounded simply perfect, and we put Richard Hell's current girlfriend, Roberta Bayley, at the door to collect the admission money which I think was two dollars.

We decided how to run the club based on the idea of a double feature at the movies—we would only have two bands play per night and each would play two sets. We would not kick people out between sets. Tom came up with that idea because we wanted a place where we could build an audience and that meant playing more often. I think we were jealous of the Beatles in Hamburg.

Say, for instance, the bill was Television with Talking Heads as the opener. That meant Talking Heads went on first and third—third was prime time. Television went on second and last—so both bands received prime slots. We tried to organize bands that were different enough but would still cross-pollinate the audiences. We certainly had growth in mind. In a way we were like a younger Max's Kansas City, where the audience was as creative as the musicians. Our audience consisted of new photographers, new journalists, new fanzines, new moviemakers, new audio engineers, new painters and other musicians who were dying to play there.

Roberta was supposed to check out new acts that sent audition tapes. CBGB's was sent so many tapes to check out that Roberta eventually refused to listen to them. Terry asked me to do it, and I said that if someone else threw away the obvious garbage first, I would listen to the others and help to decide who should get placed in the rotation as well as who got to play there once or perhaps twice.

I was sitting in CBGB's one day and somebody said, "There's a new band you might want to see." It was a dull night so I went up with them in a cab to 20th Street where the Ramones attempted to play a set eight times. Johnny and Dee Dee nearly had a fistfight between songs. I could tell instantly that the Ramones BELONGED and deserved to be in the CBGB's rotation immediately, and so they started to play CBGB's.

Television was not the first band to play CBGB's. As I mentioned, I had already seen a couple bands play there. One was called Leather Secrets, a kind of quasi S&M band that played in black leather. The lead singer was a chick with a whip. There were also the Stilettos, with Debbie Harry. Fred Smith was their bass player.

38 Tom in the Middle and Island Records

Television continued rehearsing and, to our credit, no one was ever late or missed a rehearsal. I would always show up, not only because of my own dreams and wishes, but because I didn't want to let down the other three members. I'm sure they felt the same way except for Tom perhaps, who had a secret agenda. He didn't really want to be in a band—he wanted to command a band, and when we finally got signed, he asked to be signed by himself as Television.

By the time we were playing regularly at CBGB's, I was a raging alcoholic and with two sets I had to be careful because if I didn't drink before the first set I would be shaky and the second set would be perfect; or I would start drinking before the first set which would be perfect and our last set would be kind of woozy—at least on my end. But no one noticed, because we weren't too good just yet with Billy Ficca going crazy on the drums and Richard Hell playing the bass. Tom and I, the two guitars, tried very hard to keep time which sometimes went sideways. Sometimes we sounded like the Sex Pistols when they started playing—very nearly out of control.

After a series of Sundays, we eventually got Thursday, Friday and Saturday. Many other bands began to play at CBGB's as well. There were good bands that made it, and others were good, but simply didn't make it. We did a lot of shows with Talking Heads and other bands. You can look it up in any gig history of CBGB's.

Terry Ork was still managing us, and we were becoming increasingly interested in getting a record deal. We were trying to get people down to CBGB's, which was underneath a flophouse where bums would congregate on the steps outside the place. They weren't dangerous and they just wanted to bum some money to pay the $1.65 it took to get a bed upstairs in a huge dormitory. I tried several times to go upstairs to look at the place but was stopped. They would only let the bums in.

Getting uptown people down to this dump of a club was rather difficult. We had to bring in people who were used to being at Max's in the back room which, of course, included the Uptown people—the people with the power to sign bands. They certainly had a great reticence about going to a club on the Bowery. Getting the suits down there was a real ordeal.

In the meantime, Terry Ork was beginning to realize that managing a rock club and rock band was not his only life goal, especially with this band Television, because Tom was taking charge, more and more. Terry was also deeply into filmmaking.

Richard Hell's songs were being played less and less onstage. Originally, I stood dead center, and sang two songs in our 10-song set, Tom sang four, and Richard sang four. Eventually Tom asked us, or rather told us, that he wanted to stand in the middle because he was now singing the majority of the songs. Tom insisted. I didn't particularly like that, but I moved over to stage left where I stayed for the rest of my career in the band.

Richard was getting angrier and angrier because he was

getting pushed out of the band. The final straw was reached when we recorded a demo with Richard Williams of Island Records. He brought Brian Eno in to oversee the production because he said he didn't know anything about production. As far as we were concerned, we didn't want any input into our songs, our arrangements, or our sound. We were taken into the worst studio in New York. It was completely dry with no reverb. I was put into a booth with my guitar and amp, and when I played the music, it felt like I had fallen right down into the carpet and disappeared. Listening back at the demos, everything sounded clunky and plunky. I was embarrassed even hearing it.

I didn't know it at the time, but Richard Williams had gone back to England with the demo, and Island Records loved it. Tom told me that Richard Williams called and asked him when we could all come back and do the other half of the record. Tom freaked out and told him that it was just a demo and that we were not happy with the way it sounded. So we turned Island Records down. In terms of recording, the demo stood up against all the other crap that was coming out of the punk scene, but it would have been awful to start that way with our best material sounding like shit.

We kept trying to get business people down to see us, and our audience grew and grew until it was completely packed at CBGB's when we played there. Terry Ork began to investigate getting a partner in managing the band. Some of the people he considered bringing in were certainly not appropriate. Terry brought in Bob Plotnik, proprietor of Bleecker Bob's Records in the Village, which sold rare 45s and albums, one of the few stores where you could find that kind of music. Bob was a difficult man. He had two

Doberman Pinschers and they were really mean to everyone but him. I've never seen a case where a man and his dogs were so similar in personality. Bob could be acerbic and yell, and he caused real pain. Frankly, he was a pain in the ass, and none of us liked dealing with him, but for a brief period he was a co-manager. Nothing much happened during that period, so when he left, we were none the worse for wear.

In the meantime, Lenny Kaye brought Patti Smith down to CBGB's and she soon fell in love with Television. Patti especially fell in love with Tom. She wrote an article which upped our audience a little bit, but we were already packing the joint. Lenny claims that he talked to me in the summer of '73, and I had told him about CBGB's and my band at the time, named Crossfire, but I can only remember playing one gig with him—we were invited to play it at a Policeman's Benevolent Association block party, and we were paid in alcohol and food.

It was a riot—I never saw so many shiny shoes or smelled so much gunpowder in the air. There were mobsters and police all lovey-dovey having a great time, and we played six songs ending with Bob Dylan's "Like a Rolling Stone." During the second verse, I staggered into the mic and fell over but kept singing the song while lying in the street. I was too drunk to get up, but it was hilarious.

I don't remember Crossfire playing CBGB's, that's for sure. We only did the one gig, and I was too far into my alcoholism to want to lead a band, although I could be a lead guitarist in a band so long as there was somebody sober who could take care of the business end of things. Tom never drank or smoked pot or anything—back then I only saw him drink one or two drinks a year. He told me his brother had become a junkie. Tom had tried psyche-delics and didn't like them, so he didn't do anything. Everybody called us junkies when we were an early fixture at CBGB's, but that was off the mark because I wasn't using heroin during that period. I also found out that I could not smoke marijuana and play successfully on stage.

Being onstage was a very different thing than re-hearsing because we could let our hair down and really freak out. As soon as we started playing in front of people a lot of that went away. First off, there was a certain amount of self-consciousness that made us less eager to freak out, and we began to stabilize onstage. Second, Tom was constantly demanding that we stand still because Richard Hell and I were a distraction to him while he was trying to sing. That was a lot of hooey but Tom had a will of iron, and he would keep at it and keep at it until he got his way.

By this time Richard had been pushed out of the band, i.e., he quit, which is exactly what Tom wanted. I was going to quit then as well because I felt Richard was an important part of the band. He was in charge of the looks, the public-ity, the posters and the ads we took out in the papers. He had the crazy movie star look, and the action to go with it.

We didn't have a band name when we first started re-hearsing, so we decided that everyone should go away and write down potential names. In the meantime, we called our-selves "Goo Goo." That name only lasted about two and a half weeks until Richard Hell came in one day with about 30 names typed out on a piece of paper. There were asterisks around the word Television. He suggested that was the best name for the band, and that convinced Tom because the name also could be seen as his initials: T.V.

I thought Television was a great name for the band but I was worried people might think we were a television station and would ask us what network we were on, and some people did do that. But, "to tell a vision" is also one of the meanings, because both songwriters at that time, Tom and Richard Hell, wrote fantastic lyrics that were full of double and triple entendre. I didn't bother to write anything down because I was sure anything I came up with would've been thrown out.

As I've mentioned, Richard and Tom shared an arrogant contempt that is hard to describe, and that became the politic of the band which I could not break—even though I was easy to talk to and friendly. Tom wasn't necessarily friendly at all and would never go to CBGB's unless we were playing there. Richard Hell, on the other hand, would hang out there, but not as much as I did. I was there almost every night unless I was up at Max's. My life was generated around those two clubs mostly—partying, rock music and sex and not necessarily in that order.

When we were naming ourselves, we wanted something that would not be translatable into another language but still ubiquitous like the word Radio or the word Sony or the word Kleenex—a name that wouldn't get translated into another word.

By the time we had the band name, Tom and Richard had changed their names and wanted me to change mine. Richard wanted me to change my first name so there wouldn't be two Richards in the band. I completely blocked that idea. I told him, "Since you've changed your last name, why don't you change your first name too, what difference would it make? I have two first names because my name is Richard Lloyd and I'm not going to change it for anybody,

TELEVISION

plus THE RAMONES at
The Truck & Warehouse Theatre
79 East 4th St, between 2nd and 3rd Avenues
Midnight Fri. Nov. 22nd
$3.00 at the door

I'm sticking with it." This was a big brouhaha, but I stuck to my guns, and so there were two Richards in the band for a while. To this day people get us confused, but I don't care.

Why was Richard Hell so enamored with his first name? How the hell would I know? All I know is that he wanted me to change my name so that he could be the only Richard in the band. And I said, "No, I've already got a suitable name for rock 'n' roll—go fuck yourself, try changing your first name." I found that a compelling argument. And I guess they found it compelling enough because they didn't pursue it too far.

We didn't want to only play at CBGB's. We tried renting out a few other places as well. We rented a small actor's playhouse on the north side of Fourth Street. We were planning to have the Ramones open for us, and we had a poster made up that said "TELEVISION plus THE RAMONES," which is probably pretty rare because the Ramones backed out after Johnny Ramone decided to go to Florida to visit his parents. We had Talking Heads play instead. The funniest thing about the show was the raked stage—it slanted down to the scrim. It was about a 15° slant, so that when we put the amps up they fell over. We had to get braces for the front of them. During the show it felt like we were playing on a hillside.

That reminds me of the first time I met Velvert Turner—the evening when we went to a Jimi Hendrix show out in Queens, at Flushing Meadows. It was connected with the '64 World's Fair, and had a revolving stage. The stage was built to revolve at a certain speed which was supposed to be amenable to concertgoers so they could sell the whole ring with no bad seats. The band was twirling, so that half the time we could see them and half the time we were looking at the back of the amps. That was the first time I ever saw a wave. As Jimi went around, I could see people standing up and freaking out as he did his thing, and when Jimi rotated beyond their view they would sit back down.

After the show, Velvert and I tried to go backstage but were confronted by security. Velvert began to argue that he was a friend of Jimi and he was on the list and blah, blah, blah, and I made the mistake of opening my contentious mouth and arguing with the security guards. Eric Barrett, Jimi's roadie, attacked me and began kicking the shit out of me until he was pulled off. I guess he had had a bad day, and Jimi was in his dressing room dizzy, throwing up and swearing and saying that he would never ever work on a rotating stage again. But the show was amazing—it was like looking into a nuclear reactor. It reminds me of that Television show where we played on an angle. My shins hurt for two weeks afterward from standing at that angle for an hour.

As we played more shows, we began to think that if nobody was going to sign us we might as well put out our record—a single. Patti Smith had put out a 45 called *Piss Factory* and she had told Tom about her manager, Jane Friedman, who ran a company called Wartoke Concern. Tom decided the band should sign with them and leave Terry behind with his cohorts. That was personally very sad for me because of my relationship with Terry. But when we put out a first single, it came out on Ork Records and we dedicated it to Terry Ork so he could start a record company of his own. We also dedicated our debut LP, *Marquee Moon,* to Terry.

Terry was gay, Danny Fields was gay and the Beatles manager, Brian Epstein was gay. I thought to myself, who would want to further the career of young men playing weird music? I figured that it would either be gay men, the sharks connected to the Mafia, or cutthroat business people who would rip us off. A significant number of the great managers in rock music history were gay, and it didn't bother me one whit. Jane Friedman turned out to be alright.

As I said, I called myself a try-sexual at the time because I would try anything a couple of times to see if I liked it. For a while I supported myself as a male prostitute, just like Dee Dee Ramone, around the corner of 53rd and Third. One time I got picked up by a guy who later turned out to be one of our lawyers. When he saw me walk in with the band at a show he took a blanche, but we never let on that he had been a trick—a John.

After we had been playing CBGB's for a while, and garnering an audience, a number of celebrities started to come to see us including Paul Simon, David Bowie and Lou Reed.

We were backstage when somebody came up and told us that Lou Reed was in the audience. We said, "That's nice," and then they said, "But he's got a tape recorder and is planning to make a new record in a couple of weeks." We hadn't recorded our first record and were quite paranoid about people stealing our ideas, so Tom asked me to join him to visit Lou in the audience. We told Lou how glad we were that he came to see us but that he had to turn over the tape recorder because we didn't allow taping, and that we would give him back the tape recorder at the end of the show. Lou said, "I don't have a tape recorder." We both chimed in, "We've been told you do and were going to have to search you." Lou replied by saying, "Well, I do have a tape recorder but it doesn't have any batteries in it and there's no tape to record with." We asked him to show us the tape recorder and lo and behold it had tape and batteries in it, all ready to record. We said, "Lou, we're sorry but we don't allow taping. We will give you back the tape recorder at the end of the night." I thought it was hilarious but Tom was livid, always thinking that people were stealing his ideas and style. There were several instances of that. Tom thought that David Byrne had stolen his vocal style and that Talking Heads were a cheesy version of Television— he also blamed many others for stealing elements of his songs and styles.

Some months later I ran into Lou in an after-hours club and we got to talking. We spoke for about three hours but later I couldn't remember a thing because I had been in an alcoholic brownout. When I spoke about it to Lou later, he couldn't remember what we talked about either. At the time it seemed rather important—stuff about the world and our various psychiatric experiences, but neither of us could remember a damn thing.

When Paul Simon came to see us backstage, we greeted him warmly. I couldn't believe how short he was. There are many rock stars that are short in stature, especially the English rock artists, but Paul was really short. Sometime later when I was on jury duty the judge in the case said, "Mr. Lloyd, there's word around the building that you are quite a good guitarist. I confess that I have not heard your work but it's too bad you weren't here last week because we had Paul Simon." That just adds to the irony of the whole thing. Another time I was up for jury duty and a district attorney told me he knew of my work and wondered if I could render a verdict because I was such a counterculture figure—and I asked him, "What culture am I counter to?" And all he could say was, "Dismissed, oh and I'm sorry because I enjoy your work."

39 Hell's Syringes

I started on the way to becoming a full-fledged junkie while I was in Television. Terry Ork would go out every couple weeks and skin pop heroin. Richard Hell and I started bugging him to take us along, and eventually he relented, and the three of us would get stoned.

It had been a long time since I had taken heroin in my youth, but this was Mexican brown—it had a large morphine content which would make your insides itch as you felt it moving up your veins. Shooting dope is a very different experience than snorting it. It started as an every-other-week thing, then became weekly, and then I started shooting up every few days.

Eventually Richard and I found out where to cop ourselves. We went over to the lower East Side, parts of which were quite dangerous. It was called Alphabet City then—it still is, but now it's quite a ritzy and fashionable neighborhood. Back then it was dangerous to even go there during the daytime. You could get robbed quite easily, either for your dope or your money or for both.

Richard and I went down there one day and copped. While we were on our way back across Houston Street we were stopped by two undercover cops who pushed us into the lobby of a tenement building and started searching us. I knew they would find dope on us, but Richard also had a syringe. They started grilling us about what we were doing there and what was in the bag and what was a syringe doing on our persons. Richard was completely cavalier. When they asked him about the syringes he told them he collected antique syringes. When they asked him about the tracks on his arms he told them he was a masochist, and enjoyed having his friends poke him in the arms and other places with needles. I think the cops thought we were nuts—too nuts to bother with because after threatening us they let us go—but of course they kept our dope and the syringe. That was a bummer, but it was better than being arrested in the days of the Rockefeller laws. Somehow, with all the crazy stuff we did, we never got busted.

40 Management, Flash Forward to Meltdown and Television's First Single

Our new manager, Jane Friedman and Wartoke, also managed Patti Smith and John Cale. That was about the time that Patti was getting a lot of notice—she had been doing poetry readings with accompanying musicians—Lenny Kaye on guitar and a pianist or keyboard player. Meanwhile, Television was filling up CBGB's—packing it on our own.

Normally our bill would be something like Television and Talking Heads or Television and Blondie or some other configuration. It was just at that moment that Patti decided to start playing at CBGB's, first as a trio, but soon she got a drummer and bass player as well. Patti always called me by my last name Lloyd, which is something that people hadn't done since high school. I was once at a party with Lloyd Cole and he had grown a beard so I didn't recognize him. I was introduced to him as "Lloyd,...Cole." Both of us were completely confused until I looked much closer and saw that it was Lloyd Cole. The guy who introduced us omitted my first name and his first name and with our two last names I was introduced to him as him.

It was always irritating me that Patti didn't use my first name. I could be standing right next to Tom and Patti would be gushing over Tom—it was as if I didn't even exist. She barely said hello, and only if necessary. I didn't like being

197

treated as a nonentity by her—as though I had no part in the magic that was Television. Boy was she wrong.

She still does that—calls me Lloyd. In 2002 she hosted the Meltdown Festival in London that had been going on for several years. She was the coordinator and curator that year, picking the bands that she wanted to play. Television was an obvious choice because we had already played the Meltdown Festival at the invitation of David Bowie or perhaps, Tortoise.

David Bowie had always shown a strong interest in the band. He came out one night to Club 82 which was a seedy dyke bar in a basement on East 4th Street. It was just another place we found to play at. Bowie came to talk to us, and especially Tom. He said he wanted to produce the band. Of course Tom said no. Bowie went on to produce Iggy Pop with great success. He was looking for some artists to work with, and he thought we were perfect. It was another opportunity passed on by Tom who said no many more times than he ever said yes.

Tom also said no to Tommy Mottola who had been brought to see us by Hall and Oates. They thought that Tommy would make a great manager, and he would have. We sat in Tommy's beautiful living room while he made a pitch to manage the band, but Tom squabbled with him over percentages—Tony wanted 20%. I figured 80% of a million dollars is better than 90% of a hundred dollars, but I was outgunned.

When we hit the street I asked Tom why he wouldn't go with Tommy Mottola and he said "I don't want to end up playing Vegas, do you?" Well, I couldn't fight that, so I said, "Okay, I understand."

Anyway, Patti curated this Meltdown Festival and Television played there. It was a weeklong festival in London at really nice halls. Tom was playing with Patti at the time, but sitting in a chair off to the side of the stage with a hat on, pretty much incognito. He claimed that he had been in a car accident in Nashville and hurt his leg and never really recovered, so carrying things like his own guitar got to be too much for him. He was playing with Patti and Television at the festival. The last night of the festival was going to be a Jimi Hendrix tribute. The headliner was Jeff Beck who was scheduled to do five songs. There were a lot of other acts and Patti asked Tom to do a Hendrix song—she wanted him to do "The Wind Cries Mary."

At the time, Television was rehearsing in my space where I had a rehearsal studio as well as recording gear. This is where I eventually made four or five records of my own and produced a couple of others, including Rocket from the Tombs' *Rocket Redux*. Television was in my studio working on new material and every time we got something good, Tom would drop it to try something else, and he never sang because he didn't have any new lyrics.

Tom mentioned to me that Patti asked him to play the song "The Wind Cries Mary," so I said, "I know all those songs from 1968 when Velvert taught them to me. I'll show you how to play it properly. I demonstrated a version and Tom looked at me and probably thought to himself, "Holy fuck, I would have to work to learn that damn song. Why can't I do 'Wild Thing' that only has three chords?" Tom told me that I ought to do it. The next day he was having lunch with Patti and he asked her to have me play it and Patti extended the invitation. Then I heard that Jeff Beck had decided that one of his songs was going to be "The Wind Cries Mary," so I had to think of another song.

I chose "I Don't Live Today" from Jimi's first record. I felt that I needed a strong song. "The Wind Cries Mary" was sweet, but a ballad, and it wouldn't make the kind of impact I wanted to make. "I Don't Live Today" is about the plight of the American Indians. Jimi was 1/8 Cherokee—one of his grandmothers was a full-blooded Cherokee. I boned up on the song.

The Television show went very well. After the band left, I talked over the Hendrix song with Tony Shanahan and Jay Dee Daugherty. Tony Shanahan was Patti Smith's bass player and a very good musician, as was Jay Dee. Tony could learn things very quickly—and he knew the song. The beat isn't that hard, so I was going to do it as a trio—no reason to have a zillion people onstage. But one thing I wanted to be sure of was that Patti would also be onstage, because otherwise I figured she would sit in the dressing room and wouldn't hear what I had done. I asked her to sing the chorus with me, and she agreed.

So that night we played the song, and it went over very well. At the end of the night Patti was asked what her favorite performances were and she said Lloyd and Flea—Flea did a bass solo of "Castles Made of Sand" which was quite good. I was proud to hear Patti say I was one of her favorite performances. In fact, she approached me and said, "I didn't know you could sing so well," so I finally got a measure of respect from Patti after 30 fucking years—which is one of the reasons why she invited me to join her onstage at the last night of shows at CBGB's when it closed.

After the show, I met Jeff Beck and one of his band members came up to us and said to me, "Was that you on stage? I thought for Christ sake that it was Jeff!" Jeff said

"That's quite enough of that"—a little bit of an ego scrape. Jeff did very well but his songs reminded me of how Jimi differed, because Jimi was always on the edge, and by this time Jeff Beck was just perfect. I like to imagine there are two circuses in town, and one of them is full of danger, while in the other, it is guaranteed that nobody can get hurt. Which one would you buy tickets for? Do you want to see something which is perfectly organized rock 'n' roll? I like to be on the edge of my seat, not knowing if the musician is going to actually get through the song.

Back to the mid-seventies. Patti was still head over heels for Tom, but Tom was not head over heels for Patti. Very early on they became an item, but it didn't last long because Tom, the antisocial Tom, pulled away from her.

Since Patti had put out her own record, we decided it would be easy for us to do the same. We set up a little four track machine at the Wartoke offices in one of the side rooms of the Brill building. Fred Smith, Television's new bass player, operated the tape machine and we recorded three or four songs. Tom wanted to put out "Little Johnny Jewel," but it was too long for a single. We ended up putting the song on both sides of the 45—"Little Johnny Jewel Part One" and "Part Two."

I wasn't so sure that "Little Johnny Jewel" portrayed the band in as good a light as another song we did called "O Mi Amore." That song was clearly more rock and pop, plus I had more to do with it—I played the leads. But Tom was adamant about the single being "Little Johnny Jewel," and I was extremely depressed about that. It was true that the song showcased Tom's extraordinary guitar talent but my part consisted of six notes and two chord changes which I did in inversions to make it interesting. We argued, but Tom, being Tom, forced the issue. We took a vote and I lost. I actually quit the band briefly over what I thought was a really bad business decision in regard to getting us noticed.

Hindsight proves that I was wrong, but at the time I was adamant. I said, "Fuck this," feeling that I didn't even have a say. In the meantime, Peter Laughner, who was the original guitarist in Rocket from the Tombs, was vying to replace me. However, he was going off the deep end. He and Tom were playing together and Peter was quite a good guitarist and similar in lead style to me in some ways. One day Peter showed up at Tom's house with a loaded gun and started waving it around—or it could have been at the hotel where Peter was staying, The Washington on 23rd and Lexington. That was the end of Peter's chance to take my position because Tom freaked out and I really can't blame him. Sadly, Peter died shortly thereafter of acute pancreatitis due to alcoholism.

A couple of weeks after I quit, I walked into a coffee shop and, lo and behold, Tom and Fred Smith were sitting there drinking coffee. I said, "Shall I join you? What's going on?" They said, "Not much, what's going on with you?" I said, "Not much—why don't I rejoin the band? I'll let this thing go and we will put out 'Little Johnny Jewel' as you wish." And that's what happened—we put out "Little Johnny Jewel." It was on our own label but we called it Ork Records in Terry's honor. We began selling copies by mail order at two dollars apiece, and the orders trickled in.

Then the weirdest thing happened. We got a one paragraph review in *Penthouse Magazine*. It seemed weird that a skin magazine reviewed our little 45. I thought no one ever read it but just looked at the pictures. It became apparent that people do read the fucking thing because orders started pouring in by the bucket load. The orders went to Terry Ork's post office box in Cooper Union. He brought back shopping bags full of orders from all over the place. We would cut out two cardboard pieces and put the record in the envelope, write the addresses, lick the stamps and send the damned things out ourselves. We did that for two hours every day. That was the beginning of interest in the band outside New York City.

We started to receive press in England, and it's a funny thing because England is a very small country. It had three weekly magazines that were devoted entirely to music, and they had to provide filler for these magazines—for a country the size of Ohio. Many Americans feel as though England is huge, but it isn't. CBGB's was beginning to get substantial coverage as well and the interest there began to churn—this eventually played to our advantage.

We began to do double bills at CBGB's with Patti Smith, and it made sense because we shared the same manager. We did about eight weeks in a row on that bill. It became a standard bill with Patti on top. That irked me a little because we had done so much of the ground work at CBGB's, and Patti came in and stole the thunder out from under us. But that's so much water under the bridge.

41 The Laws and CBGB's

Music is especially interesting because the two most important laws which govern reality are embedded in music. One is in the Cycle of Fifth/Fourth's—the Law of Seven with its skewed asymmetry. This law explains why you might go to the store for butter and return with fish.

The other law, the Law of Three, determines musical movement which is driven by the dissonance of the tritone or Devil's Interval: Lucifer in the role of the "Cosmic Sacrifice of Satan." This is the Cosmic Equivalent of the Earthly Christ Lord Jesus and His Sidekick Scapegoat Judas Iscariot, without whose seal we would not have the ancient play first written in Egypt and then played out in real life by the Passion.

One of the questions journalists usually ask is, "Did you know that this CBGB scene was going to be as influential as it has become?" I'm the only person I've ever heard say, "Yes, I knew it was going to be something huge." Even Tom Verlaine would say no, although hesitantly. But I had the whole thing organized like an Einstein thought experiment, only it was not an experiment. I didn't name the bands, but Terry Ork and I booked the place for three and a half years—that is I gave him some help when he was unsure about a band.

Terry Ork and I are more responsible for the success of the club than Verlaine and Richard Hell or Television itself. Ever since I was a child I have been able to join with someone and begin something that would turn into a large crowd. I had a force like an enzyme or catalyst—more like an enzyme, which is something that causes other things to happen without changing itself. Some people have implied that the success of CBGB's and Television was due to being in the right place at the right time. I bristle at that, because they are demeaning my involvement of which they know very little.

42 Hello Cleveland, This Is Not Earth Music

Television's first show outside of New York City was in Cleveland. Peter Laughner was a music journalist, and as I've mentioned, the guitar player with Rocket from the Tombs. He had written about Television in a Cleveland paper and invited us to go play with his band if they could open the show. They booked the gig for us on the ninth floor of a building called the Piccadilly.

Billy had a car and we stuffed everything into it, including ourselves. There was absolutely no room to move, and Tom lent me a book called *The Beginning Was the End* wherein some nutcase put forth the theory that fast evolution was driven by warfare between tribes of monkeys who would bash their enemies over the head, then eat the brains which had a lot of sex hormones and intelligence in them. I found this book highly amusing and read it on the way to Cleveland, which took the length of the ride—about nine hours. We were staying at one of the band member's houses and we were very disappointed that it was way outside of the central part of the city, which Tom and I were desperate to see. We didn't sleep that night and in the morning we decided we would take various buses downtown to see the city itself, ignorant of the fact that it was definitely not a pedestrian city like New York.

There was one amazing moment when we were on a bus going downtown along with all the other people going to work. I looked at Tom and we started giggling and then laughing and then laughing uproariously without being able to stop. I think it was because we were on this bus for the first and only time, whereas all the other people rode the bus every day and had their spots where they were glued down onto the seats and would probably never leave Cleveland.

For some reason this was incredibly funny. We felt like ghosts passing through who were looking at the insect people. It took about three buses to get downtown and when we arrived we were sorely disappointed. There was nobody walking around, and the place seemed deserted except for cars going back and forth. After walking around and looking for a place to have breakfast, we got back on the buses and returned to where we were staying. That night we had a gig, so we slept during the day until it was time to go for sound check.

When we got to sound check the members of the other band, Rocket from the Tombs, were having some kind of an argument—it seems that some of them had taken acid. Cheetah Chrome, whose name at that time was Gene O'Connor, was one of the guys flying on acid. The singer, David Thomas, was going by the name of Crocus Behemoth, and was a rather large fellow. He was practically having a fist fight with Cheetah.

We did our sound check and then I stayed to watch theirs. It was wild rock 'n' roll, heavy and powerful, and I remember thinking to myself that I would like to join their band if it wasn't for the fact that I was already in a band on the ascent. It's ironic that 25 years later I ended up as a member of Rocket from the Tombs. Peter Laughner, the very guy who wanted my place in Television, died young. As it happened these were their last shows—they broke up in fistfights afterwards. There I was, years later, replacing Peter in his own band.

Rocket from the Tombs dissolved into two bands that became famous in their own right, Pere Ubu and the Dead Boys. The Rocket shows went very well even if some of them were flying on acid. When we played the next day, the same thing occurred. We arrived at the sound check and they were fighting amongst themselves yet again. It was hilarious.

We went back to New York and began the usual planning of dates around the city. My mother came to a show at a club called Mother's which was on 23rd Street on the West Side. Tom's Jazzmaster fell apart and he proceeded to pull all the strings off one at a time à la Pete Townshend. I tuned down my low and high E strings, pulled them off the neck, and then pulled on them to make them sound like a sitar. We had a blast and Tom finally knocked his amp over which ended the show.

We were still trying to get a record deal. We did a number of demos for different companies after the Island fiasco. One was for Arista, which was produced by Allen Lanier, a good friend of Patti Smith and one of the members of Blue Oyster Cult. Anyway, Clive Davis couldn't see it and passed on us. Atlantic Records' VP, Jerry Wexler, really wanted to sign us. He didn't want to hear a demo but asked for a live performance instead. We went up to Atlantic Studios on 60th Street and Broadway. There was a blizzard that weekend, but we stalwartly loaded our gear into taxicabs and went to the audition.

Keith Richards was in the control room mixing the

Stone's tune, "Crazy Mama," which meant that we had to hang around because nobody tells Keith what to do, or when to stop, until Keith is finished.

Luckily, the Atlantic people weren't there either. We set up our equipment in the main room and waited. The engineer couldn't pay us any attention because he was working with Keith. Eventually Keith found the mix he liked—it sounded so much better than what came out on the *Black and Blue* record—and he called for his limousine. Charlie Watts and Billy Ficca chatted and decided to go to a jazz club later that evening—I think it was the Blue Note.

The engineer eventually called us around and said he had no time to set up a PA in the main room. That's when the Atlantic big shots walked in. The head of Atlantic, Ahmet Ertegun, was a short Turkish man. The group of them looked like a gaggle of geese, each one taller than the next. They had just come from a Sarah Vaughan session and they apologized for being late and asked to hear something. The engineer could only put the vocals in the control room, while the instruments were playing through the amps in the main room. The Atlantic people had to walk back and forth between the control room and the main room, listening first to the music, and then going back to the control room where they heard only Tom's voice.

I think that must've been a shock to hear Tom's voice alone. At one point I had to go to the bathroom and passed by the control room. The door opened and I heard Ahmet say to Jerry Wexler, "Jerry, I can't sign this band. This is not earth music."

He had an accent and earth music sounded like "oith

music." I thought it was one of the greatest compliments we had ever received—"This is not earth music." That compliment has stayed with me forever. It's too bad they didn't sign us, because Atlantic would've been a good label for Television.

43 Richard Visits the National Council on Alcoholism

When I heard about Keith Moon's death, it did not come as a surprise. What came as a surprise was that he had been using medication designed to help him stop drinking, and this was a very serious medication which causes you to get tremendously sick if you get any alcohol in your system. I don't believe that he mixed alcohol with this medicine but rather that he took too much medicine. I felt badly that he had gotten caught between the alcohol and the wish to retire from its use, which he was clearly not able to do—at least on his own.

By the beginning of 1974 I was doing my own fair share of drinking, and when I say fair share I mean something like the following. Some statistics show that 20% of the population drinks 90% of the alcoholic beverages. Of that 20%, 8% of those drink 90% of that alcohol. A smaller percentage of those people account for most of the alcohol consumption, at least on this planet. I was in this select group. I used to tell friends that if I stopped drinking the liquor industry would collapse and stocks would fall.

After Television formed toward the end of 1973, and we began practicing a lot, I realized that my drinking had gotten considerably worse, or rather, that my drinking—which probably hadn't changed because I was an around the clock drinker—was having more deleterious effects than it had in the past. My upper right quadrant was giving me a sensation of dull pain and fullness (that is where the liver is) and my alcohol use was interfering with my ability to practice and play guitar, especially now that I was in a band. I had also started taking heroin with Terry Ork and Richard Hell once or twice a week

Sometime that fall I called the National Council on Alcoholism and asked them to put me in touch with the most knowledgeable doctor in the field of alcoholism. It was a hotline, and they kept me on the phone for a long time, asking me question after question, and trying to ascertain the magnitude of my problem. I already knew the magnitude of my problem, or I wouldn't have called them, and at that moment the problem was that they were reluctant to give me the information that I needed—they insisted that I come in for a visit with one of their counselors. I made an appointment.

Their offices were in midtown Manhattan, and my appointment was around 10:30 in the morning, which was rather early for me. I generally woke up between 2 and 6 in the afternoon. I often woke up at dusk and was never really sure if it was dusk or daybreak, except that if it were daybreak I had screwed up and slept through the whole 24 hours.

I walked into the place and told them I had an appointment. I waited until the guy came and got me, and we went into his office. He offered me a very nice chair and sat behind a nice desk. He started asking me questions that had been asked a thousand times before. I always answered these questions honestly. I knew that I was an alcoholic—I wasn't trying to figure out what to call myself.

But he felt he needed to make an assessment, and he asked all those questions that you get on self-tests. Is drinking affecting your relationships? Of course it is—it is creating them, and then turning them into horror movies. Do you drink before noon? What, are you crazy? I drink in three 8 hour shifts—when I wake up till I pass out. It is usually two or three times in any given 24 hour period. Do you think I have a job or something? He asked some more questions to which I gave him answers that made him flinch. Finally we reached conclusions.

"Richard, I think you know you have a problem. Would you like to do something about your problem?"

"Of course I would. Why on Earth would I have made an appointment to come all the way up here and have you grill me if I didn't want to do something about my problem?"

"Richard, have you considered a 12-step program?"

"Yes of course I have considered a 12-step program and I don't want to have anything to do with one at this time."

"Richard, why would you not want to go to a 12-step program?"

"Because I know that people that go to a 12-step program stop drinking. I never said I wanted to stop drinking. Not once. I called because I want to be given a reference to the best doctor you know who has a specialty in alcoholism, and I would like to see that doctor if possible. I have made no bones about it. That's what I said on the telephone when they insisted that I come see you, and that's what I'm telling you now. I want to learn more about my alcoholism. As you can see, I'm studying alcoholism diligently from one angle—from the inside. Now I would like to get the opinion of an expert. I have been sitting across from you for 45 minutes answering your questions politely. I do not wish to seem rude, but you do not seem to me to be an expert in alcoholism. Nor do you seem to be an expert in talking to alcoholics. But perhaps you *are* an expert in talking to alcoholics. That I might not deny, but I have no interest in talking to an expert who is an expert in talking to alcoholics, especially those who spend their time talking to alcoholics trying to convince them to go to a 12-step program or otherwise solve their so-called problem. My patience is wearing thin. I have answered your questions truthfully without hesitation, and with great endurance, and you have steadfastly refused to answer the *one* question which I have, which is to please give me a reference to the best doctor you know who deals with the study of alcoholism."

He began talking and I interrupted him.

"Are you going to make me sit through this for an entire hour before you give me the name of a doctor I can go see? If I sit through this entire hour and you don't give me the name of a doctor, I am going to be very, very upset."

He kept talking, and then he relented.

"Alright, I'm going to give you the name of a man here in New York. He is a very good doctor and has written a number of books on the medical aspects of alcoholism which are considered to be standard textbooks on the subject. I am also going to give you my number and if you ever want to talk some more I would be more than happy to meet with you."

After some fiddling with the papers he gave me what I had come for and I told him:

"I am not likely to be calling you, but I do promise you

that I will make an appointment with this doctor. Period. That's all that I came to you for, and I thank you very much. You have extracted quite a payment from me for this one single piece of paper with a phone number on it."

"Well, we're here to help," he said.

I couldn't think of a clever retort so I simply said, "Thank you," as I shook his hand and turned to walk out of the National Council on Alcoholism, bent on finding the nearest bar. Man, I needed a drink.

Days later, I called and made an appointment to see this doctor who turned out to be a very nice older gentleman with great manners. He had written the only book recognized in the medical literature as a textbook on alcoholism. Previously, as he explained, in medical schools alcohol was treated as a subject for about four hours on one day, and that was it.

"Well that's ridiculous," I told him.

"It certainly is considering the extent of the problem."

He then explained to me the medical facts of alcohol's effect on the human body—that it was a poison to the liver, kidneys, stomach, pancreas and brain at the very least. The only time you feel "high" from alcohol is when you have overburdened your liver and the alcohol builds up in your blood. The liver is not meant to handle the amounts of alcohol that the alcoholic puts into himself, and thus he is poisoning himself slowly but surely.

The doctor then told me that he'd seen people die from alcoholism and when doing the autopsy their brains fell out of their skull just like mush. I was enthralled. He said that the first problem with the alcoholic and his brain is that the alcoholism causes the brain to develop lesions, which turn into holes. He made a joke that any serious alcoholic has a hole in his head.

Then he got to the nitty-gritty and he asked me if I felt that I could stop drinking, and I told him no. Surprise, surprise because he said:

"Good, because what kills my patients more than anything else is called the herky-jerky—that's when the person stops and starts and stops and starts, and starts and stops, and then they die. It's like being in a plane that is in a nosedive. When you stop drinking you go through a healing crisis which is like pulling the plane out of the nosedive. After the gravitational stress on the wings and airframe from recovering from the nosedive, the airplane is eventually flying straight and level again. If you then add alcohol you go into a nosedive again and have to pull out of it time after time until, after a while, all that residual stress of pulling out adds up, and the plane falls apart."

Well, that certainly made sense to me, in fact it was a very sensible description and explanation of the binge drinker dying earlier than the steady drinker. He told me that, if I couldn't stop drinking, then just stop drinking the hard stuff—to come down in proof, and drink beer and wine. I asked him what other substances were poisonous to the liver and the rest of the organs and he declared that certain fats tended to clog the liver especially in an alcoholic. These included fried foods like French fries, or even butter. Well, I ate dry toast for four years after that and avoided French fries and anything fried or deep-fried, but I didn't stop drinking. I did however switch to beer and wine as he had advised me, and things began to get better.

44 Judy

I asked the doctor at the National Council on Alcoholism about narcotics. He said that narcotics are something you could take for the rest of your life without them killing you, but that street drugs are cut with all sorts of dangerous nonsense. It is the cut that kills you, of course unless you overdose. Terry Ork and Hell and I had begun injecting ourselves with heroin several times a week. I wanted to make sure that the narcotics were not adding to the deleterious effects of alcoholism. Actually, I felt that they were conquering it. If I did some heroin, it did the opposite of what you might think it would do. Instead of nodding out, it increased my energy and I could drink all night and fuck all night and play guitar all night, all at the same time. That's when the girls at CBGB's wrote on the wall of the bathroom that I was like Mr. Machine, that I screwed like a machine, and by God, that's what I did.

Down in the basement of CBGB's was a boys' room that was in complete shambles, but the girls' room was kind of nice—because they kept it nice. Because I was one of the top dogs at CBGB's, I began using the ladies room exclusively. On one of the bins they had a giant chart naming all the rock and punk musicians and their ratings. They would have annotations like, "Big Cock, but comes too quick" or "Beats on women"—and that's just a few examples. It was a huge chart and everybody was on it. I wasn't rated that badly, in fact, I had a pretty high rating but I was also pretty picky and didn't go out with every woman in the place.

It wasn't too long after we were playing CBGB's regularly that I moved in with Judy, who was a real CBGB's girl—the kind that'll throw drinks at you and toss dishes at the wall when they get angry or drunk or stoned. Judy liked downers such as barbiturates, which aren't too good for your health, especially when mixed with alcohol. It could drive her insane and I had to pick her up out of the gutter many times to get her home in a cab.

Judy loved to screw and gave powerful blowjobs. We had sex all over the place and she was something of an exhibitionist who did not mind having sex in public. One time, we were at a party and the bathroom was occupied so we just lay down on the living room floor and started screwing. We were getting stares from all the people who were otherwise occupied with the party. The host of the party came over to us and said, "Do you really have to do that there? I've got several bedrooms you can use." We got up and moved into a bedroom where the bed was covered with coats. We climbed on top of them and went at it like animals. Humans are animals anyway.

I lived with Judy for about two years, but we weren't faithful to each other, and we both knew it, so I guess we had an open relationship. She loved the way I screwed her. Once she was talking to one of her girlfriends who was going to be coming to New York, and she got to talking to her about a ménage à trois. She talked me into it too. She didn't need to twist my arm.

Judy's girlfriend came to visit. She was a good-looking girl with big boned breasts and hips. They started making out and I joined them, fingering Judy and her friend. Then they went at it for real and the clothes came flying off. Judy motioned for me to come over and screw her while the other girl watched and counted her orgasms—I think she counted eight. Judy could have orgasm after orgasm and I could feel her twitch and vibrate. When Judy was finished and told me she was exhausted, I was encouraged to go on with Judy's girlfriend. We French kissed and I felt her up and then we began to screw. Suddenly Judy went ballistic, freaking out because I was screwing her friend in front of her. It had been her idea to begin with, but I guess she was stoned and just snapped. She started throwing things at us. I pulled out, and we all got dressed and went out to get something to eat and drink. Weird girl, that Judy.

Judy and I liked it all the way around the world if you know what I mean, and Judy had a sweet ass and a big pussy, but tight like she was the Kegel champion of the world. She could actually hold on to me between her legs so that I could barely get it out. She had a long tongue as well, and beautiful big teeth—a real Italian female stallion. But of course, nothing lasts, and eventually she got to be too much for me with her propensity for throwing things at me, and the falling down stoned and drunk.

There were a number of girls like that at CBGB's connected with guys who were like that too. Some of them are famous for their bad attitudes. I don't have to mention them because they are well represented in other books.

45 Growing Up

When I was growing up, I didn't want to grow up. Sometimes I wished I had been born a woman so I didn't have to face the issues that faced men. Remember I told you about certain practices that I did including sacred silence? Around the age of six or seven, most children are separated into sexual groups. I already said that I was never a child. I was playing the role of a child, or baby, to please others.

I had a conversation out on the playground because some kids started razzing me over having platonic girlfriends. I spent my time with the girls almost as much as the boys. I remember one conversation where I wagged my finger at another boy about age seven, like me, and I said, "Mark my words. In a few years you're going to become interested in girls in a different way, and you're going to remember me telling you this. This anti-girl prejudice is temporary and skewed. In five years or less, you will be so interested in girls and you will be pulling yourself off."

I had this different prescience about the growth of children and how they would reach puberty and become interested in sex.

When I first met Velvert, I felt he was one strange bird. He was a tall, scrawny black kid who was somewhat effeminate, but not homosexual. Around his 18th birthday I asked him what he wanted and he said he wanted us to have sex. I told him that I was not gay, and that I didn't want to have sex together, to which he replied, "Do you want to succeed or not?" I told him I did want to succeed, and he said, "This is a fear you have. You have to get over it."

You have to prove yourself. I'd try sex with anybody because when I was young, I was ambidextrous in more than one way. Before entering school, I had to figure out whether I wanted to be right-handed or left-handed. I remember my family meeting to decide which would be better—the pros and cons. The kicker for me was that when you write with your right hand you can read the words you've just written because we write from left to right. If you write left-handed you're covering the words you just wrote. However, that lets you move from the left side of the page to the right side of the page in Chinese or Arabic.

Tools come right-handed if they are chiral. In a pair of scissors the bottom part is bigger than the top part and the top part is where you put your thumb. Right-handed people had more tools and left-handed people had more accidents. I decided to be right-handed, although I bat left-handed in baseball. In the same way, sexually, I didn't know what I wanted to be.

For a long time, by looking up at the adults around me, the thing I wanted to be the least was a man. "Man" had a special connotation to me—of underarm BO and crummy bars, and whistling at women, and locker room talk. An adult is not what I wanted to become. I looked at men in general, and I thought they were specious, stupid and cruel to one another and very hypocritical. The last thing I wanted to become was one of them—plus they had responsibilities.

Men had to get jobs, and I was terrified of having a job—to me that was like standing in a block of cement that solidified around you. I wanted to be free more than anything. I could see, much to my dismay, that all these "grown-ups" seemed to be hypnotized, or asleep or in a trance. And I can remember when I was completely open. I had these chakras open and I wanted a clear conscience. I was born with an almost completely clear conscience, and when I looked up at other people I didn't see a clear conscience, or consciousness. I remember being terrified that it was like a virus or a cold or invasion of the body snatchers and that I was going to catch it.

I saw the "grown-ups" around me exploding in bouts of anger and for the life of me I could not figure out what they were doing. I searched inside myself but I couldn't find any anger in me. I'm sure I cried like a baby for my bottle, and I cried for my toys, but I couldn't find anger in me like what I saw when I looked up at them.

One day I saw an exchange between two of them, and one of them got angrier than the other and the other backed down. The first one got what he wanted. Then I understood that anger is like a tool—like a screwdriver or wrench or crowbar. It is applied pressure that can be used to get your will accomplished in the world. In ancient Chinese medicine they say that anger is an appropriate response to a thwarting of one's will, and that it is stored in the liver.

I decided that I would try out this "anger" to see if it worked to get me what I wanted, although I was born with the lack of want—there was nothing I wanted for. My only wish at the time was that mankind could be helped out of the terrible dilemma it was in. For a couple of weeks I thought about what I could ask for that I didn't really care about, but would not be given. When I was told no, I could pitch a fit and see if this "anger" would work.

I don't remember what I asked for but my mother said no and I got "angry" and acted out all the symptoms of anger—and she buckled and gave me what I had pretended to want. The tool of anger had worked, but I noticed that on my inside it was sticky. I tried this experiment again a few weeks later and noticed that it was trying to grab hold of me. Then there was the first time I got angry without quotation marks. That time I *was* anger—that is, identified with the anger which had gotten its teeth in me. It has taken the rest of my life to get free of it. That's how addictive it is—just like all the other negative emotions. I consider myself lucky because I don't suffer grief the way most people do, and I experience fewer negative emotions than many people I encounter.

46 Sire and Elektra

Sire records really wanted to sign Television. Seymour Stein, who was the head of the company, had signed the Ramones and Talking Heads. He had a deal in England to deliver six albums a year at $10,000 per album. He would come backstage at CBGB's after a show and say things like, "I love your band and I'd like to sign you. Here is the contract—why don't you sign?"

He carried blank contracts around with him. I remember hearing Johnny from The Ramones saying, "I think we ought to see a lawyer about this," and Seymour said, "Oh that's too bad because I'm going to England tomorrow. I won't be back for three months and my tastes change, so I don't know if I will want to sign you then." This is how he induced bands to sign on the spot, with a $6500 recording budget, and a thousand dollar advance. He received $2500 just for signing a band, and he took no risk whatsoever. Both Talking Heads and the Ramones signed that way, as did Madonna. He was desperate to sign Television but Tom didn't want to talk to him. Tom told me to go talk with him, but that no matter what, I was to say no.

I went up to Sire's offices where I was led in to see Seymour. He proceeded to talk to me for about three hours, trying to get me to sign with Sire on behalf of the band. I kept saying, "I don't think so—we want a reasonable recording budget and support, and you are signing bands for peanuts."

He explained that his company was not wealthy—it was one of the last independents—and that was all he could afford. He told me that Television would be the Grateful Dead of the future, and that 25 years in the future we would still be famous and have people follow us around on tour. This is exactly what happened and I knew he was correct, but I had to say no because we wanted the right record deal, and Sire could not provide that.

Eventually, a woman named Karin Berg from Elektra Records came down to see us at CBGB's. She brought her boss, Joe Smith, who was the head of Elektra. He liked us enough, and she was pressing to get us signed. He came backstage after a show and said "I'd love to sign you to Elektra, if we can get the details worked out." This was very good news because Elektra had the Doors, Love, Paul Butterfield Blues Band, Tim Buckley and other really good, artistic bands. It seemed like the perfect fit for us—which it turned out to be—sort of.

Joe left while Karin stayed on to provide some of the details. We were offered a much better contract, although we made a mistake by hiring a lawyer who had been one of the Beatles' lawyers. He also worked for record companies and I think there was a conflict of interest. We ended up with a really crappy deal, considering what we were looking for. The deal called for six or seven records. I think that was the limit you could ask for in a contract from a major label. As I mentioned before, Tom wanted to be signed alone as the band Television. The record company balked and Tom had to sign along with all the rest of us—myself, Billy Ficca and Fred Smith. Fred, who was previously the bassist with Blondie, joined Television after Richard Hell had quit the band.

Patti Smith had been signed separately to Arista, and her band has always been on retainer as sidemen, but her band was always called Patti Smith Band. Television was not known as Tom and Television, but strictly as Television. We all thought we were a band except for Tom, who was vying for all of the power, little by little.

47 Anita and Keith

One night Anita Pallenberg was brought down to CBGB's to see Television. I was introduced to her after our set, and it was platonic love at first sight. I've known very few women with whom I have not had sex with but still love deeply. Anita and I immediately fell in love with each other in that way.

I still had the bleached blonde hair with bangs and I looked quite a bit like Brian Jones. When I was out in Montauk where the Stones were rehearsing at Peter Beard's house, I was sitting around in the kitchen. Mick Jagger passed through and caught a glance of me and did a double take. I think he thought he saw a ghost.

After seeing us play at CBGB's, Anita invited me up to where she was staying, which was a fancy hotel where they had an entire floor. It was somewhere on Fifth Avenue around 60th Street. I showed up and she was the only person present except for some little kid—it was her son Marlon who was about the age of four. He was riding a tricycle all around the apartment. That reminded me of the kid in *The Shining* because of the size of the apartment and the fact that it was otherwise deserted except for Anita.

Anita had the shining as strongly as anybody else I'd ever met, and I've met my fair share of rock stars and other famous people. I've met three heavyweight boxing champs of the world, including Rocky Marciano, who served me a slice of pizza. I was on the Upper East Side of New York and stopped in a pizza joint. I didn't notice the name of the place, but ordered a slice of pizza from the little guy behind the counter. When he turned to put it in the oven I looked around on the walls. They were filled with boxing pictures of the world-famous Rocky Marciano. This time it was me who did a double take because it seemed like they were pictures of the guy behind the counter.

While he was getting my slice I said, "Rocky?"

"Yeah?"

"Rocky Marciano?"

"Yeah that's me. Whaddya you want?"

I told him I couldn't believe that it was him working in a pizza joint.

"You must own the place right?"

"Yes," he said.

"And you must be able to have people working for you right?"

"Yeah, of course."

I asked him why he was working in his own pizza joint.

"I like pizza," he said.

This was unbelievable. I was being served a slice of pizza by Rocky Marciano, one of the greatest boxing champions of all time. I asked to shake his hand. He gave me one of the firmest handshakes I've ever known, except for a few other heavyweight champs such as George Foreman, whom I met while hanging out in the green room at a TV show. All three champs I've met had the same type of handshake; they would put their hand firmly in yours but not squeeze it aggressively. This is the gentleman's handshake and I have taught it to other men. It's quite different than the ordinary handshake of some weak-willed or overly strong idiot who tries to break your hand with his overpowered handshake.

Back to Anita. I went to visit her and Marlon a number of times in the hotel until she moved back to Keith Richards' house in Connecticut. After that, when she wanted to see me, she sent a limousine to pick me up on Thompson Street where I was living. It was very kind of her to send me a limousine. It was one of the stretch limousines that you knew somebody famous was in, only it was just me, and I was driven up to Connecticut. Keith, Anita and Keith's mother were there, along with some other people who seemed to live there and do work around the house—but they certainly didn't act like servants.

Before I was introduced to Keith, Anita took me into the kitchen where Keith's mother was sitting at the kitchen table. She introduced me by saying, "This is Richard. He's in a band called Television and they're going to be huge." Keith's mom, Doris, then said, "Perhaps, but you will never be as big as my boy Keith." She pronounced Keith as "Keef."

I replied by saying, "You are absolutely right, Mrs. Richards. Nobody will ever be as big as Keith," and she smiled. There were a couple of pictures taken but I don't know what happened to them. They are around somewhere and I value a picture of me with Keith's mom more than I value a picture of me and Keith, which I never asked for. I never asked anyone to take a picture with me, and I never asked for an autograph. I was looking for something else, something far more elusive, and I got it.

After saying hello to Keith's mother, we went back into the living room where Keith was sitting on a couch. He was very friendly, we shook hands, and he offered me a seat and I sat down in a comfy chair facing the fireplace. I looked around and I saw no guitars. Strange, so I asked him about that and he said, "I see guitars so often that I like to have some time where I don't—would you like to have a play?" I said, "Yes," although I was a bit nervous to be jamming with Keith.

Keith asked Larry, a guy who worked around the house, to go out to the barn where they kept all their equipment and get a couple of guitars and bring them back. In the meantime, Keith went into another room and brought out a cassette which he had drawn on. He gave it to me as a gift. I still have it, and it contains some rehearsals of stuff like "Beast of Burden," as well as a reggae tune that I'm still crazy about, but which has never been released called "Chucky No Looky."

Two acoustic guitars soon arrived. This shocked me a little bit because I was used to playing electric guitar and hardly ever played acoustic. I always say that I play the electricity while the guitar plays me and the three of us dance while the music comes out.

We took the two guitars into the kitchen, and began to play with each other, feeling each other out—just jamming on some blues. I wanted to show Keith this ska reggae tune I had written which had two parts, a back scrape rhythm and the bass part. The rhythm was so simple that anybody could do it, but the bass part was more interesting so I taught it to him. Anita looked at me later with her jaw slack and said, "I've never seen that before," and I asked, "What?"

"You told Keith what to do and he did it!" she replied.

I didn't think much of that, but in retrospect, it's true that Keith is his own man and doesn't usually oblige anybody. He is in the eye of a hurricane where there is no wind, but there is a storm wall and people that get close to him can get caught in the storm wall and destroyed. He's like the cliffs of Dover, made of granite, where the sea can bang up against them forever and nothing happens to them. Keith has been on the next-to-die list so long that the list died, and he is still with us.

Late in the day, Keith invited me to go to Jamaica—that evening. Unfortunately, or perhaps fortunately, I didn't have my passport with me and I told him I'd have to go back to New York to get it. Keith asked how long it would take and told me that they were leaving in two hours. I could never have made it. Keith told me that it didn't matter and that I could come anyway, but something in me decided to stay with Anita and the child. I'm glad I did, because I'm the kind of person who would've definitely gone down the tubes being around Keith for an extended time.

Anita continued sending limousines for me every once in a while. I enjoyed visiting them very much and they were always warm and inviting. One time while I was there they were waiting for somebody who worked at a chemical laboratory and who was bringing some pure pharmaceutical-quality cocaine. When this person arrived, Keith was handed a little brown bottle marked with the name of the pharmaceutical company and the word cocaine on it. Keith asked me if I wanted some, and I said sure. There was plenty of cocaine around then, but it was never pharmaceutical-pure, so I asked him to pour me out a line.

I was planning on snorting it with a rolled up dollar but Keith said no, and then demonstrated how to do it. He made a fist and showed me the indentation between his thumb and knuckle of the forefinger. I imitated him and he poured some into the little indentation. He said I should

232

put it up to my nose and open my hand while I snorted it.

I can hardly tell you what happened after that. Cocaine is an anesthetic used in eye surgery to numb the eye, but snorting it this way numbed my "I"—I mean it anesthetized ME—my sense of "I Am." Frankly I didn't know whether I was alive or dead. All I knew was that I had been numbed and only my body and all of its faculties remained—but the "me" was missing. Keith asked me if I'd like another hit.

"I'll let you know after I figure out if I'm alive or dead," I replied.

They all laughed except for me because I was too stoned to know what laughter was—and I was a person who had laughed so hard I thought I was going to kill myself from laughter. But this time I couldn't figure out how to laugh, so I just sat there numbed. This state lasted about 15 or 20 minutes and then started to wear off. To tell the truth, I never tried that again. I have too much invested in my "I" to see it wander off and disappear.

One time I was at Keith's house when his father was visiting—an old sea hound with a pipe constantly in his mouth. He seemed to be a likable person but was quiet. I went to the bathroom and came out to find Keith lying on the floor next to the couch blocking the way to the kitchen. I asked the people there how I should get into the kitchen. They said, "Just step over him," and I replied "I am not stepping over Keith Richards to go into some kitchen." I walked around a long couch and made my way into the kitchen where there was never very much food anyway. When I came back, I asked them why they didn't put Keith to bed. They said that Keith would be very angry if he woke up in bed, or if they tried to undress him. They told me that Keith would stay up for four or five days straight and then simply keel over and conk down on the floor and nobody ever tried to do anything except walk around him or over him. For some reason I found this funny, but I suppose I had done the very same thing myself when completely stoned out of my mind. Once I rolled a joint, or attempted to, and I was so stoned I put the marijuana on the paper and lit a match—only to look down and see that I had not rolled the joint yet. Other times I have been in conversations with people and closed my eyes while continuing the conversation. When I opened my eyes, I would be shocked to see that they were gone. I closed my eyes and continued the reality in a dream.

I had this crazy girlfriend who went to Keith's house with me once. She seemed to hit it off with Anita—she had been invited behind my back. Keith caught her asking questions with a hidden tape recorder in her jacket. I heard that Keith knocked her out and then kicked her out. After that I was somehow blamed and became a persona non grata to Keith, although not to Anita. She still sent limos to pick me up from time to time and got me into Stones' concerts. One time she sent for me and I was in the kitchen trying to find something to eat but all the cupboards were bare and I was starving. I asked to be driven back home where at least I could eat something.

We used to go to Keith's birthday parties—one was held in an ice-skating rink. Anita had also invited Cheetah Chrome. Anita, Cheetah and myself were going around the rink—I'm a pretty good ice skater—when all of a sudden I noticed that Cheetah had disappeared. I went round and round but I couldn't find him. I learned later that he had fallen and broken his arm in about three places and had to be taken to the hospital. At the time he just seemed to vanish, and I spent a good half an hour looking for him to no avail.

Another time Keith's birthday party was at his house and I showed up wearing a tie. I didn't own a tie at the time and never had, so I thought I would wear one for the occasion. Keith was not amused. He said he had spent the week with people who wear ties and asked me to please take it off. I said, "Sure, but would you mind cutting it off?" He sent somebody to find a pair of scissors and they snipped my tie in half. I took the rest of it off and threw it in the fireplace.

Somebody had given Keith a samurai sword for his birthday. I took it out and was playing with Marlon when it knocked against the fireplace wall and broke in half. Richard had once again embarrassed himself, although Marlon thought it was groovy.

I knew Marlon from the age of four until he was about 12. I still keep in touch with him and see his mother whenever I'm in London. Anita and I still love each other deeply—although there's never been anything sexual about it. It's just two people with magic—big magic around them. Anita had "It" as much as anybody I've ever met, and she could get anybody to do anything.

One time Anita convinced me to jump off a cliff that was about 80 feet high. We were visiting a lake near their home in Connecticut. There were some jocks diving into the water from that great height. Anita egged me on, saying, "Richard, I bet you can do that," and of course I said, "Yes, I can."

I was used to diving, but from that height I couldn't dive hands first because I might have slipped over, and a belly flop would have been like hitting concrete. I went feet first and held on to my testicles so there would be some protection around them when I hit the water. I slid slowly off the side of the slanting cliff until it was too late to climb back up and I had no choice but to jump. And jump I did.

The jump seemed to last forever. I was looking around at the lake and it seemed like I was floating, so I looked down, and at that moment my body hit the water. The impact tore off the underside of my upper lip—that little flap that holds the upper lip. I came to a complete stop deep below the waterline. I didn't think to swim back up, so there I was, motionless, trying to hold my breath and wondering when I would float back up. I eventually swam upward and broke the waterline. The jocks were so close that one nearly hit my head coming up. Several of them, thinking I was in trouble, had jumped into the water after seeing blood on the surface.

One of the jocks put me in a lifesaver's super grip which I could not free myself from. Lifeguards are taught this grip because people, in their panic and frenzy, have tended to drown themselves *and* the person attempting to save them. I screamed at him, telling him that I could swim to shore (the one stroke I was good at was the side stroke) and he was ruining my good time, but he wouldn't let me. By the time we got to shore, I was so pissed I could spit. I realize now that he was doing what he was taught to do, and he thought he was saving my ass.

"Saving my ass, my ass," I said to him at the time, "You didn't do anything except ruin my dive, thinking that I was weak and was going to drown—you fuck."

Anita was suitably impressed.

48 Recording *Marquee Moon*

Television had signed with Elektra and it was time for us to record an album. We had been playing the songs for three years straight and had pretty damn good arrangements for all of them. Tom picked the songs we were going to record. He struggled with Elektra because we wanted to produce the record ourselves. After Brian Eno, Allen Lanier and the rest of the producers we tried to work with didn't pan out, we realized that we knew our own sound the best. We wanted a younger producer who was also a top music engineer.

I found out later that Tom had considered Rudy Van Gelder, but he wasn't available. The next choice was Andy Johns. Andy was the brother of Glyn Johns who had produced many of the English invasion bands like the Rolling Stones, Led Zeppelin and the Who. Andy had become Glyn's assistant and second engineer. On some projects, he was the engineer and handled the mixes as well. We knew we wanted him because he had recorded some of the greatest guitarists alive, and some of the greatest bands in existence.

I was excited about having Andy record our record, and Tom and Fred went around looking for an appropriate studio. They finally chose Phil Ramone's studio on West 48th Street mostly because it was shaped like the loft in Chinatown where we rehearsed—Terry Ork's loft. It had a very archaic recording console with helicopter controls. I don't believe it had any real panning or equalizer (EQ).

The day came for us to begin recording and we had a start time of 2 PM. We had arranged for our equipment to arrive at the studio the night before. Our stuff was there when we dutifully arrived on time—but no Andy. We didn't know how to get in touch with him, so we just waited a few hours until he showed up. He apologized for being late and told us that he had been in the studio the night before setting up the drums and recording some of the drum tracks. He asked if we wanted to hear them. Of course we said yes.

I asked him how he recorded with nobody to play the drums—who played the drums? He said that he did it by pushing the record button and running into the studio room and laying down some drums and then running back and turning the tape machine off. We all went into the control room to listen. Oh boy, what came out sounded just like Led Zeppelin's John Bonham—a huge drum sound. I liked it but Tom freaked out and said, "Oh no, no, no! We don't want big drums! We want small drums without all the effects on."

Andy got miffed and said he was going to go back to England and that he would quit because that drum sound was his signature. He kept asking us if we wanted to sound bad or what—was it some kind of New York thing where we wanted to sound as awful as the Velvet Underground? I said, "No Andy, we chose you because you've recorded the greatest guitarists on earth, and we are a guitar band and we want the guitars to be heard with the drums as support, not the other way around."

He was still kind of angry. Andy and Tom went out

into the hallway and talked for a while and smoothed things over. Andy came back to do his job with the kind of "harrumph" you use when you're going to do something you don't want to do. He also said he couldn't record without some outboard equipment. We rented a couple of 1176's and an LA2A, which were standard in the recording industry for compressors. Andy said he could not work properly without an 1176, and the LA2A was perfect for vocal recording. We also brought in a Pultec equalizer. That was all that was used on the recording until the record was mixed. It's one of the reasons the record sounds so pristine, even today.

I can't remember what song we started with, but we eventually got underway. I loved Andy Johns' rock 'n' roll style, although Andy could not figure out our all-business style. He had come from Rolling Stones and Led Zeppelin recording sessions were there was a party before, during and after the recording. With Television, nobody was in the studio except the band, Andy and the assistant engineer, Jim Boyer, whom I had known since high school.

One day we came in and Andy was asleep in his chair snoring with a bottle of wine dangling from his left hand and several empty bottles on the floor. He had ordered a case of wine for himself and us—but he drank most of it while I drank some too. He had a burned out cigarette between the first two fingers of his right hand. We didn't want to wake him so we asked Jim if we could tiptoe around him and record a song because we were eager to get started. That song was "Prove It." When we felt we had a good take we came in and listened at low-volume so as not to wake up Andy. It felt good so we played it again a little louder, and then again even louder. Suddenly Andy snorted and woke

240

up. As paranoid as he was about producing the record, he looked back and forth and forth and back and then asked, "Did I record this?" We all nodded yes and winked at Jim who told him, "Yes Andy, you recorded that—you don't remember?" Andy's tension drained away and he proclaimed, "I am very good, aren't I?"

The truth was that the microphones and all the wiring had been set up by Andy, so in a way it didn't matter whether he was awake or not for that recording. During one take I broke a string and left the studio in order to go to the bathroom and get another string, and I caught Andy in the control room sleeping. As soon as he heard me go by he snapped to attention and turned the music back on. While we were recording he had the control room on mute—the control room was completely silent. It was really ridiculous—but that was Andy.

Another time, Andy didn't show up until five o'clock. When he finally arrived, he told us he had been mugged. When we asked him more about it he told the truth which was that he had invited a couple of prostitutes up to his room. They had handcuffed him to the bed, taken his money, his credit cards and ID, then blew him kisses, said, "Thank you," and left. Andy had put the "Do Not Disturb" sign on the hotel door and wasn't found until the maid finally came in at 4 PM. Then he called his wife in England and told her that he had gotten mugged on the street and to please send him some money. She sent some money via Western Union and that's what took him until five o'clock to get to the studio. We were all laughing—including Andy.

During the session, I sat behind Andy whenever we weren't recording. I asked him what he was doing while he was setting up. I wanted to know what microphone and what signal path he was using into what track. Finally, in exasperation he turned to me and he said, "I can either do my job and record the fucking album or I can teach you how to be an engineer, but I can't do both at the same time!" And I retorted, "Andy, it has to be this way. I'm the only one paying attention to how you are making us sound, and I want to know exactly what you are doing at every step. Tom is busy with other things and I've appointed myself in charge of keeping track of what is going on in the control room." He begrudgingly told me what he was doing. Over the next couple days he started to enjoy it and he showed me all kinds of tricks that I still use today as an engineer and producer. I'm not going to go into what they are except to say that I like short wire—meaning without a lot of crap in the signal path in order to get the sound I want from the microphone selection and placement.

Andy was a real rock 'n' roll child and I enjoyed his company greatly, but Tom was miffed and clearly disgusted about him drinking so much. I didn't care because the record was coming out great. Tom had been talking about making a sort of live record—a document of how we sounded and I was thinking it was sad and pathetic to go into a recording studio just to make a live record, so I began thinking of ways that I could make it into a recording rather than a document.

After we finished "Venus" I asked if I could double my part and told them I could reproduce anything that I had already done perfectly. Neither Tom nor Andy believed me, and they both said it couldn't be done. I said, "Give me a shot, it'll only take 10 minutes to find out." They looked at each other and then ok'd it. I went back into the recording room alone, put on the headphones and in one pass I doubled the complicated melodies and filigrees that I had put on "Venus." When I came back into the room they were saying they couldn't believe it, but it sounded perfect. Tom wanted me to do it on everything, but I knew that it was a kind of ear candy that should come in and out of the various songs to make it a real record. So, I refused to do it in some instances, and in others I did double or more.

My guitar solo on "Elevation" is double tracked, and you can only hear that by listening to the very end of the solo where the two parts diverge just a little. Otherwise you can't even tell that there are two tracks. On "Guiding Light" I play a melody for the last minute of the song. There are eight tracks of me doing it which is why it sounds powerful and thick. I did my very best to make it a record—not a live document.

We went into the Record Plant to mix the album because they had more modern equipment and lots of EQ and compression. We didn't use that much—a dash of EQ mostly with the Pultec and we had discussions over whether it would be used on the guitar or the voice. The voice always won out because Andy would say that it is the most important part of the record, and I had to agree, although during some of the solos we used the passive EQ as well.

The record company told us that making the album sleeve and cover took the longest. They advised us to get that done before we went in to record. Patti Smith was good friends with Robert Mapplethorpe so we hired him to take the photographs, one of which went on the front cover. We wanted everybody to have some copies of the photos taken—all four of us—so somebody had to go out and find a Xerox machine. I offered. There weren't that many copy machines in New York in 1976 and the Xerox machines that did exist were huge. After about 40 minutes of searching, I found one and requested the clerk to make the copies.

When the guy doing the copying came back, he said that he was having difficulty because the colors were all wrong, and that I could keep the messed up one and he would try to make another one that was a proper duplicate. Instantly I spied the advantage of having the color skewed so I asked if I could come back to the Xerox machine and twiddle the knobs. I took the skewed ones and some copies that were true to the original color back to the band, and everyone loved the color-skewed Xerox copies. We chose one of the skewed photographs we liked, and that became the cover of *Marquee Moon*. To this day, the Mapplethorpe foundation is uncertain about the copyright to the photograph, as I changed it so dramatically from the original.

We delivered the quarter-inch tape of the album to Elektra records. Then we had to have it mastered for vinyl. Our choices of mastering agent came down to Bob Ludwig or Greg Calbi. Bob was busy so we went with Greg Calbi. He did a great job. Bob wouldn't allow anyone in the studio with him while he worked, so we waited for the acetates, which are soft plastic copies used for artist approvals. They are playable a few times before they start to go south.

I put the acetate on my record player and broke into tears because it did not sound as robust as it had sounded to me or the rest of the band in the studio. It was the best translation, but something was missing. I realized that no one who bought the record would experience how good it sounded in the studio. Over the years there have been some remasterings in the digital realm and on vinyl. Some of them sound much closer to the way we heard it in the studio. Thank God. *Marquee Moon* was released on February 7, 1977 and immediately received rave reviews in England.

49 Peter Gabriel and the West Coast

The first thing Elektra did for us after we recorded *Marquee Moon* was get us out on tour with Peter Gabriel, who had just left Genesis. It was a 30-date tour all across the country. The tour ended up on the West Coast. Then we did a tour of our own on the West Coast.

Peter and his band were wonderful people—among other musicians he had Robert Fripp playing on the sidelines and Hunter and Wagner as the official guitarists. Robert Fripp used to come to our dressing room and talk about being a three guitar band—he really wanted to join Television. We turned him down saying that would be too crowded, and that we did fine with two guitars. That might have been an interesting mess and I don't think it would've worked because Fripp had strong ideas, as did Tom, and Tom wouldn't stand for anyone telling him what to do.

The tour had some very funny incidents. While we were onstage people would yell out for Peter Gabriel. At one show his fans even threw things at the kids who got up and danced to our music. When Peter Gabriel finally came out, everybody screamed and yelled and applauded. Then, about three songs in, we began to hear shouts of "Genesis, Genesis" and "Play some Genesis!" It seemed like neither act could win, although Peter was fantastic, and we were no slouches either. We had a good set down but opening acts are notoriously ridiculed by audiences who are not familiar with them.

When we had a day off, Elektra decided to send us out to do radio promotion. We divided in half and went to two different stations. Billy and I were sent to Texas. We had to take three planes to get there, and on the third flight, I was sitting next to a businessman who said, "You look awfully tired." I told him that it was the third flight of the day and I didn't get much sleep the previous night. He asked me what I did and I told him I was a rock musician, and then he asked me where I had played the previous night, and I couldn't remember. Just then, Billy Ficca was coming down the aisle with his duffel bag, which he always had filled with carrots and nuts and berries—Billy's food—along with his clothes. I said, "Hey Billy, where did we play last night?" He thought for a minute and said Chicago. About 10 minutes later he sauntered up from his seat and asked me, "Where are we playing tomorrow night?" "Denver," I said. On tour you don't need to know where you are, and if you ask the tour manager, the likely response is "Look at the itinerary." This was a break from the itinerary, how-ever, and we had lost all sense of direction. I still don't know what day of the week it is because I've never had a real Monday through Friday job. The word for work for a musician is "play." I can think of only three careers where the word for work is play—musicians play instruments, actors play roles and athletes play sports. If you can think of a fourth career where the word for work is play, you've got me beat.

When we arrived at the radio station we were met by an underling of the record company who was a real local yokel. He told us it was important to treat the radio people as though they were as important as the artists, or more so, and he kept going on about how important he was in talking about payola, which still existed in one form or another. I don't think he expected us to pull out a roll of hundreds, but it was clear he was saying he had to give them gifts at Christmas and take them out to dinner to try to get a record played. We visited the radio station and the people there were very nice but knew nothing about us. They played three songs from *Marquee Moon* while asking us stupid questions. I did most of the talking because when Billy started talking you couldn't tell where it was going to go.

The Peter Gabriel tour ended on the West Coast where we unpacked our things and said goodbye to all the guys. Television then went on our own tour of the West Coast, from Seattle down through Portland and San Francisco and then to Los Angeles.

We began the tour in Seattle, and I remember Seattle being sunny almost every time we played there. Television did well there and in Portland too. There is a recording of our second tour in Portland, but nothing captured the first one.

A great place for us on that tour was San Francisco, where we played the Great American Music Hall with seating for about 600. We played there a number of times over the years, and it was always full. I went on a San Francisco radio show and one of the journalists asked such dumb questions that I decided to go mute for the entire show. He kept enticing me to talk by telling the audience that he had me in the studio, but I remained silent. I don't think that went over well with the journalist, but I didn't care because he was so stupid.

In Los Angeles we played the Whiskey a Go Go, where the Doors and Love had had their start. We were very happy to be there, and the place was packed. I hadn't seen Velvert for a long time and he visited me backstage. The single photograph that shows us together was taken there. After that tour, I decided to stay for an extra week at Velvert's house.

50 Visits with Velvert

Velvert said he was going to be an extra in a movie, so he asked me if I wanted to be an extra too. I said yes—it sounded like another adventure. I explained that I was not in the extras' union and he said it didn't matter, neither was he, although he was trying to break into acting.

The movie was called *Mara* starring Telly Savalas. It was a horror movie, and the extras were all supposed to be ghosts or spirits or some such thing. The movie crew had this huge piece of sackcloth and they had cut holes out for the heads and hands. They had us hold candles for a scene where Telly slaps the leading lady, who is an evil witch. After she gets slapped, she falls back on the bed and the lights come up exposing these terrible spirits holding candles. It was terrible agony and hard work just to stand there for hours while they did take after take. I think making movies is harder than making a record. There are more people involved in different power structures—with the extras at the bottom.

During a break I saw Telly walking across the set. I had brought along a copy of *Marquee Moon* which I wanted to sign and give to him, so I walked up to him and introduced myself and showed him the record. Suddenly I was accosted by one of the assistant directors who pulled me away and chewed me out for talking to one of the principles—the lead actor. "How dare you!" he said, and he threatened to take my union card away. I told him I wasn't in the extras' union and couldn't care less. He asked me how I had gotten the job if I wasn't in the union, but I didn't tell him. I didn't want to expose Velvert to any heat. Since I was in the lineup he just put me back with the extras, and told me to shut my mouth—in fact he told all the extras to be absolutely silent and not to talk to anybody, and to stay away from the craft table. The craft table is a table full of garbage candy and food that the stagehands insist on having around to munch on—and which the actors get fat on. There was an attempt to stop it, but the stagehands' union blocked it and kept the craft table, which still exists on movie sets.

No one could get the lighting right or the smoke machine to work properly. There were stand-ins for Telly and the woman who played the witch while the technicians tried to solve the problem. In the meantime, all of us poor extras were kept under the sackcloth, with our hands sweating. After hours and hours, they still couldn't get it right, so they decided to take a break and opened the huge iron gates that closed the set from the daylight. That's when I decided to leave. The assistant director chased me down and asked me what I was doing, and I said I was leaving. He told me that I would never work in Hollywood again because I would be ruining all the takes they had with me already in the picture. I told him I didn't care if I ever worked on a movie again, at least as an extra. He made a final threat about my union card, and I told him I didn't have one and was leaving. I told him to do the job himself.

In the meantime, Velvert was given a speaking role as one of the demons, so he stayed on and I split back to the place in Hollywood where we were staying. I never did get to give my record to anyone, but I was thankful because they wouldn't have appreciated it anyway.

When I had first come to Los Angeles on my own in the early 70s, Velvert had been talked into buying a famous house in the Hollywood Hills with 18 rooms. His music career was taking off. He only had two girls living with him, so I asked him if I could stay with him and he said no. I couldn't believe my best friend told me that I couldn't stay with him in his mansion, but there was nothing I could do. I left and didn't see Velvert again until the night Television played at the Whiskey a Go Go years later.

Velvert told me how he lost the mansion and got into drugs. He said he was found at the bottom of the swimming pool, breathing water, where he had fallen asleep for two hours. After some of the things Velvert had shown me in the past—the things that Jimi had taught him—I didn't doubt his story. During that visit, Velvert was into Angel Dust which is one of the worst drugs you can possibly encounter. I started to get high just from the fumes. One day he had two girls over, and when I walked in he was screwing one of them, who was stoned on Angel Dust, and was yelling, "Fuck me, you black devil."

This reminds me of the seedy side of Los Angeles. Back when I lived there, I worked as a male prostitute around the Hollywood bookstore. Luckily, I never got arrested, but one time I got picked up by two guys in a two-door car. I sat in the back and they asked me where they could find girls. I told them of all the places I knew, and they began calling me a fag. The driver said, "Show him." The passenger opened the glove compartment, took out a gun and waved it in my face while calling me a homo fag. He asked the driver if he could shoot me. The driver said, "No, wait a while." They drove around on some side streets and eventually turned onto a very dark street. They told me to get out and not look back. I thought they were going to shoot me in the back of the head, but they didn't and I walked away with my heart thumping. A couple days later I read in a newspaper that the thugs had been caught. They had committed several murders on a crime spree. I recognized them from the pictures. This was when I was staying in an area called Silver Lake with the music critic Richard Cromelin, who is still a friend of mine.

51 The Ice Kings of Rock

Television was getting a lot of favorable press in England, so along with Elektra's plans, we decided to do a tour there. Because of all the attention we were getting from *Marquee Moon* we were able to play the bigger theaters, and we were selling them out. Most of the other punk or CBGB bands went over to England and played clubs, but we started out at the top over there.

We arranged to have Blondie as our opening act. They had never been to the UK either and the tour started in Glasgow, Scotland. We flew to London and then took a train up to Glasgow. It was all very exciting to be in new places and I had always wanted to visit Scotland because I have Scottish relatives whom I can't understand, because their accents are so thick.

The first gig in Glasgow was in a large, beautiful old theater. We did our sound check and then it was Blondie's turn, because the opening act does the sound check last, allowing them to leave their equipment set up. Well, the people with Blondie asked us to move our equipment, and Tom said no, that they should set up in front of us or around us but that we were not striking the drums (taking them down or moving them) nor any of the amps. They were very upset over not being able to use the whole stage. There was nothing I could do, and I agreed with Tom that it was important that we stay with the set-up we had for our sound check.

It really wasn't so bad, but they took it hard. We had stolen their bass player Fred Smith, and now we were acting—according to them—arrogantly. Tom can be arrogant and I am a gentle soul, but it was important for me to stand behind Tom because a band must have only one political stance, and in this case, it was Tom's opinion that mattered, as he was the singer and guitarist in the middle of the stage.

Other than that, Blondie and Television were friends, although I very nearly got in a fist fight several days later with their keyboard player, Jimmy Destri, when we were both drunk after a show. He kept mouthing off about how unfair it was, but that's a lot of water under the bridge now.

Blondie didn't get a very good reception. People were yelling for Television, and when we came on we didn't disappoint. It's a shame nobody recorded those gigs properly as we could've developed a live album out of that tour—it was absolutely brilliant. That was a tour of standing ovations, jaws dropping and people who stopped breathing. In Glasgow, the security would not let our audience dance in the aisles so they had to sit down or stand up in their chairs because the theater was very ornate—an old Majestic theater. The disc jockey who played music between the two acts called us "The Ice Kings of Rock" because we didn't move at all, but the music moved the audience tremendously. I don't know if he meant it as a slur, but it came out as a slogan that worked to our advantage.

By the time we got to London we had played a series of seven or eight shows in various parts of Great Britain, and then in London, we did two nights, both sold out, at the Hammersmith Odeon.

52 Television Takes Europe

The biggest problem on tour in England was getting something to eat because most people cooked at home. There
were no malls and fast food places there at the time. At one
restaurant, I asked for scrambled eggs. The cook broke two
eggs into the boiling oil that they used for French fries
which they call chips. Then he used the soup ladle to get the
eggs out and put them on a dish. It was disgusting. I had to
tilt the plate to get rid of all the grease. Everything there was
greasy and you could only get a bite to eat at certain times
because restaurants were closed most of the afternoon. If
you missed lunch you were out of luck.

Billy never suffered because he kept his vegetables,
nuts and berries in his duffel bag. Billy ate so many carrots
that he got carotenemia. His skin turned carrot color which
is why he looked orange on the cover of Marquee Moon. I
told him he should look in the mirror and he slowed down
on the carrots. The doctor told him the same thing.

The tour had been a massive success and I stayed for a
few more weeks at the house of the drummer from Elvis
Costello's band while he was out on tour. Twenty-five years
later I found out that he thought I had gone to bed with his
wife, which I hadn't. I don't do that disrespectful shit. It
wasn't until we did Rock in Rio with Elvis Costello's band
and were staying in the same hotel that he and I went
together for coffee. I explained to him that all this time he'd

been thinking wrong about me, that I had never hit on his wife and never would. That was a giant weight lifted off his shoulders. For 30 years he thought he had been cuckolded, and then he found out that it was not true and that everything was on the up and up. It's funny how people reach conclusions without investigation—some kind of a bad rumor I guess.

I found English girls delightful, but wouldn't try anything with someone's wife. Once I was having sex with a girl who claimed to be single when the door opened—there was her husband with a gun. I never got my clothes on and split as fast as I did that day. It's a wonder he did not shoot both of us.

Even in London the food was boring and we ended up eating Italian or Middle Eastern all the time. I still eat that kind of food when I'm in England. The last time I was there, I found out that they had all the same roadside amenities that we have in the states—giant malls full of restaurants and snack bars. I guess they've come a long way towards Americanization. Rather a pity, because England was quite quaint, if you know what I mean.

Punk was exploding in England during our first tour there, and although we weren't punk—just "new-wave" I guess—we got the same audiences but they were a little more dignified. *Marquee Moon* went to #28 on the British music charts. We ended up playing England quite often. After we played London, we took some time off. Then we toured Europe. In Stockholm, the kids stood on their heads in the seats and went absolutely frantic. That was one of the craziest things we ever did—playing our songs while watching kids do headstands in their seats.

We were booked in Hamburg, but never did the show

because the police were afraid of a riot. They insisted that the PA be placed behind the band which would have led to nothing but feedback. They said an artist had played there two weeks before but ended up doing an instrumental set. No way were we going to do that. Our tour manager was a tall English guy that looked like a Hell's Angels member gone wrong, with missing teeth and scraggly hair. He looked like he could kick anyone's ass, so at least we got paid everywhere we went. Unless someone pulled a gun on him he was going to get paid for us, and luckily no one's ever pulled a gun on us. Oh sure, we've been cheated, but never on that tour and very rarely anyway.

That tour manager also went with us on the Peter Gabriel tour. Because it was an airline tour, the time schedule for waking up and meeting in the lobby to go to the airport was very tight, so our tour manager figured out an angle. Our phone would ring at 10 minutes to nine and a voice would say that we had to be in the lobby at nine o'clock. At 8:55 he would have the maid open the door, and if we were still in bed, he would turn the mattress over and dump us on the floor. It was kind of hilarious but I didn't want that to happen, so I always made it into the lobby on time.

The first place we played in Germany was Munich and the guy from the record company told us that we must try the three S's. I asked, "What the hell are the three S's?" He said it was schnapps, schnitzel and snuff. When we got to Hamburg he took us to the Reeperbahn, the red-light district where there were underground garages full of stripper poles with whores on each one of them. They would all try to entice us by saying "I do you both ficky ficky 50 marks," and other such nonsense. There were transsexuals and transvestites and girls, girls, girls. I had never paid for sex before and I wasn't planning to start. That's what I told the record company guy and he said, "That's okay, I'll put it on the expense tab for the record company." The record company paid for us to go to that whore house. Everyone else took the money and took a walk, while I went through all the girls and finally picked one who took me upstairs and insisted on washing me off, all the while trying to jerk me off and telling me that she had to get me to come in five minutes or else I would have to pay more money. Well that's no way to run a railroad. She was doing anything she could with her hands to prevent anything else from happening. I realized she had that beaten-down look in her face. So I didn't do anything. I just put my clothes back on and left, and that was the end of that in Germany.

Half way through the German tour, I was in the hotel lobby and I put my feet up on a table. One of the employees in a business suit ran over and said, "You will put your feet down on the floor! This is Germany where we have rules and you will obey them. This is not your home where you can put your feet up; this is Germany so take your feet off the table and put them on the floor now!" That kind of Germanic insistence really didn't leave a good taste, but the hotel was fine once my feet were on the floor and the angry German man huffed off.

We played Nuremberg in a barn 20 km from the middle of town. They had run electrical wire the entire 20 km for the amps and the PA. Outrageous. It turned out to be one of the best gigs, with kids hanging over a balcony and freaking out. All the other punk bands that came over had been spat on, which the English thought was a kind of holy water. They called it "gobbing." We weren't going to have

any of it, and we agreed that if even one person did anything, like throw something or spit at us, we would leave
the stage immediately and that would be the end of the
show. Amazingly, or perhaps telepathically, no one ever did
anything like that to us, even though the next night another
band would be there and they would get "gobbed" on. I
remember Bob Quine came back to New York saying he
couldn't see through his glasses because he and the
Voidoids had been gobbed on so much during the shows.
Richard Hell had to duck when he was touring. We heard
about this and we were having none of it. We were the Ice
Kings of Rock.

53 New York, What a Place

My junior high was deep in the heart of West Greenwich Village. You would think it was a groovy school and in some ways it was, but it was TOUGH, populated by young Turks and promising gang members. You quickly learned that you had to negotiate your way through a kind of maze in order to prevent yourself from being mugged and robbed of your lunch money even before the first school bell rang. I was mugged with knives, chains, brass knuckles, zip guns, and bare fists, all in the seventh grade. I saw knife fights in the auditorium and huge brawls on the street before, during and after school hours. It was difficult to buy drugs because it was easy to get beat, that is, somebody would take your money and say they were coming back with drugs and never return. If you went up to them the next day, they would give you some bullshit excuse or just say, "Listen I ripped you off. Go fuck yourself."

One of the cleverest characters was Quickie. He was this guinea white trailer-trash kid who had some kind of incredible magic to his scams. He could separate anyone from their money. He always had lots of shady characters looking for him and he was permanently on the lam from somebody. Sometimes he would just rob you cold. He was not averse to simply coming up to you and demanding your money. In fact this was a law. If a guy was bigger than you, he was allowed to walk up to you and say, "Gimme what you got. What I find I keep, right?" The answer was always, "Right." Any answer other than that got you into deeper trouble than losing whatever you had in your pockets. You learned that you had better keep some steel will in one place and something else hidden in your underwear or socks—somewhere they wouldn't want to search in daylight.

Aside from the fact that Quickie would rob you plain and simple, he was far better at working the convoluted scam around our inevitable desperation to get some kind of drug. Quickie always had a good connection, but we never got anything out of the deal. I mean never. Maybe once, just to set you up. It was always. "What are you looking for? I can get it for you—just give me the money and I'll be right back." But he was never right back—you would see him a couple days later if you could catch up to him (he wasn't named Quickie for no reason), and if you asked for your money back, he would give you some bullshit story so that he could work some more green out of you. Or he would tell you to your face, "I beat you. So what are you gonna do about it?" And he would lean into your face—you know, the animal stare down. Then it would all start again in a couple of days. He had incredible charm, that much is for sure. I'll bet he could talk almost anyone out of his underwear.

I had forgotten all about Quickie, but a couple of years ago I could've sworn I saw him panhandling on the subway. He didn't look too good. I think he had gone to one of those schools with a teacher who teaches you to wear garbage bags for clothing and get down on your knees in the middle of the crowded subway and start crying and whimpering and moaning. I knew the kid that started that scam. One day that kid appeared naked except for black garbage bags as clothes, and he crawled on the floor of the subway cars begging for clothes, food or money. I bet he made a pretty good living of it.

One day I was on East 58th Street and a lady had bought him a fancy outfit—oversized shoes, plaid pants and a schoolboy uniform jacket. He looked like Howdy Doody. She was walking along with him, sympathizing with his plight, and then I saw her throw his garbage bag clothing in the trash can. I could swear I saw the desperation in his eyes and I could hear him thinking, "Oh no, my precious garbage bags, gone!" A couple of days later he was back on the train, back in the garbage bag clothes business. A few months after that I started to see a couple of imitators pop up, so I think they started a school. I wonder what they charged for tuition?

A couple years later I was walking down Broadway when I bumped into a guy, or rather, he bumped into me, and the impact knocked over what he was carrying. All over town there were delicatessens with huge buffets where they sell food by the pound and business people buy their lunches. Anyway, this guy started freaking out.

"Yo, you knocked into me and knocked over my food. That food was for my baby's mama. She's sick and we got no more money. She's waiting for me at the welfare hotel and I was getting her some food and now you gone and ruined everything. What you gonna do about it? I paid $8.95 for that food. Yo, you gonna make good on it? What am I supposed to tell my old lady?"

I looked down at the sidewalk where there was a pile of cabbage and assorted salad type things. I look back at the guy—he was starting to freak out even more, raising his voice and getting angry. I reached into my wallet and pulled out a 10. "Here, this will more than take care of it. I'm so sorry. Have a nice day." He grabbed the money out of my hand, spun on his heel, and walked away. I was a little shaken up because you never know what people are going to do when they explode on the streets of New York.

I continued on my way, and a couple of blocks later I looked down and noticed another pile of cabbage in one of those plastic containers. Over the next couple of days, I became a cabbage magnet. I saw piles of this crap all over town. Then I witnessed another one of these interactions, where a guy ran into a lady and then blamed her for the mishap. I ran over yelling, "Don't give him shit, it's a big fucking scam!" I got between him and the old lady and I told him to get the fuck out of here—and that I knew what he was up to. He started blathering about his sick girlfriend and I offered to call a cop, so that the cop could escort him back to his hole and help his girlfriend. He gave me a stern look and I gave him one back. "One of your asshole friends already got me with this scam. You're not turning this trick with this nice old lady." With that it ended. The lady thanked me and tried to give me the money she was going to give him but I didn't let her. It had been far too much fun. What a place, New York.

One of the things I was told when I was growing up was that Central Park was okay during the day, but at night it was a dangerous place. Using logic, I decided that if I went into the park after dark, it would mean that I was dangerous. So one day I did, and you should have seen people run away from me. Occasionally, a Lone Ranger would play a game of chicken. We would walk towards each other until he gave up and walked in another direction. I never gave up because I was dangerous for Christ sake. That's what walking in Central Park after dark will do for you. It will make you powerful and dangerous, but you've got to know what you're doing. You don't go in with a camera hanging around your neck and tickets to a Broadway play sticking out of your pocket. That's a sure sign you're a tourist and you're going to get screwed.

One time I was walking down 51st Street between Eighth and Ninth, and I heard a woman scream. Then a guy ran right past me. Without thinking I turned and ran after him. When I caught up to him I turned and punched him flat out in the jaw, knocking him down. Then I jumped on him, holding him on the ground with my knees against his shoulders—I had him pinned pretty good. He started whimpering and telling me he was a junkie and I said, "So am I, and you're not going anywhere until the police get here." He started pleading with me, telling me he dropped the purse as soon as I turned to chase him. He had dropped the purse and the woman did get it back. She and her husband were just looking for someplace to eat in the Theater District. For all I knew, this guy could've had a knife or a gun, but my intuition turned me around and my conscience made me run him down. Eventually the police turned up and he continued his whining and crying about how sad his life was. So I said, "Now you're going to get mugshots and a cot—ain't that nice, and the taxpayers are going to pay for it, you lucky son of a bitch."

When the police got there they thanked me and I went home and forgot all about it. There's nothing like a good deed that's done on the spur of the moment, without any judgment or thought of repercussion. You just act—that's when you find out if you're brave or cowardly. You never know what you're going to do, or not do, until that moment.

Another time I was down on the lower East side trying to cop some heroin when an asshole Puerto Rican guy caught me in the lobby and pulled out a knife. He said, "I'm robbing you—give me what you got." I only had two dollars. If I'd had a reasonable amount of money I would've given it to him—after all he was robbing me at knife point. For some perverse reason two dollars was too little to turn over and I refused. He lunged at me with the knife and caught me in the chest. I didn't see any marks on my leather jacket so I chased him three blocks until he lost me. But I still had my two dollars. Then I felt a warm fluid on my stomach. I opened my jacket and there, by God, I'd been stabbed. The knife must've been so sharp it pushed the leather into the wound. I walked to the hospital where the guy who stitched it up told me that it was two centimeters from my heart and could easily have killed me. I didn't care—I'd be damned if someone was going to take my last two dollars.

54 Girls and Other Girls

There was one absolutely gorgeous girl who took me home with her for a romp under the sheets that lasted for a couple of hours of love. I asked to go to the bathroom and she pointed it out to me. After I had finished going, I couldn't find any toilet paper. I called out to her to get me a new roll and she called back, "I don't use toilet paper! It's bad for the environment." I could barely believe my ears and said, "What? You mean there's no toilet paper in the whole house?" She said no, so I asked her what I was supposed to do and she told me to use the sink. What a mess, but she was too beautiful to give up, and I returned time after time to her apartment—bringing my own toilet paper.

Another time in Columbus Circle I met a girl who turned out to be a stewardess—a younger woman—who took me to her hotel room where we quickly got hot and steamy. While we were screwing, the phone rang. She picked it up and put her finger to her lips, whispering to me that it was her boyfriend in Florida. I stopped what I was doing, but she encouraged me to keep on screwing her. So that's exactly what I did as she calmly talked to her boyfriend as if nothing was happening. I could barely believe it.

Another girl whom I met in New York took me to her hotel room on 58th Street. She was the daughter of a movie star and she told me her mother was in the adjacent room so we needed to be quiet. The bed was squeaking so much we ended up on the floor with my hand over her mouth lightly to prevent her from squealing with pleasure. During another visit she kept talking about how her mother, who was a washed up actress and not very nice, might actually come in. I knew that if she caught her daughter having sex with me she might throw her out of the hotel. Well, as pleasurable as it was on the bed, I didn't want to be the cause of that, so we made love silently on the floor. At least the floorboards didn't squeak.

When Television was in Los Angeles on our first West Coast tour we had some days off. I met a girl who was a real sex freak. She liked it every which way, and I took advantage of her lust which almost matched my own, or maybe surpassed it. She was a real dynamo. She asked for a ride to San Francisco, where we were headed for our next show. I agreed on the condition that she would do me a favor and blow me all the way there in the back of the car.

Our tour manager drove and Billy Ficca took the front seat. I was in the backseat with this girls' head in my lap the whole time—she fell asleep with me in her mouth. I felt badly when we got there because when we checked into the hotel in San Francisco, I told her she couldn't stay. I didn't trust her with my stuff, and I had to go out. She said that was okay and that she had places to go anyway. Sadly, I never saw her again.

Another girl I was having sex with eventually invited me over to her place. It was a large loft on the lower East side. She had a trapeze set up in the middle of the floor. I thought that was weird—maybe she worked at the circus. I got really excited and ran as fast as I could towards the trapeze. I grabbed hold of it and then flew up. I was so stoned on Valium, which is also a muscle relaxant, that my hands gave way and I ended up landing on my head on the floor with a cracking noise that sounded like a gunshot.

The people on the floor below actually called the police thinking they had heard a gunshot. She asked if I was alright, and I told her no. She asked if I thought I needed to go to the hospital and I told her yes. Then she asked me if I was going to go by taxicab or ambulance and I replied, "Ambulance."

That foolishness cost me 11 days in the hospital with a hair-line fracture in my skull and bleeding out of my left ear. The hospital staff put a bag over my left ear to catch the blood and kept me there for observation. I hadn't lost consciousness, and they wouldn't give me any pain medicine because it was my head that was damaged. While I admit my head was damaged, it wasn't because of that fall. But the fall dislodged my jaw so that my teeth would not fit together for about a year. I had to work on biting down hard and moving my jaw and teeth until they aligned again. Even today, when I open my mouth wide, it moves to the left instead of straight down. That's another permanent reminding factor of a lovely event that didn't happen. We never got to the love-making given that the first thing I did upon entering her loft was to run over to the trapeze and fall on my head.

Because I am inherently shy, I'm amazed when I look back at all the sex that I've had. I've never regretted any of it, although I have regretted opportunities that I let pass me by. As a teenager, if I had carried condoms I would've had three times as much sex as I did, but back then I was real shy. I recall in the fifth grade walking home after school with a friend of mine. A gaggle of girls behind us were laughing and giggling and pointing at me. I felt completely embarrassed, but my friend pointed out that they were looking at my butt, which I guess they found quite interesting and humorous. That's the way girls reacted to their budding sexual urges back then. Giggling.

Although my life has been one of sex, drugs and rock 'n' roll full tilt, I've always been mature, even as a child. I didn't lose my virginity until I was 15, and it was with a woman who was my pot dealer. She lived in my building and was roommates with Roger, who was the guitar player with Leather Secrets. We were on the 9th floor and she was on the 14th floor. I used to go up to buy marijuana from her and one day she started coming on to me. I begged her off, saying I had to go down and do my homework. She could see right through that and invited me to sit on the bed where she spent most of her time. She then seduced me and when we were finally going at it she asked, "Are you sure you're a virgin, because you seem to know what you're doing?" I didn't know quite what she meant by that. I thought it was all about kissing and caressing your partner while staying with the rhythm until they were satisfied.

There's a joke about a wonderful leather-bound sex manual that's three pages long. The first page is just a title page, "Sex Manual." The next page is Chapter 1 "IN." Then you turn the page to Chapter 2 and you find the word "OUT." When you turn to Chapter 3, all it says is, "REPEAT IF NECESSARY." That's the whole book—in, out and repeat if necessary. But there's a whole lot more to it than that. It's important to make your partner feel wanted and lavished and ravished. They need to be given exactly what they want. If they want it soft, it should be given soft. If they want it hard, then it should be given hard. If they want to be tied up, then tie them up, but do not go further than your partner wants to go. That's the one important thing I learned—to always please your partner before you please yourself, otherwise it's just sex and not love, and I like making love, not war.

I'm lucky enough to have once had sex with a girl who was a sword swallower by profession. She loved to swallow my sword, and my God, she was gorgeous with a delicious mouth. When I was young I only wanted to screw, I never wanted a blowjob. As I got older I learned to enjoy both fellatio and cunnilingus. The only problem with that would be my tongue tiring out or getting chafed by my lower teeth. I really don't know how to solve that problem except, perhaps, by getting in a bar fight for the purpose of getting my front teeth knocked out. Toothless people probably have a great time with their tongues. Mine is not that long.

There was one girl I knew—her name was Ruth—who claimed to have been the mistress of a famous painter. When she mentioned his name I had no idea who he was. She didn't believe me, because the painter was really quite famous, but I wasn't following art at the time. She had been going out with Jackson Pollock—Jack the dripper. I had no idea who he was but she was a real woman—an older woman who would ask to be tied up and ravished and eaten out.

One time she said, "Maybe you could bring a friend over and we could have a ménage à trois." I thought about who might join us, and since Richard Hell was still in Television, I invited him. I didn't have to twist his arm too hard when I told him who it was. We went over to her place on 14th Street and knocked on the door. She let us in, wearing her bathrobe with nothing under it. She got out the ropes and Richard started to balk while I developed an outrageous hard on. I screwed her first and then Richard decided he didn't want anything to do with this scene anymore—and he left. Afterwards the gossip was that she said she screwed half of Television, and one band member couldn't get it up and the other band member couldn't get it down. I know who is who, but sometimes people's egos force them to lie, which is what happened when a certain book was written by another member of the band. Our roles were reversed in that book.

I fall in love with girls easily—and when I say girls I mean women—not jailbait. "Girls" are too young for me, and besides, they're flighty and don't know what they want—whereas I do know what I want. I want girls with experience—although I am not averse to sharing my experience. There was one girl who came to me for guitar lessons. I had a strict rule not to make love to girls that came to me for guitar lessons, but to only give them guitar lessons no matter how beautiful they were. It's the same rule I have for my hypnotic subjects. This particular girl kept pressing and pressing the issue, getting close to me and trying to induce me to put my hands on her like a golf instructor. She pressed the issue to the point that I finally broke down and began making love to her. I asked her what she liked and she said she liked pressure so I pushed hard and she said, "Ooh la la, I love that." She was thin, almost anorexic, which is not my preference because I dislike making love to bones.

Some men like breasts, other men like legs—I like faces. But not perfect faces. I like faces with real life in them. When I was young, my cousin had a girlfriend who wore what seemed like a quarter inch of thick makeup on her face. She looked like a Japanese doll. Eventually she screwed him over and he joined the Marines and asked to go to Vietnam. He was sent right over. Luckily, he made it back and is still alive—older, but wiser. Like Dylan, I'm younger than that now. I always feel as if I'm getting younger rather than older, becoming more childlike rather than childish. But I don't like competition and I am not greedy, so I would never try to take a girl away from another guy—let the girl decide. I know what I stand for, and it's good—there's nothing bad about it. Anyway, that's some of the many girls I've known—and just some more of the peculiar things that have happened to me during my wacky life on this lunatic asylum planet.

55 Recording *Adventure*

After touring the United States and Europe, Television still wasn't getting much radio airplay. We decided to turn our attention toward a new album. We had a number of songs from our live sets that could've been recorded for the record but Tom wanted to experiment in the studio. He wrote most of the songs on *Adventure* while in the studio goofing around. Tom said we wanted to make a live record but what he really meant is that he wanted us to finish our parts so he could diddle around in the studio for six months on our money.

Adventure was recorded at the Record Plant with a new producer, John Jansen, who had worked on some Jimi Hendrix material towards the end of his life and after his death. I had never met him. The atmosphere in the studio was much more like what Tom wanted—just a serious engineer/producer who was all work—not like the party animal Andy Johns. I missed Andy but there was nothing I could do about it. We spent a lot of time waiting for Tom to come up with lyrics for his silly little songs. Tom's songs no longer faced outward. They had become introverted like an ingrown toenail. From my perspective, Tom is a "crazy maker" in the studio—someone who drives me insane with his shenanigans.

I ended up in the hospital during part of the recording of *Adventure* and the band did a couple of basics without me. "The Dream's Dream" is a song I had very little to do with. I had a great deal to do with "Ain't That Nothin'," and the song "Adventure." That song never made it on the record because Tom never finished it, and also, I suspect, because I had too much input into playing leads on it.

The song "Adventure" was on the reissue of the album. The only reason the song was saved at all was because John Jansen made cassettes for Tom and I so that we could go home and work on them—me on leads and Tom on lyrics. John was quite a good engineer. One time Billy was playing all over the place on drums and Tom wanted nothing but a steady beat. John said he had an idea that would take about 20 minutes, so we let him run with it. First he told Billy that his floor tom was ringing and to please put some tape on it. Billy dutifully put some tape on the drum and that made it sound duller. Then he asked Billy how many times he hit this particular drum and whether he could do without it. Someone came in the studio and took it away. Then John said the ring was coming from someplace else— perhaps the rack tom? He managed to get rid of those and some of Billy's bigger cymbals. Billy was finally down to the barest minimum—kick drum, high hat and snare drum, but he still managed to hit the sides of the drums and the hardware in his own inimitable fashion. We were in the control room laughing at this wonderful trick John played on Billy.

I wasn't in the hospital that long and I returned to the studio to finish my parts which completed the recording. I did not like *Adventure* as much as *Marquee Moon* because of the silly songs with throwaway lyrics. There was nothing I could do about that.

Slowly the band was coming apart at the seams. Tom

was asserting more and more dictatorial power and there wasn't much the other three of us could do about it. We were dependent upon him for lyrics. Our old method of voting when there were disagreements had gone out the window.

Adventure entered the English charts at #7, but the timing of our tour for the record was all wrong. While on tour we received a sample of The Cars' new record. That's when we knew we were done for in terms of mainstream radio airplay. We were sitting on the tour bus while listening to it and Tom threw up his hands and said, "Well that's it—that's a commercial Television. Elektra now has a band that is commercial and they are going to forget about us." Tom was partially correct and what Seymour Stein had prophesied was beginning to come true—that we would not have mainstream commercial success but would have incredible longevity. That's something we have enjoyed along with a rabid audience which has only grown over the years.

Frankly I'm sorry that the song "Adventure" did not make it onto the record *Adventure* because of all the songs we had, that's probably the one that would've gotten on the radio. Too bad, but we broke up later that year anyway.

56 Television Dissolve

In the early summer of 1978 I received a phone call from Tom Verlaine. That in itself was unusual because we met at rehearsals or at shows, but didn't share a social life outside the band. We were together 24 hours a day on tour, and principally we all got along, eating together, staying in the same hotels and performing together. So it was a bit odd to get a call from Tom. He said, "I have some bad news to tell you—I'm leaving the band." This was a bit of a shock but I also felt relieved. I told Tom that I had been thinking of leaving myself but didn't want to leave the rest of the guys, himself included, in the lurch. I told Tom that instead of him leaving the band we should simply dissolve the band.

We decided that we would play the shows which we were obligated to play and then go our separate ways. We decided not to tell anyone at all except Billy and Fred, so it was kept among the band members.

The last three Television shows were at the Bottom Line. We knew these were the last shows but our audience did not. They were very good shows, all sold out, with enormous audience involvement. Many of our friends and longtime fans were there. We got together for lunch in Chinatown at one of our favorite restaurants the day after our last show. The food was cheap and plentiful, and we bid our farewells to each other. I felt rather odd leaving the restaurant both sad and exhilarated for myself—for some time I had been writing songs that did not fit with Television's image. Chris Stamey asked if he could use one of my songs for his first single with the dB's—of course I said yes. I was going to sing it but Elektra had me under contract and wouldn't let me. Chris sang it from my guide vocal and the dB's performed it live. I had also been writing songs that would end up on my first solo record, *Alchemy*.

As Television went our separate ways I believe everyone suspected we would eventually get back together, which we did in 1992.

57 The Hats, Atlanta and the B-52s

Sometime in 1979 the B-52s made it up to New York and played CBGB's. I knew immediately that they were going to make it big time. They had me hopping and hollering and jumping up and down on the tables. Around that time, Terry Ork had taken on two music business partners who called themselves "The Hats" because they were Jewish and wore yarmulkes or some kind of hat at all times. Terry very badly wanted to sign the B-52s to a record deal with Ork records and decided to send The Hats down to Athens, Georgia to meet with them. He suggested that I go along because I knew the band by then, and could perhaps convince them to sign with Ork Records if The Hats couldn't.

We flew down to Atlanta, rented a car, and drove to Athens where we had booked rooms in a house that I recall was owned by some friends of Terry. The Hats observed the Sabbath on Saturdays, which meant that they could have no money on them, no drugs and no car keys beginning on Friday night at sundown. They gave me all that stuff to hold on to for them. But they would play all sorts of funny games like "I want some cocaine but I'm not allowed on the Sabbath. But if by accident you hold the spoon under my nose, I still have to breathe, right? That won't be breaking the law. And if I get thirsty and want to drink some whiskey or other alcoholic beverage and I just happen to have my mouth open by accident, and you poured it in my mouth, I would have to swallow as a natural reaction and that would not be considered to be 'work'."

This was a hilarious premise and I went along with it, holding the spoon of cocaine underneath one or another of their noses or pouring a glass of tequila down their throats. They were required to observe all the Jewish rules and regulations but had figured out ways to get around them. It was a total scam.

Friday night I took the car out and drove around all night long while drinking various beers, wines and liquors. When daylight came up, I decided I had better drive back to the house. When I saw the sign for the street where I needed to turn I was going a little too fast. Instead of going straight and going back around the block, I turned the wheel fast and hard. The car jumped the curb and continued right on up the guide wire of a telephone pole which got caught underneath the front wheel base. When I got out of the vehicle it was hanging at a 45° angle and the front seat was six feet off the ground. From a short distance, it looked like the car was suspended by nothing, so there was all this rubbernecking going on. I thought of going to ask Ari, one of The Hats, for the camera to take a picture, but I realized the police and ambulance were going to arrive and I knew I was in trouble.

I ran back down to the house as fast as my legs would take me and told The Hat that was awake that he needed to come with me posthaste—that there had been an accident with the car and that he wasn't going to believe what he was going to see. We ran up the street and, as the car came into view we saw the cops, the ambulance personnel, and neighbors standing around scratching their heads. It was a one in a million chance that the wire would catch the inside of the front wheel rim pulling the car up like a roller coaster. It was a station wagon so the back of it stayed on the ground while the front of it was about 12 feet off the ground.

I told The Hat, "This is an emergency and you have to take the keys and claim that it was your car and that you were driving."

"But it's the Sabbath and I can't drive on the Sabbath."

"I know that but just take the keys and tell them you were driving so we don't all get into trouble."

I explained to the cops about how the car came to be standing at 45° angle. The cops were actually amused. They called a tow truck to get the car down and let us go—no ticket, no nothing. And because The Hats were sober at the moment, there was no DUI for me.

The next day we went to meet with the B-52s at Maureen McLaughlin's house which was outside of Athens in the country. Maureen was their manager. Of course, I insisted upon driving and did pretty well. It was a dark moonless night, and we ended up on a dirt road trying to find her place—which was near to impossible. At a certain moment we thought that we had passed it, so we decided I should turn around. I put the car in reverse and, as I tried to turn around, the car slipped into a deep muddy rut. The three of us tried to get the car out but nothing we did worked, so we walked to Maureen's house and asked the B-52s for help. "Certainly we will help," they told us and we all walked back to the car. It took every person pushing and pulling on the station wagon to get it dislodged from the mud and back on the road. This time I turned around much more carefully and we went to Maureen's house. By this time I was pretty stoned and I don't remember much of what took place at her house except that we tried to convince them to sign with Ork records. But, they ended up signing with Warner Brothers instead, which was probably a good thing for them. They deserved all the success they got and I knew they were going to have a lot from the first second I saw them. That was some adventure, with The Hats. Although we didn't get the B-52s to sign, I enjoyed the outrageous experience of the two idiots trying to worm their way out of the Sabbath by using me as a 1/3 party to the evil deeds. I loved it.

58 Dr. Steve and Various Overdoses

By the end of 1978 I was a full-blown junkie. It was a very strange thing that happened to me. I'd been shooting up heroin and cocaine together, a mixture called speedball, and boy oh boy, that can get you so stoned you don't know which side is up. I kept looking over my shoulder for the addiction to get me but it never seemed to. I could go several days without anything until I got the hankering—but I never felt any sickness. Then we went on tour with Peter Gabriel and I was sure that I'd be sick because I couldn't take any dope with me for the entire month. But I was just fine and dope free. I didn't feel sick until after we flew back to New York and I took a cab to my house on the Lower West Side. The cab passed through the neighborhood where I would cop drugs. All of a sudden I started to dry heave. I had the cab pull over while I ran upstairs to a slimy tenement house to get myself a couple of bags of heroin which I practically did in the cab. But I didn't—I waited until I got home and got myself straight.

That's when I knew I was hooked. A true junkie. Around '77 and '78 there was a huge supermarket of drugs on the Lower East Side that opened every day at seven in the morning. There'd be a line around the block like it was a hit movie. There were businessmen and old ladies and young people of all ilk standing in line waiting for their

285

chance to get to the door where you put your money in the top slot and your dope or coke came out the bottom. The building was locked tight.

There were runners going up and down the line saying, "No singles, five dollar bills and up. Know what you want before you get to the door, put your money in the slot and tell them what you want and get your stuff out of the bottom of the door and MOVE ON. Don't stay on the block; there are shooting galleries nearby if you need them, but do not do it in the street in front of this place." About 1978, right after Television dissolved, I would often see my friends in line. At that time, I was working on the material that would turn into *Alchemy*, my first solo record on Elektra.

The machinery of this drug business was rather incredible—they could service 100 clients in 10 minutes. I would walk up to the door, say "Three dope, two coke," put in my $30 and out would come the bags at the bottom lickety-split. I would grab them and run home to get off. I caught my first case of endocarditis from one of these places. It's an inflammation surrounding the heart—bacteria gets into the heart and starts eating away at the valves. The first time I talked with a doctor about this, I told him I had recently been to the dentist. I had researched ways you could get endocarditis and really there were only two—either through shooting up bad dope with Streptococcus on it or through bad dental surgery where the germs get in through the gums. I lied to him because I didn't want to go into the junkie ward. I was placed in a really nice semi-private room in Beth Israel Hospital. While in the hospital, Deerfrance brought me the I-Ching, and the first hexagram I ever threw was number 33—Retreat. Boy, that couldn't be any clearer. But did I listen? Hell no.

What did I do? Well for one, I sold pot from my hospital bed and secondly, every night, I would go scouting around the hospital. The nurses' station had thousands of syringes. I would steal a box every night and then have somebody take them home for me the next day. That probably saved me from getting AIDS because I obtained thousands of syringes during that visit.

I also telephoned a photographer—David Godlis, and asked him to come up and take pictures of me in the hospital, which he very kindly did. We were walking along the hallway and I saw an oxygen tank and a big sign on the door about the dangers of flames. I decided to smoke a cigarette and have David take a picture of me next to this oxygen tank. He was afraid the whole thing would explode so I had to explain some chemistry to him. Oxygen does not burn—it facilitates the burning of carbon and hydrogen and anything else that can burn. I explained to him that the worst that could happen would be that the cigarette would burn down in two puffs if there was a leak, which there wasn't. After about 20 minutes I convinced him to take the photo—that is the one that became iconic. I was at the hospital about two weeks and then released. It was years later that I had a second bout of endocarditis while I was living with a doctor in his penthouse on East 57th Street and First Avenue.

This was Dr. Steve—he was a real Dr. Feel-Good who prescribed drugs for a lot of rock stars. He had a duplex and his office turned into his bedroom, so he let me stay upstairs. He was a neurologist and most of his real patients had Tourette's syndrome. Now can you fathom the waiting room? One time Keith Richards was upstairs shaving and taking a shower while downstairs in the waiting area were myself, Mick Taylor, Anita and Felix Pappalardi, and three or four patients with Tourette's Syndrome. I really feel bad for the Tourette's people—they have a neurological illness where they cannot control themselves. They may have tics or involuntarily speak or shout certain words—often swear words.

Dr. Steve would be in his office and we would hear "shit fuck piss shit fuck piss shit fuck piss mother fuck" or some other nonsense, while all the rock music people were waiting for their prescriptions and their chance to see him. I lived there for about two years, upstairs by the roof. Dr. Steve gave me the PDR—the *Physicians' Desk Reference*—which listed all the drugs that a doctor could prescribe. He said, "I will do anything to get you off the needle addiction. Look through this book and if you see anything that you like, I'll prescribe it for you." I would wake up in the morning and there'd be a little tray next to my head with the medicines of the day—six or eight Percodans, some Tussionex narcotic cough syrup, maybe a few Dilaudids, and some benzodiazepines—usually Valium. I tried other things too, but that was my main meal—pills.

While I lived with Dr. Steve I took so many pills that my jaw muscles atrophied and I couldn't chew—I just wanted drugs. For food I lived on crushed bananas, yogurt, and a few other foods that could be made really soft so I didn't have to chew too much. For protein, I would take a couple of raw eggs and drink them. Outside the penthouse, Dr. Steve had a little garden with herbs, and I started going out there and sun gazing while eating different herbs or drugs to see what effect it would have on my eyesight, and whether it would change the colors in the rainbow.

Dr. Steve was a closet gay and chased me around his desk a couple of times before giving up. It was enough to have a good-looking boy living with him. I used to be his runner, going to the specific drugstore that would fill all of the bogus prescriptions. Then I'd come traipsing back and take my share before giving it to Dr. Steve who then handed them out to the various rock stars who came to visit.

Anita Pallenberg first turned me on to him. One of the things we tried to help us get off of drugs was a transcutaneous electronic nerve stimulator, where you would put the pads on the bones behind your ears and it would cut the signals of dope sickness from reaching your brain. That worked okay, but the one that really worked was a medicine called Klonopin. It's a benzodiazepine and it could relieve withdrawal, but we were so deep into the narcotics that these were only temporary measures.

Once, Anita invited me down to Montego Bay in Jamaica where she rented a villa. We were planning to stay for two weeks and kick drugs. We took just enough with us to stave off the withdrawal for a couple of days and then we ran dry and started freaking out. We went to a local doctor and asked him for some narcotics and he said he didn't have any. We asked him for some syringes and he said he didn't have any and that the closest narcotics and syringes he knew about would be in Kingston—about a five or six hour drive. So we drank alcohol and smoked pot and used the electronic transcutaneous nerve stimulator and Klonopin. We just about got through the two weeks without driving ourselves crazy. There we were in Paradise, but so sick we couldn't enjoy it.

The moment we got back to New York we went and copped drugs because by then we were totally hooked and I mean totally. I would go through withdrawal once in a while and it was total torture—like in the movie, *The Man with the Golden Arm,* where Frank Sinatra plays a junkie who has to be handcuffed to a radiator to prevent him from going nuts. It was that serious, but every time I withdrew I knew what I was doing—I was suffering consciously because when I took the heroin I would fight to remain conscious, and mostly I did.

I overdosed a number of times. One time I turned blue and the people I was with were going to roll me out into the hallway and let me die. But one of my girlfriends put me in the bathtub and gave me hot and cold showers and slapped me around and walked me off of it. Similar instances happened a couple of times. Once I overdosed and a girl was smart enough to stick an ice cube up my ass which woke me up. I remember one time when I did a speedball so strong that I thought I was going to die—the only thing keeping me alive was the cocaine which only works for about 25 minutes. So as soon as I did the cocaine I would start preparing the next shot because if I didn't get it off in time I would nod out and maybe not wake up.

In 1979, I went on a promotional tour of England. I was so drunk after the flight that they wouldn't allow me into the country until I sobered up. I was searched from top to bottom for drugs because no one believed that I was that stoned just on alcohol. I had been traveling with a girl named Connie, one of Dee Dee Ramone's girlfriends, who could drink just as hard as I could, and we did nothing but consume alcohol and laugh through the whole flight. She made it through customs. I don't know why I was picked on, except that I was so stoned I didn't really care. When I got to London, and after I sobered up, I went to see the lead singer of the Only Ones, the band that opened for Television on the *Adventure* tour. He happened to have some very strong heroin. I had no idea how strong it was. He offered me some and told me it was really strong. He took out a tiny spoon and half-filled it and put it in my hand. I said that I could do more than that and he warned me, but I insisted. He gave me a larger amount. I did the whole thing at once and immediately keeled over.

The next thing I remember was waking up to a white ceiling and feeling great—like the whole burden of the world was lifted off me. Then I looked down and saw that my beautiful clothing had been cut open. There were nuns walking around. I started screaming about the fate of my clothing, and then one of the sisters came over and said, "You're in hospital. The doctor will be right over in about five minutes." So I looked up at the ceiling, still feeling great, and an Englishman came over in a white suit—you know, like a proper Doctor. He proceeded to tell me a tale.

"Mr. Lloyd, right? You were brought in last night and you were dead on arrival, right? So we tried to bring you back and if we took your clothes off in a nice manner you would still be dead, right? So we took your clothes off as soon as possible to put the paddles on your chest and we gave you a shock to start your heart again but it didn't work. We tried again and it didn't work. We gave you injections and they didn't work and I was just about to give up on you when one final electric shock caused your heart to go into sinus rhythm and saved your life, right? So I hope you will accept my apologies for cutting your clothing off but we were in a hurry, because you were dead for quite a while."

Suddenly I felt like shrinking down to a one-inch sized man. I was so embarrassed for complaining about my clothes when this man had saved my life. But I was also annoyed because I had no out-of-body experience whatsoever—no white light, no black light, no nothing. I had had visions before but I guess I didn't deserve any that time. Still, I felt absolutely marvelous—they had been giving me Narcan, which offsets the deleterious effects of the heroin. Elektra Records sent a limousine to pick me up in my tatters—and that's what I was dressed in—tatters. Luckily the people I took the heroin with had called the ambulance right away and had not been afraid of being caught. In England it's not quite like the USA—when a man has overdosed the medical professionals will come and take him away without the police interfering.

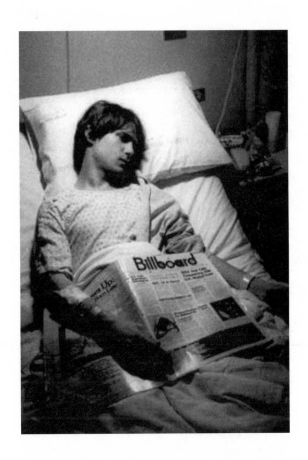

59 *Alchemy* and the Downward Spiral

Because Television had been signed as a group, all four of us individually were contracted to Elektra for a certain number of records. So, when Television broke up in 1978, Tom and I each made a record. I don't know how Tom's relationship with Elektra went, but they asked me to do a demo, and I went into Blue Rock studio and produced four songs which I thought would seal the deal.

Unfortunately, Elektra turned that demo down, although all four of those songs eventually ended up on *Alchemy*. My artist and repertoire person at that time (A&R) was Maxanne Sartori. She was the Boston disc jockey who had brought the Cars to Elektra, and she believed in me quite strongly. Maxanne convinced the company to let me do another demo, this time produced and engineered by a fellow named Michael Young, and we recorded about 16 songs live at CBGB's.

This demo eventually got me the "okay" to make a third record for Elektra under the original Television contract. The Television contract also increased the amount of money available to record and also provided an advance for each new record; I received an advance as if I alone was recording the third Television record. I assume Tom did also for his solo record.

Maxanne and I hit it off platonically and she spent a lot of time going to clubs where I was playing, especially a new club called the Mudd Club. One time we went there and got into an argument about some trifle. She stormed out of the club, and I went to chase her in the car she had rented because I had the keys. I began driving the wrong way up Broadway which is a one-way street downtown. About two blocks up was a hot dog stand where the cops usually got their doughnuts and hot dogs, so of course there was a police car parked there. They hit the siren and pulled me over. They asked me if I had been drinking, and I said, "Of course, do you think I'd drive up Broadway if I wasn't drunk?"

When they found out that I was driving a rental they simply took it off of me and made me walk away. This was before the days of severe penalties for DUI, and I suppose the cops couldn't be bothered writing up such a ridiculous ticket as citing a man for driving up Broadway the wrong way. I got away with it because of my angel face and completely honest demeanor. I didn't try to hide anything from them and I told them the exact truth. I was drunk, actually smashed, and I could have gotten myself and others killed. I often drove without a license when drunk and never drove sober. But that was back then.

Maxanne had warned me that the one thing that would splash the deal with Elektra was my being on drugs, which of course I was already completely into—and heroin addicted. But I told her I wasn't and got away with it for a time. After the contract for my solo record was fully negotiated and signed, she found out about the drugs. She decided to have me record outside of the city so that I couldn't get drugs while recording. It would've been better if we had recorded in New Yok City, but she reserved Bearsville Sound Studios near Woodstock, NY, and assigned Michael Young as my producer.

Michael and I got along at first, and I had taken some drugs with me up there because I was going to be far from the city for at least two weeks before taking a break. But I ran out after several days, and told the band to record a basic backing track without me while I took a bus back to Manhattan to get more drugs.

Bearsville was a studio in the woods with an apartment where we all stayed while we were recording. I hated it— Todd Rundgren was recording next door in the larger studio, and we were in the next largest space. There was a refrigerator in the apartment, which stunk, and the stink got worse and worse and worse as the days went by. Nobody opened it until finally the smell became the stench of death. When we opened it we found a chicken that had been left from the last recording session, and the refrigerator was turned off, so it'd been in there rotting. We all freaked out and made the studio itself clean up the place and spray it with disinfectant.

One day during the *Alchemy* recording session, I was awakened by Fred Smith, who was playing bass with me and Tom at the same time. He knocked on the door until he woke me up and told me that Michael Young was down in the studio putting keyboards on my record and that the studio door was locked.

I got dressed and went downstairs and indeed the studio door was locked, and I could hear the sounds of crappy synthesizers from behind the door. I knocked and knocked and banged and kicked on the door, but it would not open. I called Elektra and tried to fire Michael, but he also called Elektra and told them that I was stoned on drugs and that he was saving the record. I was angry about those keyboards for a very long time. In retrospect, I understand that perhaps he was contributing to, rather than detracting from the record, and *Alchemy* stands as a pop classic.

After we finished recording, I gave Elektra the title and the cover photograph which was in color. When they sent me a copy of the cover to approve, it was in black-and-white with a ridiculous black-and-white to gold word "Alchemy" laid across the top. I couldn't stand that, and I demanded that they use the color photograph, but Elektra said they had already printed 10,000 record sleeves and, if I insisted, they would use the color photograph—but the record wouldn't get released on its release date—and maybe not at all.

Elektra had me strong-armed, and I had also been forced to work with Michael Young until the completion of the record. We took about a month and a half off to try to sort it out but couldn't come to any new arrangement because Elektra had already paid Michael his full fee and told me that if I wanted to work with another producer I would have to pay for it out of my own pocket. I wasn't interested in doing that, although perhaps I should have. The advance I had received was enough money to do so, and more money than I had had at any one time in my life, but I really didn't know what to do with it except burn down the house.

Elektra released the first song on the record, "Misty Eyes," as a single and it soon began to get radio play in the Northeast and became a "regional breakout," which means that it should have gotten increasing radio airplay all over the country. Elektra wanted to hook me up with a strong management company and arranged a very big meeting for me with a well-known company, to see if we could get along. That would have shot me to the top, but the morning of the meeting, I did my usual heroin—only it was much stronger than I expected and I began to nod out. I debated with myself whether I should call the company and tell them I had stomach troubles or simply go to the meeting and try not to nod out. I decided to go to the meeting, which was an unfortunate decision.

I went to the big meeting and proceeded to nod out, and I remember someone from the management company saying, "They must be working him awfully hard because he's falling asleep." But everybody knew what the real deal was and I lost that opportunity. The next time I went to Elektra's offices, my posters were all gone, and from then on I could not get anybody from the company on the telephone. I had been dropped. This was another in a long series of setbacks in my music career, not all of which have had to do with drugs. I had plenty of opportunities after I got sober that were ruined by various events.

After Elektra dropped me, I spiraled out of control with my drug use and the huge amount of money that I needed to buy drugs. I decided to protect myself from myself, so I went out and bought some expensive furniture that would be difficult to pawn or sell. Eventually I ran through my money anyway, and was once again broke. I remember Johnny Thunders and myself going to the pawnshop to pawn our guitars in order to have money to buy dope. Then, when we had a gig, we would get an advance off the money in order to go back to the pawnshop and redeem our guitars. I'm lucky I never lost my guitar that way but it was probably safer in the pawnshop than it was with me. I played a lot of gigs in 1979 and 1980 but they were mostly around New York, because I no longer had a record company backing me. There were some great shows at places like the Mudd Club, and as far away as Philadelphia and Boston, but that's about as far as I got.

Alchemy eventually got phased out and became a "cut out"—meaning that Elektra sold off their reserves at a very inexpensive rate, and my royalties became zero. In the meantime, Maxanne had insisted that I had to have a good lawyer and accountant, but the people I ended up with were crooks. The accountant never paid taxes. Blondie had the same accountant and ran into serious trouble with the IRS some years later.

My lawyer was a scoundrel and a cocaine addict. Eventually I couldn't get him on the telephone and he owed me a bunch of money, so I harassed him by calling his office over and over again until finally he picked up and said flat out, "I stole your money and it's all gone. I bought cocaine with it, so sue me." This lawyer was eventually disbarred, but there was nothing I could do about recovering my money—it had simply disappeared.

A lot of the places I played in Manhattan around that time were run by rock club manager Jim Fourrat, who is credited with inventing the "rock disco." Years later he helped me get off of drugs by suggesting that I go to an acupuncture clinic in the Bronx, which I did on a daily basis, and it really helped—but that's getting ahead of myself.

I also played at the Peppermint Lounge, Ungano's, CBGB's and other places in New York City. Eventually I came to be living with Dr. Steve, and went into a manic episode. He prescribed an antipsychotic called Haldol, which is extremely strong and causes all sorts of side effects.

The thing that finally put the kibosh on my real career was a show at CBGB's. Before the show, Dr. Steve gave me my Haldol by injection, and he gave me 10 times as much as he was supposed to. I began to go into spasms and begged them not to make me go on stage with that in my system. I was pushed onto the stage and I could barely talk, or play guitar, and the place was packed. After that, I lost much of my NYC audience for live shows. I continued on a downward spiral until I got sober in 1984.

On a personal level my years from 1980 through 1984 were like the Great Depression that occurred in the 1930s in the United States. I could hardly draw people to gigs and I was thoroughly addicted to heroin. During that time, I met a girl named Susan who lived with another fellow who was a heroin importer and he used mules—fat women who would smuggle heroin from Thailand. This was pure heroin and also very strong cocaine that Susan and I got for free. I was still living on Thompson Street in the Village, but every day I would get up and go to this guy's house where Susan and I would shoot up enough heroin to kill 14 people. By then, the drugs no longer got us stoned but only prevented us from getting sick. When I didn't see Susan, I would go to the Lower East side, Alphabet City, and cop for myself.

I didn't hit the bottom until late 1983, and after that I began to get sober, but it took me until July 1984 to get completely sober and clean. It was shortly after that I was given the opportunity to go to Sweden for a year where I made my second solo record, *Field of Fire*, and I had another chance to get on top of things.

60 Endocarditis and Bob Marley

The second time I got endocarditis it was much, much worse. I was still living with Dr. Steve, who was providing me with enough narcotics to prevent me from going back to the syringe. But when I got some money, I had the craving for some cocaine. We lived on First Avenue and 57th Street., so I went out and started walking downtown towards Alphabet City where I knew I could buy some cocaine and a syringe. I walked about 10 or 11 blocks when suddenly I heard a voice within me say, "You have an angel on one side and the devil on the other, and they are vying for you now."

I thought about appealing to Jesus Christ. Since there is no such thing as time, Jesus is now just as he was then, and so I made an appeal. Instantly the craving left me and I turned around and began walking uptown again. But after a couple of blocks, the devil spoke to me and said, "How long do you think you will last? You know I am more powerful than you are, and you are alone. How long do you think this release will last?"

I walked two more blocks as I was having this battle within myself. I turned around and started walking downtown. Then I turned around again and started walking uptown, but eventually I found myself walking downtown and succumbing to the darker impulses. I paid a high price for that impulse and very nearly died. If it weren't for Bob Marley, I would have. I will explain as I go along.

I went downtown and bought some cocaine. When I got home, I crushed up a Dilaudid, a very strong narcotic, and mixed it with the cocaine. I put the mixture into my veins, shot it up and got that incredible rush that is called the speedball. I can't describe the pins and needles inside the body and the exhilaration that took place in the brain except to say that it is virtually unbearable—except for the fact that it is bearable. However, it leads only to more and more craving. Sometime later, I began to get sick with what I thought was the flu. I started feeling worse and worse and sicker and sicker until I had no choice but to tell Dr. Steve, who thought I should go to the hospital right away. He took me there by cab and immediately put me on intravenous antibiotics. Then he turned me over to the care of the doctors at Beth Israel.

I was in a ward with very sick people, some of whom died and a few of whom lived. Some had cancers and others had tuberculosis and all manner of other deadly diseases. When they got my blood back from the labs; the doctor came in to see me and told me I had one of the worst cases of endocarditis he had ever seen—what he called quadruple bacterial endocarditis. He said that I would have to be on intravenous antibiotics for months in order to get better. But I didn't get better. I got worse. The bacteria had clung to the valves of my heart and was eating away at them. I was either born with, or developed a grade B heart murmur when I was five and had rheumatic fever and whooping cough. During that brief second when the heart pauses between beats, the bacteria from the injection clung to my valves and began destroying them.

I kept getting worse and worse. I had been there more

than two months when the doctor came to me and said, "You're not getting any better and you're getting as many intravenous antibiotics as everybody else on the floor combined, and we're afraid you may die. So I want you to brace yourself for what I'm about to tell you. We are going to go in and replace your valve and clean out your heart. I've reserved an operating room for Monday morning. We are going to use a valve from a pig, which is the closest thing to human tissue as we know, so you will have to take anti-rejection drugs from now on. That's the only way you will stand a chance."

He left me with that bleak news and frankly I did not want a pig's heart or any part of a pig in me. I wanted my own things in me. The things in my body all have a con-sciousness—even the valves of the heart and the heart itself has a separate consciousness and conscience.

It was Friday evening, and I began to sing Bob Marley songs to myself. The songs were from his early days with the Wailers and I fixated upon one song which ran over and over in my head until it became a mantra. The lyrics were from a song called "African Herbsman," and I re-peated them over and over again. I couldn't quite remem-ber the words, so I sang:

African herbsman, biding your time,
Letting the wind blow through your mind;
While that old white slave trader,
    with a transplanted heart,
Well guess how soon him have to part.

I could feel that this was Bob sending me this song about a transplanted heart in the old slave trader because I had done him a favor and turned Albert Anderson on to marijuana, which allowed him to become a member of Bob's band. From Friday night until Sunday night those five lines ran through me, singing their way through me while I sang them low, under my breath, or out loud depending if people were nearby. I knew the melody and I kept to it.

The doctor came in early Monday to examine me before the surgery. When he put his stethoscope on my heart he looked startled. After examining me for a while he said, "I don't know what happened to you, but whatever it was, you'd better hold onto it, because it seems as though you've turned the corner and are getting better. I'm going to cancel today's surgery but I'm going to reserve the operating room every day at 10 am in case you take a turn for the worse."

Bob Marley had sent me the help I so desperately needed to beat the devil. As surely as I know I have fingers, I believe that. I kept singing the same song for weeks while I got better. After three months the doctor said I was ready to go home. Dr. Steve came to pick me up. I never again put a syringe to my arm, and I believe that Bob and I have settled our debts toward each other in the spiritual realm. I know deeply that he saved my life with that song and that, without it, I would be a dead man.

61 *Field of Fire:* Part One

I finally got clean and sober at the beginning of July in 1984. I'd been trying since the previous October when I had "hit my bottom." I had come to a conclusion that I could not go down in flames by myself because I was taking my loved ones with me.

An incident occurred which I will not recount except to say that I was in a fight with one that I loved. Afterwards I could not talk for about an hour except to say, "It's over" and when asked why, I said, "Everything. Everything is over."

What I meant was that I could no longer take drugs and alcohol the way I had for 20 years, and I began to try to get sober. The siren's song was very strong and it took me six months to begin to pull free of that centripetal force, but I finally achieved it that July, and stopped everything.

As I began to wake up, I didn't know what I should do with my life. Should I start over as a scientist, or go back to school or get a job, or continue being a musician? I just didn't know, so I wrote down a prayer when I was about 45 days sober and clean. Then a miracle happened.

I thought about prayer and how powerful it could be, but I felt that simply saying words out loud or left unsaid would allow one to escape the prayer, so I decided to write it down. It went something like this—

"Dear God, I wish to become the best me I can be, not only for myself but for all those who care about me. Tell me which direction I should go in and what I should do with my life. Amen."

I was looking down at the piece of paper. I wondered if God would send a message in a still, small voice that I might not hear, or that it might be something I just didn't want to hear. Then the phone rang. This was 4 o'clock in the morning. I knew that the phone call had something to do with the message, because who would call me at 4 AM? I was staying at the house of a woman named Gail, and hardly anybody knew my phone number. I picked it up and it was the overseas operator who asked me if I would pay for the call, and I said yes.

"Hello, Richard? This is Keith and I am in Sweden and there's a guy over here who owns the biggest independent record label in Scandinavia, and he wants to fly you over to make a record. Do you want to come over and make a record?"

I looked down at the piece of paper with the prayer written on it. It had been less than 10 minutes since I wrote it down, so it was obvious that I should say yes. So I said, "When?" And Keith said, "As soon as you are able. He's going to be in New York in a couple of weeks and would like to meet you for coffee."

That was about the extent of the conversation. It was my friend Keith who had gone to Sweden to escape his own problems. He knew a girl over there and did what we call the "geographic"—except for the fact that wherever you go, there you are.

A couple of weeks later Peter Yngen came over and met me at a coffee shop and told me point blank that he would like me to make an album for him, and that he had a really nice recording studio in Stockholm where I could record it. I asked if he wanted to hear any demos, which I didn't have at the time, and he said, "No, I've heard your work and I trust you." Well this was surely the answer to my prayer—I was destined to be a musician, to play music, even if it was rock 'n' roll, with its prurient interest and egocentric "search for stardom." I could not deny this, so that January, Keith and I left New York to go to Stockholm. It was 18 below zero when we arrived. But the cold in Sweden is different than the cold in New York. It's so cold that it's a dry cold and easier to bear.

62 *Field of Fire:* Part Two

I thought we would stay in Stockholm to rehearse the record, but no. Peter Yngen sent us to a small town called Orebro, in the center of Sweden. A band named Lolita Pop, who was also on his label, had a rehearsal studio where we could rehearse for a month before recording. We each bought a pair of "Strumkrumpers," a kind of padded shoe that keep your feet warm, and we began to rehearse with the band that Keith Patchel had put together for me. It was Keith and I on guitars, and two Swedish guys on bass and drums.

I did not feel the rhythm section was that good, and I despaired of not having brought in my own musicians. Peter Yngen said that he couldn't afford to bring Americans over and put them up, although he did have room for me and Keith. We stayed together in an apartment and went to Lolita Pop's studio every day, trying to whip the band into shape. I kept trying to give them that certain something that I've always tried to give the musicians I work with. I have never been able to give it away, teach it, or to even impart it—that's the special "It" that is the aura of stardom. That includes the ability to play with the kind of energy I needed. But after a month it was time to go into the studio and we made an album that I called *Field of Fire.*

This was in 1985, and we began touring Sweden. I've probably been to more parts of Sweden than any Swede I know. We also toured Norway, where we flew inside the Arctic Circle to play Tromso, the northernmost university town in the world. People went crazy during the shows—we were wildly successful. Then I was given an apartment in Stockholm, and a dear friend of mine named Anders loaned me a bicycle. As summer came around I used to cycle around all night because there was very little darkness, and I'd visit the various girlfriends I had accrued. Sometimes I visited three girls in one night. One time I was in my apartment with a girl when one of the other girls showed up, and I had to pull that ridiculous stunt of making the first girl disappear so the second girl wouldn't get jealous.

I spent about a year in Sweden, and then headed back to the United States, bringing a new drummer and bass player with me. On the song "Field of Fire," which has a five minute guitar solo, we had to replace the drums and the bass because they were out of time with each other and with my guitar. The guy who replaced the drums was Sanken, and he is still a good friend of mine and runs the major record company there. He came over to America as my drummer because, when we had planned to tour Finland, we couldn't find Peter the drummer. We were to take a boat over from Stockholm to Helsinki, but nobody could find Peter, so the three of us left and hoped that somebody would find Peter and fly him over before the show. I had to find a new drummer fast and the best one I ever found was Sanken.

We did an 18-city tour in the Unites States. At the time I was on fire and we did magnificent shows—I felt that I was at the height of my powers. We were invited to open for Iggy Pop who was playing the old Ritz which is now called Webster Hall. It was sold out, and I did very well opening for Iggy, with whom I've always had a pretty good relationship. Once upon a time we talked about working together, but he ended up working with Steve Jones of the Sex Pistols instead.

It was during that tour that Nancy Jeffries from Virgin Records wanted to sign me very badly. She was in A & R and also wanted me to work with Mick Jagger. He was doing a solo record and he wanted to get a good guitarist and Nancy recommended me. Jagger was in the audience on the second night I opened for Iggy, and I put on a damn good show, and Iggy put on an amazing show of course, but Mick Jagger did not come back to visit me.

I was a bit perplexed, but Nancy came back and explained. The rumor was that Jagger left when they started playing Rolling Stones records on the PA because everybody knew that he was there and he became uncomfortable. Later on it was reported to me that Mick passed on using me because he said it seemed as though I was uncomfortable on stage. If that is true, then frankly he was gemlike-spot-on.

I realized that when I went onstage I carried baggage with me of my own personal sadness, reticence and self-deprecation, and that everyone unconsciously could smell it—my inner bag of shit—and Jagger had noticed it. This was painful for me, suffering this dismissal by Jagger whom I had met earlier, in part because I was friends with Anita Pallenberg and Keith Richards. But it benefited me enormously because it was true—completely and utterly true. It was one of the reasons why I hadn't been able to reach the audience that I might have reached without carrying that sadness with me. It was measurable, which made people unconsciously adversative.

When I was younger, I lived in extreme poverty and was also mentally ill, neurotic, and sometimes psychotic. What I realized was that I was hoping to be rescued by a woman, and as long as I stayed in that position of neediness I would draw someone to rescue me. This was a replication of some very early abandonment issues that I had been trying to cure by remaining sick. I realized that this was a completely erroneous methodology. Balanced people are not attracted to people who are needy and self-pitying. Balanced people are attracted to people who are successful, happy and well-adjusted. I realized the futility of being in need of rescue because it only drew complementary people who needed to rescue other people for their own psychological reasons.

We finished up the 18-date tour, and while we were in Los Angeles, we did a private audition for A&M records. After about 20 minutes we were told to stop, and I thought they were going to pass, but the president of the company shook my hand and said, "Welcome to A&M. You can tell anyone you want that you are an A&M artist and we are going to make you huge. There's just some paperwork we have to do and then we'll get started."

A few days later I heard that the contract wasn't going to materialize because my manager had gone in asking for too much. This was just at the time when *Field of Fire* could've done enormously well in the United States—when stadium rock was happening, but I had snatched disaster out of the jaws of success once again.

63 Matthew and the Little Kernels

One day I was sitting around playing my guitar—it must've been about 1988, and I got a call from Anton Fier. Anton had been one of the drummers in the Feelies, and he had his own band, The Golden Palominos. He told me that his guitarist had quit and he had three dates that weekend. He asked me if I could learn 17 songs in three days. I said "No, but if you tell me the keys of the various songs and I can play mostly lead, no one will know that I don't know what I'm doing." He said that would be fine, and so I ended up in the Golden Palominos for three shows.

This was a band of singers and various instrumentalists. One of the vocalists and bass players was Matthew Sweet, who sang three songs in the show. I enjoyed playing the material and we became friends and sent postcards back and forth. When he was making his second record for Columbia he asked me to play on it, and so I played lead guitar on at least one song called "The Alcohol Talking" which was about a girl who was drunk and talking nonsense. I enjoyed it very much and so did Matthew—so when he was ready to record his next record *Girlfriend*, he asked me to play on it. I ended up playing on three tracks—"Divine Intervention," "I've Been Waiting" and "Evangeline."

Girlfriend is a very special record. It was recorded with

no reverbs, and no effects on the instruments. The band did use effects during the mixdown, but they spent a lot of time listening to *Revolver* by the Beatles and tried to capture that sound with loud lead guitars. The album was produced by Fred Marr, who had met Bob Quine, Lou Reed's guitarist, when he programmed the drums for one of Lou's records. Fred and Bob ended up playing cards together in a kind of card club of which I had no part. I had learned my lesson early and I don't gamble.

That's how Bob Quine got on the record as the other guitarist. He's the guitarist that played on "Girlfriend," whereas I played on the opening track, "Divine Intervention." My work with Matthew turned into a long-term collaboration where I ended up playing lead guitar on a number of his records—about seven—including three tracks on the Sid and Susie records which he made with Susanna Hoffs.

Matthew asked me if I would play live with him during some promotional shows, and I agreed. It was a lot of fun, so when he started touring I became the lead guitarist. We did a number of tours together, including Australia.

Matthew didn't like flying. When the record company wanted to send us to Toronto to do press, I was sent with him. We got to the airport and he began to feel sick. He said he couldn't go. I called the record company to tell them Matthew could not get on the flight. I should've sat him down and used some hypnosis, but things were moving quickly, and the flight was about to leave, so I didn't have time. We missed that flight.

When we finally went to Australia, he knocked himself out on the plane, and slept the entire way. Matthew's shows there were packed. The cities in Australia are far apart—

separated by scruff and desert and kangaroos. Matthew refused to fly even though the rest of the band flew. After the shows, Matthew was immediately, within 15 minutes, headed off in a car driving 24 hours to the next show. I thought it was insane but there was nothing to be done because Matthew really, and I mean really, didn't want to fly.

We did several American tours and Matthew became a teen idol. His shows were attended by young pubescent girls who idolized him. I could have set myself on fire onstage, or played the greatest guitar in the world, and no one would've noticed me because they had their eyes pinned on Matthew. I called them little kernels, and they were jailbait. I was asked by someone in the band what I meant by "little kernels." I explained that their teeth hadn't really come in so they looked like kernels on a baby corn. If a girl came on to me and I examined her teeth and she had little kernels, I steered clear. There were enough mature girls to get by.

Matthew was pretty shy. He mostly spent his time in the back of the bus listening to music, watching videos and playing video games. I had gotten into the study of Gurdjieff's ideas and spent my time in the front of the bus reading books that I had sent to me from a company that sold Fourth Way material. It was a very productive time for me.

Matthew and the band did a gig in New York where everybody got very drunk, except me. It was a complete train wreck, but wonderful. Fred Marr played drums and nearly fell off the drum seat. This was at Wetlands, a club on the Lower West Side—way lower, near Canal Street. We did another gig there with Jody Stephens, the drummer from Big Star. He hadn't played in a while so he was nervous, but we thought he sounded marvelous.

During the *Girlfriend* tour, Matthew's management team wanted some of his shows to open an act that was breaking nationally. They chose Melissa Etheridge. What we didn't realize was that the first six rows were reserved for members of the Melissa Etheridge fan club. She hadn't come out of the closet yet, but was very clearly gay. Many of her fans were lesbians who screamed and yelled hate messages at us because we were young men., This was in spite of the fact that the lead guitar player and co-writer of some of Melissa's songs was a man, and she had other men in the band. But we got the worst of it. We used to arrive and look out the bus window at all the lesbians arriving— the butch dyke, the pretty submissive, the cowboy, the biker chick, you name it. They came in while we were onstage and there were always girl couples making out in the front and giving us the razz. One band member started making cartoons of all the different kinds of lesbians and then putting them up on the bus. Matthew had an audience who bought tickets as well, but they were in the back. We could hear them screaming "Yes!" but all the lesbians in the front would hiss and boo and yell out for Melissa to get on stage.

During that tour we got stuck in an Ohio town because Melissa lost her voice from screaming and had to take a week off. The entire tour ground to a stop. It must've cost her half a million dollars with all of that equipment, stage gear and the opening act sitting around doing nothing. Matthew wrote about 56 songs that week. Man, he was prolific and I suppose he still is.

The only reason I stopped touring with Matthew was because Television got back together and I couldn't ride two horses. Bob Quine wouldn't tour with Matthew because he said he was too grumpy and cranky, which he was. Matthew asked me who I would suggest as my replacement. I suggested Ivan Julian, who had been in the Voidoids with Bob. I felt Ivan was kind of in the middle between my style and Bob Quine's. Matthew told me that Bob had suggested Ivan as well—that's how Ivan got the gig with Matthew Sweet.

At the time, Ivan was probably not quite as good as me or Bob, but he dressed like a rock star and Matthew really liked that. Bob and I wore relatively ordinary clothes. I like to look smart and always had a good sense of fashion—but I never wore spandex or bandannas. That bit about Jimi Hendrix wearing a scarf around his thigh comes from prostitutes in Paris who wore scarves around their thighs to tell their customers that they were available. If they got a John that they liked, they took the scarf off. Hardly anybody knows that but it's a true story.

After we recorded Matthew's next record, *100% Fun*, Matthew and Bob had a falling out. Bob felt his guitar was too low in the mix. He was right. Mine was too. Bob Quine started chewing Matthew out, saying that he had made Matthew by playing guitar on *Girlfriend* and how dare Matthew allow him to be buried in the mix. I'm not sure if they ever talked again, but because he didn't use Bob on the next record, he didn't ask me to play on it either. Ivan did, which led to some uneven sounds, in my opinion. Following that, Matthew made some records where he played almost everything himself. Some years later Matthew began asking me to play on his records again.

I had been sober for many years but I started drinking again because I was so alone. One time, while I was driving on a road along the Pacific Ocean, I hit water that was on the road from a sprinkler. I lost control of the car and slammed into a light pole. When the cop got there, he wanted to arrest me for drunk driving. I refused to give him a breathalyzer test. I collapsed on the scene and had to be taken to the hospital. I looked pretty horrible, and felt worse. Matthew had the idea of putting me in his new video for the song "Sick of Myself" while I played guitar in my hospital bed. I agreed, although I probably shouldn't have.

64 The Coke Cat

I was in one of those 30 day detoxes. It wasn't a place like Hazleton—not some fancy place for millionaires and celebrities. It was one of those dingy, state-funded, run-down Mother Theresa type places where it is only through the charitable hope of unknown soldiers that the wracked bodies, paralyzed emotions and twisted thinking of the addict might find solace. If he or she is fortunate, the lucky addict may find the tunnel going up from the depths that they have dug themselves into. Every man is given a shovel and can dig his own grave as deeply as he wants, but it is hard to fill up the hole. A few may find a shovel to tunnel up through some of the many levels of Hell that Dante speaks of.

This was not my first rehab, but even with my powers of memory, the time frame of this one remains mushy. I'm thinking perhaps it was '90 or '91 after I'd slipped out of my sobriety in the best possible way—by having a relapse.

There I was, savvy to the game but wanting to get sober and straight again. My relapse taught me that it could spin me like the spin cycle of a washing machine—where the fluid is being squeezed out by centrifugal motion—and what is squeezed out is success, ambition, social graces and friends. I was glad to be there.

I've always loved experiences. If you are like me, where everything in life is a worthwhile adventure, even if you're being crushed by a Catherine wheel or losing your toes to frostbite, then being in rehab or a mental hospital is better than being at the movies, because after all, the characters are written in vivid colors. They are stereotypes beyond belief, and yet everyone—and everything—is real.

There was a Hispanic guy at the rehab that I took a liking to. We can call him Rafael. He tried to put on a rough and tough exterior like a gang member but really, he had a soft heart and was a real sweetheart inside. He was the kind of man that was putting up a false front of hardness, but it was so transparent as to be translucent, and what came through the translucence were screams of, "Lost, I am totally lost."

I took him under my wing and allowed him to become my friend because he was a misfit of a sort that doesn't develop friends easily. One day he said that his eyes hurt, and the next day he said the same thing. On the third day, I was talking to him and he started moaning.

"Oh, my eyes hurt. My eyes hurt!"

"Let me have a look," I said, and I moved him so that he was in the light and I looked into his eyes.

"Are you wearing contact lenses?" I asked him.

He answered, "Yes."

"When the last time you cleaned them?" I asked.

"What do you mean, 'clean them'?" he said, and I could barely believe my ears.

"I mean, when did you last clean your contact lenses—you're supposed to clean them every day. They look filthy!" I told him, and he said he had never cleaned them and had had them in for two years.

"How often are you supposed to clean them?" he asked.

"EVERY DAY!"

I told him to clean them and to ask for contact lens solution at the nurses' station, and to tell the nurses that he hadn't cleaned his contacts in a long time. Rafael did not even know what contact lens solution was, and he insisted on not cleaning them. I told him I would teach him how, but he refused and admitted to being scared.

"Listen, your eyes are hurting you. You haven't cleaned your contact lenses in two years and you're supposed to clean them every day. You're lucky you haven't gone blind. If they get infected you could lose your eyesight, and it could happen very quickly. Especially if you say your eyes are hurting, you've got to get that done," I told him matter of factly.

"I can't, I'm too scared."

I looked at him for a moment and realized that on the inside he was a child. He had never grown up and wasn't going to be able to take care of himself, so I offered to clean his contact lenses for him.

"Take out your contact lenses, and I will clean them for you," I said.

"I don't know how—I've never taken them out. I didn't even put them in, the doctor did," he replied.

Oh brother!

Reluctantly, I pulled him in to the bathroom where I washed my own hands and stuck my thumb and forefinger in his eyes and removed his contact lenses. They felt like Brillo pads, utterly filthy with grime on both sides. No wonder his eyes hurt.

"Hey, my eyes feel better!" he said suddenly.

"Well of course they do. We've gotten two years of crap out of your eyes."

I washed the contact lenses with plain water. He didn't

want to go to the nurses' station and tell them what happened because he thought he would get in trouble, so I just went along with him. When I put his contact lenses back in his eyes, he blinked a couple of times and was amazed that he could see. His contact lenses were so filthy that he had thought he had cataracts but was afraid to tell anyone. He could barely see two feet in front of him. When his vision returned to normal, I warned him that he needed to learn to wash them himself—and that he didn't have any choice. Then I asked him how he got in the rehab place, and he told me a sad and incredible story.

"I was living with my girlfriend in the Bronx and I was doing a lot of crack cocaine and I was starting to lose my mind. My girlfriend is a hairdresser and she was out working. I was sorting through my cocaine when her cat jumped over the table. It was this big, white, super long-haired cat. When the cat jumped over my crack, I thought the cat had stolen some of it, so I cornered it in the closet. I grabbed the cat and started shaking it, but no crack fell out, so I got a comb and started combing through the cats hair, but still I couldn't find my crack. Since my girlfriend is a hairdresser, she had a drawer full of barber's tools and I took a pair of electric clippers and I shaved the cat. It looked like a scrawny little rat and I had a big pile of white hair. I was going through the hair with a pair of tweezers trying to find my crack when I realized my girlfriend was coming home soon. I got scared that she would be mad at me, so I took the cat and the hair into the bathroom, where there was a bottle of crazy glue, and I tried to glue the hair back on the cat so that she wouldn't find out, but the cat ran out of the bathroom, and I guess it died. When my girlfriend got home, she freaked out when she saw her dead cat with tufts of hair glued all over him and she called the police. They took me to jail, and later in court the judge said that I could either go to jail or come here. So here I am, and I don't know if she's still my girlfriend, or if I have a place to go when I get out of here."

I had heard a lot of war stories by then, and seen and heard a lot of crazy things, but I had never heard a story like this one. I looked at him for a moment and then I said, "I want you to understand something. That cat is now your guardian angel. You owe that cat big time, and you are now at a crossroads. You should never forget that cat and what happened, because if you do, the cat will be waiting for you when you die and it will do to you what you did to it. If on the other hand, you never forget that cat and make the cat part of yourself, then the cat will watch over you and protect you and forgive you. It will understand that you were sick and didn't mean to hurt it. But if you forget that cat even for a moment, and do something undignified, there will be hell to pay. That cat died for you, and you know you owe it now to act as if that cat has become human in you. That's the only way of paying it back."

There were a lot of incidents like that in rehab where I tried to help others. I never told anybody about any of these events because they were mine and the other person's. They are secret tales I'm only telling now because this is my memory, truth to tell.

Sometimes I tell my students to open their wallet, take out a dollar, and throw it over their shoulders and then not look back. Why? First because it is hard to do—to give up even one dollar because we are so attached to money. More importantly, the found dollar is worth more than the earned dollar. When you earn a dollar it's simply that—you have earned a dollar, but when you find a dollar on the street you feel happy and that happiness is worth something. I tell my students to throw it over their shoulders and not look back no matter what. If somebody runs up with the dollar and says, "Excuse me, you dropped this," they are to say, "No, that's not mine—the wind blew it up against me, but it's not mine so I guess it's yours." Then they are to turn and walk away.

If the lowest denomination in your wallet is a five or ten, do the same thing. It only hurts for a moment and is a good deed done in secret. Even if the bill finds its way into the sewer you have still gained an advantage, because money is like a crocodile's mouth—it tries to close itself around you and eat you alive. And for many people it does. Money becomes the drug to which they become addicted.

I once took a dollar and tried to eat it. Of course, that was useless, so I tried to blow my nose and wipe my ass with it, but it was too slick to work as toilet paper. So I threw it away. Money is just paper, and worthless. Why do some people work an hour for one dollar and other people work an hour and get $1000? The value of money is nonexistent—and he who craves it is thoroughly addicted to it. To throw away one dollar is not much, but it is an act of bravery and charity. Not many people can do that or even think of it.

I have never allowed myself to be trapped by objects, so when my place on Thompson Street was burglarized and my large television was stolen, I didn't care. And because I don't care, things cling to me and it's hard for me to lose things. On the rare occasions when I do lose something, I become its slave if I look for it. It is easier to realize that it still exists and is somewhere, and will turn up eventually.

Everyone should live like that, without clinging to things or people. Clinging to people only makes them want to get away from you as quickly as possible. Learn to become anyone's friend. Look over at a stranger and figure out who you would have to be to be their friend. Try to become that person, even if just for a moment. Loosen yourself from yourself. You won't regret it and you won't die. You'll just come out of the trance a little bit. That's the deadly trance that keeps so many people from living. Our friend Rafael now has a chance to live, whereas before he only had a chance to die.

65 John Doe and SXSW

It was 1990, and I was sitting in my apartment in New York minding my own business, with nothing much going on, when I received a phone call from an A&R man from Geffen. It was Gary Gersh, who had struck gold with Nirvana. He was the top A&R person at that time, and he asked me if I knew who John Doe was. I said, "No," and then he asked me if I had heard of the band X, and again I said, "No," which was true—I had stopped listening to music unless I was working on it, so I had missed the entire Southern California punk movement.

Gary said he had signed John to a solo deal and that they were trying to make a record but John kept leaning in the direction of American Western and he needed a New York ace on the record to give it some "street smarts." I wasn't doing too much so we negotiated a price and soon I was flying to LA for rehearsals.

I really liked John—he was a great guy and had a terrific voice, but yes, his songs were on the country-western end of things, and I didn't really hear a hit. Anyway, we rehearsed a bunch of stuff and, as Geffen was loaded with money at the time, we had a huge budget to record with. John and his manager, a cigar smoking scoundrel, had picked the producer for us—a guy who had worked with the Bangles and other acts that received lots of radio play.

The studio was one large room with an isolation booth for the vocals and one for a guitar. There was none for me because we had two guitarists, myself and John Dee Graham. Tony Marsico was on bass and the drummer had been Dwight Yoakam's drummer—that tells you a little bit about the country-western influence.

They built a little box for me in the studio to put my amp in, which of course took away any ambience we might've had, but allowed me to turn it up and use some distortion pedals. The producer began calling me Princess, and I didn't give a shit so I allowed it, although it was patently disgusting. The producer went on to say how he had convinced a female singer who had a number one hit that she would sound better if she sang nude, which she apparently did in a darkened room. This producer was getting on just about everybody's nerves as he went on and on about himself. John is very slow to anger and a real gentleman with an incredible voice, so I guess he just put up with it.

We had a $5000 food budget—we went over it and Geffen didn't care. We were ordering cartons of cigarettes, bottles of ginseng and huge plates of sushi. We tried and tried to hit that $5000 budget by ordering liquor and all sorts of other things. I wasn't drinking at the time so I don't remember exactly what was ordered, but I got a bunch of vitamins, cigarettes and ginseng.

Recording the album went well and everyone seemed pretty pleased with what I added to the mix. That album became known as *Meet John Doe*—I guess it's a takeoff on the Capra movie, and that's what John called it.

A tour was being organized and I flew back to New York in the meantime. They decided on a single and wanted to make a video, so I got a call from John's manager who told me that he wanted me in the video even though there was no money in it—but it would be good for my career. What a load of hooey. I told him it would be good for John's career if I was in the video, not the other way around, and to call me when there was money for me in addition to airfare and hotel for the three days it would take to shoot. We got in a screaming match and the asshole manager hung up on me. About 15 minutes later he called, and after trying to talk to him sensibly, we again got into a shouting match and I hung up a second time. He finally called me back a third time and agreed to my terms.

So I flew out to LA, we rented a bar and shot the video which came out pretty well. There was also a song on the record where John gave everyone in the band a writing credit, but I never saw a dime from that, as usual.

For some crazy reason, when it came time to tour on the record, John didn't want to take a bus out on tour. I guess it would have cost too much because we were playing larger sized clubs. He didn't want to go out in a smaller vehicle because we would have to tow the equipment with us, which is dangerous and we would be liable to get it ripped off. John decided on a recreational vehicle, an RV. I had never heard of a rock band going on tour in an RV before, so it was of interest to me as an experience.

All the shows were crazy-packed. We were touring in the summer, and it was so hot that I often felt like I was going to pass out from heat stroke. A roadie began keeping buckets of cold water on hand to dump over our heads between the main show and the encore.

Things went well until we were driving along in Iowa and the bus—the RV—broke down and nobody could fix it. We were driving to Minneapolis and had a show that night. John and the tour manager started walking, looking for a garage or some place to rent a vehicle. They were hoping for another RV, but when they finally found a rental place, the only thing the guy had available was a big locked-back truck, the kind that dead immigrants are found in because there are no windows or air vents. Meanwhile, the rest of us were waiting around in a field two miles from where Buddy Holly, Ritchie Valens and the Big Bopper went down in an airplane crash. We were being eaten alive by mosquitoes.

John decided to rent the locked-back truck. The story goes that he gave the rental guy his credit card. The guy looked at the credit card which said "Exene" on the front—the singer of X. On the back was the signature of D.J. Bonebrake—the drummer of X. Then the rental guy looked at John and asked him his name. John said, "John Doe." That was the last straw. The guy said, "Wait here just a minute," and went in the back to call the police, who arrived posthaste. They were going to arrest John and the road manager for fraud and theft. John called his manager in Los Angeles to get the thing explained away. His manager gave him another credit card number and luckily it checked out. The credit card John was carrying was his band's—which is why it was signed by one person in the name of another and neither of them were John Doe.

In the meantime, we were waiting by the side of the road, running back and forth, trying not to get eaten alive by the clouds of mosquitoes and cursing out John and everybody else under earth and above heaven because they were taking too long. Finally they showed up. Everybody looked at the truck and I said. "Oh no—we're not riding in the back of that!" It was explained that there was room for only two in the front, the driver and John. The rest of us and the equipment had to go in the back—and then the door would be locked on us.

When we climbed into the dinky back of the truck we heard the corrugated aluminum door come down and the snap in the lock. I couldn't see my hand in front of my face, that's how dark it was. We just talked and talked and every bump we hit was like a bad roller coaster. It's a wonder anybody got out of it alive, but eventually we pulled up in front of the Minneapolis gig and breathed fresh air. It was 8:45 P.M. and our gig was supposed to be at nine, so we didn't have much time.

We unloaded our gear, set up the mics and immediately started the set. It was the best set we had done so far. Everybody agreed that it was incredible and we discussed the possibility of never doing sound checks again. After all, what was the point if we sounded better just going on and playing? Of course we did return to doing sound checks as soon as they were available.

About a week later John came into sound check in a foul mood—something I'd never seen before. His face was white as a ghost. I wondered what the hell was going on with him. I found out a day later what had happened.

John had been on the phone with Gary Gersh who said, "John, we made the wrong record." An artist hates to hear that, especially from an A&R man that made him do demos over the course of two years before allowing him to make the record. The worst part of it was that Gary told John that the record company had decided to pull their tour support. John was told he could go home or carry on with the tour, but would have to pay for the tour himself because Geffen had quit the record. No wonder he was ashen white after that phone call. We were in the middle of a sold-out tour and John didn't want it to end. I guess he bit the bullet because we kept going.

We especially wanted to get to New York where we were booked on David Letterman's show. We got there and it turned out that Ronnie Wood had purchased the old property of the 82 Club and turned it into an art gallery for his own artwork—that's where we played our regular show. It was the hottest show yet in terms of the temperature onstage. Tickets were oversold and the place was packed with hot bodies. I thought I was going to pass out from the heat which is something that had never happened before. We were all dunking ourselves in ice water while the drummer begged us not to do an encore. He did that every night because he was so used to doing country sets. We did encores and that's that—get used to it buddy.

After we played David Letterman's show we started getting recognized by gas station attendants in Georgia and everywhere else we went. At the end of the tour, everybody said goodbye—I still love John and always wish him the best whenever I see that he is doing something new. I heard that X is doing a reunion someday. Maybe I'll finally get to hear them.

I went to the first three SXSW music festivals. They were excellent. Then they got too packed and ridiculous. The last time there were too many bands, and rather than listen to any single band, people were busy looking at the lineup to see who was coming on next and talking with each other about which bands they had seen that were good. I spoke on a panel at the first one and ended up sitting in with a number of people, including John Dee Graham, from the True Believers, who was also the other guitarist with John Doe. That is a great band—The True Believers.

I also got to play lead guitar with Ronnie Lane of the Faces, who was living in Austin. I had never met him before, and he had multiple sclerosis and was using a wheelchair at the time. But he could stand up, and he came out on stage, stood up and did a couple of songs including "Ooh La La." I played the leads and cried during the whole song because there he was with MS singing the lyrics, "I wish I knew then what I know now." It was an incredibly moving moment.

66 Television Reunite

Television decided to get back together in 1992. Tom's manager and my manager had met at a party and asked each other what we were doing and both said not much. So they got Tom and me together. I decided that I would take Television to my lawyer, Fred Davis, Clive's son, to try to get us a new record deal. Fred had been planning to shop my demo around, but I figured I could always do that later—Television would be a big paycheck.

We told people that we only got together during the eclipse cycle of 11 years. The cycle is one of 18 and 11 years so it was kind of a fudge, but there was no way to tell the journalists that we just got back together because we weren't doing anything much individually. When we got back together we sounded like we had never split up.

Fred Davis began meeting with record companies. He was known as a shopper—a lawyer who will take an artist on consignment for a percentage of the deal he gets them. Twenty-three labels were interested in signing Television, but as the bidding went up, the labels started dropping out. We ended up with two—A&M and Capitol Records. We went with Capitol because they offered a bit more money and their president was Hale Milgrim. Hale was a true music fan who had 25,000 vinyl record albums in his collection. He would go on tour with the Grateful Dead on his vacations. That's a man of music, and he loved us.

I loved him back—he was a great fellow.

Tom put the screws on Fred Davis, whittling his percentage down, so Fred would never take my calls again. When it came time to talk about producing and promoting the record, Tom actually got up on the table in the conference room and started walking around, saying how he knew everything about the music business because he had released a lot of records. None of those records have sold anything near what *Marquee Moon* has sold. I was completely embarrassed.

We made a deal with Capitol where no one was allowed in the studio from the record company, and we produced it ourselves. Actually, Tom produced the record along with Fred Smith, because Fred originally joined Television wanting to produce us. Fred found out how rigid Tom was later on. But Tom and Fred became good buddies and have stayed that way, as far as I know.

We made Capitol promise to release the record on vinyl, but one day Hale Milgrim brought us into his office. He was ashen white. He told us he had just come from the bean counters' offices where they went over the money. Vinyl was down to one percent of Capitol's sales so Capitol could not make a vinyl version of our new record. Hale had pleaded with them, but they said that CDs were the wave of the future, and that Capitol still made a lot of its money from the Beatles and Frank Sinatra, which allowed them to move forward. They wanted a band like us, but they could only put the record out on CD. We were disappointed. In the end, they may have printed a small number of vinyl copies which would be pretty collectible these days.

Tom chose Sorcerer Sound in NYC for us to work in. They had two different studios, a big one on the first floor and in the basement, and a smaller one on the fifth floor which we took as a buyout. A buyout is when you pay a certain amount of money per day and no one else can use the studio. That way a band doesn't have to move their equipment from day to day. The company was refurbishing the fifth floor studio where we worked, so we couldn't start until noon when they were supposed to be finished. Oftentimes we would get there and the studio would be a different shape. It was very strange.

I negotiated a percentage of the publishing for the band before we went in to record. That took about a year of keeping my foot down until Tom resigned himself to the fact that the band was justified in getting a percentage of the publishing, which is where the real money is. Before that, Tom had been very tight and even stole some of my deserved publishing. When we did "Fire Engine" on what was to be a cassette-only release called *The Blowup,* Tom took the writing credit right out from under Roky Erickson's nose by writing a few extra words and changing the name of the song to "The Blowup." When I recorded the song myself, I credited Roky as the writer. I've heard there are challenges all over the place as to who wrote that, but as far as I'm concerned, Roky Erickson did the writing.

Bands usually borrowed money to make a video or support a tour because at that time tours usually lost money. To build an audience, the band borrowed the money from the record company. The goal was to build a strong enough audience to support touring and sell enough records to pay back the company and make a profit. Tom never had the long view on this. He would never take money from the record company for anything that he didn't have to. Whenever Tom did anything, he wanted to be paid right away. I thought this was foolish and prevented a lot of greater successes. What I didn't know at the time was that Tom had been playing this game since the very beginning, so that he could be in charge of everything and say no whenever he liked.

Back in New York in the seventies, toward the end of the New York Dolls' days, they decided to dress up in red leather with a hammer and sickle backdrop behind them. It was completely nuts. They had Malcolm McLaren managing them—the guy responsible for the Sex Pistols. When the Dolls came back to New York, they were afraid they would not sell out the theater they were going to play, so they asked us to become what's known as a co-bill. That means that both parties are equal and both bands get top billing, although one band has to go onstage before the other. We were happy to go on first so we could get out of there early. This is when Richard Hell was still in the band. We did six straight nights with them at some place that was like the Copacabana.

Malcolm McLaren fell in love with Television and especially Richard Hell and his look. But when he talked to Tom, Tom said "no way" to Malcolm managing us. This was right before McLaren formed the Sex Pistols—they were a kind of mix between the way Television looked and the Ramones sounded. We were still wearing torn T-shirts, sometimes held together with safety pins. Malcolm called his wife, who had a clothing store called Sex, and told her about the look. She started selling T-shirts with zippers and safety pins holding them together. This merchandise was a big hit there, and kids started hanging around the store. Malcolm took a few kids that looked good and had raw talent, and turned them into the Sex Pistols. He would've done that with Television and made us all millionaires almost overnight, but Tom said no. One of his underlying reasons probably had something to do with the fact that he was finished with Richard Hell, but hadn't told anyone yet.

Tom and I were walking along the street after Malcolm had made his pitch to manage the band. I asked him why he turned Malcolm down. I explained that I thought Malcolm, although a con man, was like Elvis's manager and could make us all rich overnight. Tom looked at me, laughed and asked me, "Do YOU want to end up in red leather?" Of course I said no, and that was that. Tom had gotten away with saying no again.

I didn't like the recording of the third Television record very much. To me it sounded like "Television lite," where everything is soft and muted. When I had a talk with Tom before recording about potential studios and engineers, he stood up and screamed at me, "I am not going to make a pop record or a rock record!" This was disheartening to me. Tom was always doing things which embarrassed me and were against my code of ethics. The best part of the Capitol Records deal was that we started to play again, and we kept playing from 1992 through 2007, when I left the band.

Our manager at the time was John Telfer, a very amenable Englishman who ended up living in São Paulo Brazil where he married a doctor and was quite happy. He always joined us on tour. The first thing Capitol did was send Tom and me on a promotional tour to Europe. At the time, I had a malady that caused me to yawn fifty to a hundred times a day. This drove Tom nuts and I remember overhearing him talking with John Telfer long-distance and saying that I was falling asleep and yawning at business meetings, which was far from the truth. It's true that I yawned a lot, but I also gave plenty of input. John Telfer trusted my business sense which was far more realistic than Tom's. So I always had John's ear and I told him about Tom, who traveled without luggage, but with his clothing in garbage bags and plastic bags from various supermarkets and stores. All Tom did was smoke cigarettes, drink coffee and look like a bum. He was an absolute embarrassment to be around, but I had no choice.

Tom lost one of his plastic bags of clothing when we flew into Germany. I used to jokingly call them his Gucci bags, just to make things lighter. Tom could be one of the funniest people on earth and the record company person who met us at the airport was very nice. She said, "Where are your clothes, Tom?" Tom told her he lost his clothes and only had what he was wearing. Being the record company person she said, "You can't be seen in those clothes. We have to get you some new ones." Tom said "I have no money," so she offered to put the clothes on her personal credit card. I have never to this day seen it again, but behind her back, Tom actually rubbed his hands together like he had put one over on her.

She took us into some very nice stores where Tom picked out very expensive things. If Tom bought something with his own money it was usually for 10 cents or a dollar. He would walk into rehearsals saying things like, "How much did you pay for that shirt Richard?" When I would tell him, he would say "I got mine for a dollar, ha, ha, ha!" I began refusing to tell him what I paid for anything because I like to pay full price for nice things.

After Tom finished shopping, we went to meet the publicists and journalists. It all went pretty well, but when he got back to New York, Tom found a bill waiting for him asking for repayment of the amount that was spent on his clothes. God, he fumed over that. The next time he came to rehearsal, he kept complaining about it and talking about how he wasn't going to pay. I don't know if he ever did pay.

We eventually went on some short tours to support the third record. We did very well in certain cities like Chicago and San Francisco, while in other places we didn't do as well, which means we didn't really do well at all. I remember the first time we went to Chicago by airplane, and in the cab ride into town, Tom rolled down the window, stuck his whole upper body out and sang "Chicago, My Kind of Town" in a ridiculous Frank Sinatra imitation while gesticulating to all the other people in cars who were looking at us as if we were crazy. We were crazy and we knew it and I nearly pissed my pants from laughter. Tom could be that funny and he could also be gracious—but it was very rare. He never lost his free-floating contempt for anything or anybody that wasn't him, and he thought people were copying him. For the longest time he felt that David Byrne and Lloyd Cole were copying his style.

We never had a hit single on the radio, in no small part because of the singing. I always thought Tom could have improved his singing a great deal, as well as his stamina, if he took a few voice lessons. Whenever I suggested it to him he would scream at the top of his lungs that his voice had character and that he was not going to take any god damn vocal lessons no matter what, and I had better shut up. So I shut up, and as a result we suffered no radio hits whatsoever. What Seymour Stein had said in comparing us to the Grateful Dead came true—rabid audience but very little radio play.

When *Marquee Moon* came out we asked Elektra to send records to college radio, but they told us that college radio airplay didn't sell records. We also asked them to let us print up T-shirts which would act like advertisements for the record, and also merchandise we could sell at gigs. They turned that down saying, "We are not in the merchandise business—we're in the recording business." A couple of years later both those things became the norm—college radio and bands selling merchandise with their pictures on the T-shirts. College radio was an open format that played bands like Television—and they did play us a little. But in those days it was nothing like major radio. Nothing.

We toured the Capitol record on the East Coast, then Chicago, Minneapolis and Cleveland, and then the West Coast, including Seattle, Portland, San Francisco and LA. In Los Angeles, we played a theater that asked us to turn the volume down. We found out later they were using a limiter on the entire mix to keep us from being extremely loud. This took away our punch to that audience, which was full of record company bigwigs. It was also our doomsday because Tom had seemingly never ending technical problems that had me standing around onstage for about half the set. It was completely boring. We used to start our shows with one of our songs, but during this tour Tom didn't want to sing, so we would start with "Swells"—a long jam that allowed Tom to postpone his singing. By this time, I could tell that Tom hated singing and would do everything he could to shorten the set by cutting songs left and right. That night it was a disaster and I think that was the end of Capitol Records having an interest in us. Tom really stunk that night, both in playing and singing. His Jazzmaster fell

341

apart—the bridges on those guitars are notorious for collapsing. They aren't really meant for rock 'n' roll because you can't hit them that hard.

However, when the equipment worked, the combination of my Stratocaster and Tom's Jazzmaster created an incredible mix that could not be beat.

67 The Awakening of Kundalini

A couple months prior to Television's first tour of Japan I was in a bookstore and I noticed a book on kundalini. I stopped to look at it and became nervous. I wondered what about it frightened me, so I picked it up and read it. It contained a series of exercises designed to awaken the kundalini. I figured I had stuck needles in my arms, gone to acupuncture, Rolfing, the Alexander technique, shiatsu, reiki and other modalities so I pushed aside my fear and began doing the exercises. This was at the same time I was doing a 20-minute breath counting meditation every day. The kundalini exercises took about 40 minutes for the full course. I had read all the classic works on yoga—almost all of which spoke of kundalini as a major goal. After about a month I began getting noticeable results, shimmies through my nervous system and strange feelings of rumblings in the deepest part of my body.

Television went to Japan in 1992 and we stayed at the Prince Hotel which was next to a Buddhist shrine, which was nice for me because I went over and rang the bells and did some of my meditations there. We toured a number of cities in Japan and an event happened when we were in Osaka, a strange town with huge underground malls where you could buy an apple for eight dollars or a cup of coffee for five. Everything was very expensive there as their economy was booming at the time.

As a result of the kundalini exercises and my breath meditations I was experiencing extreme psychosexual orgasms that were not centered in my genitals but occurred anywhere in the body. One day I was sitting in a chair in my room. I had already done the 40-minute exercise. As I was doing the 20-minute breath counting exercise I suddenly experienced a moment of void—my "I" seemed to simply vanish, and I felt like flint had hit steel in my solar plexus and suddenly a huge rush went downward from my solar plexus through my body and my legs and into the floor and kept going. Judging from the sensation of it, I would say that this downward movement extended about 200 yards below my body and then turned and began roaring back up towards me. I thought, "Oh my God, here we go," as the rumbling, like a freight train, reached my feet and moved up my legs and through my torso and out the top of my head. All of a sudden, my breathing stopped and my heart when into fibrillation. I sat there for a moment and thought to myself, "Everything they said was metaphorical is *actual*."

I could barely believe it and so I lifted my right hand and touched my left hand which was cold as ice and I put my hand on the top of my head where there was a small circular bit of warmth. The rest of the body was as if dead. It felt as if all movement in my body had stopped like someone going out and turning out all the lights in the house one by one. All the so-called chakras stopped rotating and stood in stasis. I remained in this condition and position for some time before the "kundalini" which was over the top of my head came back down into the body bringing with it a surge of sexual pleasure into every cell of my corpse.

I opened my eyes and stood up and noticed that my "I" had, for lack of a better term, herniated. "I" was everywhere. Everything, including the body, was just a small part of it. I worried that I was not going to be able to speak or come down from this and we were scheduled to perform in Osaka that evening. I decided I needed ballast—that is, some heavy food like meat or something else to bring me down.

I walked out of my room and got on the elevator where thankfully no one else was present. I walked through the lobby and out onto the street. I *was* the street and the street lamps and even the people. The only place I was not present was within the deepest part of the people I passed by. Somehow, I withdrew my presence from them, allowing them a certain decency of privacy. About two blocks away I found a store. They had nothing to eat but bananas and yogurt, which is what I took back to the hotel and ate, and that brought me down a little. I smoked a cigarette and that brought me down a little more. But I— the "I" that I was accustomed to—was still spread out all over the room and outside the hotel. I mustered all my strength and slowly I began to come down to the point where I was able to go out and speak to my bandmates, albeit haltingly and in simple sentences. By the time the show was to go on I was okay and we gave a great performance, but when I came back to the hotel and lay down to go to sleep I kept getting rushes of sexual energy coursing up and down and through my body.

The next day I called a friend of mine in New York and explained what it happened. He said he knew nothing about this type of event but that I better find a kundalini yoga teacher when I got back to New York, which I did. I found a man who taught what was being called kundalini yoga and started to go to classes every day. The funny thing was that everyone else was trying to get their kundalini open and I was trying to get it to close. I took those classes for about two years on a daily basis.

Once I went on a retreat with a group of students and the teacher. Everyone stayed with a roommate and I was the odd man out so I stayed with the teacher. I was awoken during my sleep by his breathing—he was doing a complicated breathing exercise. The next day at breakfast I asked him if he knew that he had been doing breathing exercises in his sleep and he said that he did not but asked me to describe it, so I did. He said that this was an exercise he had been doing six months prior but quite extensively.

This proved to me that breathing exercises can be dangerous in the sense that one might make an instinctual habit out of holding one's breath for an undue length of time and actually die in one's sleep. I was always the one who researched and took great care in what I did. I did various kinds of yoga to the point of seeing its real effects. I had a golden rule; if the result of the exercise was good for other people besides myself I would continue, but if it was only a kind of onanism, I would stop. I suppose this kept me, and still keeps me, out of a lot of trouble with white and black magic and tantra, because I always had a conscience that spoke loudly within me.

Now it is many years later but I can still remember distinctly what happened and it took about 18 months for me to turn the valves so that the experience would disappear. I remember thinking that if I had five or six months alone I could've gotten into a position where I would have been able to keep the kundalini experience and still be in the world. But my duty was to be in the world and I did not have that five or six months so I stopped what I was doing, like so many other times in the past when I had reached the brink.

68 Leaving Television

In 2007, I finally left Television. I had begun work on *The Radiant Monkey*, which turned out to be one of my favorite solo albums. I played everything but the drums.

The principal reason I left Television was because I was tired of having my income determined by someone else—namely Tom Verlaine. Also, Television had not made a new record since 1992. That record was exciting to play live, but I call the record itself "Television lite" because, except for a few dynamic moments, it was quite a subdued recording. Some might call it sublime but it had none of the spunk or force of *Marquee Moon* or even *Adventure*. During rehearsals Tom always talked about a new record, but year after year passed and nothing ever came of it. This was coupled with the fact that Tom had no new lyrics and would piddle about on the guitar trying to find amusement for himself. It was clear to me that we were no longer a band, and that the rest of us—me, Billy and Fred—were being treated as sidemen.

I told the band I was going to be leaving after our scheduled show in Central Park, but I got ill and missed that show as well. This caused me no grief whatsoever because my intention and impact were brought to bear on *The Radiant Monkey*. During the years since the "Television lite" record, I have put out six records, while Television has not recorded any new material to speak of.

Tom would only go on tour when the money was substantial. Of course, when we did go out on tour, I profited from this state of affairs, but I was sick of it. From the very beginning I wanted to tour extensively even if it left us in debt, because that was a way of building our career, but Tom declined anything except instant money.

I was terribly saddened the year before I left the band because Tom released two new records without a thought to recording a new Television record. Then Tom gave an interview in which he talked about deciding early on that he did not want to pursue "the career thing." That was the last straw. I realized he had never been in the band except in the very beginning and that after *Marquee Moon* he drifted into his own realm and left the band to stagnate. There was no point in me arguing with him, so I decided to quit the band and go it on my own.

About two years after I left, Jimmy Rip took my place and learned my parts. Television began a series of tours where they played nothing but the material from *Marquee Moon* and a new song we had been doing for a couple of years called "Persia." I was represented because Jimmy had to learn all of my parts and solos. This was somewhat gratifying, and the records continued to sell so I continued to get artist royalties, but I was shafted by Tom who was not paying me any of my publishing. I had gone for years allowing this to continue in order to keep the band going, but I was absolutely at my wits' end when I left.

The band, which calls itself Television, remains a vital force in music with the rhythm section of Fred Smith and Billy Ficca, but Tom now meanders and jokes around.

69 Suffering

I have suffered all my life knowing that it is a valuable aspect of being human. I did not choose to become a human being as far as I know, and when I came out of the womb, the doctor held me upside down and slapped me on my ass because I had not yet turned from an aquatic creature into an air breathing creature. When he smacked me it was as if he said, "Welcome to the world, Richard—this is what you can expect from it." Then they cleaned out my airways, cut my umbilical cord and I remember them putting some ridiculous hat on me and tying it under my chin and I hated it.

My mother had been put to sleep with an anesthetic, and although it wasn't supposed to go through the umbilicus, I'm sure that I had come out woozy—already stoned a bit. The next day after my mother woke up, they took me to her and I remember looking at her and wondering what the hell had happened—where was I, and what kind of trouble did I get myself into? Who are these people and who is this woman? After a brief period of staring at her with my old soul eyes I realized I was expected to be a baby, I softened in her arms and played the role of a baby even though I was fully conscious. I played the part of a young child and eventually I lost myself in my role as a teenager and young adult, but I never lost touch with the fact that I suffered. This kind of conscious suffering earned something.

Some sort of unseen substance was generated by this kind of conscious suffering. Even in my madness during manic attacks I never hurt anyone. I had gone crazy over rock music, and this was to be my life so I wouldn't have to grow up—I was already mature inwardly. I was a highly precocious and intelligent child who learned to walk and talk and interact with the adults even though I could see that there were problems with them that I could not solve. I suffered for the world, as much as my measure would permit.

I am no Dalai Lama or saint—it's as much as I can do to be generous and help others, but this has caused me great suffering as well because no one wants to wake up. Everyone is in a comfortable sleep, dreaming away in their imagination and creating personalities with which they walk around in an arrogant unconsciousness.

All my life I have tried to teach others what I recognize now as the famous "It," and all my life I have failed to teach even one person, or to transmit to even one person who does not have it, that elusive quality of "It." Whereas, I had "It" to the point of "agony"—a word that means trial from the ancient Greek. I see this life as a trial. Life on the earth can be Heaven or Purgatory or Hell, but life in the world is nothing but Hell or Purgatory—there is no Heaven in it. It is a fleeting thing which lasts both seemingly forever, and also wilts like a flower, having its short season in the sun.

I have enjoyed suffering and have learned how to suffer knowing that it earns me something unseen and un-knowable by others, except by taste. Where I come from, the Pearl is known as the tears of the suffering of the oyster, because an irritant gets into the oyster and it begins to form a cyst of mucus around it, which only makes it bigger. It suffers more and more as the Pearl becomes larger. Finally it is drawn out of the sea and cracked open which kills the oyster but releases the Pearl.

This is the Pearl of great worth—the knowledge of the value of suffering. Everyone in this world wants to be free and people have all sorts of ideas about what that means, without realizing that it means abiding by the law—and I need not speak of the laws of society which change from culture to culture or even the laws of nature, which hold us as tightly as Gulliver is held by the threads of the Lilliputians. But I need to speak of THE LAW— WHEREBY ALL THINGS ARE CREATED, HELD TOGETHER AND DESTROYED, LEADING TO NEW THINGS.

This law is like sunlight—both good and evil. There are areas of the Earth where the Sun can kill you in four hours, and yet without the Sun there would be no life. And there would be no life without the Moon, which acts as a stir stick upon the seas in the primordial ooze and soup of life. All movement comes from the stir stick—the Moon, which traverses around our planet like a weight swung by a discus thrower, slowly moving further and further away from the earth year by year, decade by decade, century by century and millennia by millennia. Scientists know that when the Moon was formed, the Earth's day was only six hours long, and the Moon was much closer, producing a drag which gradually slowed the Earth's orbit down as the Moon moved away.

The Earth's orbit is still slowing down as the Moon moves further away even today, only it is so slow that no one ever notices. The Moon looks the same as it did when man first beheld it. It is a place where nothing changes, and nothing will ever change except for perhaps a few of man's footsteps and other trash. Forgetting myself for moment, or perhaps remembering myself, I ask what is to become of man, who soils the nest—the world contaminating the earth while reducing its entropy in some places.

Human brain: three and one-half pounds of gelatinous substance. It is the single object in the universe with the lowest entropy we know about. It can soar to the heights, or sink to the depths and visit all places in between. Look up! Does not the Moon and the planets in their turn affect you?

Man is engaged in war at all times, but the wrong war. It is that war which is caused by the planets in their turn. War breaks out like a rash on the earth but man does not have war with himself. Instead he allows himself to lavish praise upon himself and contempt upon others. How can this be permitted? The laws of the universe permit it, but not forever. Soon it will become unnecessary, as language gives way to the very first thinking, which is by form, and which is telepathic. Language is the language of lying and it cannot help but be so because the word is not the thing. It is nothing but a symbol which was a piece of clay broken in half and sent by messenger to its recipient. By putting the two together the recipient could verify the message.

I receive messages from on high and from below, and I mix them here together in this third realm. I suffer this mixture in me, not deigning to change it and not trying to change it. It is the person of Richard Lloyd, a creature born to woman just like all other men. A chemical and sexual entity, who has access to worlds unseen, and like Swedenborg, I can sense my angels and demons nearby as they contest for my soul. This is the value of suffering—the Pearl of great worth, the treasure hidden in the garden which is worth more than the world. How long do we traverse here in a world which is a pain factory, a lunatic asylum, a topsy-turvy upside down image which a mere insight can change. In that insight the suffering becomes bliss—two sides of the same coin. Like Janus looking both ways, man is a god in a pantheon of beings. ALL things are living, even a stone. Even the Moon. And up the scale, we need to reach the human brain, and its dreams and hopes—no, not its fears which are useless in the face of things, but its understanding which is a suffering unto itself.

Man is a repository of experience—the impressions he receives he can keep and digest in his memory or not. Those things that are not remembered have not existed, and at the end of his days what does a man have left? How can he justify his existence? Here is another mystery—a suffering which is waiting for each man. Even having an illness is practice for the immune system and practice for death, when the entire world and everything a man loves is loosened from him. Is this not a suffering? To cling, to capture, to own. I own nothing—not even myself—I only own the memory and the suffering I have accumulated.

Why do you think I used drugs the way I did? Was it to escape? No, it was for the inevitable suffering that follows. When a man learns to walk he must learn to fall, and so perhaps falling comes first in learning. Learn to fall and do not be frightened of the heights from which you fall. Thou art nearer the Earth than ye suspect, as ye are part of the Earth and its nature and cannot escape. I recognize that having been born I am like a butterfly whose wings are trapped and awaits the catharsis of freedom while in the throes of suffering gladly. I would that all men understand this.

Part II
Outtakes

I remember my first funeral at age 7. My cousin's mother had been in a terrible car accident—decapitated on her way back from her honeymoon, so it was a closed casket. There were many family members there, including my cousins, Billy and Ronnie. Ronnie seemed to be in shock, saying nothing and looking ghostly. Billy was bawling his eyes out crying for his mother. All the other adults seem to be grieving and even the children had a sullen look on their faces. I thought to myself, how can any of this help the person who has died?

About three quarters through the funeral I went and sat in the first pew in front of the coffin and thought about what I could do to help. Inwardly I told the woman that she could go now and was free, and not to let anyone's own wishes try to hold her back from her own fate, which was to play out in another realm. I sat for about 20 minutes paying attention to my breathing which became quiet and almost disappeared. I concentrated hard on sending blessings to this soul who had been taken so abruptly. She was probably still hovering around trying to console her children. I told her that this was not necessary and that she had to give up the world and everything and everybody in it and move along following the cords of destiny to wherever they might take her.

I could never understand grieving. It is one thing to feel sad for the loss of a life the dead person might have enjoyed. But most grief is self-pity—I could see that clearly. All the adults and children there were only thinking of themselves and their loss of mother, child, sister or cousin. This seemed to be duplicitous to me in my innocence. I have never grieved as others do over the death of anyone. Life leads to death which is inevitable and death leads to life which is also inevitable.

A couple of things happened to me during second grade that were very strange. One of them involved a boy whose eyes rolled up inside his head. He would try to strangle other children. This happened during a recess one day. He had his hands around a girl's neck and would not let go. She passed out and the nuns pulled him off of her—four or five nuns. The nuns trapped the kid behind one of the heavy doors at the entrance of the school. It took all of the nuns to hold the door against him. An ambulance pulled up a little later and men in real white suits came out and put him in a straitjacket. Then they transferred him into the ambulance and we never saw him again.

By then I had learned to read very well. We were reading the Dick and Jane readers. We were given a pretty thick book with over 200 pages in it. Each page was very short with large print. I used to read ahead of the class but I would keep my finger in the spot the rest of class was reading so that if I was called on I could easily find my place. One day I was reading very far ahead and my fingers slipped out and I lost my place. Then I was called on by a nun. Being an honest child I said, "I'm on page 178, but if you tell me the page you're on, I'll be glad to take up the reading." The nun ran over and started screaming at me. She told me that I was a conceited, self-centered, sinful child who was going to go to hell and that I should help other students who are not doing as well. She told me that the class only went as fast as the slowest pupil.

I would have been glad to help another student but that would have interrupted the class so I sat silently absorbing this insult. I was never hit by the nuns but I did see them hit other children on the knuckles with their rulers—and the nuns screamed a lot. Even the younger nuns looked like dried up old prunes in their habits. I wondered a great deal about what happened to the religious. Clearly these professional religious people had had something happen to them that was not good at all.

◇◇◇

I got into my first and only fist fight in the fifth grade with a guy named Mark. I don't remember why the fight started. We got into quite a good punch up until we were pulled apart by other children. I snapped while fighting and went into berserker mode. I realized I could kill this other child without any qualms. I thought this was interesting because I was a very nonviolent person

◇◇◇

One time in the sixth grade a child brought a camera into school. He kept pointing it at me before class began. I told him not to take my picture and I put a newspaper in front of my face. As soon as I put it down I heard the click of the camera. I began chasing him around the room. The teacher came in and tried to stop us. We ran around her desk several times and knocked her over. I picked up her chair, raised it above my head and ran out into the hallway after this sixth grade paparazzo. I threw the chair at him and then heard the word STOP! I stopped, turned on my heels military fashion, and found myself looking at the principal. He took us both into his office. The other kid told him there was no film in his camera. The principal got very hot under the collar. I got out of trouble and was sent back to class and the other kid got suspended.

◇◇◇

My cousins Billy and Ronnie decided they were going to form a rockabilly band around '58 or '59, so they bought a guitar. I took one look at it and fell in love. I desperately wanted to play it but was shy and I didn't know how to play anything. One night I went over to their house for a sleepover. While we were talking in the evening, Billy and Ronnie passed the guitar back and forth. They played some acoustic numbers from the Everly Brothers and some Elvis—not my kind of music at the time but better than nothing.

I asked to play the guitar and they handed it to me. They taught me three chords: G, C and D. Every time I got my hands on that guitar I would practice those three chords. My left hand was out of shape and refused to obey me, so I would use my right hand to move my left hand fingers to form the chords. Billy and Ronnie didn't let me play much because, frankly, I sucked. That night after everyone had gone to sleep, I got hold of the guitar and started practicing. I was told to cut out the noise—everyone was trying to sleep. I went into the bathroom and played those three chords and lost track of time.

Then there was a knock on the door and I heard Billy say, "Get out of the bathroom, I need to use it!" I stopped playing, opened the door and there I stood with the guitar in my hand. Billy told me it was morning. I had no idea it was the morning. I had played those three chords as best I could all night long and wasn't sleepy in the slightest. I probably could have gone on a three chord marathon for three more days but I was embarrassed. I put the guitar down and let Billy have the bathroom. That was my first experience with a real guitar.

I had played the ukulele because my stepfather had one that he had gotten in Hawaii while stationed there in the Air Force. He didn't like me playing it because it was one of his prized possessions. I used to play it with a pick made of a coin instead of the thick felt picks that are usually used to play ukuleles. This was hard on the strings and my stepfather started to hide the ukulele in a closet. In the middle of the night I would take a chair and climb up inside the closet to find it. Then I'd bring it down and play it for a few hours before putting it back. I had no idea how a ukulele was tuned. My stepfather said that it was tuned to the song "My Dog Has Fleas" but I could never remember the song melody so I just played it the way I found it. I really wanted to play the guitar and I was playing the uk-ulele as if it were a guitar.

When I was about nine, I got an AM radio and started listening to it. There were two main stations—WMCA and WABC, with Cousin Brucie and other disc jockeys who have since become famous. I started listening in about 1959, but the music then was absolute pap, pure sappy garbage as far as I was concerned. Every once in a while, a novelty song would interest me but for the most part I listened and waited and hope for intelligent life to appear. Some of the R&B music was good, and occasionally the three big female bands had good production, but Paul Anka and even the Righteous Brothers were not my style.

In about 1962 that began to change, and we began to hear Motown and much better black music and even the beginning of some rock and blues on the radio. But it wasn't until 1964 that the door got smashed open with the Beatles. Around about January of 1964 a friend of our family came over for dinner and asked me if I'd heard about the Beatles. He told me that they were going to be huge and soon they were going to appear on the Ed Sullivan show. I had not heard of them, but in that knee-jerk reaction style of "I didn't eat the cookies" I said, yes, I had heard of them. Of course I had—they had reached the radio and were coming like a tsunami wave, but I hadn't really noticed it until I saw the excitement that occurred when they first arrived in New York. The attention they got was crazy—no other rock band had ever gotten that kind of attention. There had been a kind of rock 'n' roll going on in the United States for quite some time, but not white boys singing love songs with simple pronouns in their titles like "Please Please Me" and "Love Me Do."

I prepared to see them on Ed Sullivan, and when the time came, I sat down in front of the television like an anthropologist from another planet, and wondered how four young men could induce such adulation and interest. After that, it became a worldwide phenomenon with the strength of the energy that war uses up, only in another direction—the direction of togetherness and peace and love.

It was nearly unbelievable that at the time there was still war going on in the world, but there was also this other war—a war on for music and fashion and youth culture. I went to Be-Ins and Love-Ins in Central Park, witnessing the birth of the hippies. I was too young to be a beatnik by several years, and I was also too old to fall for becoming a hippie, so I was in between. My intelligence said to me that I was not yet part of this culture, but a witness to it, like an anthropologist, and I wondered what made the Beatles so special. After all, they were just four young fellows in a rock 'n' roll band, mostly singing juvenile songs of puppy love. But I suppose the '60s were ripe for that sort of thing. Anyway, shortly on the heels of the Beatles came the Rolling Stones. I suppose if you had to ask whether I was a Beatles or a Rolling Stones person I would say the Rolling Stones—they were much more steeped in the blues and, although I couldn't understand the sexual implications of their music, it drove me deeply in a way that the Beatles music didn't. That is not to say that the Beatles music didn't have an effect on me. It did, and in a very powerful way, but the Rolling Stones were singing about adult love and I was intrigued.

One time in the village and I saw Charlie Watts of the Rolling Stones walking down the street. I opened the door to the music school where I was studying drums, and there were a bunch of girls tuning up their violins and cellos. I made the mistake of saying "Guess who I just saw outside? Charlie Watts from the Rolling Stones!" The girls dropped their instruments—and half the guys did too—and ran outside. Charlie saw them coming. He started running and they started running. He ducked around a corner and they followed him. I don't know if they caught up to him, but I doubt it. This is a confession—I'm sorry Charlie. I didn't mean to get you chased down the block.

◊◊◊

During one summer vacation—I was about 14—I got caught with some marijuana because I had planted some seeds and they grew. I was very proud of my plant and kept it on the windowsill. But I had to go to summer camp for two weeks, and I asked my grandmother, who was visiting, if she would take care of my plant. I told her that it was a palm tree. She believed me and dutifully watered my palm tree. But while I was away, the New York Post printed a huge picture of a marijuana plant on the cover with the caption "Parents Beware." When I came back from camp and went into my room, I looked at the windowsill. My plant was gone and instead there was the picture of the pot plant from the newspaper taped to my window—and my parents said they needed to talk to me. Oh brother. I had to admit that I was using, but so were they—legal prescriptions for sleeping pills and ups and tranquilizers—mother's little helper, and daddy's too.

◊◊◊

My cousins, Billy and Ronnie, lived in McKeesport, Pennsylvania while I stayed with my grandparents in Homestead. They were my best friends, and I used to eagerly await my time with them. One of the last times that I went to Homestead for summer vacation was memorable. Billy had bought himself a car and I'll never forget the name of it. It was a 1956 Chrysler Crown Deluxe Windsor Limousine and he was very proud of. It was a fixer-upper and so he began working on the car at all hours. We used to go driving and it was quite a thrill, but one time the thrill was almost too much. That part of Pennsylvania is very hilly and we were going down a hill that snaked down the mountain to the interstate that ran in front of the steel mills. We were going down the mountain and the brakes failed and we began careening faster and faster down the road, trying to not crash. The biggest danger was at the bottom of the hill where there was a sudden left curve and then a traffic light in front of the highway. When the traffic light was red there were often cars piled up waiting for the light to change. We were scared to death, or half to death, and when we turned that final corner, thank God the light was green. We couldn't stop and we ran right out onto the highway and jumped the divider between the two lanes. Billy straightened the car out in the right direction and slowed down until we could pull off to the side. These are the kind of crazy adventures we got ourselves into.

◇◇◇

Sometime in the 11th grade I decided I was no longer going to take schoolbooks with me to school, but only my guitar in a hardshell case. I remember my physics teacher walking over to me after he asked people to take out their schoolbooks, and I simply sat there because I had no schoolbooks with me.

"Mr. Lloyd, I don't see your schoolbooks. Where are they?"

"There in the case," I said.

He asked me to open the case so I put it on my desk and opened it. There was my Stratocaster guitar and nothing else.

"I don't see any schoolbooks," he said.

"That's the only book I am studying at the moment. You have me for 45 minutes so why don't you teach and I will pay attention and you can give me any test you want and I will pass it. But I'm not bringing schoolbooks to school anymore and I'm not doing any homework because that's the book I'm studying—the guitar."

PART II: OUTTAKES

◇◇◇

Up at Danny's house there was a clique that was based around doing all sorts of drugs, mostly psychedelics and pot, and listening to the records of the day. One day his father, who was a psychiatrist, came into the room and started lecturing us, saying, "You boys—you boys do nothing but sit around all day listening to this crazy music. You live in the most exciting city in the world. You could go to the library; you could go to the museum, you could go to a movie or visit the parks. We have wonderful parks in New York City, but all you guys do is sit around and listen to music. I just don't get it."

After he left the room we all broke out in gales of laughter because he didn't know that we were already adventurers, mystics, criminals, saints, chemists, doctors and all manner of other things rolled up into one. We laughed and laughed until one of us got nauseous and went to the bathroom. When he came back, he had a jar with a piece of protoplasm in it and declared, "Look, I've thrown up my stomach." We all looked at it and certainly it looked like a chunk of flesh from his intestines—but he lived.

One day we all went down to the "League for Spiritual Discovery" because we had heard that Timothy Leary was visiting. When we got there, Leary was sitting on a bunch of silk pillows lecturing to a group of people who were also sitting on pillows and were looking at him rapturously as though he were some kind of savior. We asked around and there were no drugs and I thought, "What the hell is this? League for spiritual discovery and there are no drugs?" We walked out—we knew more about drugs than Leary did, that's for sure.

Another time, a member of our clique said his family had a farm about an hour outside of the city and that we could go there and trip. He said he had some drug that he called Martian Energy Powder, or MEP. This was supposedly even stronger than STP. Six of us went up to the farm, including Velvert who refused to take the drug. It was like LSD for the first half hour, and then like STP for around 20 minutes, and then the bottom dropped out and I remember hearing God say, "So you wanted to know what reality looks like—well, here it is." Suddenly I was on the deepest trip I had ever experienced. It lasted about eight hours until we all came down and began telling each other about our trips. We discovered that we all had the same experience. Velvert stated that he had gone on the same trip, even though he hadn't taken the drug. I guess it was synergistic and affected him because he was with us. One will never know, but there are stranger things in heaven and on earth than we can ever think of. With LSD I could write down the secret of the universe, and then the next day look at the paper unable to figure out what the hell I was trying to convey. But with STP and this Martian Energy Powder I couldn't even write.

One time I was at my friend Maynard's house. Maynard's Aunt Bea let all the kids hang out. This time there were three kids there, one of whom was the younger brother of a friend—he and the others decided to eat some belladonna. The belladonna was sold as Asthmadora, and it was meant to be smoked for asthma. I'm pretty sure you can't get it anymore, because the only ingredient was the leaves of belladonna plant, which contained scopolamine and other alkaloids that were used in witchcraft during the

Middle Ages to go on devilish trips—like the one I had gone on with my friend by taking 20 Sominex.

I tried to talk them out of eating this stuff but my friends' minds were made up and they stuffed it into their mouths and began chewing it and swallowing it even though it tasted like shit. Pretty soon they were bouncing off the walls. Maynard left me in the basement of his house with these three kids who were walking into walls, talking nonsense and completely freaking out. I had to stop them from walking out of the house where they said they were going to "walk over cars to Boston in the middle of the street." I knew they would get themselves killed, so I had to stop them. Imagine me babysitting three kids who were all on complete hallucinatory bummers—at least they were bummers for me. I was very angry at my clique for abandoning me with these kids but I had a conscience and I could not leave them alone. Message to my friend whose younger brother I looked after: you probably never heard about this but you owe me a favor for saving him from the ravages of getting hit by a car or causing himself brain damage by banging into walls!

One afternoon I was invited up to the Record Plant by one of the girls who knew Jimi—probably Devon Wilson. We went into the studio and about 10 people were there including the engineer Gary Kellgren who was sitting with Jimi at the consul. Most of us either sat or stood at the back of the studio while the others went about their business. There were no drugs in evidence. First, they listened to the previous days' takes. Since engineers stored the tapes tails out, Jimi asked the engineer to put the tape on backwards, which he did, and we listened to an eight-

367

minute version of "Isabella" backwards sans vocals. It was quite amazing to be in the inner sanctum where these great works were being created. It turned out that Jimi always had a group join him in the studio until they got ready to do their actual work and then people were asked to leave. After listening to the tape backwards Jimi turned to Gary and said he had an idea about a song he wanted to do.

He wanted to do a song that would be eight bars forwards and then eight bars backward, back and forth, until the chorus which was to be 16 bars backwards and eight bars forward. Gary rolled his eyes, shrunk in his chair and told Jimi that it would take a year of cutting tape to create even one song that way. Jimi slumped in his chair, disappointed. He asked why and was told about the limitations of tape, meaning that to do such a forward thinking dramatic effect would take an extraordinary amount of work with pieces of tape all over the floor, and since Jimi was paying for the time spent in the studio— literally the only place he got to spend his money for real— it was an insurmountable task. The conversation continued about what could be achieved and then they decided to get to work.

All the people who had been hanging out and listening —friends of Jimi's and friends of friends like myself—got our coats on and left quietly, not wishing to disturb them. This was only one of several times I got to spend in the studio, usually at the beginning of the session before the real work started. Jimi was very shy, especially about singing. He didn't want anyone in the studio except the engineer and the rest of the band, and perhaps Chas Chandler, but by this time Jimi was doing the producing. *Electric Ladyland* had just been released but they were working on new material all the time, some of it rather silly, like the tune "The Three Bears," but also the important things that ended up being released posthumously. It's a shame that Jimi didn't make it to the digital era where he could've easily accomplished a forwards-backwards song structure and all sorts of other tricks that I bet he would have been very happy to use.

◇◇◇

One time in Boston I took a downer and it didn't work quickly enough, so I took another. They were very strong, and when they hit me I was wobbling out on Boylston Street where I decided to lie down. I nodded off until I was shaken awake by a lady who was looking down at me and saying, "Don't worry, I've called the ambulance." I was outraged and terrified but I managed to get myself on my feet, and I walked away going from building to sidewalk edge to building in a giant weave until I couldn't see her anymore. I looked down at the cigarette I'd been holding. It had burned down between my fingers and burned a hole in my shirt. Damn, that was a nice shirt.

◇◇◇

The last time I stayed at Velvert's house in LA, angel dust was being manufactured there. One day I saw one of Velvert's friends, a former member of Jimi's band, obviously intending to pull off a burglary. I told him I saw him and that I was going to tell Velvert. He backed off. That's the kind of nonsense they were getting into back then.

◇◇◇

Velvert played on one of Arthur Lee's records and was staying at his place during the recording. Velvert told me that one day he woke up to find all kinds of feathers flying around the room. When he looked up, he saw Arthur in the doorway with a gun—he had just shot his pillow. Arthur was apparently screaming at Velvert, "You stole my crack!" Velvert rolled out of bed and jumped out the window on the second floor before Arthur could get off another shot. LA is that kind of place—it's plastic and unreal, and very weird things go on there.

◇◇◇

One night I was hanging out at CBGB's when Joey Ramone came in all excited because Arturo Vega had purchased the building around the corner and Joey had his own space for the first time since living with his parents. He wanted to show me his "apartment." I said sure and asked him if he had a guitar there and if we could write a song together. He said he did and we went around the corner and he showed me his place which was a studio on the first floor. After showing me around, I asked him about the guitar and he said, "Oh Richie, you don't want to see my guitar." I said that I did and we bantered back and forth. I insisted and he finally went into the closet and pulled out a guitar with two strings on it.

I asked him if he had any new strings and he said, "I don't know." I offered to put them on and tune them up if he did. Then he admitted that he had no strings except those two. I asked him how he wrote his songs, and he said, "On those two strings!" I asked him why he didn't put a regular set on, and he said, "Oh Richie, I can't play more than two strings." It was quite endearing actually—he wrote all those melodies on two strings. After a while it was pointless to stay there and we went back to CBGB's. He was really happy that he had gotten to show me his new place. What a sweetheart in a sweet soul.

I hung out a lot with Dee Dee, and I think I loved him the most of all the Ramones—him and Joey. We had both worked as male hustlers around the corner of 53rd and Third but we never ran into each other so it was funny to find out that we had that in common. He was always as friendly with me as I was to him and we used to drink a lot together.

◇◇◇

Television was a band that just didn't care—we played our music and all the rest could go to hell. Many bands in that era *did* care and were desperate to become famous and rich. It's sad really, because pretending they didn't care was a pretense. Television truly didn't care about what people thought of us.

◇◇◇

There have been some rumors floating around that I was in Alex Chilton's band: Alex Chilton and the Cossacks. At one point Alex moved to New York and he and I talked about forming a band together called the Cossacks. I can't remember much aside from the fact that we played together a couple of times and I might've played live with him once at CBGB's. When he began calling his band Alex Chilton and the Cossacks, I was definitely not involved—Chris Stamey was, and a number of other people. There is a recording floating around that sounds like me playing, but it is Alex playing the guitar—I guess he got something from our jamming together.

◇◇◇

One time I went to see the New York Dolls at Club 82, which was a seedy downstairs bar run by two lesbians. It was frequented by a number of transvestites but was not usually very crowded until Television and other bands started playing there.

On this particular night Johnny Thunders asked me if I'd like to sit in on a number with the band. I said I didn't know any of their songs. He said, "Surely you know some songs," and I replied, "Nope, I only know the ones I've written or that Television does. I don't know anything else and I've never been in a cover band." Johnny said, "Let's do 'Shotgun,' because it's only one chord."

The Dolls played their set and then it was time for me to join them. I stepped onstage, plugged in, and we began. We played for 15 minutes. At about 10 minutes in, Arthur Kane, the bass player, started turning in circles. What he didn't realize was that an amp cable was coiling around his ankles. I realized that if he tried to take even one step he would fall over. I started yelling first but Arthur wasn't facing me, so I tried to get Johnny's attention, which I did, and I pointed at Arthur and his ankles. I said, "Stop him before he hurts himself." Johnny was just about to move towards Arthur when Arthur tried to take a step and fell right off the stage onto the concrete floor face first. Then he rolled onto his back and kept on playing. He didn't seem hurt, so it was one of the funniest things I've encountered with the Dolls.

Another time Johnny invited me to his home where he actually had acoustic guitars and we had a play. I was surprised at what a proficient guitarist he was because he was known for being a total wreck on stage and having one or two licks that he would play over and over again, while yelling, "More reverb—more reverb in the monitors!"

Any sound engineer knows that there is no reverb in the monitors but only in the house, but Johnny would continue to yell it no matter what. "More reverb, More Reverb,

MORE REVERB!" Nobody could do anything to help him because there was no monitor reverb and when they turned it up in the house so that he could hear it onstage it always became a giant mess. This was a constant in Johnny's performances after he left the Dolls. At his house, he played me some of the songs that ended up on *So Alone*, his first solo record. They were really fine songs, and I left with a great deal more admiration for him.

◇◇◇

One time Anita and I went down to Alphabet City in her limousine and the people on the block started screaming, "Get that fucking limousine out of here. You want us to get busted? Get that fucking limousine out of here now!" We drove around the corner and I got out, walked back and copped. While walking back to the car I saw a couple of guys running towards me and I knew right away they were undercover police. I got scared half to death and jumped in the limo and threw the dope underneath the carpet in the back.

By the time police got there all the doors had been locked by the limo driver. He rolled down the window and refused to let the cops in. They said they had probable cause. That was debatable because they only saw me quickly get into the limousine. That was one savvy limousine driver because after about five minutes of back and forth, the cops gave up and went away. We were driven back to my house where we shot up and got high.

◇◇◇

A groovy event happened in Chicago during a tour stop there in the 90s. I was approached by Cynthia Plaster Caster, who is known for her molds of the appendages of rock stars. She wanted to get a mold of my appendage, and although I can be shy, in this case I was quite forthright and agreed—in part because she was to bring in someone called a plater—a woman who is to give the rock star an erection. That sounded pretty exciting.

I went over to Cynthia's studio and she introduced me to a beautiful woman who wanted to be the plater. We messed around a little, I got a hard-on, she blew me, and then she asked if we could have sex. The most important thing was not to ejaculate, so that I could keep my hard on for the casting. This was not a problem for me, and they came over with a bucket full of dental paste and told me that I had to keep my hard-on for three and a half minutes and that it was very cold and that if I lost my hard on it would pull the dental paste off. They slammed the bucket onto my groin and held it there while the plater kissed me. I didn't need that, but I liked it, and I held my hard-on the whole time. When they pulled the bucket off, the plater and I went back to having sex. Later on, Cynthia told me that it was the second best job she had ever done—that I had a great one, second only to Jimi Hendrix in her collection.

◊◊◊

During Television's first tour in Japan the promoter took us out to dinner. He talked about all the orgies he had organized for the bands that had been there the previous year. He told us that he couldn't do that for us because all the Japanese women were afraid of AIDS. I hate being told I can't do something—it really rattles my cage and I will often do it anyway just to prove that it can be done without dying. I've been clinically dead a couple of times so what difference does it make to me? I like experience.

Appendix A
Meeting Mr. Gurdjieff

I can tell you that I have had many existential moments, like when I found out that I was not the only Richard in existence, but that Richard was a common name. And if there are many Richards, how can I be Richard? Clearly, I am not my name.

I have always been unsettled existing in the world—being in a physical body has always irked me. My body certainly does things on its own: breathing, heartbeat, digesting, eliminating. I seem to have no real control over this body of mine. I cannot stop my heartbeat, although I have tried. I can cease breathing for a good length of time, and then an irresistible urge comes from somewhere and I am forced to breathe. So my body can go on living without "me." Therefore I am not my body per se, I am rigidly connected to it—I cannot escape it and I am subject to its whims. I have thoughts, but if I look at them carefully they are not mine—they are just thoughts that "happen."

So I have always been interested in what might be called other-worldly things—not science fiction, but a compelling conviction that although I am connected to the body and operate through it, I am not "it" or any of its parts. Even if I am called Richard, it is just a label. I cannot be Richard or I would be all the Richards or any of them instead of this particular Richard.

So again, my question arises: who am I, and what is my purpose, my function? No matter how grandiose my daydreams might be, no matter how successful I might be in my chosen field, there is something else. Something nags at me and makes me wonder: do I have an obligation or am I free to do as I please with no consequences? I tried religion but it only tells me how I should act; it does not explain how I am to achieve these goals. Besides, I have a pretty strong ego which lives in rebellion. I can't imagine that I am the devil himself either. I am just an ordinary person—some good, some bad, all mixed up. In my search I have gone through all the religions of the world. I have tried all the disciplines that are to be found. I have done yoga and stood on my head for long periods of time, but it hasn't gotten me anywhere, not really.

I spent years reading in libraries and buying books with nothing in them but fools' gold and mixtures—new age concoctions. Then I found the ideas of Mr. Gurdjieff. The more I read, the more intrigued I became. The vitality of Mr. Gurdjieff and his ideas began sinking into me through the writing of Mr. Ouspensky and others. I began to think that Mr. Gurdjieff was a person who could answer any question—any question about anything at all. I wanted to know more but the books said that one needed to find a group, or someone who actually knows. I am clever enough to understand that it is easier for me to see the faults of others than it is for me to see my own faults. I could read all about the ideas and understand them intellectually, but I could never see myself properly, be-cause I am that thing that I call myself. It is actually a pretty funny picture. I, Richard Lloyd, was on a two-year long round-the-world rock 'n' roll tour spending all of my free time reading books about the Gurdjieff work which were sent to me from a mail-order house dedicated to books about this "Fourth Way"—and which all told me that there was no hope alone—that one needed to work with others who have gone further on the path.

I began looking to visit a group even though I was on the move. I actually spent $120 taking a taxicab to some meeting out in the suburbs of Detroit in order to experience an advertised introduction to the Work . It turned out to be a hoax, where the people acted like robots and told me that their leader was conscious, but that no one else was, and that I would never find another place as wonderful as theirs. To this remark I replied that I didn't care at all if their leader was conscious—all that mattered to me was whether or not he could help me to become conscious. They also offered me a glass of wine. I'm an alcoholic and I don't drink but these people insisted, and as they came towards me with a glass they pretended to trip, spilling the contents all over me. Instead of wine, the glass was full of confetti. They expected this to prove to me how gullible I was, but I didn't flinch and was not taken by surprise because this was important to me—in a sense, this was life and death for me, and their parlor tricks only convinced me that they were idiots following a fool.

When I reached New York at the end of the tour, I decided I would stay there and try to find a real Gurdjieff group. I went to a number of advertised groups mostly filled with what I would call "wackos," gullible young people who thought that they were going to be "special," full of esoteric and occult powers. I even joined one of

377

them and paid them some money, but after the first month, when the price went up and I realized they were "the blind leading the blind," I went on my merry way.

The woman from whom I had been buying books told me that I was lucky because New York had a real Gurdjieff Foundation, but at that time there was no way to find them—they were not listed in the phone book and there was no internet. I asked the woman for the address and she gave it to me with the warning that the people at the Foundation did not like people just showing up and knocking on the door—she advised me to write a letter. I wrote a two-page letter—I still have a copy of it. I was afraid that the letter would end up in the dead letter section if the address was wrong, so I pretended to be a messenger and hand-delivered it. The building had no sign, just the street number. I knocked on the door and waited. I knocked again and waited. I told myself that I would knock one more time and wait five minutes, and if no one came to the door I would turn around, walk away, and throw my letter away. I was just about to turn around when an elderly woman opened the front door and said, "Yes?" I handed her my letter and asked her if the address was correct. She said it was, so I turned around and walked away leaving the letter with her. The next day I got a phone call from another woman suggesting that if my interest was real, then perhaps we could meet.

In the meantime I had been going to weekly meetings with some other people who seemed more real, genuine and sincere. Then I met the woman from the Foundation who became my first teacher of the Work. She told me I was very lucky because they were starting something they called an exploratory group, which they did not do often, and if I should like, I could attend this group. I did so, and for a little while I went to both groups. But I soon recognized that I could not ride two horses, and though I felt the first group was sincere, I felt that the group which was connected to the Foundation was gold, so I chose that route.

At the time I was very disgusted with my life—I played rock 'n' roll guitar and to my way of thinking, this was juvenile—an egotistic self-serving lifestyle, but in talking it over with my teacher she said something very interesting which has taken on more and more truth as time goes on. She said that the conditions of my life were what I was supposed to study, and if I tried to change anything, I wouldn't be able to study what was real, because I would surely change or try to change in the direction that would make me "better." If I did that, I would not be able to truly study how I was in reality. She explained that there were two of me—the one that other people could see from the outside, and the one I wanted to be on the inside, but that the one I wanted to be was imaginary and was the enemy. I had to see myself exactly as I was, warts and all.

She also told me not to change careers because there were very few people in the Work who played rock 'n' roll, and if I just waited long enough perhaps I could be useful to the Work because of my unique position. This I could not understand—it was very humbling, but as the years have gone by I see that it's true. I am somewhat of a public figure who teaches and plays rock 'n' roll. My life has been an open book—anybody can look it up and find out that I was a huge drug user for many years. I could say that I was studying consciousness by making myself unconscious and fighting against it, the way a writer named René Daumal did, but it doesn't matter. I don't do drugs anymore, but I feel as though it prepared me for where I am now.

I am eager to help my fellow man, but I feel my tremendous smallness. Among six billion human beings I am completely invisible, and yet I do feel that my own work, which is based on quality rather than quantity, is extremely important for the future of mankind. Nature makes millions of acorns, but not all of them have a chance to become a tree, and of those who do find themselves in the position of being able to become a tree, not all of them bear fruit. Although this story has been about my search, and the undeniable fact that for me, I have found the pearl of great worth, the secret of the perpetual motion machine and how to make gold out of the mud of my own existence, I hope this resonates with some seekers who may feel as though they need a stable path and a sure way out of the existential terror of useless existence—and who wish to find a way to become truly useful to the Earth, the planets, the solar system and to the life which exists here.

There is a way. It is narrow, sublime and elusive, but it can be found by the serious and the sincere.

Appendix B
The Depth of Wish

Star light, star bright,
first star I see tonight;
wish I may, wish I might,
have the wish I wish tonight.

Wish is the most powerful thing in the world. Higher than God.
—G.I. Gurdjieff

The true wish requires and even demands an emotional component. It can be said that the true wish comes from the heart rather than the mind. But the mechanics are as Jesus declares. The New Testament discusses this fully and calls the resultant of wish by the word faith: "if thou had faith as large as a mustard seed and said to the mountain, move, then the mountain would move.

Then one has to think in terms of time, the supreme objective subjective – and when one makes a true wish with conscious faith it is already in the past, except that the past has not arisen yet – in this way it is like a foretelling of a demanded future whereby quantum collapse all other possibilities fall away. This is what Michelangelo meant when he was asked how he constructed the statue David. He said "I only took away from the marble what was not David." Wish must operate in the same fashion.
—Richard Lloyd

Life is real only then, when "I am."
—G.I. Gurdjieff

A New Adventure

There is a new adventure, yet it is also an adventure older than time itself, and I'm invited to participate in it should I wish. We are all a ray of this wish. It is embedded in us so deeply that we languor in the forgetting of its promise. We make our own wishes at birthday time and then turn away from their meaning with the extinguishment of the candles. We then return again to a belief in the world that has trapped us.

A friend of mine, when discussing wish, said that when he was a child he distinguished the coin of wish. He said that he knew the difference between little wish, which cost pennies, and big wish, which may cost more than we can pay.

These wishes are not entered into lightly, he said, for we have been allotted a certain amount of wish money— yet the exact amount is always kept hidden from us. I asked him if there was ever a wish for which he knew he could not pay and he said yes. He said that when he was younger he had wished to be on a rocket ship to the moon, and as he said this to me, all his cares fell away from him, he lit up with glee and became himself in a way which I had never seen before, and I knew in that instant that his wish had been answered. In that moment I also had a wish answered, and was given a moment free of gravity and Earth's laws of Encumbrance. I also left behind the shackles of myself and my self-imposed sorrow.

Perhaps the only wish worth the honor is that for which we have no means to pay.

There is a new adventure beckoning me, as old as I

AM, and it is made of starlight. There is a passage in "Fragments," by P.D. Ouspensky, which interests me.

Mr. Gurdjeff told Mr. Ouspensky that for a man to move up in the Work, that man must put another man in his place. This is a law. I had always taken this to mean that one had to find another man in order to pass on a kind of understanding. Now I believe that there is a trick being played here—how to escape the laws which bind me here. I do not know what I have done, but I have come to be here. The Moon, the Earth and the Planets need me, demand me and will hunt me down with redoubled efforts if I should abandon my place and try to run. If I am to escape in this fashion another man is needed—a dummy to take my place.

This is the "other man" whom I must put in my place. There is a Zen saying: *Before enlightenment, chop wood and carry water; after enlightenment, chop wood and carry water.*" I cannot change this. But I can have a wish. And I can fashion another man—an inner man, fed by wish, not subject to the fears and demands of the moon. For the outer man it is too late and has always been too late—he will always get angry. The moon has made him so. He is made of dust and I cannot cling to him. But I shall make him a shell. Empty. Slowly I shall move within my wish.

I shall slowly build an ark to live in so that the waters will not overtake me. At the same time I will leave myself exactly where I am. It is only in this way that one may pay for this journey. This is the taking up of one's cross. This is the payment demanded for such a wish. One must obtain oneself at the cost of oneself.

My friend has forgotten how to wish. I also have forgotten how to wish, but now I see a little, and my wish comes back, lingers a little and then fades. This is my work: to gather myself against the tide and beckon to my wish.

The Depth of Wish

As human beings we are each endowed with the same organic format and limitations. This is the result of being living, physical creatures who breathe, eat and think. We take in food, air, sensations and impressions. We excrete behavior and we have an inner life. In this inner life exists our thoughts and desires including unspoken and unconscious urges. What is the nature of wish? What is the meaning of this action within us which can be stronger than hope? Where in our inner nature is the platform upon which we can examine the nature and meaning of WISH which seems so fleeting against the mundane world? What happens in each of us as our ability to WISH is tempered by the facts of material existence?

One may speak of dreams, of innermost desires—of the deepest longings of the heart. Even when crushed by the weight and gravity of our ordinary existence these longings still have the power to renew us, to facilitate a surge of forgotten energies within us, to cause us once again to fall in love—not with any other person, or even with ourselves, but with an idea, with a hope of the unrealized potential within us.

When we wish, when we truly come to recognize that within us is a WISH (not simply a made up desire or objective, but a surge towards a longing which lives an independent existence from us), then for that moment we open to a life that is ordinarily denied us, and we have access to a power that can organize us into wholeness. This power can move mountains on our behalf. Even if only for this reason, we owe a debt to ourselves to go within and search for the meaning of WISH.

All myths and fairytales of the ages contain tantalizing remembrances that there exists the hope of a primordial connection with wish and the realization of one's destiny. This is destiny as opposed to fate and as opposed to conscious intent. Destiny is the unfolding of the greatest possibilities out of the unformed potentialities contained within a given life. This is why the image of the genie, the fairy godmother or the wizard are such profound symbols of how the deepest inner wish in a person can be independent of all of the actualized aspects of a person, for the true wish comes to us from an entirely other level. This also points to the reason why the true wish can never be mistaken with simple desire or objectives which may be self-realizable. The creative force always erupts into consciousness from a level outside of it. Wish has a power while simultaneously being disregarded in ordinary life. This is because the wish can only await its actualization—it can never "do." This also means that one cannot influence the wish in any ordinary way. Yet wish is strongly differentiated from hope, which contains within its jurisdiction the element of happenstance upon which we may rest our hope. Wish, on the other hand, does all, contains within itself all authority for what is to be, and yet "does" nothing.

What is the goal of Wish? There are many levels upon which wishing may be said to reside. There is the wish blown upon the birthday candle. There is the wish sent with a coin into the fountain. There are the teaching wishes granted by the Jinn where the fallacious nature of desire is revealed by the foolhardy wishes of the recipient and where the last of the granted wishes is almost always a fervent plea to return to the state which existed before the wishes had been granted, but which can bring at the end a hard won maturity. There is a coin of wish, and all know that the spending of this coin can be foolish or wise. There are the unrealizable wishes, verging on fantasy, but which can still be perhaps amongst the wisest of purchases. For those who dare to wish to fly to the moon or to have secret powers of wisdom, perhaps the wish pays its dividends in unearthed energies and ideas leading to invention. At the very least, the fabulous and sweeping wish which is scarcely to be expected brings within it a delicious inner thrill, and it is a sad thing that so many have forgotten its delights. The highest wish in a person is the "true wish"—and its goal is far away but has a substantially more concrete form.

The myths and fairy tales of the ages suggest that one cannot exert an influence over the form of this true wish. Power in wishing must be bestowed upon a man—and it is not necessarily bestowed by overtly beneficent forces. The bestowed power to wish is almost always a test. This test is not designed to separate good from evil but to separate the innermost essential in one from everything else. Tradition holds that any wish other than one connected to the essential treasure of the heart—and which also moves one in the direction of one's hidden destiny—will be a wish that will bring a dismantling of elements within the self which are false. The false wish, when it comes true, brings decay which, objectively speaking, is healthy and true, like a pull upon the reins of the wayward horse. Only elements which do not belong to the true and essential self may be ruptured in this way.

The Alchemical axiom is: "Gold does not fear the fire."

For those upon whom this wish is bestowed, the event is one of a preternatural winnowing fire out of which none but the purest intention can emerge unscathed.

In my own case I was born with a certain gnosis such that when I was asked at the age of five if I believed in God I answered, "No, I know." This caused the adults some consternation and they asked me what I meant by this homonym. I said that I did not need to believe because I knew, and that knowledge trumps belief and that belief depends upon the hope and faith of something unseen, whereas knowledge is an immediate apperception of the truth.

I also trusted that, just as a mother is given a baby shower with gifts before the child is born, that my guardian angels and forbearers and archangels also gave me, the child, what I term "wish money." They may even put wish money in a trust fund that will bear fruit later in life. This is the reason I did not want to spend any of my wish money on frivolous things. On my third birthday when they brought the cake out and my mother asked me to make a wish and blow out the candles I said, "No." My mother pleaded with me but I told her that I had nothing to wish for—that I was housed, fed, clothed, and loved, and that I needed nothing further. She pleaded with me and told me that I did not have to tell anyone my wish. I thought for a moment and came up with a wish that was proper and blew out the candles. I wished that everyone else present would get their wish and that if I benefited it would be collateral.

Later, as a teenager growing up in the 1960s, I made my first wish. It was that I should become a world-renowned electric guitar player and have an irrevocable impact on the history of rock 'n' roll. I gave everything over to this wish, even making a pact with Lady Poverty and threw myself on the mercy of the Holy Ghost to fulfill my wish. I knew that my wish was going to come true and so I began speaking about the future as if it was the present. Adults would ask me what I wanted to be when I grew up. I told them that I already *was* what I wanted to be when I grew up—a renowned electric guitar player who made an irrevocable impact on rock 'n' roll history. This got a lot of laughs, but my wish was formed and it never changed.

I recognized that once one made a true Wish the deal was sealed. Gurdjieff said that anything which hinders you towards reaching your goal or helps you to reach your goal is serious, "AND NOTHING ELSE!"

I lived in a divine comedy where everything that happened to me was predicated on reaching this aim, goal or wish—all of which I consider to be the same thing.

For those who have come to recognize their wish, the journey towards its fulfillment is an odyssey of epic proportions. Against this truth every man is the hero—set upon the seven voyages, or demanded to fulfill twelve tasks and to return with a proof not given lightly. Almost always, mythical forces are set against this adventure—the dragons of the unconscious guarding the precious treasure.

For one who is set out on such a quest, tradition allots years of search for guidance, and a journey of unimaginable distances through dark and dangerous places. One's own resources are never equal to the task. One must search for tools with which to perform the tasks which are strewn against the intent, and in almost in every case the tasks cause the supplicant to detour and to undertake Herculean tasks which on the surface seem to have no connection to the goal.

The man on a mission seems, to the outside observer,

headed in the wrong direction—perhaps he seems to be even a dolt or idiot. On top of that, these tasks are usually formulated to be well beyond the ken of the seeker. They cut perpendicular to their strengths and abilities and require the assistance of magical elements and a guiding guardianship.

Remember: The true seeker of WISH has magic in his pocket. This is the compass or lodestone which guides him unerringly towards his goal. The rest move like lemmings convinced of their direction while the seeker of the true WISH of the Heart moves in a direction wholly opposite to expectations.

Appendix C
Poems

In a Land

I once lived in a land where no one was negative;
where no one was angry,
and where no one lied.

The inhabitants loved each other beyond description,
so that they always told each other the truth;
which meant that all people were always in pain.

This suffering they welcomed as the deepest love;
a burning off the dross of their imperfections;
and they strove to constantly feel this burning,
which made them shine in the glistening of their
suffering like diamonds.

And the Endless Father of all
looked down upon them with great kindness,
for this was one of his favorite places.

And then I awoke, or was it that I slept?

And I found myself alone in a darker place,
where everyone was angry, and afraid.

Where every person was afraid of suffering,
and they lied to themselves to avoid the pain.

They lied to each other,
so that they would not be caught in their own lies,
and they never talked about it.

It became impolite to stare —
because everyone was hiding from the fear;
and everyone became alone,
so that none were truly friends,
because none could bear the truth.

Then again I slept, or was it that I awoke?

And I could remember,
like a distant dream that other place,
my home.

The Flame's Wish

consider the image of a candle flame, burning
the blue below, the orange red above
lingering, and pressing upwards.
the wax
the material which feeds the flame
is below it, underneath
yet the flame yearns upward.

what is the flame's wish?
it wishes, to reach something which is above it
in an unquenchable ardour,
it flickers, hopes and presses up
looking for its lover.

we,
are the flame of a candle
aching towards a potential
which remains above us.

yet sometimes
a spark breaks off.
it floats away,
lands,
and catches fire.

Appendix D
Discography

All songs written by Richard Lloyd
unless otherwise noted.

Alchemy (1979) Elektra
Misty Eyes
In the Night
Alchemy
Woman's Ways
Number Nine
Should Have Known Better (Lloyd/DeNunzio)
Blue and Grey
Summer Rain
Pretend (Lloyd/Mastro/Smith/DeNunzio)
Dying Words

Field Of Fire (1985) Mistlur
Watch Yourself
Losin Anna
Soldier Blue
Backtrack
Keep On Dancin
Pleading
Lovin Man
Black to White
Field of Fire

Real Time (1987) Celluloid
Fire Engine (Erickson/Hall/Sutherland)
Misty Eyes
Alchemy
Spider Talk
Lost Child
Number Nine
The Only Feeling
Soldier Blue
Field of Fire
Pleading

The Cover Doesn't Matter (2000) Upsetter Music
The Knockdown
Ain't It Time (Leonard/Lloyd)
She Loves To Fly
I Thought
Strange Strange (Johnson/Lloyd)
Torn Shirt
Downline
Raising The Serpent
Submarine
Cortege

Field of Fire Redux (2006) Parasol-Double LP
1
Watch Yourself
Losin' Anna
Soldier Blue
Backtrack
Keep On Dancin'
Pleading

Lovin' Man
Black To White
Field Of Fire

2
Soldier Blue (Revisited)
Pleading (Revisited)
Watch Yourself (Revisited)
Backtrack (Revisited)
The Only Feeling (Previously Unreleased)
Losin' Anna (Revisited)
Tobacco and Corn (Previously Unreleased)
Lovin' Man (Revisited)
Black To White (Revisited)
10. Field Of Fire (Revisited)
11. Keep On Dancin' (Revisited)

The Radiant Monkey (2007) Parasol
Monkey
Glurp
There She Goes Again
Swipe It
Only Friend
Kalpa Tree
Amnesia
Carousel
Big Hole
Wicked Son
One for the Road

The Jamie Neverts Story (2009) Parasol
Purple Haze (Hendrix)
Ain't No Telling (Hendrix)
Spanish Castle Magic (Hendrix)
I Don't Live Today (Hendrix)
May This Be Love (Hendrix)
Little Miss Lover (Hendrix)
Wait Until Tomorrow (Hendrix)
Castles Made of Sand (Hendrix)
Bold As Love (Hendrix)
Are You Experienced? (Hendrix)

Lodestones:
Nuggets From the Vault (2010) Sufi Monkey
Secret Words
The Knockdown
King of Fools
Fooling
Lowdown
Already Gone
Highway Signs
I Will Show You Mine
Shimmer
Oh Paige

Rosedale (2016)
Crystal Mountain
The Word
I Want You
Every time it Rains
Tasting Quicksand
Murder Boogie

DISCOGRAPHY

The Real Girl
Easy
Devils Design
Tired Old Morning

With *Television:*
Marquee Moon (1977) Elektra
Adventure (1978) Elektra
The Blow Up (1982) ROIR (1992) Capitol
Television (1992) Capitol
Live at The Academy 1992 (2003) Ohoo Music
Live at The Old Waldorf (2003) Rhino

With *Rocket from the Tombs:*
Rocket Redux (2004) Smog Veil/Morphius
Richard Lloyd: producer, guitar

With *Bibi Farber:*
Firepop (1978) Glowtime
Richard Lloyd: Producer, Guitar

With *Matthew Sweet:*
Earth (1990) A&M Records
Girlfriend (1991) Zoo
Altered Beast (1993) Zoo
Son of Altered Beast (1994) Zoo
100% Fun (1995) Zoo
Time Capsule: The Best of Matthew Sweet (2000) Volcano

With *Stephen Eicher:*
Carcassone (1993) Barclay

On Compilation albums:
Where the Pyramid Meets the Eye:
   A Tribute to Rocky Erickson (1990) Barclay
10 ROIR Years (1990) ROIR
New York Rockers (1991) ROIR
Great New York Singles (1992) ROIR
Saturday Morning - Cartoon's Greatest Hits (1995) MCA
Poptopia! - Power Pop Classics of the 90s (1997) Rhino
This Note's For You Too! A Tribute to Neil Young (1999)
    Inbetween Records
Ork Records: New York, New York (2015)
    Numero Group

Other Appearances:
Walter Stedding: Red Star Records (1981) Red Star
Chris Stamey: It's Alright (1987) A&M / Coyote
Michael Callen: Purple Heart (1988) Significant Other
Imperiet: Tiggarens Tal (1988) Mistlur
John Doe: Meet John Doe (1990) Geffen
Pierce Turner: It's Only a Long Way Across (1990)
    Beggars Banquet / RCA
Rage To Live: Blame The Victims (1990) Bar/None
Health & Happiness Show: Instant Living (1995) Bar/None